THE MARKS OF CAIN

Tom Knox is the pseudonym of the author Sean Thomas. Born in England, he has travelled the world writing for many different newspapers and magazines, including *The Times*, the *Guardian*, and the *Daily Mail*. He lives in London.

To find out more about Tom Knox and *The Marks of Cain*, visit: www.tomknoxbooks.com

By Tom Knox

The Genesis Secret
The Marks of Cain

TOM KNOX

The Marks of Cain

HARPER

Harper
An imprint of HarperCollins*Publishers*
77–85 Fulham Palace Road,
Hammersmith, London W6 8JB

www.harpercollins.co.uk

A Paperback Original 2010
3

Copyright © Tom Knox 2010

The author asserts the moral right to
be identified as the author of this work

A catalogue record for this book
is available from the British Library

ISBN 978 0 00 734261 7

Typeset in Meridien by Palimpsest Book Production Limited,
Grangemouth, Stirlingshire

Printed and bound in Great Britain by
Clays Ltd, St Ives plc

Mixed Sources

Product group from well-managed
forests and other controlled sources
www.fsc.org Cert no. SW-COC-001806
© 1996 Forest Stewardship Council

FSC is a non-profit international organization established
to promote the responsible management of the world's forests.
Products carrying the FSC label are independently certified
to assure consumers that they come from forests that are managed
to meet the social, economic and ecological needs
of present and future generations.

Find out more about HarperCollins and the environment at
www.harpercollins.co.uk/green

Author's Note

The Marks of Cain is a work of fiction. However, it draws on many genuine historical, archaeological and scientific sources.

In particular:

The monastery of Sainte Marie de La Tourette stands in the forests and vineyards of central France. Designed by Le Corbusier, the building was constructed in the 1950s. Five years after completion the building was threatened with closure, as so many of the monks were suffering mental problems.

Eugen Fischer was a German scientist, famous for his studies in human heredity, firstly amongst the Basters of Namibia, and then for Hitler and the Nazi party. He survived the Second World War, and continued his work without prosecution.

In 1610, the King of Navarre asked his physicians to examine twenty-two of his 'Cagot' subjects.

Acknowledgements

I would like to express my gratitude to everyone who helped in my Namibian research: especially the people at Canon Lodge, Namib Desert Lodge, Luderitz Nest, and Klein-aus-Vista. Extraordinary places all. The staff of EHRA, who showed me the stirring Damara landscapes of the Namibian desert elephants, were invaluably helpful.

Thanks are likewise due to Mark Kurlansky and Paddy Woodworth for their highly informative books on Basque culture, everyone in Zugarramurdi in Navarre, the scientists of Stanford University's Human Diversity Genome Project (which closed, amidst controversy, in the 1990s), and the Dominican monks of the Priory of La Tourette.

My editors, Josh Kendall in New York, and Jane Johnson in London, have been patient, assiduous and insightful over many months: I am vastly grateful to them; I am similarly grateful to Eugenie Furniss, my agent at William Morris, and Jay Mandel at WME New York.

Finally, I want to thank Marie-Pierre Manet Beauzac, who allowed me into her house in Tarbes, in southern France, and revealed her remarkable ancestry.

This book is for Marie: *the last of the Cagots.*

The voice of thy brother's blood crieth unto me from the ground.

Genesis, 4:10

1

Simon Quinn was listening to a young man describe how he'd sliced off his own thumb.

'And that,' said the man, 'was the beginning of the end. I mean, cutting off your thumb, with a knife, that's not nothing, is it? That's serious shit. Cutting your own thumb off. Fucked my bowling.'

The urge to laugh was almost irrepressible; Simon repressed it. The worst thing you could do at a Narcotics Anonymous meeting was laugh at someone's terrible story. Just not done. People came here to share, to fess up, to achieve some catharsis by submitting their darkest fears and shames: and thereby to heal.

The young man finished his story: 'So that's when it, like, kicked in. I realized I had to do something, about the drugs and the pop. Thank you.'

The room was silent for a moment. A middle-aged woman said a breathy *thank you, Jonny*, and everyone else murmured: *thank you, Jonny*.

They were nearly done. Six people had shared; pamphlets and keyrings had been distributed. This was a new group for Simon, and he liked it. Usually he went to evening NA meetings nearer his flat and his wife and son in Finchley Road, the London suburbs. But today he'd had to come into Hampstead for business and *en route* he'd decided to catch a new meeting, try somewhere fresh; he was bored of the boozers at his usual meets, with their stories of guzzling lighter fuel. And so he'd rung the NA hotline and found this meeting he'd never been to before, and it turned out it was a regular lunchtime job – with interesting people who had good stories.

The pause was prolonged. Perhaps he should share his own story now? Give a little change?

He decided to tell the very first story. The big one.

'Hello, my name's Simon and I'm an addict.'

'Hello, Simon . . .'

'Hi, Simon.'

He leaned forward – and began:

'I was a drunk . . . for at least ten years. And I wasn't just an alcoholic, I was . . . a polydrug abuser, as they say. I did absolutely everything. But I don't want to talk about that. I want to . . . explain how it started.'

The leader of the group, a fifty-something man with soft blue eyes, nodded gently.

'Whatever you want. Please go on.'

'Thank you. Well. OK. I . . . grew up not far from here, in Belsize Park. My parents were pretty affluent – my father's an architect, my mother was a lecturer. My background is Irish but . . . I went to private school in Sussex. Hence the stupidly middle-class English accent.'

The leader offered a polite smile. Listening attentively.

'And . . . I had an older brother. We were rather a happy family . . . At first . . . Then at eighteen I went off to university and while I was there I got this *frantic* phone call from my mother. She said, *your brother Tim has just lost it.* I asked her what she meant and she said, *he's just lost it.* And it was true. He'd suddenly come home from university – and he'd started talking absolutely mad stuff, talking equations and scientific formulas . . . and the maddest thing of all is that he was doing it in *German*.'

He gazed around the faces, gathered in this basement room. Then continued:

'So I shot home and it turned out my mother was right. Tim had gone mad. Genuinely cracked. He was doing a lot of skunk with his chums at uni – maybe that was a catalyst – but I think he was schizophrenic anyway. Because that's when schizophrenia usually kicks in, between the ages of eighteen and twenty-five. I didn't know that then of course.'

The middle-aged woman was sipping from a plastic cup of tea.

'Tim was a science student. Seriously bright – much brighter than me. I can barely say *bonjour* but he could speak four languages. As I say, he was doing a physics PhD, at Oxford, but he'd come home suddenly . . . without warning – and he was ranting, quoting scientific formulas in German. Doing it all night, walking up and down the landing. *Das Helium und das Hydrogen* blah blah blah. All through the night.

'My parents realized my brother had a pretty serious problem – and they took him to a doctor, and they prescribed Tim the usual drugs. The wretched little pills. Antipsychotics. And they worked for a while . . . But one night when I was home for Christmas I heard this *muttering* noise and . . . and it was this voice. Again. Yes. *Das Helium und das Hydrogen*. And I lay there wondering what to do. But then I heard this terrible scream and I rushed from my bedroom and my brother was in . . .' He closed and opened his eyes. 'My brother was there in my mother's bedroom and they were alone because my father was away . . . and . . . and my brother was *attacking* her, hacking at my mother, with a machete. A big knife. A *machete*. I don't know precisely what

3

it was. But he was chopping away at her, our mother, so I jumped him and I held him down and there was blood everywhere, just everywhere – actually sprayed up the walls. I very nearly throttled him. Almost killed my own *brother.'*

Simon drew breath.

'The police came and they took him away and . . . my mother went to hospital and they stitched her up, but she lost the use of some fingers, some nerves were severed. But that was all, really, which was incredibly lucky. She could have died – but she was alright. And then we had this *terrible* dilemma as a family – should we press charges? My father and I said "Yes", but my mother said "No". She loved Tim more than the rest of us. She thought he could be treated. So we agreed with her, stupidly, crazily, we *agreed.* Then Tim came home and he seemed OK for a while, on the drugs, but then one night I heard it: *Das Helium und das Hydrogen . . .'*

Simon could feel the sweat on his forehead; he hurried on with his story.

'Tim was muttering, again, in his room. And of course *that* was *that.* We called the police – and they came straight round. Then they put Tim in an asylum. And that's where he is now. Locked and bolted and shut in his box. He's been there ever since. He'll be there the rest of his life.'

As his conclusion approached, he experienced the usual relief. 'So that's when I started drinking – to forget, you know. Then sulphates and then pretty much *everything . . .* But I finally stopped the boozing six years ago and yes I did my course of NA antibiotics, my sixty meetings in sixty days! And I've been clean ever since.

'And I now have a wife and a son and I dearly love them. Miracles do happen. They really do. Of course I still don't know why my brother did what he did and what that means but . . . I look at it this way: maybe I haven't got his genes, maybe my boy will be alright. Who knows. One day at a

4

time. And that's my story. And thanks very much for listening. *Thank you.'*

A murmur of *thank yous* filled the warm fuggy space, like the responses of a congregation. The ensuing silence was a coda; the hour was nearly up. Everyone stood and hugged, and said the Serenity Prayer. And then the meeting was finished, and the addicts filed out, climbing up the creaky wooden stairs, out into the graveyard of Hampstead Church.

His mobile rang. Standing at the church gates, he clicked.

'Quinn! It's me.'

The phone screen said *Withheld*, but Simon recognized the voice immediately.

It was Bob Sanderson. His colleague, his source, his man: a Detective Chief Inspector – at New Scotland Yard.

Simon said a bright *Hi*. He was always pleased to hear from Bob Sanderson, because the policeman regularly fed the journalist good stories: gossip on high profile robberies, scuttlebutt on alarming homicides. In return for the information, he made sure that DCI Sanderson was seen, in the resultant articles, in a flattering light: a smart copper who was solving crimes, a rising star in the Met. It was a nice arrangement.

'Good to hear your voice, DCI. I'm a bit broke.'

'You're always broke, Quinn.'

'It's called freelancing. What do you have?'

'Something nice maybe. Strange case in Primrose Hill.'

'Yes?'

'Oh yes indeed.'

'So . . . What is it? Where?'

The detective paused, then answered:

'Big old house. Murdered old lady.'

'Right.'

'You don't sound very enthusiastic.'

'Well.' Simon shrugged, inwardly, watching a bus turn

5

left by the Tube, heading down to Belsize Park. 'Primrose Hill? I'm thinking . . . aggravated burglary, thieves after jewels . . . Not exactly unknown.'

'Ah, well that's where you're wrong.' The policeman chuckled, with a hint of seriousness. 'This isn't any old fish and chip job, Quinn.'

'OK then. What makes it *strange*?'

'It's the method. Seems she was . . . knotted.'

'Knotted?'

'Apparently so. They tell me that's the proper word.' The policeman hesitated. Then he said, '*Knotted!* Perhaps you should come and have a look.'

2

Beyond the hospice window stretched the defeated beauty of the Arizona desert: with its vanquished sands, stricken creosotes, and blistered exposures of basalt. The green arms of the saguaro cacti reached up, imploring an implacable sun.

If you had to die, David Martinez thought, this was a fitting place to die, on the very outskirts of Phoenix, in the final exurb of the city, where the great Sonoran wastes began.

Granddad was murmuring in his bed. The morphine drip was way up high. He was barely lucid at the moment – but then, Granddad was barely lucid most of the time.

The grandson leaned over and dabbed some sweat from his grandfather's face with a tissue. He wondered, yet again, why he had come here, all the way from London, using up his precious holidays. The answer was the same as ever.

He *loved* his Grandfather. He could remember the better times: he could remember Granddad as a dark-haired, stocky, and cheerful man; holding David on his shoulders in the sun. In San Diego, by the sea, when they were still a family. A small family, but a family nonetheless.

And maybe that was another reason David had made it

all the way here. Mum and Dad had died in the car crash fifteen years ago. For fifteen years it had been just David in London, and Granddad living out his days in distant Phoenix. Now it would just be David. That sobering fact needed proper acknowledgement: it needed proper goodbyes.

Granddad's face twitched as he slept.

For an hour David sat there, reading a book. Then his grandfather woke, and coughed, and stared.

The dying patient gazed with a puzzled expression at the window, at the blue square of desert sky, as if seeing this last view for the first time. Then Granddad's eyes rested on his visitor. David felt a stab of fear: would Granddad look at him and say, *Who are you?* That had happened too often this week.

'David?'

He pulled his chair closer to the bed.

'Granddad . . .'

What followed wasn't much of a conversation, but it *was* a *conversation*. They talked about how his grandfather was feeling; they touched briefly on the hospice food. *Tacos, David, too many tacos*. David mentioned that his week of holiday was nearly up and he had to fly back to London in a day or two.

The old man nodded. A hawk was making spirals in the desert sky outside, the shadow of the bird flickered momentarily across the room.

'I'm sorry . . . I wasn't there for you, David, when your mom . . . and your dad . . . y'know . . . when it happened.'

'Sorry?'

'You know. The . . . crash, what happened . . . I'm so damn sorry about all of it. I was stupid.'

'No. Come on, Granddad. Not this again.' David shook his head.

'Listen. David . . . please.' The old man winced. 'I gotta say something.'

David nodded, listening intently to his grandfather.

'I gotta say it. I could've . . . I could've done better, could've helped you more. But you were keen to stay in England, your mom's friends took you in, and that seemed best . . . you don't know how difficult it was. Coming to America. After the war. And . . . and your grandmother dying.'

He trailed into silence.

'Granddad?'

The old man looked at the afternoon sun, now slanting into the room.

'I got a question, David.'

'Yes. Sure. Please.'

'Have you ever wondered where you come from? Who you really are?'

David was used to his Granddad asking him questions. That was part of their relationship, how they rubbed along: the older man asking the grandson about younger things. But this was a very different question – unexpected – yet also very acute. This wasn't any old question. This was *The Question.*

Who was he really? Where did he really come from?

David had always ascribed his sense of rootlessness to his chaotic upbringing, and his unusual background. Granddad was Spanish but moved to San Diego in 1946 with his wife. She had died giving birth to David's father; his father then met his mother, a nurse from England, working at Edwards Air Force Base in California.

So, for the first few years of David's life there had *maybe* been a certain sense of who he was – an American of Anglo-Hispanic parentage, a Californian – but the Latino surname and the dark Spanish looks still marked them out, as a family, as not *quite* your normal one hundred percent Americans. After that they'd moved to Britain, and then to Germany and then Japan, and then back to Britain – with his father's career in the US Air Force.

By the end of this world tour, by the time he was ten or twelve, David hadn't felt American, British, Spanish, Californian – or anything much. And then his mum and dad had died in the crash – and the sense of being cut off, of being alone and anonymous and floating, had only worsened. *Alone in the world.*

Granddad repeated the query. 'So . . . David? Do you? Do you ever think about it? Where you come from?'

David lied and shrugged and said, *No, not really.* He didn't feel like getting into all that, not right now.

But if not now, then when?

'OK. OK,' the old man stammered. 'OK, David. OK. And the new job? Job? You like that? What are you doing, I forget . . .'

Was Granddad losing it again? David frowned, and said:

'Media lawyer. I'm a lawyer. It's OK.'

'Only OK?'

'Nah . . . I hate it.' David sighed at his own candour. 'I thought . . . at least reckoned it might be a bit glamorous. You know . . . pop stars and parties. But I just sit in a dismal office and call other lawyers. It's crap. And my boss is a tosser.'

'Ah . . . Ah . . . Ach . . .' It was a wrenching, old man's cough. Then Granddad lay back and stared at the ceiling. 'Didn't you get a good college . . . college degree? Some kinda science, no?'

'Well . . . I did biochemistry, Granddad. In England. Not a lot of money in that. So I turned to law.'

Another hiatus. The light was bright in the room. At last his grandfather said:

'David. You need to know something.'

'What?'

'I lied.'

The silence in the room was stifling. Somewhere in the hospice a gurney rattled.

'You *lied*? What does that mean?'

He scrutinized his grandfather's face. Was this the dementia, reasserting itself? He couldn't be sure, but the old man's face looked alert as he elaborated.

'Fact, I'm lying now, son . . . I just . . . just can't . . . get past it, David. Too late to change. *A las cinco de la tarde*. I'm sorry. *Desolada*.'

This was perplexing. David watched the old man talk.

'OK I'm tired, David. I . . . I . . . I . . . Now I need to do this. Please look in there . . . Least I can do this. Please.'

'Sorry?'

'In the bag at the end . . . of my bed. Kmart. Look see. Please!'

David got up smartly, and went to the assorted bags and luggage stored in the corner of the room, beyond the bed. Conspicuous in the rather forlorn pile was a scarlet Kmart bag. He picked it up, and scoped inside: there was something papery and folded at the bottom. Maybe a map?

Maps had been one of David's passions as a child, maps and atlases. As he unfolded this one, in the desert light from the window, he realized he was holding a rather beautiful example.

It was a distinctly old-fashioned road map, with dignified shading and elegant colouration. Soft grey undulations showed mountains and foothills, lakes and rivers were a poetic blue, green polygons indicated marshland beside the Atlantic. It was map of southern France and northern Spain.

He sat down and scrutinized the map more closely. The sheet had been marked very neatly with a blue pen: little blue asterisks dotted those grey ripples of mountains, between France and Spain. Another single blue star marked the top right corner of the map. Near Lyon.

He looked at his grandfather, questioningly.

11

'Bilbao,' said the old man, visibly tiring now. 'It's Bilbao . . . You need to go there.'

'What?'

'Fly to Bilbao, David. Go to Lesaka. And find José Garovillo.'

'Sorry?'

The old man made a final effort; his eyes were blurring over.

'*Show him . . . the map.* Then ask him about churches. Marked on the map. Churches.'

'Who's this guy? Why can't you just tell me?'

'It's been too long . . . too much guilt, I cannot, can't admit . . .' The old man's words were frail, and fading. 'And anyway . . . Even if I told you, you wouldn't believe me. No one would believe. Just the mad old man. You'd say I was mad, the crazy old man. So you need to find out for yourself, David. But be careful . . . Be careful . . .'

'Granddad?'

His grandfather turned away, staring at the ceiling. And then, with a horrible sense of inevitability, the old man's eyelids fluttered shut. Granddad had fallen back into his fitful and opiated sleep.

The morphine pump ticked over.

For a long while, David sat there, watching his grandfather breathe in and breathe out, quite unconscious. Then David got up and closed the blinds; the desert sun was almost gone anyway.

He looked down at the map sitting on the hospice chair; he had no idea what it signified, what connection his granddad had with Bilbao or with churches. Probably it was all some ragged dream, some youthful memory returning, between the lucidity and the dementia. Maybe it was nothing at all.

Yes. That was surely it. These were just the ramblings of

a dying old man, the brain yielding to the flood of illogic as the final dissolution approached. Sadly, but truly, he was crazy.

David picked up the map and slid it into his pocket, then he leaned and touched his grandfather's hand, but the old man did not respond.

With a sigh, he walked out into the hot Phoenix summer night, and climbed into his rented Toyota. He drove the urban freeway to his motel, where he watched soccer on a grainy Mexican satellite station with a lonely sixpack and a pizza.

His grandfather died early the following morning. A nurse rang David at the motel. He immediately called London and told his friends – he needed to hear some friendly voices. Then he called his office and extended his 'holiday' by a few days, on the grounds of bereavement.

Even then his boss in London sounded a little sniffy, as it was 'only' David's grandfather. 'We are very busy, David, so this is exceptionally tiresome. Do be quick.'

The service was in a soulless crematorium, in another exurb of Phoenix. Tempe. And David was the only real mourner in the building. Two nurses from the hospice showed up, and that was it. No one else was invited. David already knew he had no other family in America – or anywhere for that matter – but having his relative loneliness underscored like this, felt notably harsh – indeed cruel. But he had no choice in the matter. So David and the two nurses sat there, together and alone, and exposed.

The ceremony was equally austere: at his grandfather's request there were no readings, there was nothing – except for a CD of discordant and exotic guitar music, presumably chosen by his grandfather.

When the song was done, the coffin trundled abruptly into the flames. David felt the briskness like a punch. It was as if the old man had been quick to get off stage, eager to flee this life – or keen to be relieved of some burden.

That afternoon David drove deep into the desert, seeking the most remote location, as if he could lose his sadness in the wasteland. Under an ominously stormy sky, he scattered the ashes between the prickly pears and the crucifixion thorns. He stood for a minute and watched the ashes disperse, then walked to his car. As he returned to the city, the first fat raindrops smacked the windscreen; by the time he reached his motel a real desert storm had kicked up – jagged arcs of lightning volting between the black and evil clouds.

His flight was looming. He began to pack. And then the motel phone trilled. His ex girlfriend maybe? She'd been calling on and off the last couple of days: trying to elevate David's mood. Being a good friend.

David reached for the phone and answered.

'Uh-huh?'

It wasn't his ex. It was a breezy American accent.

'David Martinez? Frank Antonescu . . .'

'Uh . . . hello.'

'I'm your grandfather's lawyer! First of all, can I say – I'm so sorry to hear of your bereavement.'

'Thank you. Uhm. Sorry. Uh . . . Granddad had a *lawyer*?'

The voice confirmed: Granddad had a lawyer. David shook his head in mild surprise. Through the motel room window he could see the desert rain pummelling the surface of the motel swimming pool.

'OK . . . Go on. Please.'

'Thank you. There's something you oughta know. I'm handling your grandfather's estate.'

David laughed – out loud. His granddad had lived in a heavily mortgaged old bungalow; he drove a twenty-year-old Chevy, and he had no serious possessions. *Estate?* Yeah, right.

14

But then David's laughter congealed, and he felt a pang of apprehension. Was *this* the reason for his grandfather's weird shame: was the old man bequeathing some insuperable *debt*?

'Mister Martinez. The estate comprises two million dollars, or thereabouts. In cash. In a Phoenix Bank savings account.'

David swayed in the high wind of this revelation; he asked the lawyer to repeat the sum. The lawyer said it again, and now David experienced The Anger.

All this time! All this time his grandfather had been loaded, minted, a fucking *millionaire*? All the time, he, David, the orphaned grandson, had been struggling, fighting, working his way through university, just keeping his head above water – and all along the Beloved Grandfather had been sitting on *two million dollars*?

David asked the lawyer how long his grandfather had possessed this money.

'Ever since he hired me. Twenty years minimum.'

'So . . . why the hell did he live in that crappy little house? With that car? Don't get it.'

'Damn straight,' said the lawyer. 'Trust me, Mister Martinez, I would tell him to use it, spend it on himself, or give it you of course. Never would. At least he got a good rate of interest.' A sad chuckle. 'If you ever do find out where the money came from, please let me know. Always puzzled me.'

'So what do I do now?'

'Come by the office tomorrow. Sign a few documents. The money is yours.'

'Just like that?'

'Just like that.' A pause. 'However . . . Mister Martinez. You should know there is one codicil, one clause to the will.'

'And that is?'

'It says –' The lawyer sighed. 'Well . . . it's a little eccentric.

15

It says that first you have to utilize some of the cash to . . . do something. You have to go to the Basque Country. And find a man called José Garovillo in a town called Lesaka. I think that's in Spain. The Basque Country, I mean.' The lawyer hesitated. 'So . . . I guess the best way to do it is this: when you reach Spain you just let me know and I'll wire the cash into your account. After that it's all yours.'

'But why does he – did he – want me to find this guy?'

'Search me. But that's the stipulation.'

David watched the rain through the window, as it turned to drizzle.

'OK . . . I'll drive by tomorrow morning.'

'Good. See you at nine. And once again, my sympathies on your loss.'

David dropped the phone and checked the clock: working out time differences. It was too late for him to call England and tell anyone the bizarre and amazing news; it was too late for him to ring his boss and tell him to go choke on his stupid job.

Instead he went to the little table and picked up the map. He unfolded the soft, sadly faded paper and scrutinized the tiny blue asterisks. The stars had been firmly and neatly handwritten next to placenames. Striking placenames. *Arizkun. Elizondo. Zugarramurdi.* Why were these places marked out? What did this have to do with churches? Why did his grandfather even own this map?

And how come his impoverished grandfather had *two million dollars that he never touched?*

He needed to look for flights to Bilbao.

3

In the crowded Arrivals lounge of Bilbao airport he opened his laptop and emailed Frank Antonescu. Attached to the email was a jpeg of himself holding a Basque newspaper, to prove his arrival in the country: to fulfil the one stipulation of his grandfather's will. The entire escapade was surreal, and borderline foolish, and yet this was what his grandfather wanted. So David was happy to obey.

Despite the troublesome time difference, the lawyer emailed back, at once – and with impressive efficiency: the money was being wired over.

Clicking on a website, David checked his bank account.

There. It was really *there*.

Two point one million dollars.

The feeling was unsettling, as well as gratifying.

He was *rich* but in a garish and discomfiting way; he didn't quite feel himself; he felt like someone had snuck into his house, and painted his furniture gold. Was he even allowed to sit down?

Shutting his laptop, David yawned, and yawned again, and glanced through the wide glass terminal doors. It was raining, very hard. And he was very tired. He could do the rest of his travelling tomorrow.

Sheltering ineptly under his copy of *El Correo* David wheeled his luggage to the taxi rank; he was saved by a cheerful cab driver with a lurid Barcelona soccer shirt under a smart leather jacket, who smoked and chattered as they pulled out of the airport.

The taxi slashed along the rainy motorway. On the left was the distant greyness of the Atlantic Ocean, on the right sudden green hills reached to the clouds; in the steep dips between the hills lurked steelworks and papermills, and factories with tall redbrick chimneys churning out ribbons of smoke the colour of faded white underwear.

David buzzed down the window and let the rain spit onto his face. The cold rain was good – because it pierced the weary numbness; it roused him, and reminded him. He gazed at the Basque Country. He was *here*.

He'd done some investigating during his thirty-hour flight around the world: some internet research into the Basque Country, and the Basques.

He now knew that some people thought the Basques were descended from Neanderthals. He knew that they had surprisingly long earlobes. He knew they had a unique and complex language unrelated to any other language in the world; he knew that *Arrauktaka* meant 'to hit someone with an oar'.

He had also learned that the word 'bizarre' came from the Basque word for 'bearded'; that the people were tall and burly compared to Spaniards; that the Basques were expert whalers; that they had special cherries, a passion for rugby, their own form of linen, a wavy solar symbol called a *lauburu*, and a tiny wild horse called a *pottok*.

David buzzed the window shut. The research had been diverting enough, but it hadn't been able to give him any of the information he really wanted. Who was José Garovillo?

What was this reference to churches? What about Granddad's map?

The memory of Granddad was a discernible pain. David fought back the emotion; if he thought of his grandfather the thread of cognition could so easily lead to his parents. So he needed to *do and not think*; and he had one more severance to make, one more definite change to enact.

He picked up his mobile and pressed.

The phone rang in London.

'Roland De Villiers. *Yes?*'

It was the normal snooty, self-consciously weary locution. The same voice that David had endured for half a decade.

'Roland, it's David. I –'

'Oh for God's sake. Rilly. David. Where are you *now*?'

'Roland –'

'You do realize your desk is piled high? I don't care about your frankly peripheral circumstances. You are a professional, get a grip. I expect to see you behind that screen in the next hour or –'

'I'm not coming back.'

A pause.

'You have one hour to get back here –'

'Give my job to that guy in accounts. The one who's banging your wife. Bye.'

David clicked off. And then he laughed, quietly. He could picture his boss in his office, red faced with anger.

Good.

In front of him the motorway dipped and curved; they seemed to be cutting towards the middle of the city. Grey apartment blocks, stained by rain, stood to attention along the route.

The taxi driver looked up at David, mirrorwise:

'*Centro urbano, señor?* Hotel Donostia? *Sí?*'

'*Sí.* Er . . . *sí.* Yes. Centre of the city. Hotel . . . Donostia.'

19

The driver turned off the *autopista* and headed down into the wide and principal streets of the town. Large grey offices exuded an air of damp pomposity in the gloom. Many of them seemed to be banks. Banco Vizkaya. Banco Santander. Banco de Bilbao. People were scurrying past the sombre architecture, with umbrellas aloft; it was like a photo of London in the 1950s.

The Hotel Donostia was very much as it had appeared on the website: faded but formal. The concierge looked disdainfully at David's creased shirt. But David didn't care – he was almost delirious with tiredness. He found his room and fought with his keycard; then he collapsed into his oversoft bed and slept for eleven straight hours, dreaming of a house with no one inside. He dreamed of his parents, alive, in a car – with small wild horses, cantering across the road.

Then a scream. Then redness. Then a small boy running across an enormous empty beach. Running towards the sea.

When he woke, he opened the curtains – and gawped. The sky was bright blue: the September sun had returned. David pulled on his clothes, filled up on coffee and pastries, then called a cab, and hired a car at the railway station. After a moment's hesitation, he rented the vehicle for a month.

The main road out of grimy Bilbao took him east towards the French border. Again he thought of his mum and dad and Granddad; he averted himself from the thought, and concentrated on the route. Was he going the right way? He pulled over at an Agip service station; its huge plastic logo – of a black dog spitting red fire – was overly bright in the harsh sunlight. Parked up, he took out the old map and traced his finger over the cartography, examining those delicate blue stars dotting the grey foothills. They looked like distant policelights, glimpsed through mist and rain.

Then he half-folded the map, and for the first time he

noticed there was proper writing, in a different hand, scribbled on a corner of the map's reverse. Seen in the stark sunlight the writing was very faint, and *possibly* in Basque, or Spanish. Maybe even German. The writing was so small and faded it was quite indecipherable.

It was another puzzle – and he was no nearer to solving any of it. But at least the map told him one thing: he was going the right way, into the 'real' Basque Country. He started the car once again.

The drive was hypnotic. Sometimes he could see the blue ocean, the Bay of Biscay, sparkling in the sun. Sometimes the road ducked instead through those dark green shady valleys, where the white-painted Basque houses looked like cuboid mushrooms, suddenly sprouted overnight.

At last the road divided, near San Sebastian; thence the smaller, prettier road headed for the interior: the Bidasoa Valley. It was as scenic as his research had promised. Tumbling mountain rivers ran down shady gorges, enormous oak and chestnut forests whispered in the delicate September air. Lesaka was close. He was in the Basque Navarre. He was nearly there.

As David slowed, he noticed.

Something was happening in Lesaka. The edge of the town was marked by big black police vans, with metal grilles over the windscreens. Surly-looking Spanish riot policemen were sitting on walls, and chatting on mobile phones; they all had very obvious guns.

One of the cops stared at David, and frowned at the car, and checked the numberplate. Then he shook his head, and pointed at a parking space. Mildly unnerved, David slotted in the car. The policeman turned away, uninterested. He just wanted David to stop and walk.

Obediently, David slung his rucksack over his shoulder and paced the rest of the way into Lesaka. He remembered what he had read about Basque terrorism: the campaign for Basque independence by the terror group ETA. It was a nasty business: killings and bombings, intense and surreal atrocities, men in women's wigs shooting teenagers dead. Very nasty.

Was this police activity connected with that?

It was surely possible; yet it was hard to reconcile such horrible enormities with a place like Lesaka. The quiet air was cool and sweet: mountain freshness. The sky was patched with cloud, but the sun was still shining down on ancient stone houses, and an old church on a hill, and mild stone palazzos surrounding little squares. On streetcorners there were strange pillars, carved with the curvilinear sun symbol, like an Art Nouveau swastika. The *lauburu*. David said the word to himself, as he walked through Lesaka.

Lauburu.

Not knowing quite what to do next, he sat on a bench in the central plaza, staring at a large stone house hung with the green, red and white Basque flag, the *ikkurina*. He felt a sudden foolishness: what *should* he do next? Just . . . ask people? Like some amateur detective?

An old woman was sitting next to him, clutching a rosary, and muttering.

David coughed, as courteously as he could, then leaned nearer and asked the woman, in his faltering Spanish: *did she know a man called . . . José Garovillo?*

The woman glanced warily his way, like she suspected him of some imminent street crime; then she shook her head, rose to her feet, and walked off – scattering pigeons as she departed. David watched her shadow disappear around a corner.

For the rest of the afternoon he tried his best: he asked more strangers on the streets and stepped inside two *supermercados,* but he got the same blank or even hostile reactions.

22

No one knew José Garovillo, or no one, at least, wanted to talk about him. In frustration David retreated to his car, hauled out some clothes and a toothbrush, and booked into a little hotel at the end of the main road: the Hotel Eguzki.

The allegedly double room had a design of shepherds' crooks on the wall, and bathtaps which coughed rusty water. David spent the evening eating supermarket chorizo, watching Spanish TV quiz shows, or gazing at the indecipherable writing on the map. He could feel the loneliness like a song in the air. A wistful old folk song.

The morning found him more determined. His first visit was to the church, a decayed and musty building with a fragrance of mildewed leather hassocks. A stricken wooden Christ gazed longingly at the vacant pews. There were two fonts. The smaller of these was carved with a strange symbol, like an arrow, incised brutally into the old grey stone.

He touched the stone, which had been polished to smoothness by the centuries, by a million peasant hands, reaching in for the magic water, daubing it on grubby foreheads.

In nomine patris, et filii, et spiritus sancti . . .

Enough. This was useless. David hoisted his bag and exited the church, stepping with relief into the grass-scented daylight. Where would people congregate? Where would he find life and chatter and *answers*?

A bar.

He made for the busiest street, lined with shops and cafes; then he selected the Bar Bilbo. There was music jangling inside, and through the thick windows he could see people drinking.

A few faces turned as he entered. The dark and dingy bar was crowded. A group of teens were chattering in a corner, talking the most guttural Spanish David had ever heard. Sitting at the opposite table was a young woman, an attractive blonde girl. She glanced his way, then turned back to

23

her cellphone. The rest of the bar was dominated by swarthy, black-haired men, downing glasses of cloudy cider and laughing along to the music.

It was then that David recalled – the music. It was the same kind of music that had been playing at Granddad's funeral. Wasn't it? A vigorous, slightly discordant guitar song. What did this mean? Was there some direct link to the Basques? Was his grandfather actually . . . *Basque?*

David had never heard his granddad speak anything but Spanish – and English. And their family name was authentically Hispanic. *Martinez.* Yet the stocky men actually looked like Granddad. And David's father, for that matter.

Another mystery. The mysteries were *breeding*.

Leaning on the bartop, he ordered some *cerveza* in his conspicuously pathetic Spanish. Then David sat down at a nearby table and drank the beer. Again he felt paralyzed: idiotic. But he also remembered his grandfather's words: go to Lesaka, find José Garovillo, and ask about the map. So he should do it. *Just do it.*

He stood up, and tapped the shoulder of the largest guy at the bar.

'¿Ola?'

The man ignored him.

'Er . . . *Buenos días.*'

Several other customers, with wide brooding faces, were contemplating David's failed attempt at conversation. Faces impassive. Yet somehow surly.

He tapped the man's burly shoulder once more.

'¿Buenos días, señor?'

Again, the man ignored him.

Two of the other drinkers were now glaring at David and asking him sharp questions in their glottal accents. He didn't understand what they were saying. So David pointed at the map, and reverted to English.

'Look, I'm sorry to interrupt . . . but. Really sorry. But this map . . . I was just kinda given this by my grandfather . . . and told to come here and look . . . at these places – see, Ariz . . . kun, Elizonda? Also I need to find a guy called José Garovillo. Do you know where I could find him?'

Now the biggest man turned, and he said something very terse.

David was lost.

'Er . . . I'm sorry . . . But . . . my Spanish is pretty poor?'

The men scowled, with real fury; David realized he must have made some major error. He'd gone too far. He had no idea why or how, but he'd done something stupid. The atmosphere had most definitely intensified. The music had been switched off.

One of the cider drinkers was yelling abusively at David. Across the room the barman was jerking a thumb at the door. David knew he should take the hint. He raised both hands – and made for the exit.

But the drinkers moved first, three of them were up and blocking the way: obstructing his escape route. The big guy had been joined by a man with a denim shirt and muddy boots, and another guy with a Led Zeppelin singlet and tatts on his shoulders.

Jesus. What now?

His best choice was to just barge his way through, hope to reach the door and the light and freedom. But he made one more attempt at talking his way out.

'Look – guys – sorry – *por favor* –' It was useless; he was stammering. One of the cider drinkers was actually rolling up his sleeves.

'Stop!'

David swivelled, and saw the blonde girl. She was physically interposing herself between David and his assailants – and she was talking very quickly to the men. Her smart and staccato Spanish was accented, and the words came too fast for David to understand.

Yet her intervention was . . . *working*. Whatever she was saying – it was succeeding. The anger in the men perceptibly dwindled; scowls became sullen glares, the cold angry faces sank back into the shadows. She was rescuing him from a nasty beating.

He looked at the girl, she looked at him, and then she looked right past him.

Now David realized – maybe there was *another* reason the guys had fallen back. Right behind him, a figure was walking across the room. If the drinkers had been calmed by the girl, they were positively cowed by this new figure emerging from the shadows. Where had he come from?

The man was tall and dark. His face was stern, half shaven, and mournfully aggressive. He was maybe thirty-five years old. Maybe an athletic forty. Who was this? Why had he silenced everyone?

'Miguel . . .?'

It was the barman – gabbling nervously.

'Er . . . Miguel . . . Eh . . . *Dos equis?*'

Miguel ignored the offer. He was gazing with his dark, deepset eyes directly at the blonde girl and David. He was standing close. His breath was tinged with some alcohol, strong wine or brandy. But he didn't seem drunk. Miguel turned, and looked at the girl. His voice was deep and smooth.

'Amy?'

Her answer was defiant. '*Adiós*, Miguel.'

She took David's hand, and started pulling him towards the door. Quickly and firmly. But Miguel stopped her. He reached out – and simply grabbed Amy's throat. Her fingers loosened from David's grasp.

And then Miguel hit her. Hard. A shocking and brutal

blow across the face. The girl fell to the floorboards, sprawling in the cigarette butts and screwed tapas napkins.

David gaped. This sudden violence, against a much smaller young woman, was so shocking, so utterly and casually outrageous, David was stunned. Immobile. What should he do? He gazed around. No one else was going to intervene. Some of the drinkers were actually turning away, giving each other weak and cowardly grins.

David leapt on Miguel. The Basque man may have been bigger and taller than David – and David wasn't short – but David didn't care. He remembered being beaten as a teenager. The angry orphan. People picking on the weak or vulnerable. Fuck that.

He had Miguel round the neck, he was trying to get room for a punch.

He failed. Grabbing this man was like riding a surging bull: the taller man stiffened, swivelled, and threw him contemptuously onto the floor. David grabbed at a bar stool, pulling himself to his feet. But then he felt another, quite absolute pain: he was being struck by something metal.

As the blackness descended, he realized he was being pistol-whipped.

4

Simon Quinn paid the cabbie, quit the taxi, and shot a glance along the stucco Georgian terrace. His laptop bag felt heavy on his shoulder.

The murder house was painfully obvious: two police vans were parked outside, with forensic officers in white paper suits offloading steel-grey Scene of Crime suitcases. Festoons of blue and yellow police tape roped off the frontage of the tall, elegant London terrace.

He felt a sudden twinge of apprehension. DCI Sanderson had described the murder as a . . . *knotting*. What the hell did that mean?

The nerves were palpable, indeed visible: a faint tremble in his hand. He'd attended a lot of murder scenes in his job – crime and punishment were his journalistic meat and drink – but that word . . . *knotting*. It was odd. Disquieting.

Ducking under the police tape he was met at the threshold by the bright young face of DS Tomasky. Sanderson's new junior officer, a cheerful Londoner of Polish descent. Simon had met him once before.

'Mister Quinn . . .' Tomasky smiled. 'Fraid you missed the corpse. We just moved her.'

'I'm here because the DCI called me . . .'

'Wants his name in the tabs again?' Tomasky laughed in the pleasant autumnal sunshine. Then he stopped laughing. 'I think he's got some photos to show you.'

'Yes?'

'Yeah. Pretty gruesome. Be warned.'

Tomasky leaned an arm across the doorway, physically barring the journalist from entering the house. Beyond Tomasky's arm, he could see two more forensic officers stepping in and out of a room, with their blue paper facemasks hanging loose.

'How old is the victim?'

The policeman didn't move his arm.

'*Old*. From southern France. Very old.'

Looking up at the stucco frontage of the house, Simon glanced left and right.

'Nice place for an old lady.'

'*Tak*. Must have been wealthy.'

'Andrew, can I go in now?'

DS Tomasky half-smiled.

'OK. The DC is in the room on the left. I was just trying to . . . prepare you.'

The detective sergeant gestured Simon through the door. The journalist walked down the hallway, which smelled of beeswax and old flowers – and the gases and gels of forensic investigation.

A voice halted him.

'Name of Françoise Gahets. Never married.'

It was Sanderson. His lined and lively face was peering around the door of the room at the end of the hallway.

'DCI! Hello.'

'Got your notebook?'

'Yes.' Simon fished the pad from his pocket.

'Like I said, name of Françoise Gahets. She never married.

She was rich, lived alone . . . We know she's been in Britain sixty years, no close relatives. And that's all we've got so far. You wanna see the SOC?'

'Unless you want to get, ah, pizza.'

Sanderson managed a very faint smile.

They crossed the doorway. As they did Sanderson continued:

'Body was found by the cleaner yesterday. Estonian girl called Lara. She's still downing the vodkas.'

They stepped to the end of the sitting room. A white-overalled, white-masked forensic officer swerved out of the way, so the two men could see.

'This is where we found her. Right here. The body was moved this morning. She was . . . sitting right there. You ready to see the photos?'

'Yes.'

Sanderson reached to a sidetable. He picked up a folder, opened it, and revealed a sheaf of photographs.

The first photo showed the murdered old woman, fully clothed, kneeling on the floor with her back to them. She was wearing gloves, oddly enough. Simon checked the photo against the reality in front of him.

Then he looked back at the photo. From this angle the victim looked alive, as if she was kneeling down to search for something under the TV or the sofa. At least she looked alive – if you regarded her up to the neck only.

It was the head that made Simon flinch: what the murderer, or murderers, had done to the head.

'What the . . .'

Sanderson offered another photograph:

'We got a close-up. Look.'

The second photo was taken from a few inches away: it showed that the entire top of the victim's scalp had been wrenched away, exposing the white and bloody bone of her skull.

'And check this one.'

Sanderson was proffering a third image.

This photo showed the detached scalp itself, a bloody clogged mess of wrinkled skin and long grey hair, lying in the carpet; rammed through the hair was a thick stick – some kind of broom handle maybe. The grey hair was tightly wound around this stick, many many times, all twisted and broken. *Knotted.*

Simon exhaled, very slowly.

'Thanks. I think.'

He gazed around the room: the bloodstains on the carpet were still very visible. It was fairly obvious how the killing must have been done: bizarre – but obvious. Someone had made the old woman kneel down, by the TV, then they had forced the stick through her long grey hair, then they had turned the stick around and around, winding the hair ever tighter on the stick, chewing all her hair into one great painful knot of blood and pain, tearing at the roots of the hair on her scalp, until the pulling pressure must have snapped, tearing off the entire scalp.

He picked out one of the last photos. It was taken from the front, showing the woman's expression. His next words were instant – and reflexive.

'Oh my God.'

The old woman's mouth was torqued into a loud yet silent scream, the last frozen expression of her suffering, as the top of her head was twisted off, and popped away.

It was too much. Simon stiffened, and dropped the folder of photos on the sidetable; he turned and walked to the marble fireplace. It was empty and cold, with dried grasses in a vase, and a photo of some old people. A kitsch plaster statue of the Blessed Virgin Mary smiled from the centre of the mantelpiece, next to a small ceramic donkey. The yawning image of his brother, his hands coated in blood, came unbidden to his mind.

He purged it, and turned.

'So . . . Detective . . . judging by that broom handle . . . it looks like . . . They twisted and twisted the hair, until it ripped off the top of . . . of her head?'

Sanderson nodded.

'Yep. And it's called knotting.'

'How do you know?'

'It's a form of torture. Used through the centuries, apparently.' He glanced at the door. 'Tomasky did his research, like a good lad. He says knotting was used on gypsies. And in the Russian Revolution.'

'So . . .' Simon shuddered at the thought of the woman's pain. 'So . . . she died of shock?'

'Nope. She was garrotted. Look.'

Another photo. Sanderson's pen was pointing to the woman's neck; now the journalist leaned close, he could see faint red weals.

It was puzzling, and deeply grotesque. He frowned his distaste, and said:

'But that's . . . rather confusing. Whoever did this, tormented the old woman first. And then killed her . . . expertly . . . Why the hell would you do all that?'

'Who the fuck knows?' Sanderson replied. 'Bit of a weird one, right? And here's another thing. They didn't steal a thing.'

'Sorry?'

'There's jewellery upstairs. Totally untouched.'

They walked to the door; Simon felt a strong urge to get out of the room. Sanderson chatted as they exited.

'So . . . Quinn. You're a good journalist. Britain's seventh best crime reporter!' His smile faded. 'I'm not kidding, mate. That's why I asked you here – you like a bloody mystery story. If you work out the mystery, do let us know.'

5

When he came to, groggy and numb, they were both outside, by the door to the bar. In the mountain sun. The girl was bleeding from her forehead, but not much. She was shaking him awake.

A shadow loomed. It was the barman. He was standing, nervously shifting from foot to foot, wearing an expression of compassionate fear.

He said in English, 'Amy. Miguel – I keep him inside but but but you go, you must go – go now –'

She nodded.

'I know.'

Once more the blonde girl grabbed David's hand. She was pulling him upright. As David stood, he felt the muscles and bones in his face – he was hurting. But he wasn't busted. There was dried blood on his fingers, from where he must have tried to protect himself – and protect the girl.

'Crazy.' She was shaking her head. 'I mean. Thank you for doing that. But crazy.'

'I'm sorry.' David was wholly disorientated. She was British. 'You saved me first anyway. But . . . I don't . . . don't understand. What just happened in that bar?'

'Miguel. It was Miguel.'

That much he knew already. Now she was tugging him down the silent Basque street, past little restaurants advertising *raciones* and *gorrin*. Past silent stone houses with towers.

David regarded his rescuer. She was maybe twenty-seven, or twenty-eight, with a determined but pretty face, despite the bruise and the blooding. And she was insistent.

'C'mon. Quick. Where's your car? I came by bus. We need to get out of here before he gets really angry. That's why I tried to pull you away.'

'That wasn't . . . really angry?'

She shook her head.

'That was nothing.'

'Sorry?'

'You've never heard of Miguel? *Otsoko*?'

'No.'

'*Otsoko* is Basque for wolf. That's his codename. *His ETA codename.*'

He didn't wait for any further explanation; they ran to his car and jumped in.

David stared at her across the car. 'Where should we go? *Where?*'

'Any village that's not Lesaka. Head that way . . . Elizondo. My place.'

David gunned the engine and they raced out of town. Amy added:

'It's safe there.' She looked his way. 'And we can clean you up, you're still a bit of a mess.'

'And you?'

Her smile was brief. 'Thanks. Go this way.'

David twisted the wheel, his nerves tautened by the idea of Miguel, 'the Wolf'. The barman and the drinkers had obviously dissuaded Miguel from further violence: but maybe the Wolf would change his mind.

The Wolf?

David sped them urgently out of the little town, past the Spanish police, past the last stone house; he was agitated by all the puzzles. What had happened in the bar? Who was Miguel? Who was this *girl*?

He realized, again, that her Spanish had been spoken with a British accent.

What was she doing here?

As they raced down the narrow road, through the sylvan countryside, he sensed that he had to inquire, that she wasn't just going to tell him too much, unprompted. So he asked. Her face was shadowed with dapples of sun – light and dark shadows that disguised the bruising on her face – as she turned. His first query was the most obvious of all.

'OK. I guess we go to the police. Right? Tell them what happened.'

He was astonished when she shook her head.

'No. No, we can't, we just . . . can't. Sorry, but I work with these people, live with them, they trust me. This is ETA territory. And the police are the Spanish. No one goes to the police.'

'But . . .'

'And what would I say anyway? Mmm?' Her blue eyes were burning. 'What do I say? A guy hit me in a bar? Then they would ask his name . . . and I would have to say the Wolf. And there, that's it – then I've betrayed an ETA hero, a famous ETA fighter.' Her expression was grimly unamused. 'That would not be good for my longevity. Not in deepest Euskadi.'

David nodded, slowly, accepting the explanation. But her replies had triggered more questions: she worked with these people? How? Where? And why?

He asked again, outright, about her situation. She turned away from him, to stare at the mellow green fields.

'You want to know *now*?'

'I've got a lot of questions. Why not now?'

A pause, then she said:

'OK. OK. You did try to save my life. Maybe you deserve to know.'

Her slender face was set in determined profile, as she offered her answers.

Her name was Amy Myerson. She was Jewish, twenty-eight, and from London, where she'd been educated, taking a degree in foreign languages. She was now an academic at San Sebastian University, teaching Eng Lit to Basque kids. She had fetched up here in the Basque Country after a couple of years backpacking. 'Smoking too much hash in Morocco. You know.'

He managed a smile; she didn't smile in return. Instead she added: 'And then I found myself here, the *Pays Basque*, between the forests and the steelworks.' The spangled sunlight from the trees was bright on the windscreen. 'And I also got involved in the struggle for independence. Met some people from Herri Batasuna, the political wing of ETA. I don't support the violence, of course . . . But I do believe in the goal. Basque freedom.' She was looking out of the window again. 'Why shouldn't they be free? The Basques have been here longer than anyone else. Maybe thirty thousand years. Lost in the silent valleys of the Navarre . . .'

They were at the main Bidasoa highway; huge cement lorries were thundering past. Amy instructed him:

'Turn right.'

David nodded; his lip was still throbbing. His jaw ached where the pistol butt had smashed across it. But he could tell he clearly had no broken bones. A life of looking after himself, as an orphan, had made him a good judge of his physical condition. He was going to be OK. But what about her?

Amy was gazing his way.

36

'So. That's my autobiography, not a bestseller. What about you? Tell me *your* story.'

It was only fair: she should know too.

Swiftly he sketched his strange and quixotic situation: his parental background, the bequest from his grandfather, the map and the churches. Amy Myerson's blue eyes widened as she listened.

'Two million dollars?'

'Two million dollars.'

'Christ. Wish someone would leave me two bloody million dollars!' Then she put a hand to her pretty white teeth. 'Oh God. You must be grieving. *Stupidest* remark in the world. I'm sorry . . . It's just . . . this morning.'

'It's alright. I understand.' David wasn't annoyed. She had just saved him from a beating – or worse – as much as he had saved her. He remembered Miguel's dark eyes glaring.

'Take this left here.'

David dutifully steered them off the main road; they were on a much quieter highway now. Ahead of them he could see a wide and sumptuous valley, leading to hazy blue mountains. The upper slopes of the mountains were lightly talced with snow.

'The Valley of Baztan,' said Amy. 'Beautiful, no?'

She was right: it was stunning. He gazed at the soothing view: the cattle standing knee-deep in the golden riverlight, the somnolent forests stretching to the blue-misted horizon.

After ten minutes of admirable Pyrenean countryside, they pulled past a tractor repair depot, then a Lidl *supermercado*, and entered a small town of dignified squares and little bakeries, and chirruping mountain streams that ran past the gardens of ancient sandstone houses. Elizondo.

Her flat was in a modern development just off the main road. Amy keyed the door and they snuck in; her flat had tall windows with excellent views of the Pyrenees up the valley. With their slopes draped with ice and fog, and the summits looming blue above, the mountains looked like a row of Mafiosi at the barber's, white-sheeted to the neck.

A row of killers.

He thought of Miguel as Amy busied herself in the kitchen. Miguel, *Otsoko*, the Wolf. The immensely strong muscles, the tall dark shape, the deeply set eyes. He tried not to think of Miguel. He glanced around the apartment: the walls were sparsely decorated but the bookshelves were full of heavy-weight literature: Yeats and Hemingway and Orwell. A mighty volume called *The Poetry of Violence*.

What did she teach these kids at San Sebastian University?

Then he swivelled: she had returned, carrying paper towels and flannels and antiseptic cream, and a plastic basin of hot water; together they knelt on the bare wooden floors, and tended to each other's wounds. She dabbed at his lip with a white flannel; the cloth came away red and brown with old blood.

'Ouch,' he said.

'Not broken,' she said. 'Brave soldier.'

He waved away the absurd compliment; she bent to her task, squeezing the flannel in the water, making soft crimson blooms of his blood. Then she spoke.

'We could go to the doctor . . . but we'd just have to sit for six hours to get a stitch, maybe. Don't see the point. Mmm?'

He nodded. Her expression was serious, impassive and reserved. He guessed there were still a lot of things she wasn't telling him yet; but then again he hadn't yet asked her the truly probing question: why had Miguel attacked her, so instantly and angrily?

'OK, Amy, let me help *you*.' He took a clean flannel and moistened it with hot water. She presented her face, eyes shut, and he began to dab and wash the blood from her hairline. She winced at the tang of the water, but said nothing. As he cleaned her wound, he questioned her.

'I want to know more about that bar.'

'Uh-huh?'

'What I don't get is . . . is . . . It wasn't just that guy Miguel, the whole place was punchy. What did I do *wrong*? How did I upset so many people just by asking a couple of questions?'

Amy's head was tilted, letting him clean her forehead. She was silent for a moment, and then she said:

'OK, here's the deal. Lesaka is one of the most nationalist towns in the Basque Country. Fiercely proud.'

David nodded, and took some paper towels, beginning to dry the deep but now unbleeding scratch.

'Go on . . .'

'And then there's ETA. The terrorists. Miguel's friends.' She frowned. 'They killed some Guardia Civil, just two weeks ago. Five of them, in a horrible bomb, in San Sebastian. And then the Spanish police shot dead four ETA activists. Madrid claims they were also planting a bomb. Basques are saying it was cold-blooded reprisal.'

'Ah.'

'*That's* why there are police everywhere. It's majorly tense. The Spanish police can be *extremely* violent when they are taking on ETA. It's a vicious spiral.'

David sat back, examining his work on her wound. She would be alright; he would be alright. But there was something odd that he had noticed, something that was not quite alright.

When he had been washing the blood from Amy's forehead, he had seen a scar. A strange and complex scar: curving arcs of some deep yet decorative cuts – hidden under her bright blonde hair.

He said nothing.

Her injuries treated, Amy was sitting back. She was

cross-legged in her jeans and trainers, her hands flat on the bare floorboards.

'So you wanna know what else you did wrong?'

'Yes.'

'Let's take it in order. First you accused the guys of talking Spanish in a ferociously Basque-speaking area. That isn't so hot. And then you must remember the political tension. As I explained.'

'Sure. And?'

'And . . . well . . . there's something else as well.'

'What?'

'You said something quite provocative on top of all that.'

'I did?'

'You mentioned *José Garovillo*. That's when I came across to try and help you, when you said that. I told them I knew you, that you were a bloody idiot, they should pity you –'

'Er, thanks.'

'I had to say that. Because when I heard you banging on about José, I knew you were in *deep* trouble.'

'So . . . who is he?'

She gazed across the tepid water, in the plastic basin.

'You don't know?'

David felt increasingly stupid, and increasingly frustrated.

Amy explained:

'José Garovillo is very old now, but he's really quite famous around here.'

'You mean you actually know him? You can help me find him?'

'I know him well. I can email him today, tell him about you. If you want.'

'But . . . Great. That's great!'

'Wait.' Her face was unsmiling; she lifted a hand to slow his words. '*Listen*. A *lot* of people round here know Garovillo. Because he's a cultural icon, one of the intellectuals who

40

helped revive Basque language and culture – way back when. In the 60s and 70s. He was also a member of ETA in the 60s.'

'He's famous? But I looked him up on the net! There was nothing.'

Amy answered: 'But he's only famous amongst Basques. And in ETA he was just called José. You'd never see his full name written down . . . ETA people like to keep a low profile. And Garovillo has been a Basque radical since way back – he was interned by Germans in the war, over in Iparralde.'

'Sorry?'

She turned and waved a small white hand at the window.

'There. The land beyond! The French Basque Country, over the mountains. In 1970 he was arrested and tortured by Franco, and then by the Socialists. He used to drink in the Bar Bilbo, years ago. He's pretty famous – or notorious.' Her face was serious. 'Not least because of his son . . .'

'I'm sorry?'

'His son's name is . . . Miguel.'

'The guy who attacked us . . .'

'Is José's son. The Wolf is José Garovillo's son.'

6

David booked himself into a hotel on the outskirts of Elizondo, to wait for Amy's email to José to do the job. The Hotel Gernika was nothing special. It had a small swimming pool, a modest breakfast bar, and lots of leathery old French guests on cycling holidays wearing alarmingly tight Lycra shorts. But that was fine by David.

With his money, his unaccustomed wealth, he could have booked into the best hotel in Navarre – but it didn't seem right. He wanted to be inconspicuous. Anonymous and un-noticed: just another tourist in a nice but mediocre hotel. So he grabbed his bags and booked himself in, and spent the rest of the day staring from his humble balcony, gazing out at the mountains. The cirques and summits seemed to shimmer, knowingly, exulting in their own remoteness.

It was a hot and dusty day. In the evening he decided on a swim: he walked into the hotel gardens and stripped to his shorts, and dived in the blue inviting water of the pool. He gasped as he surfaced, the water was *freezing*, straight from the mountains, unheated.

His whole body was tingling, his heart was thumping, it was a perfect metaphor for his situation. Three weeks ago he was a bored and listless commuter, reading free newspapers on the train, drinking machine coffee at work, doing the daily rounds of nothingness. As soon as he arrived in the Basque Country he had plunged right into it, straight into this mystery and strangeness and violence; and yet it felt good. Shocking but good; bracing but invigorating. Like diving into a pool of freezing mountain water. Making his body tingle.

I am alive.

The next day Amy called him: she'd had an idea. She reckoned that he should maybe publish his story, to help with the puzzle. Amy said she knew a local journalist who was willing to write it up; her way of thinking was that the more people who knew the questions, the better the chance they might locate some of the answers.

David agreed to the idea, with only the faintest sense of reluctance.

They met again in the journalist's spare white flat; the young, dark-haired writer, Zara Garcia, banged out the article on a laptop. The piece appeared in a Spanish newspaper just half-a-day later. It was immediately picked up and translated by some English language newsfeeds.

When David finally read the published story, on his own laptop, sitting with Amy in a little wifi cafe near the main plaza of Elizondo, he felt anxiety as well as excitement. The article was headlined 'Bizarre Bequest Leads to Million Dollar Basque Mystery'.

It had a photo taken by Zara of David holding up the map; the newspaper offered an email address where people could get in touch with David, if they had any ideas that might help.

The journalist had left out the connection with José Garovillo: she'd explained that it was too incendiary and provocative in the political climate. Reading the article, David

43

decided this omission had definitely been a good idea; he already felt exposed enough by the newspaper piece. What if Miguel read it?

He shut the laptop and looked at Amy, in her purple denim jacket and her elegantly slender jeans. She looked back at him, silent, and blue eyed; and as she did, he felt the oddness of their situation – like an inexplicable shiver on a very warm day. Already they were sort-of friends: forced together by that horrible and frightening scene in the Bar Bilbo. And yet they were not friends; they were still total strangers. It was dissonant.

Or maybe he was just unnerved by the noise in the bar. The slap and laughter of kids playing *pelota*, the peculiar Basque sport, in the square outside, was very audible. Children were thwapping the hard little *pelota* ball against a high wall. The noise was repetitive and intense. She glanced his way.

'Shall we go somewhere else?'

'If you have time.'

'Academic holiday. And I'd like to help, while my students are off shooting the police.' She smiled at his alarmed response. 'Hey. That was a *joke*. Where do you want to go?'

'I want to start looking at the churches. On my map . . .'

'OK.'

'But first . . . I'd like to go somewhere I can have a proper drink.' He looked at her for a long moment, then he confessed: he was still feeling the nerves, the fear, the after-effects of Miguel's attack.

'Let's go for a glass and talk,' she said.

A few minutes' driving brought them to a hushed little village; the sign said *Irurita*. Old men sat snoozing under berets, outside cafes. Parking the car by the village church they walked to one of the cafes; they sat under a parasol. The clear mountain air was refreshing, the sun was warm.

Amy ordered some olives and a bottle of the chilled local white wine that she called *txacolli*.

The waitress served them at their shaded table with a nimble curtsey.

Amy spoke:

'You haven't asked me the most obvious question of all.'

He demurred; her expression was serious.

'You ought to know this . . . if I am going to introduce you to José.'

He drank some of his cold fresh wine, and nodded. 'OK. If you insist. Why did Miguel attack you? He came out of nowhere, then . . . assaulted you. Why?'

Her answer was fluent:

'He hates me.'

'Why?'

She pressed her hands together, as if praying. 'When I first came to the Basque Country I was . . . as I said, very interested in ETA. The cause of independence. I thought it was a laudable ambition, for an ancient people. I even sympathized with the terrorists. For a while. For a few months.'

'And . . .'

'Then I met José. The great José Garovillo. We became very good friends, he showed me where to buy the best *pintxos* in Bizkaia. He told me everything. He told me he had renounced violence, after the fall of Franco. He said terrorism was a cul de sac for the Basque people, within a democratic Spain.'

'But his son –'

'Disagreed. Obviously.' She gazed straight at David. 'But then José got me a job, teaching English at the university. And you see . . . a lot of the kids who come into my class are very radical, from the backstreets of Vittoria and Bilbao, ready to die for ETA. The girls are even more fierce than the boys. Killers in miniskirts.'

45

Her lips were pink and wet from the *txacolli*. 'I see it as my task to maybe steer them away from ETA, from violence, and the self-destruction of terrorism. So I teach them the literature of revolution: Orwell on the Civil War, Yeats on the Irish rebellion. I try to teach them the tragedy as well as the romance of a violent nationalist struggle.'

'And that's why Miguel hates you? He thinks you are working against ETA.'

'Yes. I knew he'd been abroad for a while, though I did hear a rumour he was back. But I thought it was safe to go see my friends in the Bilbo. But he must have been in the bar already. Hanging out in one of the back rooms, with his ETA comrades . . .'

'Then he heard the row.'

'Yes. And he walked out. Saw me. With you.' She grimaced. 'And did his favourite thing.'

The explanation was good, if not perfect. David still felt the echo of an unexplained space, a dark blur on the image. What else was she not telling him? What about the scar on her scalp?

He stopped thinking as the waitress placed some olives on their table.

'*Gracias,*' he said. The girl nodded and bobbed and replied in that thick guttural Spanish accent: *kakatazjaka* . . . Then she waved to a friend across the cobbled plaza, and made her way back to the bar.

'You know it's funny,' said David, half turning to Amy. 'I've not heard any Basque being spoken. Not yet.'

'Sorry?'

'I've been in the Basque Country for two days. I've seen it written on signs everywhere. But not heard anyone speaking it.'

She gazed at him from under her blonde fringe – as if he was retarded.

'That girl spoke Basque *just then*.'

'. . . She did?'

'Yep.'

Amy's denim jacket was off; David noticed the golden hairs on her suntanned arms as she reached again for her glass of wine.

'And all the guys in Lesaka,' she said, tilting her glass. 'They were all speaking Basque. Hence their anger when you tried talking Spanish.'

David cocked an ear, listening to the chatter of the waitress. *Kazakatchazaka*.

Amy was right. This *was* surely Basque. And yet it sounded like they were talking a very bizarre Spanish. *And he'd been hearing it all along without realizing.*

'Don't worry,' she said, 'it took me a while, when I first came here, to realize I was surrounded by Basque speakers. I just thought they had over-the-top Spanish accents.' She looked beyond him – at the whitewashed church walls. 'I think it's because Basque is *so* strange, the ear and the mind can't entirely comprehend what's being heard.'

'Have you learned any?'

'I've tried, of course! But it's just impossible, weird clauses, unique syntax.' She lifted her chin. 'Here's an example of how mad Basque is. What's the first phrase you learn in any foreign language?'

'"Do you speak English?"'

'Comedy genius. What else?'

'. . ."Can I have a beer?"'

'Exactly. *Une bière s'il vous plaît. Ein bier bitte.*'

'So how do you say "Can I have a beer" – in Basque?'

Amy looked at him.

'*Garagardoa nahi nuke.*'

They sat there in the sun, in tense but companionable silence. And then a gust of wind rippled the parasol. David looked left: clouds were scudding in from the west, thicker clouds were rolling down the nearest Pyrenean slope, like a white sheepskin coat slowly falling from the shoulders.

'OK,' said David. 'How do we know Miguel isn't going to just turn up here, and follow you? And hurt you. I don't get it. You seem calm. Fairly calm anyway.'

'He was drunk. He's only ever hit me once before.'

'He's done it before?'

She blushed. Then she quickly added: 'He usually hangs out in Bilbao or Bayonne – with the other ETA leaders. He rarely comes to Navarre, might get seen. We were just very very unlucky. And anyhow I'm not going to let that bastard chase me away.'

Her final words were defiant: the slender nose uptilted, eyes wide and angry.

David saw the conviction and the sense in her statement; but he still felt queasy and tense. Just sitting here in the autumn breeze. Doing nothing.

'OK. Let's go and see the churches on my map.'

Amy nodded, and rose; when they climbed in the car the first flickers of drizzle were spitting on the windscreen.

'How quickly it changes. In the autumn.'

The rain was a majorette's drum-roll on the car roof. David reached in the glovebox and took out the precious paper; carefully unfolding the leaves, he showed her the map that had brought him halfway round the world.

He noticed her fingernails were bitten, as she pointed at the asterisks.

'Here. Arizkun.'

'You know it?'

'I know *of* it. One of the most traditional Basque villages. Way up in the mountains.' She looked squarely at David. 'I can show you.'

David reversed the car. He followed Amy's lucid directions:

towards France and the frontier, and the louring mountains. Towards the Land Beyond.

The villages thinned as they raced uphill. Ghosts of fog were floating over the steeply sloping fields, melancholy streamers of mist, like the pennants of a departing and spectral army.

'We're right near the border . . .' she said. 'Smugglers used to come over here. And rebels. Witches. Terrorists.'

'So which way?'

'There.'

Amy was indicating a tiny winding turn off – with a sign above it, just perceptible through the mist.

The road to Arizkun was the narrowest yet: high mountain hedges with great rock boulders hemmed them in, like bigger people trying to bully them into a corner. More mountain peaks stretched away to the west, a recession of summits in the mist.

'On a clear day you can see right into France,' said Amy.

'Can barely see the damn road.'

They were entering a tiny and very Basque village square. It had the usual Basque *pelota* court, several terraces of medieval stone houses, and a bigger stone mansion, adorned with a sculpted coat of arms. A wyvern danced across the damp heraldic stone: a dragon with a vicious coiling tail, and feminine claws.

The village was desolately empty. They parked by the mansion, which was spray-painted with ETA graffiti.

Eusak Presoak, Eusak Herrira.

Beneath this slogan was an even larger slash of graffiti. Written in the traditional jagged and ancient Basque script, the word was unmistakable.

Otsoko.

Next to the word was a black stencil of a wolf's head.

The Wolf.

Amy was standing next to David, looking at the graffito.

'Some of the Basque kids worship him . . .' she said.

'Why?'

''Cause he's so perfectly ruthless. A brilliant killer . . . who comes and goes. Who never gets caught.'

She was visibly shivering. She added:

'And they admire the cruelty. Of course.'

'Miguel is . . . especially cruel?'

'Rhapsodically. Voluptuously. *Poetically.* The Spanish torture Basque radicals, but Miguel tortures them right back. He frightens the fuck out of the Spanish police. Even the anti terrorists.'

Amy leaned to look at the graffito. David asked:

'What kind of tortures?'

Her fringe of blonde hair was dewed with water in the mist. 'He buried one Guardia Civil guy in quicklime.'

'To destroy the evidence?'

'No no no. Miguel buried the man *alive*, in quicklime, up to his neck. Basically he dissolved him. Alive.'

Abruptly, she walked on. David jogged after her, together they walked down a damp stony path, between two of the older Basque houses. David looked left and right. Brown and thorny sunflowers decorated the damp wooden doors, hammered fiercely to the planks. Some of the wayside thistles had been made into man shapes. Manikins made out of thistles.

The silence of the village was unnerving. As they paced through the clinging mist, the echo of their footsteps was the only noise.

'Where the hell is everyone?'

'Killed. Died. America.'

They were at the end of the lane. The houses had dwindled, and they were surrounded by rocks and thickets.

Somewhere out there was France, and the ocean – and cities and trains and airports.

Somewhere.

Abruptly, a church appeared through the mist. Grey-stoned and very old, and perched above a ravine which was flooded with fog. The windows were gaunt, the location austere.

'Not exactly welcoming. The house of God?'

Amy pushed at a rusty iron gate. 'The churches are often like this. They used to build them on older sites, pagan sites. For the ambience, maybe.'

David paused, perplexed. Odd circular stones, like circles balanced on squares, were set along the path to the church door. The stones were marked with *lauburus* – the mysterious and aethereal swastika. David had never seen circular gravestones before.

'Let's try inside,' he said.

They walked down the slippery cobbled path to the humble wooden church door. It was black, old, wet – and locked.

'Damn.'

Amy walked left, around the side of the church – shrouding herself with mist. David followed. There was a second, even smaller door. She twisted the rusty handle; it opened. David felt the lick of moisture on his neck; it was cold now, as well as gloomy. He wanted to get inside.

But the interior of the church was as unalluring as the exterior. Dank and shadowy, with unpainted wooden galleries of seating. The reek of rotten flower-water was intense; five stained glass windows filtered the chill and foggy daylight.

'Curious,' said Amy, pointing up. One of the stained glass windows showed a large bull, a burning tree, and a white Basque house. Then she elaborated, still pointing at the window.

'The Basques are very devout, very Catholic. But they

51

were pagan until the tenth century, and they keep a lot of their pre-Christian imagery. Like that. That house – there –' she gestured to the main window '– that's the *exte*, the family house, the sacred cornerstone of heathen Basque culture. The souls of the Basque dead are said to return to a Basque house, through subterranean passages . . .'

David stared. The stained glass tree was burning in the cold glass light.

'And the woman? In the other window.'

'That's Mari, the lady of the witches.'

'The . . .'

'Goddess of the witches. The Basque witches. *We do not exist, yes we do exist, we are fourteen thousand strong.*' She looked at him, her eyes blue and icy in the hanging light. 'That was their famous – or infamous – saying. *We do not exist, yes we do exist, we are fourteen thousand strong.*'

Her words were visible wraiths in the chill; her expression was obscure. David had a strong desire to get out; he didn't know what he wanted to do. So he made for the little door, and exited with relief into the hazy daylight. Amy followed him, smiling, and then immediately headed left. Away from the path, disappearing behind the stage curtains of fog.

'Amy?'

Silence. He said again:

'Amy?'

Silence. Then:

'Here. What's this? David.'

He squinted, and saw her: a vague shape in the misty graveyard: female and slender, and elusive. David quickly stepped across.

'Look,' she said. 'Another graveyard . . . With derelict graves.'

She was right. There was a secondary cemetery, divided

from the main churchyard by a low stone wall. This cemetery was much more neglected. A crude statue of an angel had fallen onto the soggy grass; and a brown cigarette had been contemptuously stubbed out – in the angel's eye. Circular gravestones surrounded the toppled angel.

A noise distracted them. David turned. Emerging from the mist was an old woman. Her face was dark. She was dressed in a long black skirt and a ragged blue jumper, over which she was wearing a T-shirt imprinted with Disney characters; Wall-E, The Lion King, Pocahontas.

The woman was also deformed. She had a goitre the size of a grapefruit: a huge tumorous growth bulging out of her neck, like a shot putter holding the shot under his chin, getting ready to throw.

The crone spoke. '*Ggghhhchchc,*' she said. She was pointing at them, her goitre was lividly bulging as she gabbled, her face vividly angry. She looked like a toad, croaking.

'*Graktschakk.*' She pointed at them with a long finger, and then at the neglected graveyard.

'What? What is it?' David's heart was pounding – foolishly. This was just an old woman, a sad, deformed old woman. And yet he was feeling a serious fear, a palpable and inexplicable alarm. He turned. 'Amy – what is she saying?'

'I think it's Basque. She's saying . . . shit people,' Amy whispered, backing awkwardly away.

'Sorry?'

'She says we are shit people. *Shit people.* I've no idea why.'

The woman stared. And croaked some more. It was almost like she was laughing.

'Amy. Shall we get the hell out?'

'Please.'

They scurried up the path, David tried not to look at the woman's enormous goitre as he passed; but then he turned

53

and looked at her goitre. She was still pointing at them, like someone accusing, or denouncing, or *laughing*.

They were almost running now; David stuffed the map in his pocket as they escaped.

The sense of relief when they made the car was profound – and preposterous. David pressed the locks and turned the engine and spun the wheel – reversing at speed. They rumbled over the cobbles, past the stencil of *Otsoko* – the silently grinning black wolf's head.

Amy's mobile phone bleeped as they crested a hill: the telecom signal returning.

'It's José Garovillo. It's *José*.'

'So.' His excitement was real; his fear was repressed. 'What's his response?'

She looked down, reading her message. 'He says . . . he is willing to meet you. Tomorrow.' She shook her head. 'But . . . this is a little odd . . . there's something else.'

'What?'

'He says he knows why you are here.'

7

The tiny four-seater plane soared across the windswept fields of Shetland, heading for the rough blue sea already visible in the distance.

'It's just a twenty-minute flight,' said the pilot, above the loud engines. 'Might get a bit bumpy when we reach the coast.'

Simon Quinn was squeezed in the back of the minuscule plane alongside DCI Sanderson; sitting next to the pilot was DS Tomasky.

The speed of events was bewildering. Simon had learned only the previous afternoon, while watching *Shrek* with his son, Conor, that there was another murder case, linked to the Primrose Hill knotting. And already he was here: flying across the lonely, sunlit cliffs, with the words of his excited editor at the *Daily Telegraph* still reverberating in his mind: *you know the cliché, Simon: murder is money. Our readers will lap this up. Go and have a look!*

It was certainly a juicy story. He could envisage the headlines – and the byline photo. But there was a mystery here, too. All he had been told was that the new victim, Julie Charpentier, was also old, and she was from the South of France. But the circumstance which had apparently clinched the link, to the satisfaction of the police, was the fact that the woman was tortured. The details of the 'tortures' were, so far, unrevealed.

When he'd heard about the murder, he'd had to beg Sanderson to take him along; promising him some very nice coverage in the resulting article. The DCI had yielded to the journalist's pleas – with a laconic chuckle: 'Make sure you bring a strong stomach. They kept the corpse there for a few days so we could see it.'

The plane raced over the cliffs, out to sea. Leaning forward, the journalist asked the pilot:

'What's it like?'

'Sorry?' The pilot – Jimmy Nicolson – lifted one of his earphones, to hear better. 'Didnae catch it. Say again?'

'What's it like, living on Fowler?'

'Foo-lah,' Jimmy laughed. 'Remember what I said. Foula is pronounced Foo-lah.'

'Yep. Sorry.'

'Don't worry,' the pilot answered. 'We're used to people not knowing about us.'

'You mean?'

'Since they evacuated Saint Kilda, Foula is the most remote inhabited place . . . in the whole of Britain . . .'

Simon peered out of the window at the oceans. Chops of foam were mere flicks of whiteness against the enormous wastes of water. For several minutes they flew on in silence. He felt his stomach churn – he didn't know if it was the nauseating rollercoaster ride of the airplane, or his apprehension at visiting the murder scene. Yet he was also adolescently excited. Headlines. He would get *headlines*.

'There,' said Jimmy Nicolson. 'Foula!'

Just perceptible through the sea-haze was a small but gutsy outcrop: a looming outlier of treeless, grass-topped rock, surmounted by steep hills. The cliffs looked so enormous and the hills so daunting it was hard to believe anyone could pitch a tent on the island, let alone find enough flat space to build a house. But there were houses there: small crofts and cottages, tucked against the slopes.

And now they were banking towards Foula's only landing spot. A patch of green turf.

Sanderson laughed. 'That's the airstrip?'

'Flattest part of the isle,' said Jimmy. 'And we've never had a crash. Anyway if you overshoot, you just end up in the sea.' He chuckled. 'Hold onto your bonnets, gentlemen.'

It was the steepest descent Simon had ever made in a plane: they were plunging headlong towards the airstrip, as if they intended to plough up the fields with the propeller. But then Jimmy yanked fiercely on the joystick, and the plane tilted up, and suddenly they were coming to a stop, ten yards from the vandalizing waves.

Tomasky actually applauded.

'Nice landing.'

'Thank you,' said Jimmy. 'Look now, here's the widow Holbourne. And Hamish Leask.'

Already the red-cheeked locals were slapping Jimmy on the back, and helping him to unload stores from the hold of the little aircraft; a few of them were nodding respectfully at DCI Sanderson. A tall red-haired man, in a police uniform, came over and introduced himself to the Scotland Yard officers.

'Hamish Leask. Northern Constabulary.'

Sanderson smiled politely:

'Of course. We talked. Hello!' He gestured. 'This is the freelancer I mentioned. Simon Quinn. He's covering . . . things for the *Telegraph*.'

'Och, yes. A proper newspaper.' Leask shook Simon's hand with crushing vigour. Before the journalist could reply, Jimmy intervened:

'Terrible thing, Hamish. Terrible thing.'

Leask nodded. Without a word. Then he turned to face his guests. 'So, chaps – shall we go straight to it?'

'Yes please.'

'I've been using Jimmy's car. Very generous of him. Just over there.'

The five men strode across the meadows to a blue and very muddy four-wheel drive. The inside of the Range Rover smelt of peat, dogs and sheep-farming.

They drove past a small harbour. On the shingly beach, small wooden boats were lying on their sides, like drunks asleep on park benches. The biggest boat of all, a red metal tugboat, was oddly craned above the icy waters: literally lifted out of the harbour-water by an enormous metal claw.

Leask explained:

'They have to lift the boat up, or it would get crushed in the storms.'

'But . . .' Simon said. 'It's made out of *metal*.'

Jimmy laughed: 'You haven't seen the storms on Foula.'

The road ran through fields with dark brown sections of soil, where peat had been brutally chopped from the sward. Sheep were nibbling at the salty grass.

Finally they rocked around a corner, where the road turned into a track; beyond that a few humble, off-white cottages were scattered on the last fields, staring at the sea – some looked empty, some had smoking chimneys. And all of these homesteads had a crouched and fearful appearance, huddled against the punitive wind: like dogs too often clattered by a brutal owner.

The path to Charpentier's croft – the apparent scene of the crime – was short and soggy. Simon was glad he was wearing his walking boots.

'OK,' said the Shetland inspector. 'We haven't touched anything since the discovery.'

Sanderson said:

'Just as it was found?'

'And a wee bit grim! Gird yourselves. The body was discovered by a friend, Edith Tait. Another old lady who lives in the cottage just over that field. She's gone to stay on the other side of the island.'

The modest croft seemed innocent enough in the cool northern sunlight. Whitewashed and foursquare. There was no sign of police activity, none of the kerfuffle Simon had expected.

Hamish looked at the assembled faces; he paused, theatrically.

'Shall we?'

Everyone nodded; Hamish Leask thrust open a second door and Simon swiftly scanned the room. The furniture was austere; a painting of the Queen was hanging next to a photo of a Pope. And there was the corpse: lying on the floor, next to the fireplace.

The woman was old, she was dressed in some kind of housecoat. Her body below the neck was virtually untouched; her grey hair was long. She was dark-skinned and barefoot. But it was her face and shoulders that showed what had really happened.

Her face was shredded. Literally ripped into shreds: flaps of skin hung from her cheeks and forehead; the lips had been cut away but left to dangle, livid pink flesh showed inside the savage wounds. Her tongue had been sliced in two: it was protruding, and forked by the slice. Blood was spattered over her throat, the longest ribbon of skin draped down to her chest. Despite the complex and barbaric wounding, an expression was still visible: her face was contorted by pain.

Simon felt himself weaken, somehow, at the appalling sight: it was worse than he had anticipated. Much worse.

But he needed to stay lucid and cogent: do his job, be a journalist. He took a pen from his pocket – he needed to grasp something to calm himself.

DCI Sanderson approached the corpse. The detective stooped to look at the bruises on the neck. Blood had drained into the victim's chest, discolouring the flesh; the intense rotten odour of decomposition was quite profound. The corpse would have to be moved very, very soon.

'Hey, Tomasky. Have a look.'

The Polish DS dutifully stepped near. Simon quelled his sense of repulsion, and did the same – uninvited.

Sanderson whistled, almost appreciatively.

'*Expertly* done, again. Another garrotting.'

Simon followed the line of the DCI's pen: he was pointing at some thin weals on the neck. They were livid and painful-looking. Blood had been drawn, but the bruising was minimal, the killing had indeed been swift, ruthless, and *expert*. As the DCI said. And yet the torture looked wild and insane.

Something else caught Simon's attention. He looked down at her feet. Something there was not quite right; something there was . . . *not right at all*.

He didn't know whether to mention it.

Sanderson was off his haunches and saying, briskly: 'You'll need to get her to Pathology in Lerwick, right?'

'Aye, we're flying her out this afternoon. Kept her too long. But we thought you might want to see the scene first, Detective. Seeing as it is so . . . unusual.'

'Lifted anything?'

'Noo. No signs of forced entry – but that means nothing on Foula, people don't lock their doors. No prints. Just . . . nothing.'

He shrugged; Sanderson nodded, distractedly.

'Yes. Yes, thank you.'

Tomasky mused, aloud. '*O moj boze*. Holy Mother. *The face.*'

Sanderson came back: 'Quite something.'

Simon was puzzled, as well as horrified. He was still thinking about her feet. The weirdness of it all. He turned.

'So the big question is . . . what links this woman to Françoise Gahets?'

Sanderson was gazing about the room. 'Yup. We're on it,' he said, pensively. 'She was from Gascony. Isn't that right, Hamish?'

'Aye. French Basque Country near Biarritz. Came here with her mother when she was very young, sixty or seventy years ago.'

A sober pause enveloped them; the moan of the ceaseless Foula wind outside was the only noise, carrying the faint bleats of sheep.

'Enough?' said Hamish.

'Enough for now,' Sanderson answered. 'We'll want to speak to her friend, of course.'

'Edith Tait.'

'Maybe tomorrow?'

The Shetland inspector nodded, and turned to Jimmy Nicolson.

The good cheer of the pilot had quite departed. 'She was such a grand old gal. Came here after the war they say. Now look at her.'

He put a shielding hand to his eyes, and walked out of the room.

Leask sighed. 'Foula is a tiny wee place. This has hit them hard. Let's go for a walk.'

He led them outside into the cold bright air. Jimmy Nicolson was sitting in his car, passionately smoking a cigarette. Tomasky wandered over to join him, but Hamish Leask was already hiking in the opposite direction: up the nearest hill. He turned and called over his burly shoulder.

'Let's climb the Sneug! I feel a need to clear my lungs.'

Simon and Sanderson glanced at each other, then turned and pursued the Shetland officer.

The incline was austere, it was too exhausting to talk as they made their ascent. The journalist found his blood thumping painfully in his chest as, at last, they crested the top of the mighty hill.

The wind at the top was fierce. They were on the edge of a sudden cliff. He edged closer to the drop to have a look.

'Bloody hell!'

Seagulls were wheeling at the bottom of the cliffs, but they were minuscule flakes of whiteness.

'Good God. How high is *that*?'

'One of the biggest sea-cliffs in Europe, maybe in the world,' said Leask. 'More than half a mile down.'

Simon stepped back.

'Very advisable,' said Leask. 'The wind can whip you off these clifftops – and just flip you over the edge.' Hamish chuckled, soberly, and added, 'And yet you know what . . . what is truly amazing?'

'What?'

'These cliffs kept the Foulans going for centuries.'

'Sorry?'

'Look. See here –' The Shetland officer was pointing at some distant atoms of birdlife, halfway down the enormous rockwall. 'Puffin yonder, they nest on the cliffside. In the old days, when food ran low after a long winter, the local men would climb down the cliffs and steal the eggs and the chicks. It was a vital source of protein in the bad times. Baby puffin is very tasty – lots of fat, ye see.'

'They'd climb down these cliffs?'

'Aye. They actually developed a strange deformity. Like a kind of human subspecies.'

'Sorry?'

'The men of Foula. And Saint Kilda too.' Hamish shrugged, his rust-red hair riffling in the wind. 'Over the centuries they developed very big toes, because they used them for climbing the cliffs. I suppose that was evolution. The men who climbed best happened to be the ones with big toes, so they got wives and had well-fed children, and passed on their big toes.'

'Are you serious?'

'Quite serious.' Hamish smiled serenely.

But Simon was not feeling serene; the talk of the weird toes of the Foulans had brusquely reminded him. *What he saw*. The old woman's bare feet. He *had* to mention it.

'Guys. Can we, ah, get out of this wind?'

'Of course.'

The two policemen, and the journalist, walked down to a hollow, then lay back on the dewy turf. Simon said: 'You mentioned toes, Mister Leask.'

'Aye.'

'Well. It's funny but . . . Julie Charpentier's toes . . . Did either of you notice?'

Leask looked blank. 'I'm sorry?'

'You didn't see anything unusual about the victim? Her feet?'

'What?'

Simon wondered if he was making an idiot of himself. 'The toes of her right foot were deformed. Slightly.'

Sanderson was frowning.

'Go on, Simon.'

'I think the word is syndactyly. My wife is a doctor.'

'And syn . . .'

'Yes. Syndactyly. Webbed toes. Two of the old woman's toes were conjoined, at least partially. It's rather rare, but not unknown . . .'

Sanderson shrugged. 'So?'

Simon knew it was a big guess. But he felt sure he was onto something.

'Do you remember the woman in Primrose Hill? What she was wearing?'

The change in Sanderson's expression was sudden.

'You mean the gloves. The fucking *gloves*!'

Before Simon could say anything else, Sanderson was on his feet and speaking on his mobile; the DCI took his phone a few yards down the sunlit slope, talking animatedly all the while. The wind was too boisterous for Simon to hear the conversation.

He sat in the cool yet dazzling sun, thinking of the woman's pain, her lonely screaming pain. Hamish Leask had his eyes shut.

A few minutes later, Sanderson returned, his normally ruddy face whiter; quite pale with surprise.

'I just called Pathology in London.' He turned towards Simon. 'You were right. The gloves were concealing a deformity; Pathology had already noted it.' He looked away again, staring at the distant ocean. 'He said it was digital syndactyly. The Primrose Hill victim had two . . . webbed fingers.'

The sea birds were calling from the cliffs below.

8

They took the Bidasoa Road through the misty green valley, chasing the tumbling river downhill, and then shaving a sudden right, up into the hills, into another Basque Navarrese village, past the obligatory stone fountain and the deserted grey *fronton*. David could sense the small tightness of anxiety: what did José Garovillo know? What was he going to say?

The village was called Etxalar.

David said the word *Etxalar* out loud, practising the pronunciation; Amy smiled, very gently.

'No. Don't say the x like an x, you say *tchuhhhh*.'

'Etch . . . alarrrr?'

'Much better.'

They were stalled behind a cattle truck. Amy seemed distracted. She asked him, apropos of nothing, about his past life, London, America, his job. He sketched a few details.

Then she asked him about his lovelife.

He paused – but then he confessed he was single. Amy asked why.

The cow in the truck stared at them, reproachfully. David answered:

'I guess I push people away, before they get too close.

Perhaps because I lost my parents. Don't trust people to hang around.'

Another silence. He asked, 'And you? Are you attached?'

A silence. The cattle truck moved on, and they followed, accelerating past small orchards of pear trees. At last Amy said, 'David, there's something I should tell you. I've been lying. At least . . .'

'What?'

'I've not been giving you all the information.'

'About what?'

The green-blue of the mountains framed her profile. Her conflicted thoughts were written on her face. David offered:

'You don't have to tell me if you don't want.'

'No,' she answered, 'you *deserve* an explanation. And we are going to meet José, Miguel's father.'

Amy turned and regarded David; there was a tension and yet an audacity in her expression.

'We were lovers. Miguel was my boyfriend. Years ago.'

'Jesus.'

'I was *twenty-three*. I'd just arrived in the Basque Country. I was alone. Young and stupid. I never mentioned it . . . Because I guess I am . . . ashamed.'

David turned the wheel as they drove around a corner; the trees and hedges shivered in the slipstream as they passed. He had to ask: 'You knew he was ETA. And yet you . . .?'

'Slept with him?' She sighed. 'Yes, I know. *Muy stupido*. But I was young like I say and . . . young girls go for bastards, don't they? The bad boy. That Heathcliff shit, the older man bollocks. Even the glamorous violence.' She shook her head. 'I guess it had some juvenile allure. *And* he was mysterious. And he's smart and good looking and a famous guy, famously strong and active.' She forced a weak smile. 'He looks a bit like you, actually. Except older and a little thinner.'

66

'Except I don't mutilate, torture and kill people and . . . I don't hit women in bars.'

'Of course. Of course. I realized this myself after about two months, that he was just a nasty piece of work. And . . .' She shrugged, awkwardly, then confessed. 'And there was something sick about him, as well. He was kinky. In bed. I dumped him after two months.'

David didn't know what to say; her honesty was disarming. He tried another question as they sped past a farmhouse.

'Do you still have contact?'

'No. Not if I can help it. But sometimes it's inevitable. Miguel introduced me to his dad, to José, who is still a good friend – he helped me get my job. And I really love my job . . . The same way I love these mountains.' She sighed. 'But Miguel is always bloody there, lurking, he's pursued me ever since . . . You know what you did in that bar, that *was* very brave.'

'Did he hit you when you were together?'

'Yes. That's when it happened. He hit me once and that's when I dumped him. Bastard.'

He thought of the scar on her forehead. It didn't quite match a scene of domestic abuse. But he didn't want to pry further. The farms were turning into forests, they were slowly ascending the mountains.

'Amy. Thanks for telling me.' He looked at her. 'You didn't have to tell me any of this. In fact, you don't have to *do* any of this.'

'I'm in it now.'

'Kinda.'

'Not kind of,' she said. 'Definitely. And besides, I feel a . . . rapport. With your situation.'

'How come?'

'Because of my *own* family.' Light, spiteful rain spattered the windscreen. 'My father died when I was ten, my mother

67

started drinking soon after. My brother and I practically had to look after ourselves. Then my brother emigrated to Australia. And yet my drunken mum and my distant brother – that's all I have left, because the rest of my family died in the Holocaust – all those ancestors, the *cousinage*. They all died. So I guess I feel . . . a bit of an orphan.' She turned to look at him. 'Not unlike you.'

Amy's yellow hair was kicking in the cool rainy breeze through the car window. Her monologue seemed to have calmed her; she seemed less alarmed.

'Take the right here. Past the chapel.'

He turned the wheel obediently.

'I wonder,' she said, 'I sometimes wonder if my Jewishness explains my attachment to the Basques, because they have such a sense of who they are, and where they belong. They've been here for so *long*. One people, living in one place. Whereas the Jews have wandered, we just keep wandering.' She rubbed her face, as if trying to wake herself up. 'Anyway. We are nearly there.'

David changed a gear as he took a final corner. He thought of Miguel Garovillo, the lean, menacing features, the dark and violent eyes. Amy had assured him Miguel was not going to show up at his father's house. José had guaranteed he would not be around.

But the way Miguel had come for Amy in the bar was just too hard to forget. Wild and violent jealousy. Something more than jealousy. A kind of lustful hatred.

Amy gestured. 'Slow down – it's the little road here.'

It was a shaded and very rutted track, that seemed to lead directly into the misty mountain forests. Carefully David nudged the car through the muddy narrows; just as the wheels began to slither they turned into a clearing and Amy said: 'There.'

The house was tiny, pretty, brightly whitewashed, and

trimmed with green wooden shutters. The rain had stopped and spears of sunlight lanced the evanescing fog. And standing in front of the house, proudly waving a beret, was the sprightliest old man David had ever seen. He had very long earlobes.

'*Epa!*' said José Garovillo, looking at David very closely as he climbed out of the car. '*Zer moduz? Pozten naiz zu ezagutzeaz?*'

'Uh . . .'

'Hah. Don't worry, my friend David . . . *Martinez!*' The old man chuckled. 'Come in, come in, I am not going to make you speak Basque. I speak your language perfectly. I love the English language, I love your swearwords. Fuckmuppet! So much better than Finnish.'

He smiled and turned to Amy. And then his smiling face clouded for a moment as he regarded the fading bruise on her face.

'*Aii*. Amy. *Aiii*. I am so so so sorry. *Lo siento*. I hear what happened in the Bilbo.' The man shuddered with remorse. 'What can I do? My son . . . my terrible son. He frightens me. But, Amy, tell me what to do and I will do it.'

Amy leaned close and reassured him with a hug.

'I'm fine. David helped me. Really, José.'

'But Amy. *El violencia?* It is so terrible!'

'José!' Amy's response was sharp. 'Please. I am completely OK.'

The elderly smile returned.

'Then . . . we must go and eat! Always we must eat. When there is trouble the Basques must eat. Come inside, Davido. We have a feast to satisfy the *jentilaks* of the forest.'

There was no time to ask any further questions; as soon as they sat down they were presented with food and drink, endless food and drink.

Fermina, José's much younger wife, turned out to be a

69

fervent cook; with dark eyes and bangled arms she served them traditional Basque food from her miniature kitchen, all of it rapturously introduced and explained by José. They had fiery nibbles of Espelette chillies skewered with *tripotx* – lamb's blood sausage from Biraitou; they had a *Gerezi beltza arno gorriakin* – a cherry soup the colour of claret served with a white blob of crème fraiche; then the 'cheeks of the hake' decorated with olives; this was followed by unctuous *kanougas* – chocolate toffee – and soft *turron* nougat from Vizcaya, and Irauty sheep's cheese next to a daub of cherry jam, and all of it sluiced down with foaming jugs of various Basque ciders: red and green and yellow and very alcoholic.

Between the courses of this enormous meal, José talked and talked, he explained the origins of the beret amongst the shepherds of Bearn, he declaimed on the splendours of the ram-fighting of Azpeita, he showed David a cherished ormolu crucifix once blessed by Pope Pius the Tenth, he spoke mysteriously of the cromlechs in the forests of Roncesvalles built by the legendary giants and the mythical Moors, the *jentilaks* and the *mairuaks*.

It was exhausting – but also engaging, even hypnotic. By the end David felt obese, drunk, and something of an amateur linguist. He had almost forgotten the fierce grip of anxiety, and the reason why he was here. But he hadn't wholly forgotten. He could never wholly forget. *El violencia, el violencia.*

It was hard to forget that.

David looked at Amy. She was gazing out of the window. He looked back.

José was sipping a sherry; Fermina was busy in the kitchen, making coffee it seemed. It was the right moment. David filled the silence, and asked José if he'd like to hear the story, the reason for David's mission to Spain. José sat back.

70

'Of course! But as I said in my texting message, I think I know the answer already. I know why you are here!'

David stared at the old man.

'So?'

He paused dramatically. 'I knew your grandfather. As soon as Amy told me the name, Martinez, I knew.'

'How? *When?*'

'Long time ago – so many years!' The old man's smile was persistent. 'We were childhood friends in . . . in Donostia, before the war. Then our families fled to France in 1936. To Bayonne. Where they have the Jewish chocolate. The best chocolate in the world!'

David leaned close, asking the most obvious question.

'Was my grandfather a Basque?'

José laughed with a scornful expression – as if this was a surreally stupid query.

'But of course! Yes. He did not tell you? How very typical. He was a man of . . . some enigmas. But yes he was a Basque! And so was his young wife, naturally!' José glanced pertly at Amy, and then back at David. 'There now, David Martinez. You are Basque, in part at least: a man of Euskadi! You can play the *txistu* on San Fermin day! And now, have I answered all your questions? Is the mystery solved?'

David sat quietly for a few seconds, absorbing the information. Was this all there was to it? Granddad was a Basque, but never admitted it?

Then David remembered the map, and the churches. And the inheritance. How did that fit in?

'Actually no, José. There is more.'

'More?'

Amy interrupted: 'José . . . The stuff in the papers. The bequest . . . The map. You didn't see it?'

'I never read the newspapers!' José said, his smile slightly fading. 'But what is this other mystery? Tell me! What else must you know?'

David gazed Amy's way, with a questioning expression: she shrugged, as if to say, *go on, why not, we're here now*.

So David began. He told the story of his grandfather, and the churches, and the bequest. As he did, he reached in his pocket and pulled out the map, marked with blue stars.

The atmosphere in the cottage was transformed.

Fermina was standing by the kitchen door, wrapped in a consternated silence. The old man was frowning as he stared at the map. Frowning very profoundly: almost tragically. He looked almost . . . bereaved.

Shocked by the effect of his story, David dropped the map on the table. It was as if the light in the room had dimmed; the only brightness came from the soft white pages of the map itself.

José leaned over and took the map in his hands. For a few minutes, he caressed the worn paper. Opening it, he examined the blue asterisks, muttering and mumbling. No one moved.

Then he looked up at David.

'Forget about this. Please, I beg you. *Forget about this*. You don't want to know any more about the churches. Keep your money. Get rid of this map. Go back to London. *Por favor.*'

David opened his mouth. No words emerged.

'Take it away,' said José, handing the map back. 'Get it out of my house. I know it is not your fault. But . . . get it out of my house. Never mention these matters again. Ever. That . . . that map . . . the churches . . . this is the key to hell. I beg you both to *stop*.'

David didn't know what to do; José's wife was wiping her hands on a cloth, still at the door to the kitchen. Wiping her hands over and over, full of nerves.

The tension was heightened by a noise. José Garovillo looked up; the scrunch of the gravel outside the house was distinctive.

A red car was pulling up.

Amy had a hand to her mouth.

'Oh no . . .'

José was gasping.

'But no! I told him not to come. I am sorry, I told him you were coming but I asked him to stay away. *Barkatu*. *Barkatu*. Fermina!'

The very tall man climbing out of the car was unmistakable: Miguel Garovillo. A second later he was pushing the farmhouse door and was inside the house, tall and wild and glaring – at Amy and David. And gazing at the map in David's hand. A little twitch in his eye was quite noticeable, likewise a slender scar above his lip.

'Papa!' said Miguel, his voice rich with contempt.

The son had his hand raised; for a ghastly moment it looked like he was actually going to clout José, to beat his own father. José flinched. Fermina cried out. Miguel's black eyes flashed around the room; David saw the dark shape of a holster, under the terrorist's leather jacket.

Fermina Garovillo was pushing her son away, but Miguel was shouting at his father, and at Amy and David, shouting in Basque, his words unintelligible – the only thing that was obvious was the *ferocious anger*. José shouted a few words in return – but weakly, unconvincingly.

And then Miguel shouted in English. At David. His deep angry voice vibrated in the air.

'Get the *ffffffuck* out of here. You want the whore? Then take her. You take all this shit out of here. Go now.'

David backed away. 'We're going . . . We're going . . .'

'First time I hit you. Next time I shoot you.'

Amy and David turned and ran into the yard and jumped in the car.

But Miguel followed them outside the house. He had taken out his gun, he was holding a black pistol in the air. Holding it – as if to show them. David got the strange jarring sense of something inhuman about him: a giant. A violent *jentilak* of the forest displaying his strength and anger. The gun was so very black. Glinting in the watery sunlight.

David urgently reversed. He spiralled the wheel – and at last they turned, revving in the mud, and then they rocked down the track, skidding out onto the road.

For half an hour David drove fast and hard, into the green grey foothills, just driving to get away.

When the panic and shock had subsided, David felt a rising anger, and a *need to stop and think.*

He pulled over. They were halted at the edge of a village, with a timberyard on their left. The distant Pyrenees seemed a lot less pretty now; the pinetops of the forest were laced with an insistent and smothering mist. A church, surrounded by circular gravestones, sat on a hill above them.

Everything was damp, everything around them was faintly, ripely, perceptibly rotting away in the damp.

David cursed.

'What. The. Fuck.'

Amy tilted her face, apologetically.

'I know. I'm sorry.'

'What?'

'Sorry . . .'

'It's not your fault.'

'But . . .' She shook her head. 'But it is. Maybe you *should* go home, David. Miguel is my problem.'

'No. No way. This is my problem too.'

'But I told you what he is like. Murderously jealous. He . . . really will . . . do something. He might even . . .'

'Kill me?'

She winced.

74

David felt the surge of a rebel spirit.

'Fuck him. I want to know the *answers*.' He started the car and negotiated the road slowly for a few minutes. 'I want to know it all. My grandfather wouldn't have sent me here – sent me into all this – unless he had a reason. I want to know *why*.'

'The map.'

'Exactly. The map. You heard what José said, saw how he reacted – there is something – something –'

He was searching for a way to describe the complexity of puzzles; his next words were interrupted.

'Don't stop.'

'What?'

'Drive on.'

'What?'

David felt the cold possibility constrict around his heart. Amy confirmed.

'Miguel. In the car. Right behind.

9

Her eyes were locked on the mirror. David copied her gaze.

'Jesus.' He squinted. 'Are you sure? *Is it the same one?*'

'Numberplate. *It's him.*'

The road ahead was narrow, the fog was thickening as they climbed the mountainside.

'But . . .' David gripped the steering wheel tightly. 'Was he there all along? Following?'

'Who knows. Maybe he followed us. Or . . .'

'What?'

'He is ETA. This is real ETA territory.'

'So . . .'

'They watch the roads all the time. He has friends and contacts all over. Maybe someone made a phone call. We were just parked there by the village. What do we *do*?'

The fear was tangible. But David felt the rising defiance – again. He thought of his beloved mother and father: *who left him alone*. He thought of his loneliness: he'd had to fight his way through college, on his own, with just a distant grandfather in Phoenix. He had made it through all that shit, he had dealt with all *that*, so he wasn't going to be frightened off, even by the most demonic of murdering terrorists.

Not now. Not when he knew his grandfather's mystery was linked to his own background, his own identity. This revelation of his Basqueness.

And he didn't like being *hunted*.

'Let's lose this bastard.'

Pressing the throttle, he accelerated up the narrow, sharply curving road; the noise of the engine was painful as they shot between the stony hedgerows and the muddy slopes. Then he checked the mirror.

The red car was closing.

'Shit.'

David could taste the savour of alarm; he ignored it, and changed down a gear or two – then he surged on, as fast as he could.

'David –'

On their left was a sudden cliff-edge. The slope was brutal – a fall of three hundred metres, or more. Just a few metres the wrong way and they would spin helplessly over the precipice.

David steered back to safety – but then – *thump*.

The red car had smacked into them. The bump from behind was firm, deliberate, and destabilizing. David gripped the wheel desperately, and kept them gripped to the road – then he flicked a frightened glance at the mirror. He couldn't see for sure, but it felt like their pursuer was . . . *smiling*?

'Don't worry, it's alright –' he said to Amy.

Why was he saying this? He was *terrified*. And yet he was feeling a rush of fury as well. Not now. Don't give up *now*. If he gave up – what had it all been for? All those years of doing nothing, sitting in that sterile office, being a lawyer; struggling to make relationships, so scared that people would leave him – leave him alone, again.

His heart swelled with angry revolt; he was going to save Amy, and save himself – he could do it.

The accelerator crushed to the floor, he raced the car as fast as he dared. He felt a certain confidence as he did this – despite his grinding fears. He'd had to learn to drive when young, to get himself around. He was pretty good.

But this was a different kind of driving: they were skidding madly round bends, higher and higher. And they were being chased.

Then the road began to zigzag, turns getting tighter, until at last it slashed around a sheer rock wall, totally blind – David caught his own breath, his heart thumped, this was it – but the corner was clear.

David scoped the mirror. The red car had slowed for a moment, he'd outpaced their remorseless pursuer. He had a few seconds' grace.

As they roared along, he tried to think. If they stopped the car and got out and ran, maybe they could hide . . . but the red car was surely too near. Miguel had a gun, maybe he would chase them across the rocks. Teasing them – then shooting them. A simple execution in the forest.

'David!'

The red car was speeding towards them. David couldn't go any faster. They had reached the crisis: the terminal moment. No one would see. They were right above the clouds now; the sun was brilliant and dazzling, shining off clumps of unmelted snow. This was where they would die. A man and a woman in a car. Like his parents. Both dead.

But then David saw a chance. Up ahead was an expanse of bare rock. Three seconds later he slid the car onto a flank of raw limestone and did a squealing handbrake turn. They spun like they were kids in a nightmarish fairground ride, a vicious carousel.

And it worked. The red car shot right past. At once David took off the other way, descending fast and hard.

He was racing vertiginously down the mountain road – he could see the red car turning, in his mirror. But this time he had a plan, as he rounded the sharp rocky corner at eighty miles an hour and they raced into the grey forests. He took a wild right turn up a farm track.

Into the trees.

The track swung this way and that, catapulting them into the dark woodlands. The car bounced and groaned, and after half a mile the track stopped. David parked the car with a jolt, he kicked open the door and jumped out – Amy was already outside and waiting. He grabbed her hand and they fled into the woods, running between the trees and the rocks and leaping over a stream until they found a great boulder.

And then at last they stopped, and crouched down. And waited. Panting and breathing.

David's heart was a madman clattering his prison bars; Amy's hand was tight and clammy in his fist.

They crouched there, cold and mute. The forest crackled, under the mournful drizzle. Nothing happened. Wisps of fog drifted between the sombre black larches, like fairytale wraiths.

The low sound of a car engine throbbed in the distance. The red car, presumably – looking for them. The engine seemed to slow, somewhere on the road. Somewhere quite near. David felt Amy's fingers tighten on his. The agonizing moments marched slowly by, like a funeral parade. They waited to be found, and shot.

Or worse.

The car engine throbbed again. It was going. The red car was *taking off*, heading downhill maybe. Silence surrounded them. David allowed himself to breathe.

But his relief was aborted by a singular *snap*: the sound of twigs, broken underfoot.

10

The old women were singing through their noses, a rising carol of weird sounds; the tremulous voice of the dark-suited man at the front – warbling and waving his hands – led and yet followed the intense humming from the choir of ululating women.

They were still in Foula, about three hundred miles from Glasgow.

Simon and Sanderson and Tomasky had spent an uncomfortable night in Foula's only B&B, waiting for a chance to interview Edith Tait. The B&B owner, a middle-aged widower from Edinburgh, had been all too excited by the influx of glamorous tourists – of new people to talk to – and he had kept them up, over tots of whisky, with bloodcurdling tales of Foula's weirdness and danger.

He told them of the German birdwatcher who had slipped on some lamb's afterbirth, banged his head on a rock, and had his brains devoured by Arctic skuas; he mentioned a tourist couple who had gone to the highest cliff, the Kame, and been swept over the precipice when one of them sneezed.

All this Simon absorbed with a suppressed smile; Sanderson

was openly sarcastic: 'So the tourist death rate, is what, about fifty percent?'

But there was one thing the journalist found truly and deeply interesting: the Gaelic heritage of the isle. As the hostel owner explained, Foula was so isolated it had maintained Norse-Gaelic cultural characteristics that had almost disappeared elsewhere. They used their own Gregorian calendar, they celebrated Christmas on January 6th, and some of the locals still spoke authentic Scots Gaelic.

They did this especially at church, where the services were, apparently, some of the very last of their kind: notable for a capella nose singing, known as 'Dissonant Gaelic Psalmody', as the B&B owner explained – with loving relish.

So now they were actually in the kirk listening to the Nasal Celtic Heterophony, waiting for a chance to talk to Edith. Simon was distinctly drawn to this authentic, ancient, possibly pagan tradition; DCI Sanderson was less impressed.

'They sound like a bunch of mad Irish bumblebees in the shower.'

His sidelong remark was loud. One woman turned around and gave the DCI a stare; she was singing through her nonagenarian nostrils, even as she glared.

DCI Sanderson blushed, stood up, and edged along the pew, and bumbled out of the kirk. Feeling exposed and conspicuous, Simon swiftly followed. He found Sanderson dragging on a cigarette by the graveyard.

Sanderson dropped the cigarette, crushed it under his shoe, and gazed at the Sneck o' da Smaalie, a great ravine hard by the kirk that led all the way down to the roiling sea, which writhed like a fallen epileptic in a blue straitjacket; the earlier rain had dropped and the sky had cleared.

'Not religious then, Detective?'

'You guessed?' Sanderson's smile was sarcastic. 'Went to

a church school, because my parents were real believers. Guaranteed to put you off.'

Simon nodded. 'My experience was absolutely the opposite, my folks were . . . atheists. Scientists and architects.' An unwarranted thought ran through his mind: *das Helium und das Hydrogen*. He hurried the conversation along. 'So they never forced any belief system on me at all. Now I do have . . . rather vague beliefs.'

'Nice for you.' The DCI was glaring at a white shape. A sheep had wandered into the graveyard. 'Jesus, what a place. All these sheep everywhere. Sheep. What are they about. Stupid woolly fuckers.'

Sanderson put a hand on the journalist's shoulder, and looked him in the eye.

'Quinn. There's something you should know. If you still wanna write up this case.'

'Yes?'

'There was another murder. This morning. Heard on the wire. We're certain it's related.' He frowned. 'So I can tell you.'

'Where?'

'Near Windsor. An old man named Jean Mendia. That's why Tomasky flew home this morning. To do some knock-ups.'

The nasal singing in the church had stopped.

'Let me guess, the victim is Southern French? Deformed?'

Sanderson shook his head.

'French Basque, yes. From Gascony. But no, not deformed. And not tortured.'

Before he could ask the obvious question, Sanderson added, 'The reasons we're *sure* it's connected are: his age, very old; and the fact he was Basque; *and* there was no robbery. An apparently pointless killing.'

'So that's three . . .'

'Yep.'

'Who on earth is doing it? And why?'

'God knows. So maybe we could ask Him.' He turned.

The service was concluded. The church door had swung open, and bonneted old ladies were parading out of the kirk into the daylight, chattering in English and Gaelic.

They quickly located Edith Tait. She was spryer than Simon had expected: despite being sixty-seven, she could have passed for fifty. But the twinkle in her eye soon dulled as they told her who they were: and their reason for tracking her down.

Edith actually looked, for a moment, as if she might burst into tears. But then she buttoned her tweed coat even tighter and ushered them back into the empty church, where they sat on a pew and conversed.

She was not the witness they'd hoped for. She admitted she had heard the odd sound on the fateful night – *but she couldn't be sure*. She might have heard the whirr of a small boat in the wee small hours – *but she couldn't be sure*.

Edith Tait wasn't sure about anything – but that was hardly her fault. She was doing her best – and the process obviously wasn't easy for her. At the end of her testimony, Edith emitted a tiny sob, which she hid with her pale hands. Then she unmasked herself, and gazed at the journalist.

'I am so sorry, I cannae help any more. She was a very good friend to me, you know. My very good friend. I am so sorry, Mister . . . gentlemen. You have come all this way to see me. But I didnae see what I didnae see.'

Simon swapped a knowing glance with Sanderson. This was a sweet old lady, doing her damnedest, they'd gone almost as far as they could. There was just one more question that maybe needed asking.

'When and why did Julie come to Foula, Edith? It's a pretty remote place.'

'She arrived in the late 1940s, I do believe.' Edith frowned. 'Aye. The 1940s. We became friends later, when my mammy died and I inherited the croft next door.'

'So you don't know *why* she emigrated to Foula, of all places, from France?'

'Noo.' Edith shook her head. 'She would never talk about that, so I never asked her. Perhaps there was some family secret. Perhaps she just liked the loneliness and the quiet, just now. Some people do, you know . . . And now I really must go. My friend is expecting me.'

'Of course.'

The interview was done. He closed his notebook.

However, as she walked to the exit, Edith slowed, and tilted her head. Engaging with the question.

'Actually. There is *one* more thing. One more thing you maybe should know. A wee peculiarity.'

Simon opened the notepad.

'Yes?'

'A little while ago . . . She was being bothered by a young man, a young scientist . . . She found it most upsetting.'

'Sorry?'

'Angus Nairn, he was called.' The old lady closed her eyes – and opened them once again. 'That was it. Good Scots name. Yes. He was bothering her with phone calls, the scientist chappie.'

'What do you mean, "bothering"?'

'He wanted to examine her. He said she was a unique case. A Basque, I think. Is that right? I don't know. Basque maybe. Aye.'

'And this upset her?'

'Very much so. Much more than you would expect. She was greeting for a week. That man Nairn truly upset her. There now, my friend is waving.'

Simon pressed on: 'But Mrs Tait?'

She nodded.

'When you say this man wanted to use her in a test, what did he mean? What did he want to test?'

Edith calmly replied:

'Her blood.'

11

David peered over the dripping ferns.

It was a horse. A small, shaggy-maned horse.

'*Pottok*,' said Amy.

The little pony regarded them with an expression of ageing melancholy, then it clobbered away into the woods; mysterious and wild, and ancient and gone.

The relief spread through David's tensed and aching muscles. He gazed through the trees. The car was surely far down the hill. They were OK. They had escaped. He reached for a rock, to haul himself to his feet.

Amy whispered, fiercely: 'Wait.'

He felt the jarring fear return.

Amy hissed again. 'What's *that*?'

She was pointing. David squinted, and froze. About five hundred yards away a tall, thin, shadowy figure was treading slowly through the mist, looking this way and that; the drifting fog made it hard to identify, but not impossible.

'Miguel?'

Her question was surely unnecessary. It was surely Miguel. The black wolf, stalking them through the woods.

He grabbed her hand again. 'Come on . . .'

She nodded, saying nothing; together they backed away, slithering into the deeper darkness of the woods; slowly, agonizingly, they retreated and crawled over damp mossy logs, trying not to break the smallest twig or scrunch the tiniest leaf.

David glanced behind but couldn't be sure what he was witnessing. Was that really Miguel – still hunting them down? The mist shifted in the wind, black figures turned out to be trees, trees bent in the drizzly wind, with a forlorn mewling sound.

He turned and concentrated: searching out a route through the bleak, autumnal maze.

'Down here –'

David had no idea where he was leading Amy – just away from Miguel. For sixty or seventy minutes they descended; the forest was thick and treacherous. Several times Amy slipped; many times, David felt himself skidding on the leaves and muck. Despite the cold of the dank mountain forests, he was sweating. Amy's hand was clammy in his. And still he could hear, or he could *imagine hearing*, the soft, menacing crackle of someone behind them. Or maybe it was just another *pottok*.

The incline lessened, the black of the crowding wet trees yielded to whiteness – sky and light. They were approaching what looked like a path. An hour of crawling and fear had brought them to civilization.

'Here . . . down here.' He reached for her hand again. They were ducking under an old half-fallen oak. Brambles guarded the route. The rocky path turned and twisted, towards a little valley.

Amy spoke: 'I know where we are.'

'Where?'

'Very near Zugarramurdi.' She pointed at the clearing mists. 'A village, it's just over there, over the hill.'

'So why are we waiting – let's do it! We can go to a cafe and –'

'No. Wait!' Her voice was sharp, insistent, frightened. 'He knows these forests . . . He'll expect us to go there, to head there. We need . . .' She was reaching in her pocket, pulling out her phone. 'We need to hide,' she said, 'until someone can help, can fetch us.'

She clambered a few yards up the damp slope, apparently to improve her signal. He watched her key a number, heard her say *Zara* and *por favor* in desperate whispers; he guessed it was her friend the journalist, Zara Garcia. Moments later she pocketed the phone and gave him her attention: 'OK, she's coming to the village. It'll take her half an hour.'

'But where do we hide . . . until . . .?'

'This way.'

She was already descending with an air of quiet purpose. Bewildered and clumsy, he followed behind, grasping at tree roots to stay upright. Finally the muddy path curved and widened – to reveal a forecourt of natural flagstones. And beyond that, the gasping mouth of a mighty cave.

Amy gestured. 'The witch's cave of Zugarramurdi.'

The enormous cavern was open at either end, a natural rock tunnel with a stream running along the bottom – like a trickle of sewer water in an enormous concrete pipe. Dim grey light bounced from the bubbling water, flickering on the elongated cave roof.

'The what cave?'

Her expression was fixed.

'The *witch's* cave. Zugarramurdi. We can hide here. These cave systems are endless.'

'Are you sure?'

She didn't wait to give him an answer; and maybe, David surmised, she was right. Their escape through the woods had been exhausting, he yearned to rest; Amy looked utterly wearied, her face smeared with mud. They needed to hide out for half an hour.

Her careful steps led them along a secondary path that ducked beneath the roof of stone. It fed onto a flat rock-shelf overlooking the main cavernous space, the vast echoing tunnel. All around, shadowy recesses ate into the soft white rock, speaking of further tunnels. Amy was correct, they had entered a labyrinth of passages and chambers. Beckoning them deeper inside.

They sat down. The dry warm stone felt like silk after the chilling misery of their escape through the woods.

David rested his head against the rock, exhausted. He closed his eyes. And then he opened them, alert and frightened. He shook the sleepiness from his head and gazed out over the cavern.

'You said this is the witch's cave.'

'Yes.'

'So, why is it called that?'

She shrugged, bleakly.

'Quite an alarming story. José told me. He loved telling this story.'

'And?'

Amy's smile was replete with tiredness. 'You always want to know.'

'I always want to know. Please, tell me something. I don't want to risk falling asleep.'

'OK. Well.' She moued: thinking, and remembering. 'This cave, and the meadows beyond, this was the *akelarre*, the place where the Basque witches held their Sabbaths.'

He went to ask a question; she silenced him with a gesture. And explained.

'About four hundred years ago Zugarramurdi was the centre of a huge witch craze. A French witch hunter, Pierre De Lancre, became convinced that . . .' Amy grimaced. 'He *decided* that all Basques were essentially witches. Because the Basques were so different, the easily identifiable minority. They were the *other*.'

'You mean . . . like the Jews?'

'Of course. It began around . . . 1610. A Basque girl who had been working away from home, in Ciboure, near Saint Jean de Luz on the coast, she came back to her village in the hills. To Zugarramurdi.'

The reflected light of the stream bounced off the cavern ceiling. Stalactites pierced the emptiness.

'The young woman's name was Maria de Ximildegui. She began to denounce her friends and relatives – as witches. The local priests called in the Inquisition. Children were dragged from their families and interrogated. The kids started to report nightmares, dreams of naked greased-up witches who took them on strange flights, to the Devil's *sabbat*.

'Satan would appear as a huge billygoat, walking on his hind legs. He had intercourse with the women and children. He has, apparently, a very thick and icy black penis. Afterwards he would mark them on the forehead with his claw. The infamous marks of the Devil. Showing that he had possessed them.'

Amy stared at David, deadpan. He didn't know what to say; whether to laugh or protest. She continued the story, her voice echoing softly in the cavern. 'And so the craze began. The priests reported their findings, and the witch panic spread down the valley, into Elizondo, Lesaka, San Sebastian. *Thousands* were arrested, David, literally thousands of women, men, children . . . And then the priests went to work, putting people to the rack, pricking them for blood, torturing everyone.'

David was trying not to think about her scar. He said: 'But . . . they did the same across Europe, right, it wasn't that unusual? Around that time. It was like Salem, it was just a witch craze. No?'

'*No*. Witch crazes were unknown *on this scale*, it was maybe the worst craze in Europe. They called it the Basque Dream Epidemic. The Inquisition mutilated hundreds. Dozens were lynched by villagers. Five were officially burned to death at Logrono.'

'And De Lancre?'

Amy was staring into the grey cavern light. 'De Lancre was even more efficient than the Inquisition. As I said, he was obsessed: he thought that all Basques were witches, an evil race to be exterminated. He burned hundreds, maybe more. It was a holocaust. Just over there, in Iparralde. *The land beyond.*'

She gestured at the little brook. 'They still call this the stream of Hell. The irony of it all is that De Lancre was *Basque*. A self-hater.'

Her words dwindled away. David was about to ask another question, but his half-formed thoughts were crushed. By a very deep voice. Echoing.

'*Epa.*'

He swivelled.

Miguel. Standing there. At the entrance to the witch's cave.

David glanced left and right, rapidly calculating. The only descent from the rockshelf – further into the caves, or towards the light of the entrance – took them directly past Miguel. They were trapped.

'*Epa.*'

David knew this one word of Basque. Hello. The terrorist's smile was languid yet angry; his gun was pointing their way.

'*Euzkaraz badakisu?* Ah no. Of course. You Americans only speak one language. Let me explain . . . in more intimacy.'

The tall Basque paced along the rocky ledge – the gun trained on them all the time. He slowed as he approached – and turned. David realized Miguel had an accomplice: following behind was a short, thickset man. Miguel gestured a request.

'*Enoka? La cuerda . . .*'

The accomplice had a *lauburu* tattooed on his hand. And the same tattooed hand was carrying a rope. The short man, Enoka, came forward.

David shot a desperate glance at Amy.

They already had a *rope*? It was like they had been *preparing*.

The accomplice, Enoka, set to work. Tying Amy and David by the hands, behind their backs – while they sat there, mute and immobile, subdued by the terrorist's gun. In a few seconds they had been trussed like dumb animals, headed for the slaughterhouse.

Then Miguel spoke, with a sad and frowning passion. His shadow was long on the cave roof, cast by the flickering light off the stream.

'You know, you drive very well, Martinez. Very good. Very impressive. But you still don't really understand these hills. You do not understand this place. Our language. You *cannot* understand that. *Hikuntzta ez da nahikoa!* Is it not so?'

Miguel half-smiled, and gazed around him at the cavern, his words resonant in the emptiness.

'I told you what would happen when I found you again. And now I find you. In the witch's cave! Of all places. The little witch and her big Gascon friend. Appropriate.' He turned. 'Remember, Amy? Our marvellous picnic supper?'

He was stooping now, looking very closely at Amy. David realized, with disgust, that he was actually stroking Amy's face with the muzzle of the gun. Stroking her.

'Mmm. Amy? Didn't we? Remember the excellent blood sausage. The *tripota*. Your sweet *marmatiko*.'

She said nothing. He persisted.

'Didn't we have sex here? Or was that some other cave? It was here, wasn't it? I forget.'

Her face was averted, but the killer was using the muzzle of the gun to tilt her chin, *forcing* her to look at him. He was quietly smiling. She was scowling. He was smiling.

And now *she* was smiling.

David stared, aghast.

Amy was looking up, smilingly, almost lasciviously, as Miguel murmured:

'You know that I am going to kill him, don't you?'

She nodded.

'Yes.'

'In that case, Amy, shall we have our fun first?'

She nodded again; he leaned very close:

'*Dantzatu nahi al duzu nirekin.* Before we kill him.'

'Yes,' she agreed. 'Please yes? Fuck me here. Fuck me like before.'

Miguel laughed. A sad and gluttonous laugh. The terror iced David's veins with tiny crystals of grief. What was happening?

Again the terrorist traced a line from Amy's ear, to her lips, with the metal of the gunpoint – like a surgeon practising his incision, or a butcher marking out a fillet. Then he turned to his accomplice, skulking in the shadows.

'Enoka. *Vaya, Adiós!*'

The squat little man scuttled away, an expression of relief in his gait. David looked from Miguel to Amy, to Miguel again. Searching their faces. His heart was cold with the horror.

Amy was still smiling, upwards, smiling at the terrorist: submissive, needy and desirous. The twitch in the terrorist's eye was subtle. More obvious was the erection in Miguel's khaki trousers.

Fear and disgust suffused David's thoughts. He didn't even want to look at Amy. How could she do this? Was it all some terrible joke on him? Was she just saving herself? Or did she really want Miguel? Was this some strange psychosexual game the two of them were playing – and he was the necessary spectator?

His heartbeat juddered with anger – and contempt – and inadequacy.

Enoka had disappeared along the rocky passage. They were alone. Miguel and Amy – and David. The terrorist was unlashing Amy's hands. Immediately she was free, she reached for Miguel; she was unbelting his trousers, pulling them down, and then tugging at his shirt; she was kissing him under his half shaven chin, and caressing his jawline, like a concubine soliciting a sultan for a night of love. A witch imploring the goat for his favours.

David turned away, nauseated. He didn't want to watch; he was stuck here, tied up, he would have to listen, but he didn't have to watch.

A deep voice echoed across. 'You!'

He opened his eyes.

Miguel was on top of Amy, the great tall figure arched over the small young woman, like a dark roof. But he was looking at David, and the gun was still in his hand.

'You, Martinez. Watch or I kill you. Watch *then* I kill you.'

David was filled with a furious nausea. He narrowed his sullen eyes and watched.

Amy was on her back. She was naked from the waist down. Her lips were seeking Miguel's bare shoulders, kissing him eagerly. David observed with a grisly repulsion – as Miguel entered her. Now they were fucking, now they were really doing it, Amy was kissing him. She was putting her fingers in his mouth and he was sucking, tasting her fingers. Biting and tasting. His hips bucking wildly, thrusting at her; his face in a rictus of pleasure. He was moaning.

'My sweet red *marrubi* . . . The little girl. *Sí*? You love your Papa still . . .'

He was biting at her white breasts, his hands were dark on her white buttocks, he was a black overpowering shape on the whiteness of her flesh, nuzzling at her red nipples; his dark wolfish mouth consuming. David felt the blur of despair.

And then, grotesquely, the terrorist climaxed. His arms shivered and he slumped forward.

His head lay on her white naked breasts. She was stroking his head, caressing him.

And then she widened her eyes and stared at David with an unfathomable expression.

'Let's go.'

David was choked.

'What?'

'He's asleep. He always falls asleep after sex. Always. The deepest sleep. We have a chance!'

She was gently pushing Miguel away. David realized, bewildered, that she was right: Miguel was snoring, utterly unconscious. The terrorist didn't even stir as Amy pushed him aside, onto the sandy rockfloor.

David diverted his gaze as Amy threw her clothes on; the vortex of questions inside him was spinning: had she really done all this so they could *escape*? What kind of black and cruel comedy was this? As he looked away, he spotted the pistol, fallen from Miguel's grasp.

'My hands. *Amy.*'

Amy was already there, untying him. As soon as his smarting wrists were unbound, David leaned and picked up the gun; then checked Enoka was nowhere to be seen.

He had a chance to shoot the terrorist. Shoot the wolf. David looked at the sleeping head of his tormentor.

He couldn't do it. He couldn't kill a sleeping man, he couldn't kill a man. He was a lawyer, not a killer, the whole thing was absurd, evil but absurd; and besides, even if he killed him, he couldn't defeat him. The graffiti would still be scrawled on the walls of Basque villages. *Otsoko*. The Wolf. And the image of what he'd just witnessed would never quit.

Amy was imploring him. 'Please!'

He surrendered to her urgency. They crept down the rock-shelf, out of the cave, beyond the clearing. They were going to make it. David felt the thrill of escape even as his mind reeled at the harrowing scene he had been forced to observe; Amy was running ahead now, up a pathway, between trees and bushes.

'Zara. She'll be there – any minute.'

They raced to the end of the path, and then the path became a lane, and then the lane became a misty village road. The spire of Zugarramurdi church loomed across a desolate square.

'There!'

Amy was sprinting towards a car parked up by the church. She flung open the door and David opened the other door; Zara was inside asking questions in frantic Spanish, but Amy just said: 'Go!'

The car sped out of the square, out of Zugarramurdi, down another mountain road.

David looked across the passenger seat.

Amy was silent, but crying.

12

Zara drove them speedily to the road where they had left the hire car; it took a bare few minutes to drive what had taken them an hour to crawl. Amy was silent the entire way; she dried her tears and said nothing, despite Zara's repeated and insistent queries.

The Spanish journalist gave them a puzzled glare as they eventually stepped out into the rain. Zara was quite obviously needled by the mystery and the ensuing silence. With a wordless pout Zara handed Amy her bag: the bag she had collected, as instructed, from Amy's flat using the spare key.

Then Zara gave her friend one last searching and bewildered glance before starting up her car and driving off.

Still swathed in silence, they walked quickly up the sodden path, and climbed into David's mudded rental.

It was like they were behaving automatically. Robotically. The mist drifted between the trees. David sat at the wheel, turned on the motor, and slid the car to the edge of the road. They were at the dead and darkling heart of the forest.

He took the gun from his pocket, contemplated it for a moment, then he hurled it from the car with vigorous resolution; he pressed the throttle, and they turned a swift right, speeding away, towards France. Away from Spain, away from Miguel, away from the killer. Away from the witch's cave of Zugarramurdi.

Amy said nothing. David said: 'Are you OK?'

'Yes.' She was staring levelly out of the window, staring at the fleeing ranks of trees. 'I'm OK.'

A car rumbled into view ahead – David fought the surge of fear: but it was a farmer in a blue and mud-smeared van. They overtook the van, and he watched it disappear into the fog behind them.

Whole minutes passed. Amy gazed expectantly across the gearwell.

'We're going to France?'

'*Yes.*'

'OK . . . That's good.'

They were ascending again. After ten kilometres, they attained a grey rocky crest, a balding spot in the woods, watched over by soaring eagles with imperial wings, and then they were over the imperceptible frontier and inside France, driving past deserted old passport booths, and descending from the peaks.

David enjoyed a fraction of relief. At least they were out of Spain, where he and Amy had nearly been killed. Where Amy had been . . . raped. Was it rape? *What had just happened?*

For the fifteenth time in thirty minutes, he clocked the rearview mirror. Just to check, to see if there were any cars following. Any *red* cars.

They were alone on the road; he massaged the tension from his neck muscles. As they curved the mountain roads, he found himself thinking of the witch burnings. Of Zugarramurdi.

He could imagine the scenes of terror: a young woman being pulled, by her hair, across that dismal cobbled square; he saw the villagers shouting at her, throwing stones, with mangy dogs barking and snapping. He could hear the frightened peasant children, sobbing in the dungeon . . . Denouncing their parents. He could see the black-hooded priests, stripping the women naked, searching for the Devil's claw-marks . . .

He tried to clear his mind, focussing on the route. Now they were descending into the foothills, the sun had begun to burn through the thinning clouds; soon enough the clouds were gone. Blue autumn skies reigned over the green hills and valleys of southern Gascony.

'He was cutting trees when I met him,' she said.

David looked across the car, jolted from his reveries.

She repeated her words. Her speech was a monologue, a very necessary monologue.

'When I first saw Miguel. It was at a Basque fair. The Basques have these rustic sports. They call them *la force Basque. Herri Koralak.* Trials of rural strength.' Her fringe lifted in the soft freshet of breeze from the open car window. 'He was throwing boulders, and chopping logs, and winning the tug of war. You know, he was like this . . . *legend.* The Wolf was already a legend, everyone talked about him, the giant from Etxalar, son of the famous José Garovillo, this guy with inhuman strength. A *jentilak* from the forest of Irauty. He was bare chested when I saw him and I was twenty-three and it was purely physical. I'm sorry. Sorry. So fucking sorry.'

He wondered why she was apologizing; he wondered who she was apologizing to. He listened to her as she talked and talked, her words blurring into the noise of the engine and the strobing of the woodland sun.

'Then I realized he was clever, but . . . but, you know, a killer, truly brutal. And the strength, this famous tall guy, the *jentilak*, it was . . . tainted, it was married to a pure cruelty. But the sex was good, at first. That's the truth and I'm sorry. He used to tie me up. I bit him. He cut me once, on the scalp, with a knife. We had a sex game, with a knife. I came when he did it.'

She was staring straight ahead, her eyes fixed on the horizon of hills. 'Then I began to feel sick. Quite soon. With the sex, the taint of violence. And he was seriously troubled, mentally, emotionally, every way. Pathologically. Whenever we had really passionate sex, he always fell into this deep, deep sleep, almost comatose. What is that about? I don't know.'

Now she looked at him. 'So there it is. That was the only way I knew . . . to give us a chance. He was surely going to kill you. Maybe me too. So I let him fuck me, as I thought that might save us. Sorry. You can stop the car now if you want and leave me here. I can hitch.'

Her face was a picture of resisted tears. David felt the anger abating, it was replaced with a voyeuristic sympathy, a shared and unseeing terror of what she must have been through. So she had done it to save them; it was rape. A kind of rape. Maybe not rape. But she had saved his life.

'You don't have to talk about it any more,' he said. 'You don't have to talk about it ever again.' And he meant it. But she shook her head, her mouth trembling, as she surveyed the rolling Gascon dales, green and mellow, through the car window.

'I want to talk about it. I knew as soon as he walked in the cave he would want to do . . . something like that. The same hungry smile. He liked sex in the open, the risk of being caught, being seen by others. We did it in the witch's cave before. That's how I knew where we were. He was always ravenously sexual, like he was starved.'

'I'm so sorry, Amy.'

'Don't be. It *wasn't* rape. It was just *disgusting*. I did love him once and I can never forgive myself for that. But he was going to kill you. He was probably going to torture you. And so.'

'Is he . . .' David didn't know how to phrase it. 'Is he ill? I mean he's obviously a bastard but it feels like more than that.'

'Who knows. Psychotic maybe. The facial tic always made me wonder. And the sleep and the inexorable libido . . . He used to want sex five or six times a day. Anywhere. With lots of . . .' She grimaced, and continued: 'Like I said. Tying up. Biting. Cutting. And worse. You know.'

'OK . . .'

He reached out for her hand; he touched it, blindly, his eyes on the curving hilly road. He said nothing for a few kilometres.

Then he gave voice to obvious question, the same question as before.

'Can we go to the police now?'

'No.'

'I knew you'd say that.'

Her smile was polite.

'Sure. But it's true. No police. That's one thing José taught me. When the Basques are involved, don't trust the police *anywhere*, on either side.' She gave him another bleak and tight–lipped smile. 'You know there are five police forces in the Basque Country? All dangerous. Some are killers for Spain. Some are infiltrated by ETA . . . We might walk straight back into danger.'

'Yes, but we're in France.'

'Same difference. Let's just . . . get away. Think about it.'

He subsided. She was maybe right; he suspected she was wrong; but after the last few hours, he didn't want to question her or press her any further than he needed to.

They drove, the sun was warm, they drove.

David and Amy swapped seats, Amy taking his directions. He had a firm idea where they should go: further north and east, into Gascony, away from Spain. Towards the next towns marked on the map. Savin. Campan. Luz Saint Sauveur.

He knew where they were going, because he was more determined than ever to discover the truth about the churches and the map and his grandfather. The savagery and horror of the last days had only made him *more purposeful*. And he was, to his own surprise, excited by this velocity, this targeting, this rationale for everything. His life, at last, had a satisfying if difficult goal, his existence was speedy and directed, after a decade of anomie and apathy; it was like being on a very fast train after driving aimlessly on a beach.

Did Amy know where they were going? Probably, possibly, who could say. She seemed to fool him and beguile him at the same time. She was like a deep blue rockpool, full of deceptively clear water. When she spoke she was honest and candid and he thought he could see everything: see to the bottom, the rock. But when he dived in, he realized the truth. He could drown in the cold plunging blues, her depths were unsounded.

So they drove.

But this was big empty country, and the little French roads were slow and full of tractors and farmers' trucks. For several hours they trundled through yawning little villages and forgotten Basque hamlets, past farmyards advertising *Fromage d'Iraty* on homemade placards. In the hypnotic, mid-afternoon sunshine, David found himself wearily dreaming, again, this time remembering his childhood. Playing touch rugby in the summer with his father – he remembered his father's bright happy smile; the pungent aroma of the leather rugby ball, rough against David's hand. A big family dog cantering across the lawn. *Happiness*. And then the sadness.

At length they stopped at a vast Carrefour hypermarket on the main Mauleon road where they ate a lonely *croque monsieur* and *salade verte* in the sterile cafe; where they bought clothes and toothpaste, staring silently at each other across the supermarket aisle as they did so. They were refugees, hiding out. And they couldn't even trust the police?

At last they ascended to the little town of Mauleon Lecharre, lying alongside a pretty river and surrounded by the green Pyrenean hills.

David steered them straight to the medieval core of the town, and parked. He stretched himself, aching horribly after the long drive, after the terrors of the cave and the forest. The town was quiet and couples were wandering the twilit, cobbled streets. Amy and David joined the promenade: they walked to the riverside, and stared at the waters from the bridge. Swallows were curling about in the softening dusk of early autumn. David yawned.

'I'm exhausted.'

'Me too.'

They left the car where it was and walked to the nearest hotel, a pretty but modest two star near the main town square, with a fifty-something French manageress. The woman's fingernails were so long and over-varnished they looked like purple talons.

'*Bonsoir! J'ai deux chambres . . . mais très petites . . .*'

'That's fine,' said David. Trying not to look at her claws.

The elevator was the smallest in Gascony. David slept, but fitfully. He dreamed all the way through the night.

He dreamed the house was burning.

Voices were calling from inside the fire, asking David to help – but he couldn't do anything. He was standing in the garden staring at the fiercely burning house, at the flames licking up the walls, and then he saw a charred and black-ened face at the window. It was his mother. She was inside the burning house and she was tapping the glass, trying to touch her son, and she was saying *it's not your fault, David, it's not your fault* and suddenly church bells were ringing out wildly and David –

Woke up.

Sweating.

It wasn't church bells.

Sweating.

It was the hotel phone. Coughing away the phlegm of the bad dream, he groggily reached for the phone.

'David? Hello?'

It was nine a.m. It was Amy.

Showered and dressed, he went downstairs. When Amy came down to join him for breakfast, on the al fresco hotel terrace perched above the river, she looked at him inquiringly.

He immediately confessed.

'Bad dreams. I keep thinking about my parents' death. Baffling dreams.'

'Not surprising, maybe . . .'

'It seems relevant, but I don't know why.'

'Perhaps you should tell me. Explain. It might help.'

'But . . . what?' He shrugged, feeling helpless, a victim of his endless incoherent memories. 'What shall I tell you?'

'I don't know. You could tell me how it happened?' She smiled, and her smile had a yearning empathy. He had a desire to hug her; he ignored this. She said, 'Tell me . . . how you found out about the crash.'

'OK . . . Well . . .' Then he stopped, because it was vastly difficult. He had never really talked about it before. David stared at his half-eaten croissant, his pot of Xapata cherry jam. Amy assisted him.

'How old were you at this point?'

'Fifteen.'

Amy said slowly, and with a gentle incredulity.

'Fifteen . . .?'

'Yes,' he answered. 'And they just went away on holiday, one summer, my mum and dad.'

'That's very young, for . . . your mother and father to leave you alone?'

'Yep,' said David. 'And it was unusual. They were very good parents, we'd always had nice holidays *together*. Then suddenly – my mum said she and Dad were going away for a month *on their own*. Abroad.'

'They left you totally alone in England?'

David stared about. Just two other guests were on the terrace, a German man and wife silently buttering their sliced open baguettes. The holiday season was over. He tried not to think about Miguel. He looked back at Amy.

'They left me with friends in Norwich. Friends of my mum's, the Andersons. We were all very close, their kids and me. In fact it was them, the Andersons, who took me in when . . . when Mum and Dad . . . when they had the . . . the thing, you know, the crash. When they were killed.'

'OK.'

'But this is what's strange!' said David, his voice unexpectedly loud. He flushed, then continued more quietly. 'This is the odd thing: I remember I asked my mum, before they went, why they were going without me and she said: *we're going to find out the truth* – and then my dad sort of laughed but it was kind of different, embarrassed.'

Amy leaned a little nearer.

'To find out the truth. Why should she say *that*?'

'I don't know. I guess I've never really thought about it before. Never really wanted to think about it before.'

David sighed and shook his head. He sipped his coffee and stared across the river, at the ancient bridge. He wondered if Miguel had pursued them; he also wondered how Miguel had known they were in the witch's cave. Somehow he felt the terrorist would discover them, *wherever* they were hiding, wherever they fled.

And no wonder. With a cold shock of surprise, David

realized that Miguel was looking at them *right this minute*. From the bridge.

The medieval parapets of the bridge were sprayed with ETA graffiti. The coarsely daubed words said *Viva Otsoko!*

And next to the word *Otsoko* was a crude, huge and very effective stencil of a black wolf's head.

The Wolf.

So he was here, and watching, always watching. He was watching them finish their croissants with apricot *confiture*.

David swallowed away the bitter taste of the image, with a slug of milky coffee. He lifted his gaze, determinedly, beyond the bridge and the disturbing graffiti, across the river, to the grey mansard roofs of Mauleon.

Over the rushing mountain water he could see a church spire, a row of parked Renaults and Citroëns, and a pretty woman in her thirties coming out of the neighbourhood boulangerie, a baguette sticking out of her bag. The bakers' window advertised *gâteaux basque*, the big fat cakes with *lauburus* of white icing sugar on the soft orange sponge, and thick cherry jam inside.

He watched the pretty blonde woman, a woman like his mother.

And now, at last, the deep wound re-opened, in real-time. A *gâteau basque* sliced in two, to show the red cherry jam.

Vividly, he remembered the scene: the friend of his mother, Mrs Anderson edging red-eyed into his bedroom to tell him; the way she faltered, then sobbed, then apologized. Then at last she had told him what had happened to his mum and dad. A car crash in France.

At the time David had tried to be tough: a boy trying to be a man, but only fifteen years old. He'd refused to cry in front of Mrs Anderson, but when she had softly closed the door behind her – *then* he had yielded, at that moment something had unlinked inside him, something had snapped,

106

something had forever broken the silver necklace of life, and he had turned and buried his hot boyish face in the pillow and cried, alone, trying to muffle the noise of his shameful weak sobs.

Since then he had determinedly never come here, never visited France, never wanted to know what had happened, how exactly they had crashed, how his mum and dad had died together. Instead he had taken the feelings, the memories, these mournful thoughts and considerations, and put them in a black iron box in the saltmine of his soul, like art treasures stored by a nation when the Nazis invade; and then he had turned to work and worry and study and keeping his life on track despite it all, to protect himself – but now here he was, in Gascony. Near Navvarenx. *Near Navvarenx.*

'Are you alright?'

Amy's smile was sympathetic, anxious and incoherent and affectionate and sympathetic. And yet maybe it was none of these things. Was he even reading her smiles correctly?

'I'm OK.' His throat felt a little thick. 'It's just that . . . *I realized something. It's been staring at me all along.*'

'What?'

Muted by his own surprise, he reached in his jacket pocket and pulled out the map.

Amy watched as he spread it on the table; the soft, sun-weary map, with the little blue stars.

David was scrutinizing the little markings, the little towns marked with the blue asterisks. The map suddenly possessed a terrible poignancy; he swallowed the upwelling emotion.

'Look. Here. See the way these stars are filled out, so carefully. I recognize the style.'

'Sorry?'

'It's my *father's* handwriting. This must have been his map. And he's marked on it . . . This place.' He pointed at one of

107

the towns marked on the French part of the road map; Amy half rose from her chair and gazed down.

'Navvar . . . enx,' she said. 'Not far from here . . . and it's marked, so it's one of the places with churches. OK . . .'

'But next to that, here . . .' His finger moved a fraction and pointed at a smaller town right next to Navvarenx.

Amy looked at him.

'Gurs? Right by it.'

He nodded. His mouth was dry.

'Gurs.'

'That means . . .?'

'I've heard the name before. A long long time ago. I remember Mrs Anderson whispering it. You know, the way adults do when they're discussing something they don't want the child to hear.'

'So Gurs . . .'

'Is, I think, where my parents had the crash. This map must have been in my father's possession when it happened. When my mother and father were killed . . . *They were following this map.*'

13

In his study, overlooking the small lawn of his little house in the North London suburbs, Simon was trying to work. But his four-year-old son Conor kept running in, to show his dad a spider, and ask him what sheep liked to eat, and insist the world watch his Thomas the Tank Engine DVD.

The father found it hard to resist his son's demands; he knew he was an indulgent parent, perhaps because he had come to parenthood late: thirty-six. But he was also indulgent simply because he adored his son: the lad's trusting eyes of distant blue, the way he upbraided a recalcitrant football with a stick. Conor was a force of nature. And he could make his parents laugh at anything.

But Simon had to work. His first two *Telegraph* articles, on the linked and bizarre murders, had caused a mild stir, and his editor wanted more. Much more. Consequently he'd had to do some research, all this week, and more today.

Placating Conor with an organic raspberry drink snatched from the kitchen cupboard, he returned to his study, shut the door firmly, and let the au-pair-they-could-barely-afford deal with Thomas the Tank Engine. Sitting once more at his computer he glanced for a second out of the window at the endless suburbia, at a fat housewife hanging up her washing.

Then he started Googling.

Syndactyly.

The problem was there wasn't that much to learn. Half an hour's searching told him what his doctor wife had already explained: the deformation was moderately common, it was linked to various genetic syndromes: ensembles of ailments and afflictions, in turn linked to specific chromosomal abnormalities. The syndromes had quite resonant names: Aarskog Syndrome, Lemli Opitz Syndrome, Cornelia de Lange Syndrome.

Simon blinked at the glaring computer screen. He read the names twice. He picked up a pen and wrote the names on a pad.

Something chimed. Many of the names were French: Bardet-Biedl Syndrome. Apert Syndrome.

French?

Twenty minutes of more encouraging computer time told him why. Many of the syndromes were caused by inbreeding: 'consanguineous unions', as one website quaintly phrased it. And this inbreeding was very common in isolated mountain communities.

Such as the Alps and the Pyrenees.

That's why so many French doctors had been the first to notice the disorders, and to vaingloriously label these disorders with their own surnames. The syndromes were common in the mountains of France.

Simon stared at the pulsing words onscreen. *The Pyrenees*. The South of France. The Basque Pyrenees. Picking up his pen again, he wrote the word *Pyrenees*, fairly pointlessly, on his pad. Then he stared at the pad. He could hear his son's happy giggle in the background somewhere, but it was very much in the background. Simon was focussed. Clear headed.

Back to the screen. He quickly typed in 'Pyrenees' and 'deformity'. He scanned a few sites. Goitres were mentioned. Psychotic illnesses. Congenital ailments caused by incest, or lack of iodine, or other dietary deficiencies. And then something else flashed up, something which he wasn't expecting at all.

Up until the eighteenth century, in the Pyrenees as elsewhere, deformity was often seen as a sign of damnation, or of witchcraft.

As one flamboyant website put it: 'During the great witch craze of the sixteenth and seventeenth centuries, hundreds of innocent victims were tortured, mutilated or burned at the stake merely for the misfortune of being born with an extra finger, or a third nipple; people were literally crushed under stones because of their congenital cretinism.'

Tortured. Crushed and burned. His mind flashed back to the vile photos of the Primrose Hill victim. She was knotted. Was that witch torture?

It took four seconds. *There*. He wondered if his heartbeat was audible.

'*Knotting*. Common through the seventeenth century, this form of torture involved tying a stick into the condemned witch's hair and twisting it tighter and tighter. When the Inquisitor no longer had the strength to twist, he would grasp the victim's head or fasten it in a holding device until burly men could take over the chore. The scalp would often be ripped away.'

Simon wondered why the cops hadn't found this out themselves. Tomasky had already researched knotting, according to Sanderson. The police were being inept – or concealing things from him. Keeping elements of the case to themselves. It was hardly unknown.

He leaned to his left and wrote a little note in his pad. A reminder. Then he gazed back at the screen. What about the woman on Foula? With her face slashed into ribbons? Simon paged through a list of witch tortures: the sheer horror of them gave him pause. The Spanish Spider, squassation, the Judas chair, the shinvice, quartering by horses, the Bootikens, the Pear of Anguish – *the Pear of Anguish?* – and then, at last, he found it.

Cutting.

The reason he hadn't instantly found this torture was because it wasn't called *cutting*. The torture inflicted on the Foula victim was apparently termed 'scoring round the mouth'. And it was simply described: the witch was methodically slashed around the lips and cheek with a knife, until the face was 'a mass of appalling cuts; the skin shredded from the facial bones; the pain of this superbly cruel torture was sometimes sufficient to render the victim unconscious.'

Simon reached for his coffee, but it was undrinkably cold, so he sat for several minutes in the quietness of his study wondering what he had discovered this morning. He wasn't quite sure.

Because it didn't compute; *nothing* computed. The three murders had happened in different corners of the country, yet all three of the lonely people were of Basque Pyrenean origin; two of the murders involved elements of witch torture. But there was no evidence that these lonesome souls were actually 'witches' – whatever that might mean.

Moreover, the two tortured victims had also suffered a deformity: syndactyly, a malformation of the fingers and toes common in isolated inbred mountain communities – such as the Pyrenees. In the South of France.

Simon felt like a small child looking at a bright TV, too close to the screen: he could see the colours of the pixels, the details were implied, but he was too near to the crackling glass to get a sense of the overall image.

So he needed to sit back. Take a more objective position.

He went through the other facts that they possessed.

The manner of the murders was clinical and efficient, despite the lurid elements of torture. The killer or killers on Foula must have been very well equipped and no one had seen them come or go, by some kind of dinghy perhaps. They had presumably arrived by boat in the darkness, gone straight to Julie Charpentier's house, and tortured and killed her. Then they left the island, quitting the scene before sunrise.

The Primrose Hill case showed similar proficiency and forethought, and, likewise, a clinical garrotting followed the most extreme torture. There had been no torture involved in the slaying in Windsor, but the murder had been equally efficient. These killings were, therefore, not being perpetrated by teenage Goths high on glue, that was pretty certain. It was someone, or some agency – with a definite plan of action.

And then there was the third complicating circumstance. A truly interesting circumstance. One of the women had recently been pestered by a young geneticist named Angus Nairn who was trying to carry out blood tests.

And this geneticist had recently disappeared.

That was the most eye-opening result of Simon's research earlier in the week. He'd Googled 'Angus Nairn' as soon as he'd got back from Scotland and it turned out this man, Nairn, was himself the subject of a mystery. Eight weeks ago he had vanished.

Nairn had been working at a private London research institute called GenoMap, a research organization dedicated to the study of 'genomic diversity'. The laboratory had closed in some controversy about three months back, and soon afterwards Nairn had just . . . disappeared. No one knew where he was. His parents, his ex colleagues at the lab, his friends. Nobody.

Of course it was possible that the Nairn disappearance

113

was an entire coincidence. Maybe his involvement with Charpentier was just a *thing*. And yet something said this was surely not the case: the links were half-formed, but a link was faintly detectable. Genetics, deformity, the Pyrenees, the Basques, blood tests . . . He just needed time out to grasp the entire chain.

Checking his watch, Simon grabbed his jacket. It was noon and he had a fairly ghastly appointment, an onerous duty to fulfil.

Throwing himself in the car, he headed for the far outskirts of London where the orbital motorways met the first scruffy farms and the closely mowed golf courses. And the acres of plush greenery that surrounded the St Hilary Mental Health Institution.

Forty minutes after leaving his home, the journalist was watching a team of schizophrenics play football.

If Simon had not known what he was seeing – madmen kicking a ball – then he might never have guessed what was happening. It was only when he got close, right to the touch-line, that it became evident that there was something strange about this kickabout. Many of the players had a notable stiffness in their movements. The goalkeeper was crawling across the penalty area for no apparent reason. And a defender was arguing, vehemently and poignantly, with the corner flag.

'Simon!'

Doctor Fanthorpe, the deputy clinical psychiatrist, waved Simon's way and ran across the pitch to say hello.

The 'football cure' was Fanthorpe's pet project. Bill Fanthorpe's idea was that it helped to socialize seriously detached psychotics – to play as a team – and it gave them a reward when they scored a goal, helping with low self-esteem. Moreover, the exercise kept down the weight of the patients: so many of the mentally ill were fat.

'Hi, Bill.'

The doctor smiled; he was wearing shorts maybe three sizes too large.

'I saw your articles in the *Telegraph*. Extraordinary story. The Basque murders!'

'Yes . . . It is rather odd. Anyway, ah, how's Tim, is he . . .?'

Bill was still panting from the football.

'He's . . . OK. We had some fitting last week but this week it's not been so bad. Not so bad at all. Tackle that man!'

The psychiatrist tutted as the opposing forward slipped a ridiculously poor tackle, and slotted an easy goal. The goal was an easy score because the goalkeeper was sitting on the ground with his eyes shut.

Simon repressed the desire to laugh. But if he didn't laugh he might cry. *That was his brother out there:* the plump schizophrenic in his early forties mumbling in the corner, by the flag. The knife-attacker. There was a security guard loitering at the far end of the pitch. Simon guessed he was probably armed – this was a secure asylum.

The referee blew his whistle.

'Three-two!' said Bill, excitedly. 'That's great, good good. Let me go and get Tim.'

Half of Simon wanted to slip away right now. He'd done his duty and seen Tim – if only from a distance – and he could say his brother was alive and now he could quit, and go back to his son and the au pair and his wife and pretend that Tim didn't exist, pretend that Simon's whole family didn't have this same mad blood in their genes, pretend that the father didn't look briefly at the son at least once a day and think . . . Do you? Will you? *What have you inherited?*

'Simon?'

Tim looked very pleased to see his sibling; Simon hugged his brother. Tim's heavy white thighs looked oddly vulnerable in his blue nylon soccer shorts.

'You look good, Timothy. How are you?'

'Oh, good, good good, excellent game, isn't it!' Tim was grinning impetuously.

Simon checked his brother's face; the hair was greyer, the cheeks were even fatter and yet Tim never seemed to really age. Did madness keep you young? Or maybe it was his image of Tim that was frozen in his own mind: the image of Tim with a knife in his hand, hacking at Mum, in the bedroom. All the blood. Pints of blood.

'You played very well,' said the journalist again, trying not to hate his older brother. *It's not his fault.*

'Oh yes. Very good sporting chances. Are you here long there is a . . . yes. Ah yes doubtless. Yes.'

They both made a proper effort to chat, but sentences defeated Tim at every turn, and within a few minutes the dialogue had dwindled. Tim's attention had wandered elsewhere: gone a-blackberrying. Simon knew the distracted and pained expression all too well: his brother was hearing his voices. There were little roils of anxiety about his features, tics and blinks. Tim was trying to keep smiling but he was hearing things, all those confusing orders.

The pity welled in his brotherly heart, pity and hatred and love all at once. The sadness was drenching. He wanted to go; Tim would be here the rest of his life.

'OK, Tim, I have to go now.'

Tim offered a reproachful stare.

'Not long then? Didn't stay too long we must be busy. Busy as ever. Yes busy until . . .'

'Tim?'

'I'm busy too working of course. Excellent . . . inside the system.'

'Tim, listen. Dad sends his love.'

Tim's eyes seemed to mist with grief, standing here in the mild autumn sun by the lunatic asylum. Was his brother, appallingly, going to cry?

116

'Simon . . .?'

'Tim.'

'Rather, you know, doubtless, Mother and Father in South Africa. Simon. I . . . I . . . I made something. For you.'

'Sorry?'

Bill Fanthorpe had wandered over and was observing them from a couple of yards away.

Tim reached in the pocket of his nylon shorts. And pulled out a small object, crudely carved from wood.

'Gusty. Awfully fun. Remember Gusty remember him? I made a dog hope you like it.'

The younger brother examined the miniature wooden toy. He understood now. When they were kids, the family had owned a springer spaniel, Augustus – 'Gusty'. Simon and Tim had spent hours and days, entire holidays, playing with Gusty, going for rambles on the Heath. Running down sunny beaches.

It was a symbol of happier times, before the darkness of Tim's schizophrenia.

'Thank you, Tim. Thank you . . . very much.'

He had an urge to throw the stupid toy into the bushes. He also wanted to cherish the object, fiercely. There was an unbearable poignancy in the toy's small, pathetic crudeness.

Bill Fanthorpe stepped closer. 'Tim was doing craftwork. Thought you might like it . . .'

'Yes,' said Simon. 'It's lovely. Thanks.'

Bill stepped back; the journalist hugged his brother one more time – and then Tim beamed his mad wide anxious smile and the younger sibling got the usual horrible sense that his brother resembled his own boy, Conor – it was the same smile, *the very same smile*.

Girding himself, Simon resisted the urge to sprint down the lane; he shook hands with Fanthorpe, and slowly walked to the car. And as he walked back to the car he felt his soul keening with grief. He still held the little toy in his hand. He took out his wallet and slipped the toy inside, next to the clasp of hair he kept: from when Conor was a baby.

The sadness was so intense that he was relieved to make it to the car – and relieved to be stuck in traffic thirty minutes later; stuck in the eternal gridlock of the North Circular. The reliability of this horrible congestion was somehow soothing. So utterly predictable.

His car had been stationary ten minutes, spattered by some September drizzle, when his phone rang.

It was Edith Tait.

She told him she had just had an enormous surprise. She was mentioned in Julie Charpentier's will.

This didn't seem so surprising. Staring at the car in front, he asked the old woman to explain.

'It's the amount, Mister Quinn, the actual sum. I called the police fella to tell him, but he wasn't in . . . so, well, I thought you might like tae know. So I tried you.'

Simon changed a gear, his car moved forward three inches.

'Go on. How much?'

'Well now.' Edith laughed, self-consciously. 'It's a wee bit embarrassing.'

'Edith?'

The Scots lady drew a breath, then answered.

'Julie left me half a million pounds.'

The weather was worsening. Swathes of sour rainfall swept across the stalled and angry traffic.

14

Amy was phoning José, from the end of the breakfast terrace. David watched: her animated gestures, the way her blonde hair was harped by the freshening breeze. He could tell by the frown on her face that the conversation was odd, or difficult. She sat down. He leaned across.

'What did José say? Did you ask him about my parents? Is this all about my parents?'

Amy laid the phone on the table. 'Well . . . it was very difficult to work out. He was rambling, almost incoherent. Worse than when you showed him the map.'

'And . . .?'

'He said we had to get away. That Miguel was *extremely dangerous*. He also said not to trust the police. As I thought. And he said Miguel was probably coming after us.'

David growled his impatience.

'Is that all? We *know that*.'

'Yes. But he also seemed . . . odd.' Amy set her cardiganned elbows on the tablecloth, which was strewn with golden flakes of croissant. 'José told me he was leaving. Going into hiding.'

'José? Why?'

Her shrug expressed perplexity. 'No idea. But he was scared.'

'Of Miguel?'

'Perhaps. The police. Wish I knew.'

A raindrop hit the paper tablecloth, a grey spot next to the phone.

'Well I'm *not bloody* running away,' David said. 'I need to know what happened to Mum and Dad. If this is all linked . . . God knows how.' He stared directly into her fine blue eyes. Not unlike his mother's. 'Did he say nothing about my mum and dad, at all?'

She murmured.

'No, he didn't. I'm sorry.'

David sat back with a curt sigh of frustration. They had got as far as they could with José, yet José surely knew more. Sipping the last of his coffee, David winced at the taste of the dregs, and then he winced again, staring at Amy's phone.

The mobile.

The revelation was a mild electric shock. He reached out, grabbed Amy's cellphone, and looked at her.

'This is it!'

'What?'

'He must be using this. *I think Miguel's using mobiles.* To find us.'

'What?'

'You can trace mobiles, right? Triangulation. It's easy.'

'How . . .'

'This is the French Basque Country, you told me yourself. ETA have sympathizers everywhere around here, even in the police force. Maybe in mobile phone companies, too. Telecoms?'

Her gaze was intense.

'I made that phone call outside the witch's cave.'

'Exactly. He knows your number. And now you've called José he'll be after us in Mauleon. Probably coming here right now.'

A fresh wind swept over the terrace. David stood up – and opened the phone, and took out the sim card. Then he leaned, and took aim, and span the little card into the river. Amy stared. He snapped the phone shut, and handed it back. 'OK. Let's go. Your bags are packed?'

'They're already in the car, with yours, but why –'

'We can get another sim card! Come on!'

He led the way down the terrace steps to the waiting car. Then they drove away from Mauleon.

He pointed blindly at the map as he motored: already doing ninety kilometres an hour. 'OK. Please . . . *Amy*, work out a route. Make it a zigzag, unpredictable. Let's go and see these churches. *Right now.*'

Obediently she examined the old map, the pattern of blue stars. The forests unfurled as they accelerated. The mountains were coned with snow in the distance: a row of brooding Klansmen.

The town of Savin was easy to find. An hour of fast, anxious driving brought them to its cluster of sloped roofs. Savin was prettily situated on a crest, overlooking the grey farms and vineyards. They parked on a side street, looking up and down. For Miguel. For the red car. The street was empty.

A smell of incense enveloped David as they entered Savin church. A few Americans were taking pictures of a spectacularly ornate organ. David glanced at a rough old font, the pedestal of which comprised a trio of carved stone peasants: holding up the water. The faces of the peasants were sad. Limitlessly sad.

Then David paced around the nave, and through the choir; he peered into the chancels, where the flagstones

121

were striated with soft colour from the stained glass windows. He stepped into a side chapel dedicated to Pope Pius the Tenth. A stern portrait dominated the little chapel. The long-dead Pope glared eternally through the incensed and sepulchral gloom.

There was nothing else in the church. Amy had already given up, she was sitting in a pew. She looked tired.

But he felt curious about something. Or was it nothing? Or was it something?

There was another door, a smaller door, to the side. Why were there were *two* church doors, one so obviously humbler than the other? He stood and gazed around. He looked back. This little door was tucked away in the corner of the church, the southwest corner; low and modest. Was that significant? How many churches had two doors? Lots, maybe.

Approaching the smaller door, David touched the granite surround: the cold and ancient jamb was worn smooth. The iron handle was rusted and unused. And brutally chiselled into the lintel of the door was a slender, spindly, peculiar arrow, of three lines meeting at the bottom: the arrow was pointing down.

He stepped back, nearly bumping into a priest who was hovering behind.

'Er, *je m'excuse* . . . sorry . . .'

The priest gave him a sharp, wary glance, then paced away down the nave with a swish of nylon vestments.

David stared, transfixed, at the arrow. He was recalling the font in Lesaka. That church had possessed two fonts, and carved into one of them was a similar cruel arrow. Primitive but definite: three carven lines converging at the top: an arrow. That arrow was pointing up.

His thoughts were whirring now, the cogs of the puzzle turning fast. What about the church in Arizkun, that had two doors *and two cemeteries*. How could he forget that second cemetery? The image of an angel, with a tawny cigarette butt screwed in the eye, was lodged in his memory.

Just like the old woman with the goitre, pointing and cussing.

Shit people, shit people, shit people.

He was closer. How close he didn't know. But he was close and he wanted to keep moving. He signalled to Amy – shall we go? – she smiled in a wan way, and stood. But David kept his thoughts to himself as they retreated to the car. Because some of his thoughts were truly disturbing. Was there some direful link between the markings on the font and the markings . . . on Amy's scalp? He believed her story about Miguel: the sex game with a knife. Her painful honesty as she admitted this had been all too authentic. But the scars. The scars were odd. The marks made on the foreheads of witches after the Sabbath intercourse with Satan.

It was too much and too headily upsetting, too rich a mix of repellent ideas. David felt faintly nauseous as he walked the car park gravel. A damp grey drizzle was falling. They didn't say a word as they headed for the next town, slaloming across Gascony, trying to throw Miguel off their tracks.

Sixty kilometres of empty road brought them, very slowly, to Luz Saint Sauveur. The winding route ran spectacularly between walls of rock, with occasional side roads rudely blasted through the oppressive chasm walls: they were heading towards the Pyrenees once more. Clouds collared the black, brooding, saturnine mountaintops like white lacy ruffs around Van Dyck grandees.

Turning a final corner they saw their destination nestled in a vivid green valley. The old and sombre heart of Luz Saint Sauveur concealed another ancient clutch of low slung houses surrounding a very old church. They parked right by the church, climbed out, and entered. David just knew he was near to the sobbing heart of the mystery, at least this part of it: what the churches meant. He had no idea what the solution might be, but he could hear the noise of it, the long wailing cry of confession: *this is what it all means.*

There were two other people inside the *église parroissial* of Luz Saint Sauveur. Sitting on the rear pew with a woman who seemed to be his mother was a young and evidently retarded man. His eyes were rolling, a wet line of spittle ran down his chin, like the track of a slug. His mother's face was prematurely aged, visibly wearied by the necessity of caring for the son. The cretin. David felt a surge of sympathy; he offered the woman a helpless but sincere smile.

Amy had been staring at the altar, and the chancels. Her expression, as she returned, was despairing.

'I don't get it. There's nothing.'

'I'm not so sure . . . maybe there is something.'

'Sorry?'

He gazed her way.

'Look for two. Two of something. Two doors, two ceme-teries, two –'

'Two fonts? I saw two fonts. Over here . . .'

They walked over, their footsteps echoing in the stony silence.

This church also had two fonts, and one of them was hidden away in a cobwebbed corner, half-concealed, musty. It was small and humble and somehow melancholy.

Just like in Lesaka.

Amy said: 'But . . . Why two? Why ever should there be two?'

'I don't know,' he answered. 'Let's just keep going.'

Another tense and silent hour found them in the remote Pyrenean village of Campan, sequestered and isolated at the end of a side-valley. David buzzed down the window and stared, as they rolled down the main street.

Every house had a large rag doll grinning in the window, or at the door. Gawky rag dolls, almost the size of grown men, were sitting in shop windows. Another big doll was lying on the road, fallen from some high sill – it stared up at the wild Pyrenean peaks that imprisoned Campan.

Amy gazed at the dolls.

'Jesus.'

They parked in a side street and strode to the empty centre of the village. Their route passed a tiny, rundown, shuttered *office du tourisme;* in the window of the office was a small typed sign. Amy read it aloud, and then translated for David's benefit: the festival of rag-doll-making was apparently a local tradition, for centuries the people of little Campan had made these big effigies, known as *mounaques*, and in mid September the people would put their handmade rag dolls on display in windows and doors, in shops and in cars.

It was a village of dolls. A village of silent, impassive doll faces, smiling absurdly at nothing. The smiles felt like jeers or insults.

Not that there was anyone to feel menaced or insulted: Campan was deserted, locked up, empty, taciturn, shuttered. One old woman was stepping out of a horse meat shop; she stared their way, then frowned, and walked quickly around the corner.

They reached the main *place* of Campan. A mournful war memorial, a bus stop, and a shop, also closed, marked the centre of everything; one short road led to a bridge, over the rushing River Adour. Even from here David could see that the opposite bank of the river was utterly derelict, a field of roofless cottages and mouldering barns.

Campan was wholly empty, *and half abandoned.*

The other road off the *place* led straight to the church. A metal gate gave onto an overgrown churchyard surrounded by a tall, grey stone wall.

The church door itself was open, so they stepped straight through. The nave was adorned with cheap purple plastic flowers. Four dolls sat on the front pew, staring at the altar: an entire manikin family.

David hunted for twoness, yet he couldn't find it. Campan had one font, one door, one pulpit and four rag dolls grinning like cretins, like inbred retards.

Not *two*.

Amy maybe sensed his frustration, she put a hand on his shoulder.

'Maybe it's more complicated . . .'

'No. I'm *sure* that's it. Two. *It has to be.*' He was snapping the words angrily, and unfairly. Amy flinched, and he apologized. He said he needed fresh air and stepped outside again, into the churchyard. The overcast autumn day was clammy and oppressive, but still an improvement on the dankness of the interior.

He breathed in, he breathed out, calming himself. Staring lucidly. Working it out. The distant mountaintops peered over the plastered brickwork of the church wall.

David gazed at the wall.

If there was a second door it might be in this strange, high castellated wall, which barricaded the entire churchyard.

His search was hampered by the wet brambles that brawled between the graves. Enormous spiders scuttled from his steps.

'What are you doing?'

Amy had followed him out.

He lifted a hand, without turning.

'Looking . . . for doors. In this wall. Don't know what else to do.'

He kicked his way through the sodden undergrowth, flattening wild roses, and clambering over broken tombstones. The air was damp to the point of rain; the graves were slippery to the touch. He climbed and slithered and examined.

The wall was intact, the ancient bricks were apparently unpierced. Amy called out.

'Here!'

She was behind him, pulling back some ivy, which had draped one section of the wall. Behind the ivy was a door, shut and dead, but *a door*. He hurried over and leaned near to see: the tiny door exuded age, the stone surround was crooked, the brown wood was rotten, yet the door was somehow still firm. Resolutely shut. Shut for centuries.

David looked closer. The lintel was carved.

Urgently he ripped away the last coils of ivy and revealed the inscripted symbol in the centre of the stone.

'Here.' He was anxiously excited. 'This arrow. I keep seeing it. The font, the doors, the arrows.'

Amy was shaking her head.

'That's not an arrow.'

'What?'

'I know that's not an arrow.'

'How?'

'Because there's one on a house in Elizondo. I remember walking past it with José, one day years back. I asked him what the symbol meant. He was evasive. Oddly evasive.'

'I don't –'

'All I remember is this: what he called it, *Patte d'oie*. I remember distinctly because he used the French.'

'Patt – what does that mean. Patt . . .?'

'*Patte d'oie*. Goose's foot. An ancient symbol.' Amy brushed some more mud from the incised lines, so brusquely carved into the stone. 'This is a goose's foot, not an arrow. It's a webbed goose's foot.'

15

They were on the last leg now: heading for the last place marked on the map. Approaching the heart of the maze.

Navvarenx. Near to Gurs.

Navvarenx was north by a distance, so they pulled over at a garage for more fuel. David walked to the tiny shop, trying to work out what the doors meant. Smaller doors, smaller cemeteries, smaller fonts. Why?

It didn't make sense. Why was everything duplicated in this eccentric, almost insulting way? Was it a kind of apartheid, like benches for black people in 50s Alabama? Like old South Africa?

Or was it something else? Could they be smaller doors for . . . *smaller people?*

But that hardly made sense, smaller people could use any door.

A bell jingled as he entered the garage shop; he went straight to the till and bought Amy a new sim card, and an entirely new cellphone – just in case. The garage owner was eating red saucisson and baguette as he totted up the bill. David stared at the sum on the receipt, trying to remind himself he didn't have to worry about money.

Back in the car they were both pensive and subdued. And David felt the sadness tighten as they made the last drive. He thought of his parents. And the memories loomed in his mind, even as the mountains faded behind them in the mirror.

He was on his grandfather's sturdy shoulders, his infant mouth clouded with pink cotton candy. The blue Pacific was sparkling and his mum was young and walking beside them, and his dad was there too, and laughing. When was that? What were they doing there? How old was he then? Five? Seven? Nine? It was a blur, too faint to discern.

And the torment was: he had no one to ask. That was the worst thing. He couldn't ring his mum and say *when did we do this*, he couldn't ask his granddad and say *why did we do that*. There was no one left to give him answers, to explain his childhood, to laugh about the funny stuff, to swap memories, to say *remember when we went on that picnic*. He had been left alone and behind by the others, and David yearned, with a wild sadness, to know why. Granddad had sent him here for a reason, the reason had to explain it all.

It had to.

David gripped the steering wheel tightly. The road into Navvarenx took them through the outlying village of Gurs, which seemed to be virtually a suburb of Navvarenx.

Gurs was straggly. The long French road was lined with parallel trees, whitewashed at the base. There was some kind of strange flat area to the south of town – adorned with a series of glass structures, somewhat like bus stops. David looked at it and looked away. An enormous black crucifix loomed over the flatness; he got an overwhelming urge to drive faster. The cross was so very black.

They drove straight on, straight past the village of Gurs, tucked off the main road, and a few minutes later they were seeing a sign saying *Navvarenx*.

At last Amy spoke.

'You know, we don't have to do this now . . .' Her sadly traced smile was empathic.

'What do you mean?'

'We can wait. It's been a long day already. Maybe we should wait.'

'I'm OK. I'm fine. And if Miguel is after us I want to do this quickly.'

He wondered why he was saying this. He *knew* Miguel was after them. Probably in Mauleon right now, asking the hotel manageress. Leaning across the desk, tall and scarred and imposing. *Which direction did the English-speaking couple go?*

As they motored the last couple of kilometres Amy asked him: 'Why didn't you ever try and find out more? About the crash.'

He exhaled.

'I was young . . . I wanted to shield myself. From the agony. The knowledge.'

'That's why you didn't ever think that the map was connected.'

'I guess. Yep. Denial. Erasure. *Repression*. I avoided the details. And the Andersons protected me from the truth. I was just fifteen – and alone.'

'Understandable.'

'Zakly. But now I *have* to think about it.'

David put the car into second as he watched a man cycling down a suburban lane. There was a red car at the end of the road. He stifled the duetting cries of his grief and anxiety.

They parked at the edge of central Navvarenx; they had no choice, it was a fortified and historic town and cars were, apparently, forbidden to drive inside the *centre du ville*. So they locked the car, and they walked.

A town map confronted them at the edge of an empty grey square. It revealed that they were near the church. The last few hundred metres brought them to the impressive frontage of Navvarenx Saint Germain. It was austere and grey, with hints of Gothic arches, but no more, like a fading memory of Gothic.

The interior was virtually deserted, just like the other churches. An old priest was stacking books by the chancel; David noticed a portrait on the wall above the priest's balding head. He didn't have to go over and read beneath the painting: the portrait was exactly the same as the one in Savin. The same severe Victorian visage, frowning, disapproving, contemptuous.

Pope Pius the Tenth.

The main door of the church banged shut behind them. Alerted by the noise, the priest turned – and he stared at David. He stared with a shock of recognition whitening his aged face.

David wanted to go and talk to the man. But the priest shuffled away, and shook his head, and continued his task, as if he were avoiding their gaze, manfully ignoring their presence. He returned to stacking books.

What was this? David fretted, impatient and scared. *Was he imagining it?* Perhaps he was letting paranoia take over. And yet he knew Miguel was after them right now. He knew this because his heartbeat was telling him: *quick*-ly, *quick*-ly, *quick*-ly.

David examined the church doors. Because the plural was correct, again. There were *two doors*.

Amy came over.

'OK. Campan, Luz, Savin, Navvarenx. Two doors. Two doors each time. And two cemeteries. They're all linked. But how . . .?'

He shrugged.

131

'Two doors maybe you could explain, I guess – but two fonts, or stoups? Doesn't make sense.' He sighed. 'And the symbol. The goose's foot. I don't get it.'

As urgent hiss interrupted their dialogue.

It was the priest.

The old man was at his side and tugging David's sleeve: he was gabbling in thickly accented French, keenly, urgently, saying something important. His eyes were bloodshot and yellow, like tainted egg-yolk. David replied with a desperate, apologetic shrug: he didn't understand!

Amy stepped over; she was frowning as she listened to the priest. Then she explained, and interpreted:

'He says he . . . recognizes you. Very odd, he says *they have been waiting for you*. But now he sees your face he feels . . . different? He wants to know if your father was called . . . Edward . . .'

David shivered at the revelation. He looked first at Amy, then at the old man.

'Yes. Edward! Eduardo Martinez. *Why?*'

The old priest was crossing himself, and repeating: 'Eduardo Martinez . . . Eduardo Martinez . . .'

Amy listened closely and translated the priest's further words. 'Apparently you look just like your father. He says everyone in Navvarenx knows what happened, the accident . . . Oh . . . oh my God . . .' Amy's face was grave with sympathy. 'David . . . I don't how to put this, it was not an accident, it was . . . it was something else . . .'

'Just tell me.'

'He says your mother and father were murdered.'

Her blue eyes were wide with compassion. But he just wanted the truth.

'Ask him . . .' he said. 'Please ask him if he will sit with us. And tell me more.'

The old priest looked fretful, even frightened, but he seemed to agree.

'He says he knows a little more. But it is dangerous. The Society is waiting for us. He is meant to tell them. I've no idea what this means . . . He wonders . . . can we go somewhere else, discreet, right away?'

'*Merci!*' David snapped. 'Thank you. *Thank you!*'

The three of them walked to the blaze of light – the open door. The larger door, which had banged shut behind them. Before they crossed into the light, Amy lifted a hand and said:

'Stop.'

'What?'

There was something defensive in Amy's stance. Something very scared.

She nodded towards the square.

'A car. Just pulling up.'

He knew what her next word would be.

'Miguel.'

16

The cold terror flashed – as far as David's fingertips. Fight or flight. He visored a hand, and stared across the *Place d'Église*.

Amy was right. A red car had just swung into the square. The doors opened, Miguel got out, with two other dark-haired men. They walked towards the church.

David shrank back into the shadows. The fear was numbing. Amy had also crept away from the threshold.

'He hasn't seen us yet.'

'But he will. He's coming . . . We're trapped.'

They stared from the darkness into the ominous brightness.

Another voice intruded on their urgent dialogue. The priest was nudging Amy, saying something, very rapidly.

Amy translated:

'He says we can escape. Use the other door. The . . . *qu'est-ce que c'est?*'

'*La porte des Cagots!*' the priest stammered. '*La porte des Cagots!*'

He was hurrying across the church, taking them to the other door. Talking wildly as he did so. Amy and David followed. Amy hissed:

'Something about the door of the . . . Cagots? It leads to the medieval quarter . . . we can get out this way. He says we can escape –'

They were at the side door, the humble door, the smaller door. Amy looked at David who looked at Amy.

'David!'

He squinted, checking the square again. At a greater distance, it was hard to tell, the light was blinding compared to the darkness of the church – but it looked like the three figures had paused.

But then they walked, fast, towards the church.

'He's coming!'

'*La porte!*'

The old priest was trying the door, but the doorknob obviously hadn't been turned in decades. David helped. He pulled, and twisted: nothing happened.

'It's totally rusted!'

David's hands were sweaty with the tension – the fear – he grabbed at the old iron handle and twisted again, with all the force he could manage.

Miguel was closing in, approaching the church. Any second he would enter, see them trapped in a corner . . . and draw his gun. But the door was unbudgeable.

'Try this!'

Amy was clutching a glass phial.

'From the altar. It's oil.'

The oil oozed over the handle as David frantically twisted. The old priest was babbling, '*Votre père, votre père –*'

The metal grated – and sighed – *and then it yielded.* There were men silhouetted at the main door, but the handle of the old door was turning. With a final puff of rust, the door burst open – onto a lightwell surrounded by looming medieval houses, crooked and ancient. Various alleys led off the courtyard, disappearing into darkness.

Was that Miguel's voice behind them? A noise echoed across. The priest had slammed the door; he was still inside, blocking Miguel's way. They had a chance.

David yelled: 'Down here!'

Amy was already following. David grabbed her hand and they sprinted. He didn't dare to look back. The priest was in the church, maybe defending them, confronting Miguel. What would happen? Miguel might shoot. He would force the door open . . . and then . . . *and then* . . .

He kept on running. The alley was little more than a sheltered gutter, overhung by eaves and the bulging upper floors of ancient tenements. Shafts of sunlight speared through the slates, like rods of light they had to dodge. As he ran, half tripping, David thought of his parents. Killed. Slain. Murdered.

The fear mixed with anger; his stomach roiled with terror as he ran. At last they emerged from the alley into a space of green grass and old crumbling battlements.

'Through here?'

There was a Gothic archway – piercing the white limestone walls of Navvarenx. Beyond it was a moated dip, and beyond the dip, over a footbridge – was the car park.

'There!'

His car keys were slippery in his sweaty hands as he clicked the doors open. They piled inside. David revved and reversed – and flung them out onto the road.

South. For several minutes they drove: fast and silent. David checked the mirror. Nothing. He checked it again. Nothing. Amy sighed, urgently:

'Too much. That was *too close* . . .'

David glanced yet again in the rearview mirror as he drove. But the road was deserted. They hadn't been followed. The appalling tension eased a touch, but just a touch. They were out in the countryside, a big aluminium farm building marked a junction.

He pulled over. He handed Amy the phone he'd bought at the garage.

'Check something. Please?'

'What?'

'These people with the doors. What did he call them . . . the Cagots?'

Amy shook her head.

'*Now*? Shouldn't we just get the hell out?'

He cursed, sardonically.

'Fuck that. Where are we going to go? And if I run away . . . I will never know the answer. My parents died here; they were *fucking killed here*. It must be linked to these churches, the Cagots, otherwise why did Granddad give me the map, my dad's map, marked with the same Cagot churches?'

Amy nodded. She smiled – with unhappiness. She took a deep breath, then she picked up the phone and switched it on and went online.

'OK,' she said.

'Check the Cagots. And the symbol, the goose's foot.'

Amy went quiet as she searched the net. David looked away, and opened the car window, the damp smell of cow manure filling the car. And rotting silage. A buzzard was hunting in the distance, silhouetted by the blue distant mountains.

'Right,' said Amy. 'All I've found, not much, but it's strange. The Cagots seem to be a tribe of pariahs, that's what they're called, like untouchables. In the Pyrenees.' She paused, then added, 'They had their own doors. *Marked with symbols*. The *pattes d'oie*, of course.'

'A tribe? Of *pariahs*?'

'That's what it says. Yes. They had their own special small doors in the churches. There isn't much else. I think . . . if we want to know more –'

'Yes?'

'There's a good website here, dernieredescagots dot fr – the last of the Cagots. It's the website of a man who *is* a Cagot and he lives in Gurs. We could . . .'

David was already starting up the car. Amy protested: 'But, David . . . that's very near Navvarenx. Miguel?'

He answered, emphatically. 'Amy. I can drive you to the nearest station and give you ten grand and you need never see me again and I will totally understand and –'

She put her hand on his wrist.

'We're in it together. Now. No. Anyway I know Miguel.' She was shaking her head, the shine of fear or sadness in her eyes. 'I know him. He will come after me now, whatever I do. He will kill me and you. Separately or together. So . . .'

'So we stay together.'

David drove fast towards Gurs; Amy guided him, using the satnav on the phone.

'Down here, take a left, just here . . .'

Gurs was a humdrum place: a few sombre old villas, a disused railroad. Some desultory bungalows surrounded a tired-looking town hall, even the Brasserie d'Hagetmau was resolutely shut. It was a place sucked of life by bigger towns nearby. Or just a place no one especially wanted to live.

The sharpest corner brought another row of bungalows, with gardens lush from recent rain.

'This is it, the right number,' said Amy, gesturing at the last bungalow in the row. The bungalow was slightly isolated; it stood opposite a modern and rather ugly church, with offices attached. Beyond was scruffy wasteland.

They walked up the path. The front door was painted a self-consciously cheerful yellow. David had the sense of curtains twitching elsewhere in the silent suburban street; old faces peering. He turned. No one was looking.

He pressed the doorbell. A faintly ecclesiastic chime was heard. Nothing happened. Amy peered at the windows.

'Maybe no one is in . . .'

He pressed again. Wondering where Miguel was. Then he heard a noise. A yell. Someone was shouting at them, from inside.

'What . . .?'

The shout was heard, again. Angry and panicked.

He lifted the letterbox lid and peered.

A young woman was crouched in the hallway. And she had a shotgun. She was trembling, and her grip was clumsy, but she was pointing the shotgun at the door. At David and Amy.

17

Detective Sanderson was sceptical about Simon's mission to interview Professor Emeritus Francis St John Fazackerly, one time winner of the Willard Prize for Human Genetic Research, and now the ex-boss of GenoMap.

'Good luck. And you'll need it, mate,' said Sanderson, his cheerful voice quite clear on the mobile phone pressed to Simon's ear. The detective added: 'He's an evasive old fucker, we talked to him last week.'

'Yes?'

Simon crossed Euston Road, and stared at the gleaming offices of the Wellcome Institute: this whole area was full of medical research centres and high-tech university faculties, and young undergraduates laughing outside pubs who made Simon feel all of his forty years. He spoke into the phone:

'Doesn't he know *anything* about Nairn?'

Sanderson scoffed, 'If he does he ain't saying. Tomasky nearly got the thumbscrews out – you seeing him at the GenoMap gaff?'

'Yes.'

'He asked to meet us there, as well. Guess he prefers neutral territory.'

Simon headed down Gordon Street.

'Detective –'

'Mate, call me Bob, fer fuck's sake –'

'Bob – Detective – Bob –'

Bob Sanderson laughed. 'If you get anything on these blood tests do tell – maybe your sleuthing skills will prove a bit better than ours.'

'Bob, you make it sound like you . . . don't exactly trust him?'

The line was silent. Simon repeated his question. The DCI replied slowly, 'Not sure I do. There's just something . . . well, evasive, likesay. Check it out.'

The call concluded, the journalist pushed through the battered, paint-peeling door. He took the lift to the top floor where an old, old guy in a tweed jacket, with a wattly neck and yellowy eyes, was waiting to greet him. The man looked barely half a social class above a tramp. Yet, as Simon's research had told him, this man Fazackerly had been – once – amongst the best geneticists of his generation.

Fazackerly fixed his eyes on his visitor. The scientist's yellow-toothed smile was lordly yet repulsive, like a monitor lizard grinning after a large meal of diseased goat.

'Mister Quinn from the *Daily Telegraph*. Do come in, and excuse the mess. I'm still moving my ancillary documents. Two months later!'

Fazackerly opened a glass door and guided his guest through the main lab of the GenoMap project, as was. Evidence of the project's closure was all around. Much of the machinery had already been dismantled, there were big half-sealed crates sitting in the dusty silence, with fridge-freezer sized machines inside, waiting to be shipped.

The old professor pointed at a couple of the bigger pieces of equipment, and listed their names and functions: the thermocycler for rapid segmentation, the vast lab microwave for sterilization and histology, the DNA sequencers for analyzing fluorochromes. Simon scribbled the strange words and purposes in his notebook; it felt like he was taking dictation in Latin.

Then Fazackerly invited the journalist into a back office, closed the door, and sat down at a desk. Simon sat opposite in a steel chair. A black and white photo of a Victorian-looking man lay flat and dusty on the desk.

Fazackerly nodded in its direction. 'Just taken it down off the wall. It's Galton.'

'Sorry?'

'Francis Galton, bit of a hero. The founder of eugenics. Did some *excellent* work in Namibia.'

The scientist took up the framed photo and slid it into a cardboard box at his side; the box also contained three empty bottles of whisky.

'Well, Mister Quinn, I imagine you have some questions, like your police friend?'

'Yes.'

'To speed things up, what say I give you a little background?'

'OK.'

Fazackerly began to waffle: about human genetics and the genome project and the problems of funding pure research. Dutifully, Simon scribbled.

But the journalist was beginning to sense what the Scotland Yard detective had been implying: Fazackerly was evasive, filling the air with mellifluous but distracting verbiage, as if aiming to decoy.

He needed to hurry the dialogue along.

'Professor Fazackerly. Why *exactly* was the GenoMap project closed down?'

The interviewee sniffed the air.

'Because we quite ran out of money, I'm afraid. Genomics is an expensive business.'

142

'So there was no . . . political element?'

A flash of the yellow teeth.

'Well . . .'

Silence.

'Professor Fazackerly. I know you're a busy guy. I'll come clean.' Simon stared directly at the professor. 'I've been doing my Googling. GenoMap was set up mainly with private funding from corporations to continue the work that was begun by the Human Diversity Genome Project at Stanford University. Yes?'

'Yes . . .'

'Were you closed for the same reason as the Stanford project?'

For the first time the scientist appeared uncomfortable.

'Mister Quinn. Please remember. I'm just a retired biologist.'

'What coaxed you out of retirement?'

'I think GenoMap is a grand idea: we are, or rather we *were*, aiming to map the differences between different human races . . . and if we manage that then it could be of momentous benefit.'

'How?'

'Medicines. There are, for instance, new medicines available for people of African descent in the United States for their particular problems with hypertension. And so forth. At GenoMap we were hoping especially for some insights into Tay Sachs disease, which seems to be especially common with people of Ashkenazi Jewish origin . . .'

'But there were *political* objections, right?'

An expressive sigh.

'Yes.'

'Why?'

'I suspect you know as well as I do, Mister Quinn. For some people the very idea of there being significant ethnic

143

differences *at all* is quite anathematic. Many thinkers and politicians like to assert all racial differences are illusory, a social construct. A fable. A chimera. And certainly it's a point of view.'

'One you don't agree with?'

'No. I think young black men can sprint faster than young white men – on average. That's quite a fundamental racial and genetic difference. Of course you're not meant to say these things . . .' He chuckled mirthlessly. 'But I don't especially care anyhow. I am too old!'

'Fair enough. But a younger scientist?'

Fazackerly adopted a shrewd expression.

'For a young scholar, yes, it is different: it could be seen as career-suicide, getting into this kind of thing. It is very controversial. Koreans are better at chess than Aborigines and so forth! Eugenics died as a science after the Second World War, for obvious reasons. And it has proved very hard to revive the study of racial differences. The HDGP at Stanford was a start, but the politicians got it closed. After that many decided to avoid the field of human genetic diversity altogether. And of course, there are the endless lawsuits, as well . . .'

'The biopiracy?'

'You have done your homework.' Fazackerly's expression was almost wistful. 'Yes. You see, during our research we aimed to analyze the DNA from isolated tribes and races, like Melanesians, and Andaman islanders.'

'Why?'

'Because, like rare Amazonian plants, rare races of men might have uniquely beneficial genes. If we found an isolated Congolese tribe that is genetically resistant to malaria we could then have a shortcut to a genetically-based malaria vaccine.'

Simon wrote in his pad.

'Yet the tribesmen objected. And sued. Because it's *their* DNA?'

'Quite so. But then again, the hunter-gatherers of the Kakoveld have not done all the expensive research.' Fazackerly shrugged, impatiently. 'Anyhow some Australian native groups sued us for biopiracy, and that put the poison cherry on the already rather inedible cake for our main patrons. The Greeler Foundation, Kellerman Namcorp, and so on. They pulled the plug. And that was the end of GenoMap.'

Fazackerly gazed out of the window.

'Such a shame for the staff. We had some great people here. A fiendishly clever girl from Kyoto University. And a quite outstanding Chinese Canadian. And of course . . .'

They looked at each other. The journalist said:

'Angus Nairn.'

'Young Angus Nairn. Perhaps the best young geneticist in Europe. He had already published some quite startling papers.'

'But . . . then he disappeared?'

'After we were closed down. Yes.'

'Why?'

'I have no idea.'

'You have no idea where he's gone, or why? Or *where*?'

'No.' Fazackerly shrugged. 'I did wonder if he may have ended his life, like a good Socratic. The figures for suicide in young men are *quite* alarming. Personally I suspect he was too . . . ambitious . . . to throw himself off Tower Bridge.' The yellow smile was notably sad. 'It is an authentic mystery. I am sorry. I cannot help.'

'But what about the connection with these . . . murders? You said on the phone you'd read my articles. So you know this. Angus Nairn was testing Basques just before he disappeared.'

'The Basques are of tremendous genetic interest.'

'But, coincidentally, one of these Basques was recently *murdered*. A woman called Charpentier . . .'

The lab was silent. Fazackerly suddenly stood, and asked:

'Look, I do have a theory. About Nairn. But I don't have much more time to talk with you. So. Can we step into the square?'

'Whatever you wish.'

'Good. Maybe I can show you something there – something that will explain the concept.'

The two men turned and walked out of the now deserted laboratories; the mellow autumn sunshine magnified the emptiness of the rooms.

Fazackerly's stride was brisk for an old man. He led his guest down the steps and out of the building, across the unbusy road, through the wire gates and into the Septembery green and gold of Gordon Square Gardens. Students, tourists and office workers were taking lunch on the lawns, eating sandwiches from clear plastic packets, chopsticking sushi from little plastic trays. The faces of the lunchers were white and black and all other possible shades.

This, Simon thought, was London at its very best: the best hope of the world. All races coming together. And yet all the time people like this lizard Fazackerly were trying to divide humanity up, once again: put them in different boxes, make everyone mistrust each other *all over again*.

Simon could see why people would object. It felt wrong and depressing: racially parcelling the world. And yet it was just science, and science that could save lives. The paradox was complex. And challenging.

'Here,' said Fazackerly. He was bending to the soil. The professor reached down an old liver-spotted hand and picked something up.

In his lined old palm was a red ant, crawling for freedom.

'Watch this, Mister Quinn.' He leaned closer to the ground.

Flat paving stones surrounded a drain. The flagstones were inhabited by a multitude of black ants, many of them gathered around a discarded and glistening apple core.

Fazackerly delicately dropped the red ant amongst the dense crowd of black ants. Simon leaned further, even though he felt slightly ludicrous. He wondered if the students were laughing at them, as they in turn watched the ants.

Fazackerly explained.

'I am sure you must have done this as an inky-fingered schoolboy. Such a fascinating process. Observe.'

The red ant, evidently confused by its sudden translocation, was turning this way and that – then it began heading for the soil of the flower bed. But the route was barred by the black ants.

Simon watched.

The red ant butted into a black ant.

'And now . . .' prompted Fazackerly.

Immediately the ants began fighting. The black ant had the slightly larger red ant in its pincers. The red ant fought back, toppling the black ant onto its back – but the other black ants were mobilized now: they had gathered around the solitary and terrorized red ant, and they were ripping the legs off the red ant, leg by leg; a final black ant gripped the enemy with its pincers and pulled the red ant's head clean away. The dying ant twitched.

'There,' said Fazackerly, standing up again.

'What?' asked Simon, also getting to his feet. 'So what?'

'What you have just witnessed is interspecific competition.'

'And that is, precisely?'

'Ferocious rivalry, *between closely related species*, that occupy a similar evolutionary niche. It is just one kind of Darwinian struggle. But very destructive. Very fierce.' Fazackerly was walking to a nearby bench. He sat down on the warm old wood; the journalist did the same. The older man shut his leathery eyes and tilted his face to the sun. And continued.

'Intraspecific competition can be almost as vicious. Sibling rivalry. The Cain Complex. The murderous hatred of one brother for another.'

'OK.' Simon breathed in and out, trying not to think about Tim. Trying very hard. 'OK, I get it, and this is all rather interesting. Thank you. But what's this got to do with Angus Nairn?'

The professor opened his eyes. 'Angus was a scientist. He hungrily accepted the bitter truth that . . . you civilians will not or cannot accept.'

'And that truth *is*?'

'The universe is *not* as we wish. It is not a large version of Sweden, run by a giant social worker with sandals. It isn't even a kingdom, with a capricious sovereign. The universe is a violent and purposeless anarchy, full of piti-less struggle.' He smiled, cheerily. 'Natural selection may feel like progress, but it *isn't*. Evolution is random, it is not . . . *going anywhere*. The only law is competition, and killing, and struggle. The war of all against all. And we are no exception. Humanity is subject to the same laws of pointless competition as the animals, as the ants and the toads and the noble cockroach.'

The breeze shivered the oak trees behind them.

'And Angus Nairn?'

'People don't want to know this truth. Darwin has been around a hundred and fifty years and still people deny the ruthless truths he revealed. Even people who accept natural selection prefer to delude themselves that it is teleological, that it has a purpose, a direction, a journey to higher forms.' He tutted. 'But this is, of course, arrant nonsense. Yet no one wants to know. So our task is a thankless one. And I wonder if maybe Angus became disheartened by this. Maybe he just gave up, and went off to some beach somewhere. I wouldn't blame him.' A sad sigh. 'He was a brilliant geneticist, in a world that doesn't wish to hear the verities that are so richly revealed by genetics.' The old man exhaled again. 'Though there is a generous irony here, of course.'

'What's that?'

'Nairn was religious.'

'Sorry?'

'Yes. Bizarre. Despite his natural brilliance in genetics, he . . . had a profound faith, of sorts.' Fazackerly shrugged. 'I believe Nairn was brought up to be religious, a lay preacher father, so he acquired a great deal of rather arcane knowledge. Of course we used to have quite splendid arguments; but I'm not sure I would want his faith even if I could believe it. Angus Nairn saw no conflict between pitiless evolution and a rather . . . *malevolent* deity.'

Simon thought of his brother, momentarily. Condemned by a cruel god? The insight was fleeting, and troubling, and painfully irrelevant. He concentrated on the interview.

The old man had extracted a crimson silk handkerchief; he was delicately wiping some sweat from his brow. He spoke:

'Angus would talk about such subjects rather a lot. Towards the end. When we had . . . guests . . . some of our sponsors, they would have intense debate. The Bible and the . . . the Torah. Is that the word? I quite forget. The Jewish holy book.'

'The Talmud.'

'Yes. All rather astrological if you ask me. Runes and horoscopes! – the consolations of the foolish, like lottery tickets to the poor. But Angus did get very het up discussing the intricacies of his faith. Some strange doctrine called Serpent Seed, the Curse of Cain and so forth.'

149

'The what?'

'I don't know the recondite details. If you want to know – speak to Emma Winyard. Try her. She was very important to him. The last few weeks he was super-saturated in all this, and he would quote her. Write this down.'

'I don't understand . . . sorry . . .'

'I'm going to give you her name! She may be able to tell you more.'

Simon apologized, and poised a pen. Fazackerly spoke slowly, his aged face grey in the sunlight:

'Emma Winyard. King's College. Theology Department.'

'KC London?'

'Yes. I know he used to converse with her, towards the end. Perhaps she's important. And perhaps, quite possibly, it is nothing.'

The journalist made his notes. They were quiet for a few minutes. Then the old man said, with an air of distinguished sadness, 'The truth is . . . I rather miss him, Mister Quinn. I miss Angus. *He made me laugh.* So if you find him, do keep me informed. And now I must return to my packing. You have ants crawling up your trousers.'

It was true. A couple of ants were ascending his jeans. He brushed them off. Fazackerly was already walking swiftly away.

For a while Simon sat there. Then he got up and walked to the station and caught the train home, his mind full of images of ants. Fighting. Killing. The war between species, the war of all against all.

As he emerged from his suburban stop his phone rang. It was DCI Bob Sanderson, talking excitedly.

'Money!'

'Sorry?'

'The monies! We have a lead.'

Sanderson sounded very animated, he was talking about

Edith Tait's strange inheritance. The journalist was glad for the distraction; he paid close attention. Sanderson said:

'I got a hunch when you told me. About Charpentier. So I did some old-fashioned detecting. They *all* had money. The Windsor victim left eight hundred grand. The Primrose Hill victim more than a mill.'

Simon felt a need to play devil's advocate.

'But a lot of old people have money, Bob. A decent house in a nice part of Britain and that's half a million.'

'Yeah sure, however . . .' Sanderson drawled, merrily. 'Let's look a bit closer. Eh? Why didn't they spend it? Charpentier especially. She lived in that minging little croft in Foula, as far as we know, ever since she arrived in the UK. Yet she had a ton of dosh.'

'It is odd.'

'And she had the money when she emigrated.'

'In 1946?'

'Exactly, my old papaya. Exactly. *In 1946*. A bunch of French people, all of Basque origin. They fetch up in Britain just after the war, having lived in Occupied France, and they all have money and they all get killed nearly seven decades later.'

'Which means . . .?'

'Which means, Simon . . .' Sanderson was half laughing. 'Something happened to all these people . . .'

A tiny chill shivered through Simon, despite the autumn sun. He inhaled, quickly and deeply.

'Ah . . .'

'Got it. Someone gave them the loot – or they found it – in Occupied France.'

'You think it's something to do with the war, don't you?'

'*Yep,*' he answered. 'I'm thinking blood money. Or . . .' He paused, as if for effect. 'Or Nazi gold.'

18

The girl was shouting at them. '*Qui est-ce? Qui est-ce?*'

David turned to Amy.

'Don't move. She has . . . a shotgun.'

Amy was pale and rigid but she spoke for them both, in French. David listened keenly, trying to understand. Amy called to the girl, giving their names.

Silence. David could sense neighbours peering out of windows, behind him. He was *hyper* aware of the gun, loaded, beyond the door: one blast of that would take down the door and maybe kill them.

They had to end the drama.

'I'm sorry,' he said, through the door – feeling absurd and very scared. 'Please. We just came to talk. Don't know if you can speak English but . . . I just want to know about my parents. They died here. They were killed here. Or we can go. We will just go?'

Silence.

He glanced Amy's way. A faint sheen of perspiration shone on her forehead; a lick of her blonde fringe clung to her skin. He repressed the urge to run for the car. The door swung open. The girl was standing there. Her shotgun was broken over her arm.

'I am Eloise Bentayou,' she said. 'What do you want?'

David stared at the Cagot girl. She was about seventeen or eighteen. A small silver cross around her neck was bright against her tawny skin and her nail varnish was vivid. The girl's complexion was notably dark, almost Arabic-looking. But her black hair had that Basque look, flat against the skull.

'We . . .' David struggled to explain things. 'We wanted to know about the Cagots.'

Eloise regarded him, her young frown tinged with suspicion.

'So you have come to look at the untouchables.' She gave them a despairing shrug. 'Ahh. What do I care. Come in. Come . . . this way.'

David and Amy stepped over the threshold. A wooden clock with a picture of the Virgin Mary ticktocked, in a lonely way, on a wall. Eloise escorted them into a living room where a big, slightly old-fashioned TV flickered in the corner. Watching it was an elderly woman, sitting on a sofa.

'*Grandmère?*' Eloise spoke briskly yet solicitously, in French, to her grandmother, but the woman barely moved, she was staring at the TV. The sound was off, but she was still staring at some French game show. Finally she looked up, glanced at Amy, then David, then returned her gaze to the television. She was wearing tartan slippers.

Eloise sighed. 'Since the . . . since the murders she has not been alive. Not really. *Et . . . Grandmère? Une tasse de thé?*'

The woman kept staring at the screen; Eloise shook her head.

'Come into the kitchen,' she suggested. 'You want to talk about the Cagots? The last Cagots in the world! Before they kill the rest of us . . .' She walked to the door. 'I can make tea. English tea.'

153

The kitchen was as unprepossessing as the living room. It wasn't dirty, but it exuded neglect. A saucer of milk, set down for a pet, was beginning to congeal in a corner.

They sat at a bare wooden table as Eloise made tea. David looked at Amy, he didn't know what to say. He tried a compliment.

'You speak very good English.' Even as he said this, he felt pathetic.

'My grandmother taught me. She speaks English very well. She learned it at college . . . She was a tour guide . . . Many years before. Before it happened. Now she just sits there.' Eloise was gazing down at the mugs, now full of tea. She shunted the mugs across the table. 'Here. Earl Grey. There is lemon here if you want.'

They accepted the mugs. Eloise spoke: 'I am sorry about the gun. It was my father's before . . . before the deaths.'

Amy intervened: 'Eloise, do you mind my asking . . . about what happened?'

The girl flinched, very subtly. 'A month ago . . . my father and mother were killed.'

'My God,' Amy said.

'I'm so sorry,' David added.

The teenager's dark brown eyes gazed directly his way.

'That is why I let you in. Your story. It is very sad. I know how that feels. I sympathize.'

'How were they killed?'

'Shot.'

'By who?'

'The police do not find anyone. The police do nothing.'

'Nothing?'

'At all. They are . . . unemployed. *Chomage!* Two people killed and they find no one. It is *incroyable*.' Eloise was gulping her tea. David's was still too hot to drink. Eloise didn't seem to care. 'They were shot in the car. Just like that! Maybe because we are Cagots? We do not know why. You see why I am scared. Of everyone, even the police. The Cagots are being killed.'

The subject had been broached: the Cagots. David mentioned the website and the girl scowled.

'My father's idea! The stupid website! The last of the Cagots *dot com*. I told him it was dangerous to make that dangerous website! I told him it would attract attention. He and my mother, they said we Cagots should be ashamed no longer, that it was stupid for us to hide away. And because we were maybe the last, he wanted the world to know.' A shrug. 'He said someone had to record the fate of my people. *Les Cagots!* And so maybe my family died for it. *N'est ce pas?* Since then I have kept the shotgun. My father used it to hunt pigeons. I keep it *all the time.* They may come for us next. We are the last ones left, me and my *grandmère*. And I do not think my grandmother would care if they did kill her, it is like *she* is dead already.'

David felt hopelessly inadequate as he listened. What response could match this grief? He knew what it was like to be orphaned, as an only child; the unequalled isolation, the inner song of solitary despair. He wanted to help; he knew the girl could not be helped.

The girl nodded, with a demure sadness, at Amy's queries. Her youth and dark prettiness only made her grief more poignant.

'Yes, I can tell you . . . I do know the history. My father taught us since we were young, wanting to make us proud. Not ashamed.' She turned and cocked an ear, listening for something; maybe her grandmother; she looked back at David. 'This is what I know. This is what my father told me. We, the Cagots, we were . . . we are . . . a people. A unique race. We first emerge – is that the word? – yes, we first *emerge* in the documents around the thirteenth century. In this same region. Navarre and Gascony.'

David drank some tea. Attuned to her every word.

'By then we Cagots were already regarded as an inferior race. Pariahs!'

Amy interruped: 'Like outcasts? Untouchables?'

'*Oui*. In medieval times Cagots were divided from the . . . normal peasants – in many ways. We had our own urban districts: usually on the bad side of the river, the malarial side.' Eloise sipped tea, and continued. 'Traces of these ghettos can still be found in Pyrenean communities, if you search – like St Jean Pied de Port or . . . *Campan*.'

David nodded, eagerly. 'We saw! The old cottages and ruins in Campan.'

'Yes. The ghettos were known as cagoteries. Campan has one of the biggest.'

'What else?' said Amy. 'The doors?'

Eloise replied: 'You need to know the history, first of all. *Vraiment*. Cagot life was marked by apartness: we were separated from everyone else, hidden away, like a shameful secret. Cagots were forbidden to enter most trades or professions. We were forced to be the drawers of water and the hewers of the wood. So we made barrels for wine and coffins for the dead. We also became very good carpenters.' She flashed a sad smile. 'Which is why we built many of the Pyrenean churches from which we were sometimes excluded.'

'Like Campan again?'

'Campan, yes. Bigorre. Many other villages.' Eloise was talking more quickly now. 'Some of the forbiddings on the Cagots were strange, so strange. We were not allowed to walk barefoot, like normal peasants, and this gave rise to the legend that we all had webbed toes. Cagots could not use the same baths as the other people. We were not allowed to touch the walls of bridges. Madness, *non*? And when we went about, we had to wear a goose's foot, *la patte d'oie*, pinned to our clothes. Symbolical of the webbed foot. The mythical deformity.'

'Just like the Jews and the yellow star. In the war,' said Amy.

'*D'accord*. And one of the other ways the Cagots were treated as different and inferior *was in the churches*. In the churches, we had to use our own doors, on the left of the main doors. The small doors you saw? Yes! We also had our own fonts – the *benitiers*. Marked with the foot! And we were given communion on the end of very long wooden spoons, so the priests would not even have to touch us. To touch the dirty people.'

'But why?' asked David. His tea was finished. He wanted more tea, he wanted food, he wanted something to distract him. The pain of the girl was bringing to the surface his own subterranean grief.

'Eloise, why did the Cagots get treated like this? Why were your people so oppressed?'

The girl tilted her head, with a teenage moue of distaste.

'No one knows this, mmm? No one is quite sure *why* Cagots were so mistreated. Peasants at the time said Cagots were *psychotique*. We were *certainement* regarded, as you know, inferior, as tainted and polluted. Infectious.'

'Were Cagots . . . killed?'

'*Oui oui*. On occasions, the bigotry was brutal. Very brutal. In the early eighteenth century a rich Cagot in *Les Landes* was caught using the font reserved . . . for non-Cagots – and his hand was chopped off and *nailed to the church door*.'

Amy winced; Eloise continued.

'Shocking, *non*? Another Cagot, who dared to farm his fields, which was totally forbidden, he had his feet pierced with the hot iron spikes. If there was any crime in a village, the Cagot was blamed. Some were actually burned at the stake. Even in death, these discriminations persisted – the Cagots were buried in their own cemeteries.'

David turned to Amy: she nodded. *Arizkun*.

Amy asked: 'But where did your people come from? Who *were* they?'

'The *provenance* is not clear, because the Cagots themselves have largely vanished . . . from the records. During *La Revolution*, the laws against Cagots were, they say, abandoned – in fact I think many Cagots destroyed the archives, they stole and burned any documents that proved their ancestry. To get rid of the shame! After 1789, we Cagots slowly . . . assimilated. Many of us changed surnames. Most of us slowly died out. There were the . . . problems having children.'

David looked at the girl. He thought of his grandfather: changing identity, Basque to Spanish. More ancient shame.

Amy was still questioning the girl.

'Are there any theories? About the descent of the Cagots?'

'*Naturellement*. But the different contemporary accounts are so very confusing. They cannot even agree on what we are meant to look like! Some describe us as being short, dark and even fat. And suffering goitres and cretinism. Others say we are blonde and, you know, very blue eyed. A man, a scholar, named Michel wrote a book about this – *L'Histoire des Races Maudites*.'

Amy interrupted: 'The History of . . . the Cursed Races?'

'*Oui oui*. In 1847. It was one of the first studies. Michel found at least ten thousand Cagots still scattered across Gascony and Navarre, still suffering, still excluded . . .' Eloise stood up and took her mug to the sink. She washed it, in a lacklustre manner, talking the while. 'Since Michel, some other historians have tried to solve the great Cagot mystery, despite the French not wanting to talk about us. One theory is that we were lepers – that would explain the rules against Cagots touching anything used by non-Cagots – another that we had some contagious mental sickness. However, this theory is not good – because many other books describe us as being healthy, and robust. And intelligent. As I hope you can see? We are not lepers! We are dark. We are not lepers, we are not mad.'

David nodded.

'Of course.'

Eloise went on.

'I believe we are, maybe, descendants of Moorish soldiers left over from the eighth-century Muslim invasion of Spain and of France. That's why some people called us *Les Sarasins*. I know my family is very dark.' She paused. 'They *were* very dark. But we may never know now. It is too late, is it not? No one here likes to talk about us. There may only be a few of us left. Maybe my family was the only . . . purebred Cagot family . . . that can trace its ancestry. In the world.'

'And the name. Cagot?'

'Dogs of the Goths? That's what some say. I believe the Cagot name is a very basic insult. The dirty people. The shit people. From *caca* or *cack*. You see now? You see why we Cagots tried to hide away, to assimilate . . .'

Amy exhaled. 'The last of the Cagots. *Just remarkable.*'

'*Yes.*' Eloise closed her eyes momentarily. 'But this amazing story, it made my father and my mother . . . it made them killed.'

David wanted to ask the obvious but question: why would anyone want to kill the Cagots now? But the question, and the logic behind it, was simply *too* brutal for the query to be posed.

His dilemma was resolved by a noise. Eloise's grandmother, in her cardigan and her tartan slippers, was in the doorway.

'*Grandmère?*' Eloise was gesturing her concern.

The woman raised a frail hand. She was staring at David. She said:

'I know why you are here, Monsieur Martinez. I knew your father.'

19

He found it hard to look at Madame Bentayou. Finally, he asked, 'How did you know him?'

The old woman sat down at the kitchen table, her hands embracing an empty mug. 'I met him here in Gurs. Fifteen years ago.'

'You mean when he was killed . . . with my mother?' David felt the pounding of his blood.

'I can tell you where they both died, if you want to know. It was a few minutes from here, by the camp.'

The cat had come into the kitchen; it stalked to the saucer and began lapping at the sickly milk.

'The camp?'

The grandmother shrugged wearily. David asked: 'Please, can you show me?'

There was a tenderness in her reply: 'I can show you.'

It was a ten-minute walk through the leafy desolation of neglected suburbia, past an ugly church, past the half-hearted brasserie, and down a long straight road. They approached the old, nettly, rusty brown railway track – and crossed nervously, as if they all feared a train – though the track had obviously been derelict for decades. It seemed unnaturally flat. David wondered why the whole area felt quite so dead. So bleak and shunned.

Black insects whirled in the cooling twilight, as they crossed the open concrete and gravel, by the looming crucifix. Madame Bentayou, still in her tartan slippers, sat on the wooden bench next to her granddaughter. David remained standing, and asked the older Cagot woman: 'So . . . this is the camp? The cross? What happened here?'

Madame Bentayou waved a weary hand, indicating the vacant acres of weeds, and grey concrete footings.

'It was a Nazi camp. A concentration camp.'

She fell silent.

David gazed around. So *that was it:* that explained the desolation of the little town – no one wanted to live here any more. It was poisoned by its grievous history, like an inner-city district known for a murder house, a place where the police find bodies. *You don't want to live there.*

The old woman went on, 'The Nazis occupied . . . the southwest corner of France, right up to the Spanish border. The border with Vichy, the puppet France of Pétain, was a hundred miles east. This was the main Nazi camp in southwest France.'

'And who was kept here?'

'The usual peoples. That is a memorial to them over there, the cross, and also the glass walls.' Then she pointed to his left. 'The two buildings over there are some barracks. Preserved.'

Amy was frowning.

'They kept Jews here?'

'Yes. But also . . .' Madame Bentayou paused. 'Lots of people. When the Nazis took over it was already a prison place for refugees from the Spanish War. So it was already full of communists and, you know, the Basques. The Gestapo added Jews and gypsies. And other minority.'

The ground looked notably swampy, rancid puddles reflecting the darkening clouds. David looked to the rear of the camp: the most distant section was divided from the rest of the prison by a low wall. A second cross had been erected upon it, another memorial.

The woman noticed his gaze, and explained.

'Another shrine. Because that is the most . . . the most *notorious* part of the camp.'

'Why?'

Madame Bentayou paused, as if to brace herself.

'It was the medical section. It is very terrible. The Germans took that part of the camp . . . they did the *experiments* here . . . scientific tests. Medical experiment.'

The old woman had a handkerchief balled in her hand, ready to dab at any tears. She went on, 'Blood tests. Tissue tests. And there were tortures. People killed or tortured. Many people.'

Her words dwindled, the tears were close. David realized the ghastly and obvious truth.

'Madame Bentayou.' His words were faltering. 'Were you here?'

Her voice was whisperingly quiet.

'*Oui.* I was here. As a very young girl. And so was my mother, she was in this camp. Like so many Cagots.' She shook her head. 'So I know what you ask next. You want to know why we never moved away after the war?' The old woman flashed him a defiant, passionate glare. 'The Cagots have been here for a thousand years, why should we let them move us!? We stay. We always stay, unless they kill us.' She was wiping away the tears with her handkerchief. Then she seemed to still her emotions: 'Monsieur Martinez . . .'

'David. Please.'

'Monsieur David, I want to go home now. I am sorry. As

you must see this is very upsetting. I never speak of it normally.'

She rose. David felt the unasked questions like a pain. 'But please – I really want to know. About my parents.' He could hear the neediness in his own voice. He didn't care. 'What were *they* doing here? Where were they killed? How did you know them?'

Her face was sombre. 'Your father . . . came to Gurs. And I recognized him.'

'Because?'

'Your father looked like your grandfather. *Non?* Is this not true?'

'Yes,' he said. 'Yes, it is true. Dark hair, big shoulders. Tall . . .'

'I saw your grandfather in your father, the same way I recognized you. All three of you, you look the same . . . And this is what I told *your* father: I said to him, "Monsieur Eduardo, I was in the camp with your father, Sergio Martinez" . . .'

'My grandfather.'

'Yes.'

A new and chilly wind was raking the poplars that guarded the edge of the camp; their branches roiled, in a worried fashion, as if perturbed by the unexpected breeze.

The woman went on, 'This was a surprise for your father. He did not know your family's history, that is why he came here, to find out the truth of his background.' Her eyes were half closed. 'He did not know that your grandfather was a Basque and had been in a camp in the war. So I told him. And, David, when your father and mother learned all this, they stayed here. For two weeks. Asking more questions . . . your father Eduardo would come into the brasserie in Gurs, with your *maman*. I think my husband told him many thing, many things about the camp, and other people too.' She quietly sighed. 'I have been a widow for a decade.'

'And then? My parents were in France for a month.'

'Yes . . . Your father went to Provence, and maybe somewhere else, for a week or more. I do not know why. But . . . when he came back with your mother he was asking even *more* question. *Difficult* questions. About the camp and the Basques and the Cagots. About Eugen Fischer. About many thing. A man here, a traitor.'

'Who?'

'I cannot remember the name. I will try and remember. Later. These are terrible memories for me, for any Cagot, for anybody.'

David had to confront the final query, the necessary query. He felt he was on the disused railway track, and it had suddenly come to life, and the train was bearing down on him. Carrying the terrible truth in its rusted brown trucks.

'So where were they killed? My mum and dad?'

Madame Bentayou pointed to the main road at the edge of the camp. Beyond it was a sunflower field; the withered plants of autumn looked like tiny dead trees, made of charred and ragged paper.

'Right there. In the car. An explosion. Someone blew up the car . . . or at least that is what everyone in Gurs and Navvarenx believed. The police did not investigate properly. Just like they did not investigate . . . my son's murder, his wife's murder, weeks ago.' Madame Bentayou's voice was tremulous. 'I wonder if this is the same people killing. I wonder if I saw someone in the town, the same man, tall, both times. But I am sorry, I am talking too much, I am crazy, is that what you say? My granddaughter thinks I am losing my head. I am going now. I want some time alone. We can talk more later.'

Madame Bentayou got up wearily. She stepped close to David, and pressed his hand between her two cold small hands, gazing into his eyes. Then she turned, taking a wooded footpath back to her bungalow.

David watched her go. He also felt a need to be alone: a fierce need. He walked to the edge of the road.

Looking down at the tarmac he wondered, ludicrously, if there would still be skidmarks. Evidence of the explosion. Fifteen years later. Little quartzite nuggets of windscreen glass still sprinkled in the gutter. Patches of his mother's blood. A grass stalk smeared red.

And a car, black and gutted, with two bodies inside.

There was nothing. He stood there for ten minutes in the chilly breeze, wondering, remembering. His mother in a blue dress. Smiling and alive. He felt as if he was trying to reach out to her – here – hoping to see her ghost, here where she died. He was a small boy running along a path to the waiting arms of his smiling mother. The sadness of it was palpable, like the wind from the mountains.

The sun was gone and the air was cold.

He made his way back to the girls. Eloise was taking a phone call. Her expression was very engaged. She turned to David.

'It is my grandmother again. She remembers the name, Monsieur David. The name of the traitor. It was José. José –'

'Garovillo?'

'Yes.'

David flashed a glance at Amy: *what?*

But Eloise was now shouting down the phone. '*Grandmère? Grandmère!*'

Amy called over: 'What! Eloise! What!'

The young Cagot girl shoved her phone in a pocket.

'She says there are men coming up the drive. She says she recognizes him – it is him – the man she saw before –'

Eloise was already running across the camp.

Running to her grandmother.

Before Miguel got to her.

They all ran. The sweat dripped in David's eyes as he

sprinted after Eloise – she was fast, young, seventeen. Soon they were over the old railtrack, and sprinting past the peeling wooden doorway of the brasserie. Eloise was running to save her grandmother; David was trying to save Eloise, and maybe to save them all. As he ran, the logic of it all exploded in his mind like a speeded up film of some natural organic process: a blossoming dark rose.

It was obviously Miguel: Miguel was doing *all* the killing. It was always Miguel, the Wolf, slaughtering the Cagots, slaughtering everyone. A fox that kills all the chickens: for fun.

They came in sight of the bungalow beyond the woodlands, and David stared.

Were they too late? The twilit road looked quiet, and deserted. There was no red car. The bungalow seemed undisturbed. But then David saw – for a moment – a dark face at a window. A tall man. The head vanished. Eloise yelled – and then David grabbed her, pulling her back into the trees. He clamped a hand around her mouth.

He hissed, 'Eloise, the man in there is a psychopath. Brutal. He tried to kill us. He is killing everyone. Your mum and dad. He will kill you too –'

Eloise was half fighting, half sobbing, struggling against his restraint. What to do? *What to do?* David realized he couldn't keep hold of her – it was somehow *wrong*. If she wanted to save her grandmother, if she wanted to die doing that, then he had to let her do it. With a gasp of exhaustion, he released her – and fell back onto the soggy ground.

Amy hissed a warning but Eloise did not respond, she moved a few yards, waiting, watching – there were lights on in the bungalow– and then she ran across the road, in and out of the gloomy shadows, running to her grandmother. David stood there, lurking and shameful, paralyzed – for half a minute. He whispered hoarsely to Amy: 'What do we do? What do we fucking do?'

Amy raised a hand, and mouthed the word silently: 'Eloise.'

The teenage girl was running back, her face was stricken with terror, her young lips trembling.

'El –'

The girl shook her head. The silver cross on her dark skin glittered in the lonely streetlight.

'I see I saw I see I see –' she stammered, fighting tears, or screams '– through the window.'

'What?'

Another shake of the head. No words. Eloise stood there shivering, like a terrified gazelle, aware of a nearby predator. Amy put a hand on Eloise's shoulders; David reached in his pocket and gave her the phone. He whispered, fiercely, 'Call the police. *Call* them. Even if you don't trust them . . .'

Eloise accepted the phone, and dialled. Amy and David whispered together, trying to work out where to go, where to hide next. Everywhere they went, they got hunted down, maybe it was hopeless. Eloise was talking urgently on the mobile.

The door to the bungalow opened. David grabbed Eloise once again and they ducked into the woods.

'Come on!'

At last, Eloise spoke, 'I know . . . I know where we can go. We have to hide. Yes? He will kill us too!'

'Yes –'

'Give me your car keys!'

David handed them over; they skulked down the line of trees to David's car. Eloise hissed: 'Now!'

They jumped in. David took the back seat, Amy the front, Eloise revved the engine fiercely, squealed into reverse; and they were away: headlights dipped and racing out of Gurs, taking a narrow, rustic route, racing for the mountains. David looked behind – the road was empty; he turned and saw. Eloise's face was streaked with fierce, silent tears.

He didn't want to guess what she had glimpsed through the window. Her grandmother killed – or worse – *being* killed. She was obviously in some kind of shock. And yet her driving was good. She was crying but she was coping. Doing it. He gazed at her dark profile. There was something proud in her teenage grace; and something purely sad. Again he noticed the cross on her dark Cagot neck. It was glittering in the oncoming carlights.

Amy opened a window and the cold night air gushed in; David flopped back, quite shattered. He was covered in noisome mud, yet again, from the crawl into the trees.

But at least they were alive; *Amy and Eloise were alive*.

But they'd left her grandmother to die.

Eloise had stopped crying. Her face was now devoid of expression. She was driving, fast – with a bleak efficiency – through the back roads, the black mountains looming ahead; the clouds had cleared, so the tallest summit wore a saintly halo of stars against the deep dark blue.

They were alive. But Eloise's grandmother was surely dead.

Amy turned and looked at David, and then at his hand. He stared down: he had a vivid and bloody cut along the palm, from when they'd fallen back, so violently, into the trees.

'Ouch,' she said.

He exhaled.

'Doesn't hurt.'

'We need a bandage.'

Amy grabbed at a T-shirt, tore it vigorously in two, and wrapped the cloth tightly around his wound. 'It will have to do for now,' she said. 'Until we get to . . . wherever . . .'

The question had been broached. David nodded.

168

'Eloise. Where are we going?'

The girl did not reply. David and Amy swapped a knowing, worried glance.

'Eloise?'

The car burned down the road, the girl said nothing. Then at last she replied, quietly yet precisely: 'Campan.'

More silence. Amy filled the painful stasis: 'Eloise, look, I . . .'

'No! *Non!* Not talk about it. Please do not talk about it or I will turn the car and go back . . . I cannot tell you what I saw! *Non non non.* Please do not ever ask me.'

David glanced Amy's way. She silently nodded. They needed to distract the poor girl some other way. He spoke: 'Campan, Eloise? What's there?'

'The cagoteries.' Eloise turned the wheel to take a curve. 'No one goes there to the ruins. The ruins are stretching, down to the ravine . . . There is a house!'

'Campan . . .' David whispered to himself. The village of the dolls. Amy asked, 'You think we will be safe?'

'*Oui,*' said Eloise, with a bitter tinge to her voice. 'The cursed side of the river? Everyone avoids it and everyone never goes there. Totally safe. *Totalement.*'

David sat back, assenting, as Amy wrapped the bandage tighter around his bleeding palm. The blood looked like black squid-ink in the moonlight.

It was indeed obvious now. Who was doing it all: who had killed his parents. Who was killing the Cagots. It had to be.

He said, 'Miguel. He's doing all of it. Or most of it.'

Amy frowned, severely.

'But why? And how?'

'I don't know. I just know. Miguel killed my mum and dad. The . . .' His voice dropped to the lowest cadence. A dark whisper. 'The grandmother saw someone. A tall man? Remember? So it was him. She sensed. And she suspected the same man of killing my family and hers. This is it, Amy. This has to be it. He is killing for a reason. He is chasing us for a reason. Trying to kill us for a *reason.*'

'But what?' Her question was hushed – yet fierce. 'What's it got to do with you, with you and . . . with José? And the Cagots?'

'He saw the map in José's house.' David was working it out even as he spoke. 'Maybe he realized we were on the same trail. Following the same route that got my mum and dad killed. So he has to kill us too.'

Amy was looking out of the window at the stars. 'I suppose . . . And José knew – he knew that if we pursued the same puzzle, Miguel would come for us too. *He was trying to save us from his son*. My God.'

David nodded, feeling almost foolish. It was as if he had been marvelling at some little corner of a painting, not realizing that the actual painting was ten times the size. Now the full horror was revealed: a grotesque and Biblical tableau of the cruel and invincible son: killing mothers and fathers.

'But why?' Amy said. 'What mystery could be so bad that Miguel has to kill for it? To keep it quiet?'

'It must be something to do with his father. And the war,' said David. 'He was in Gurs. The traitor in Gurs . . .?'

The sign from Campan flashed past, momentarily red and white in their headlights. Then the car slowed.

Eloise talked, for the first time in half an hour.

'It gets difficult . . . from here.'

They were driving over a bridge. In the half-light David recognized the mournful spire of Campan church across the slated roofs; he glimpsed one of the rag dolls lying next to the bridge, smiling happily in the headlights; but now the car was headed deep into the bad side of the river, into the cagoterie. Ruined cottages with empty black windows stood on either side, tumbledown barns, derelict allotments. Thick woods approached, slowly reclaiming the ancient ghetto of the untouchables.

The road worsened, stones and branches littered the way. In the chilly darkness David got the sense they were driving underground – a ravine was rising on either side. The humble cottages were more scattered now, low grey shapes through the trees; a ghostly white owl flapped across the headlights' dazzle.

'Voila.'

It was a very large, very old stone house. Possibly medieval. And yet, despite its size, it was concealed with great efficiency: massive bushes hid the turning, thick trees formed a perimeter wall, the maze of the cursed cagoterie lay all about – and they were halfway down the black ravine.

'My grandparents brought me here only once,' said Eloise. 'To show me the house where the Cagots used to hide during the worst persecutions. This is the refuge of the Cagots. There are caves and passages beyond . . . under the house. *Les chemins des Cagots*. So the Cagots could escape here.'

They got out of the car. The night air was almost frosty, tangy with the savoury scent of the woods.

David tensed.

There was a light inside the house. A flickering light, a lantern, or a candle, inside the house. Someone was in there.

Fear fought with curiosity. David motioned to Amy and Eloise, his finger vertical to his lips, *shhh*. He approached the window and peered inside.

He started back. Two people were huddled inside the humbly illuminated room.

It was José Garovillo and his wife.

20

'I was hoping you would . . . explain the Serpent Seed.'

Emma Winyard smiled; they were sitting in a restaurant near Smithfield meat market. Then she turned to an approaching waiter, and asked for some more water, giving Simon a chance to appraise Ms Emma Winyard, the Walden Professor of Church History at King's College London.

She was pretty, elegant – and personable: in her early forties, she evidently favoured discreet jewellery, very smart shoes – and fashionable restaurants. It had been her idea to meet here at St John's, because, as she said on the phone, 'It's rather nice to lunch there when I'm doing research at the Guildhall.'

'Serpent Seed, yes . . .' She smiled again. 'This is a highly controversial teaching. It says that the snake in the Garden of Eden had intercourse – ah, here's my starter. That was quick.' She leaned back and accepted the plate.

Simon couldn't help staring at her food. It looked like a small bobbly rubber inner tube of meat, with a nosegay of parsley at the side.

Emma picked up her fork, and continued, 'The doctrine

says that the snake in Eden had intercourse with Eve, and that Cain was the progeny from this bestial copulation.'

'The snake and Eve *had sex*?'

'Yes. That is to say, Satan in the form of the serpent had sex with Eve. And therefore Cain was the son of the Devil, and all who descend from him are tainted.'

'Rrright . . .' The journalist didn't know quite what to say. His embarrassed silence was interrupted by a phone call; he glanced at the screen. It said *Fazackerly*. What did the old professor want? Nothing that important, surely. The journalist leaned to the phone, and refused the call, forwarding it to voicemail; then he switched his attention back to his lunch partner. 'Sorry about that . . .' He wondered how to get the dialogue going again; he gazed down at her plate. 'What *is* that you are eating?'

'Chitterlings,' said Emma. 'Fried intestines. Very salty, but quite delicious.'

'Intestine?'

'Oh yes.' She smiled. 'The chef here, Fergus Henderson, is famous for reviving old English meat dishes. World famous. Smithfield meat market is just down the road, of course. Been there since the thirteenth century. Do you mind if I eat my starter? It's not so good cold. Yours has yet to arrive.'

'By all means. Please.'

Simon looked on as she downed a mouthful of rubbery-looking intestine, then he pressed the question.

'Who believes in Serpent Seed?'

'A small selection of cranks, minor sects, splintered cults.' She chewed thoughtfully, and added: 'That said, the doctrine has some . . . Biblical authority.'

'Such as?'

'The idea that Eve mated with Satan, and gave birth to Cain, is hinted at in various places in the Bible. For instance, in the New Testament Epistle of John 1, Chapter 3, it states,

"Not as Cain, *who was of that wicked one*, and slew his brother". The idea of the Serpent Seed can also be found in some early Gnostic writings.' She took another forkful of intestine and chewed. Then added: 'Things like the Gospel of Philip. However, the teaching was rejected as heresy by the church father Irenaeus, and later by mainstream Christian theologians.'

Simon absorbed this. *Cain who was of that wicked one.* He thought of the two brothers, the sons of Adam and Eve: Cain and Abel. Like him and Tim. And which one of them was Cain?

He felt the gulf of sadness, and a piercing desire for a drink. So he fixed his eyes on Emma Winyard. Concentrating.

'It's a load of rubbish then? Serious Christians don't believe it?'

The waiter arrived once more, this time presenting a plate with a bone on it. Just a bone. Like a roasted kneebone.

As he was new to this strange restaurant, Simon had allowed Professor Emma Winyard to order his lunch. But he hadn't expected a bone.

Emma pointed decorously with her knife.

'The food is . . . *inside*.'

'Ah, sorry?'

'It's roasted bone marrow, Mister Quinn. That's why you have a little fork, to dig the marrow *out* of the bone. Then spread it on those slices of toast. Delish.'

He picked up the tiny fork. And put it down.

'Call me Simon.' He stared at the knee joint on his plate. 'I'll have a go at the bone in a minute.'

'Fair enough.' Emma was happily working her way through her grey-brown intestines. 'Shall I go on with my theology?'

'Please.'

'The importance of Serpent Seed is this: the actual doctrine

174

might only be *affirmed* by the tiniest Protestant sects, like Christian Identity in America, or by Midrashic strains of Judaism, but it ties in with a variant Pentateuchal interpretation which does have great significance.'

'Are you talking in English?'

She smiled. 'I mean – there is a related and controversial interpretation of the early books of the Bible which has caused much pain and anguish over the centuries.'

'Which is?'

'The problem of Cain's wife. And so on.'

'Ah . . .'

They were nearing the nub. But Simon needed to eat something – because he hadn't eaten all day. So he picked up his tiny fork and stabbed it into the surprisingly tender centre of the bone knuckle. A small, strange, wriggly blob of jelly emerged, pronged on his fork. The roasted marrow. It looked repugnant, yet it smelt quite good. He placed it on a slice of toast and took a deep breath and ate it.

It was oddly delicious, despite the revolting texture.

'See!' said Emma Winyard, her handsome face smiling. 'Not so bad after all.'

'I guess . . . Tell me more about this heresy.'

Emma had finished her intestines; she laid down her fork and knife and sipped some water, and leaned forward.

'I'll tell you in one go, as you tackle your bone. First thing to know is that there are strange hints in the Book of Genesis that Adam and Eve were not the only human beings around during the Creation.'

Simon stopped eating, halfway through a mouthful of bone marrow.

'What?'

'Yes. There are some other odd and mysterious hints in the Pentateuch of non-Adamite humans – other races of already existent human beings, apart from Adam and Eve.

175

For instance, in Genesis, the Bible tells us that Cain went out into the world: "And the LORD set a MARK upon Cain, lest any finding him should kill him." Thing is: who on earth were these people who might find him? Theoretically, only Adam and Eve were around at the time. That's in Genesis 4. So who was it Cain should be scared of?'

Simon sat back. He looked at his laptop bag by his side. He wondered if he should be making proper notes. This was really quite intriguing information: it was also quite unnerving, this Biblical idea of different humans, of people already existing, yet separate: like a tribe of pale shadows.

'That's *truly* strange,' he said. 'Go on.'

But the elegant Ms Winyard was distracted: she was sitting back once more as the waiter whipped away her starter, and placed another dish on the table. Her face lit up.

'Pig cheek and butterbeans, one of my favourites.'

The waiter now set a second dish in front of Simon. It was red and hot and looked like something . . . recently aborted.

'Ah.'

'I ordered you bloodcake.'

'That's nice.'

His phone was ringing again: very annoyingly. Simon glanced at the read-out. *Fazackerly*, it said, pulsing on and off. What had got the professor so agitated? He recalled the yellowing smile of the old man, and the over-elaborate metaphors of Darwinian struggle; he once more killed the call without answering. And this time he switched off the phone.

Emma was checking her watch, with a flicker of irritation. 'Let's kick things along?'

'Yes please. Sorry about all these interruptions.'

'Apology accepted. Now we come to the Curse of Cain. To put it very briefly, this strange passage of Biblical verse,

Genesis 9:20 or thereabouts, says that Ham's father Noah placed a hex upon Ham and his son Cain, that they should become perpetual slaves, after Ham saw his father's nakedness in a tent.'

'This is a *different* Cain we're talking about?'

'Yes. It is complex. But a different Cain, yes – this is the grandson of Noah, son of Ham. He is also known as Canaan, the founder of the Canaanite people . . .'

Simon was trying to enjoy his bloodcake, and failing. He pushed the plate away, suppressing nausea, and asked Emma to continue. She was happy to oblige.

'So what does this strange story tell us? Well, the Curse of Cain has been used by elements within the Abrahamic religions to justify racism and Zionism and especially the enslavement of black Africans. Because they were believed to be descendants of Ham and Cain.'

'But how? I'm confused. Again.' He shrugged. 'Was Cain African?'

She smiled.

'It's quite simple. The Bible itself says Ham and his son Cain should be slaves in perpetuity, for their sins – for the unseemly sexual act with Noah, exposing the drunken father. And that's all. But early Jewish and Christian scholars say God went *further,* they claim Jehovah smote Cain with blackness. The Babylonian Talmud, for instance, categorically states "Cain was smitten in his skin" – i.e. turned black. The Zohar, the most important book of the Kabbalah, likewise says "Ham's son Cain blackened the face of mankind". And Africans thereafter descended from Cain . . .'

'And it's mainly Jewish, this theory?'

'Oh no. No no. Christian church fathers were *just* as keen. An Eastern Christian work from the fourth century, the *Cave of Treasures,* openly connects slavery with dark-skinned people.' Emma swallowed a big chunk of pig cheek, and explained: 'Why all the fuss? Probably Africans were already being enslaved by this time, so foisting the Curse of Cain upon them was a good excuse to perpetuate the bondage of blacks. Throughout the Dark and Middle Ages there are many more scholastic references to Cain, blackness and slavery.'

'And people used this doctrine during . . . colonial times?'

'*Absolutely.*' Emma paired her knife and fork. 'Spanish conquistadors, British imperialists, the French and Portuguese, many American slavers, they all seized on these pseudo Biblical passages to justify the hideous trade in Africans. The idea was either that God made different inferior races, when he made Adam, or he deliberately created a caste of black slaves when he cursed Cain. Ergo, slavery is OK.'

She dabbed her lips with a napkin, and continued, 'And the theory still has potency. Mormons only renounced the doctrine in 1977.'

It was time to broach the underlying topic.

'Emma, did you discuss this subject with a guy, name of Angus Nairn, a few months back?'

Professor Winyard sat up.

'Yes, I did. But . . . How did you know that?' Her persistent smile faded. 'I thought you were just a journalist researching racism?'

'I am. But . . . there are other factors. And I need to know, what did Nairn want?'

She frowned. 'OK . . . Yes, Angus and I were quite close. He's a rather eccentric . . . but rather charming young man. Very clever scientist. Scottish Presbyterian.'

'So I understand.'

'I haven't heard from him in ages. But I have been immersed in my studies . . .'

'What did you, ah, talk about?'

'Lots. He was interested in some strange things. The history of the Curse of Cain as it related to the Inquisition, the Basques and the Cagots.'

'The Cagots?'

'Yes, a tribe of French pariahs.'

'Never heard of them.'

'Most people have never heard of them. They were one group of victims of this extreme Curse of Cain theology. Some Catholic priests thought they were of the sons of Cain, blah-de-blah, and persecuted them. There is a strain in French Catholicism which is highly racist, and sometimes anti-Semitic, to this very day.'

'Such as?'

'Remember French Archbishop Lefebvre? He was excommunicated for his extreme traditionalist views, opposed Vatican Two, and so forth. Some of his followers are outright Holocaust deniers. This strand of Catholicism had links to the pro-Nazi French puppet regime at Vichy. Some truly renegade French priests actually worked for the Nazis.'

'How?'

'As chaplains in concentration camps, for one.' Emma glanced again at her watch. 'I'm afraid I really have to go soon –'

Simon nodded. 'Just a couple more questions?'

'Fire away. But quickly please.'

'So what *else* did you and Nairn discuss?'

'Oh . . . many things. We even had dinner a couple of times.' She looked momentarily wistful. 'He was particularly keen to know what happened to the results of the doctors' tests: of the Cagots.'

'Sorry? Tests?'

'In 1610, during the worst persecutions of the Cagots, the King of Navarre ordered that the Cagots be anatomically assessed by his court physicians. To see if the pariahs were really –' Emma Winyard did air quotes, with her fingers '– "different".

179

The results of these tests were never revealed. But we know that soon after that, the upper hierarchies of the church began to emancipate the Cagots, and to end the persecutions, though it took them centuries to eradicate the bigotry amongst the lesser clergy and peasantry. Same goes for the Basques.'

'How?'

'The Basques were also persecuted, as witches. The irony is that the Basque witch burnings were stopped by the Spanish Inquisition. An Inquisitor named Salazar sacked and prosecuted the witchfinders. He had the French witchfinder, De Lancre, who was obsessed with the Curse of Cain, removed from his judicial position.' Emma smiled, quietly. 'It rather goes against the image of Rome and the Inquisition, as terrible persecutors of heretics and minorities – the truth is, the Catholic elite were actually a force for good, as regards the Basques and the Cagots, at least.'

'What happened to the results of the Cagot tests?'

'That's *precisely* what Nairn wanted to know.' Emma Winyard picked up her handbag, preparing to leave. 'I told him the Inquisition kept all their files on the Basques quite secret, likewise the records relating to the Cagots.'

'I'm guessing . . . the documents were sent to Rome, to the Vatican library?'

'Yes and no. Recall that the Inquisition was run by the Dominicans – the black friars – or the Dogs of God, as they were called, because of their zealotry and sadism. It's a medieval pun on their name. Domine Cani. Dogs of God!'

'Gotta love those medieval puns.'

'The Dominicans were the great witch burners of the medieval era. Two Dogs of God wrote the *Malleus Malleficarum*, the "Hammer of Witches" – the witchfinders' Bible. Gosh, it's nearly three o'clock.'

The lady was now standing. Simon stood and shook Ms Winyard's hand, as she apologized, elegantly.

180

'I'm sorry to dash. The Guildhall library shuts at four. But I can answer your last questions – you want to know what happened to all these fascinating archives.'

'I do.'

'Very well. Some rightwing Dominicans were especially keen on the Curse of Cain. They believe it to this day. They refused to relinquish materials which, they felt, supported their cause. At the same time the Pope didn't want a schism – Popes never want a schism! – so a compromise was reached.'

'Go on.'

'The documents relating to the Cagots and the Basques were stored in great security. They were kept at the Angelicum, the Dominican University in Rome. For centuries they were safe. But then, after the war, after the Nazis, this was not felt to be a safe place, for such . . . provocative data. You can see the problem.' She smiled, gently. 'So what happened? The rumour is that they were spirited away to somewhere even more secure. But that is just a rumour. The answer to your question, the tantalizing truth is: no one knows for sure! Scholars have speculated on this matter for decades. Deducing what happened to the Basque and Cagot materials. It's quite the theological crossword puzzle.'

'And what do *you* think?'

'Me? I suspect the archives were just destroyed and all this conspiracy stuff is candyfloss. And that's what I told Angus Nairn, to his disappointment. But there it is. And this is where I must leave you, before my entire day disappears.'

'OK . . . thank you so much.' Simon felt sated: he was still digesting the strange lunch, and the even stranger information. 'Thanks again. This has been hugely useful. *Clarifying* things.'

The professor said it was nothing.

Her smiling face disappeared down the spiral metal stairs. Paying the bill and pocketing the receipt, Simon descended the stairs a few moments later.

In the street he hailed a cab, feeling a pleasurable rush of accomplishment as he did so. He'd earned this cab ride home: he'd done some good work. He could sit in the back of the big London taxi and smoke a fat if metaphorical cigar.

But then he remembered. Fazackerly. As the taxi sped past the clock repair shops and glass-walled apartment blocks of Clerkenwell, he took out his mobile and listened to his voicemails.

The first message was long, incoherent and discursive. The professor said he was sitting in his office for the last time and he had some new theories he thought might interest Simon. He waffled about 'ecclesiastical opponents of my research'. He mentioned a Pope. He apologized for going on so long, and being a 'garrulous old bachelor rather feeling the pinch of mortality'; the voice message actually went on so long this apology was silenced by the end of the allotted timespan.

Then Simon listened to the second message.

It wasn't a message. At least, it wasn't an intentional communication as such. It was obviously a call made by accident, when the redial button on a mobile is pressed by error, by sitting on it, or knocking it in a bag.

Fazackerly had called Simon the second time by mistake. And the second call was the sound of someone in unspeakable pain. Maybe, surely, horribly – someone dying.

It was grotesque. Simon sat in the back of the taxi, the sweat like beads of clinging and frozen dew on his forehead: listening to this terrible recording.

The beginning of the message was a kind of low, groaning sigh. In the background was a buzz. Like a distant buzzsaw heard in a forest. Lumberjacks at work. The moaning was sincere and despairing, a mixture of fear and pain; then it accelerated to ferocious panting. And then came the gurgling, a rasping, choking gurgle, like someone gargling hot vomit, unable to breathe. And all the time in the background was that terrible *buzz*.

The most piercing aspect of this horrifying message was the one discernible word – 'Stop' – between the gargles and the final, terrifying rasps. That word was enough to identify Fazackerly.

'Stop,' said Simon, rapping fiercely on the taxi glass.

They were just two hundred yards from the GenoMap offices.

The cabbie braked, abruptly. And turned his puzzled face.

Simon threw a twenty pound note at the taxi driver, then he raced out of the taxi – down the elegant terraces alongside Gordon Square. He found the old battered door, it was half open. He kicked upstairs, and upstairs again, taking the stairs three at a leap. Desperate now.

Inside. He was inside the lab and the GenoMap offices. The machines were cold and unused. The hydroshear and the centrifuge were silent. It all looked normal, or the same as before. The dusty machines. The emptied desks. The place deserted. The doors open. A gonk left on a table by some departed scientist. A grinning gonk.

Where was Fazackerly? Maybe it had all been nothing? Maybe he had misinterpreted that *terrible* second message?

This panic returned when he heard the buzzing. It was the same buzzing as on the phone. Like a wood-saw heard through endless leafless trees in a snowbound forest. Someone cutting logs away over there, in the black and white distance.

There. It was emanating from the corner of the lab. It was one of the machines Fazackerly had shown Simon on his perfunctory tour of the lab. The industrial-sized microwave, used for sterilization and antigen retrieval and histology and –

He rushed over. The enormous wardrobe-sized machine

was whirring away. It was cooking, busily cooking, like a happy and humming housewife. There was something inside the oven.

Simon knew, of course, and of course he didn't want to know. He averted his face, then he turned around again, fighting the desire to run into the street, to flee in disgust and dreadful panic.

Pressed against the tinted glass pane of the vast microwave oven was a face. A cooked and sweated old face, drooling liquid from the white and crinkled nostrils. Fazackerly was inside the oven. Broiled but unbrowned. His skin was bleached and pink, one poached eye was hanging from the socket.

The buzzing stopped. The microwave pinged.

21

The wound in his hand was healing, but the pain was still there. And the anxiety was relentless.

David was standing in the sunlit garden of the Cagot house, winding bandages around his blooded hand. The garden was overgrown, with fallen trees and ivied paths and flowers growing from the tumbledown walls. But the garden was also big, and hidden from everywhere, and it got the air and light, unlike the damp and sinister hallways of the ancient Cagot house. A good place to talk. A good place to think about your beloved grandpa's *Nazi connection*.

As he tied the last bandage, David felt a grief, inside him, not far from the surface, from the conversation with Madame Bentayou. He had been mulling over their remarkable dialogue, and every time he reached the same inevitable conclusion. It *did* make horrible sense. They must all have been prisoners, at Gurs – José, Granddad, Eloise's grandmother.

The facts certainly pointed to incarceration at the Nazi camp; moreover, the hidden wealth of his grandfather, the guilt and the furtiveness, seemed to imply some kind of profiteering. Or something. Even collaboration.

It was a ghastly idea, yet unavoidable. Was Granddad complicit with the Nazis? If not, how did he get the money? And why was he so evasive at the end? Why the mystery?

David sat down on a stone bench, then stood up. The dampness of the moss was soaking into his jeans. Everywhere in this rotten and syphilitic place was so fucking *damp*. The walls were sodden with medieval humidity. The garden rioted with unlovely life: David had seen a fat torpid slow-worm the first day, sliding brazenly into the kitchen.

It was detestable. The filthy Cagot house. It made David detest *them*: the Cagots. He wanted to flush away the grime from the countless Cagots who had hid here, slept here, fucked in here, cooked their stupid Cagot meals . . .

David calmed himself. The Cagots were being killed. *They deserved pity.*

How easy it was to hate.

A kestrel swung through the sky, which was fast clouding over. David heard a noise, and turned: Amy was at the door. She frowned his way; he smiled back. She and he had been forced to sleep, these last few nights, in the same dark musty bedroom – forced by the nastier, damper, more rotted state of all the other available rooms. They had bedded down beside each other, in adjoining bunks. Nothing physical had happened between them, yet . . . something *had* happened between them.

They had talked long into the nights, alone, by the flickering candlelight. Faces inches from each other: like kids hiding under the sheets.

And here she was: open, ready, prepared. His very close friend. Something good had come out of this terror and darkness: his deepening friendship with Amy Myerson. But then he realized: she was *frowning*.

'What's wrong? Is it José?'

'No. He still won't say a word. No –' The frown was urgent and serious. 'It's Eloise.'

'What?'

'She's disappeared. At least I think she has. Can't find her anywhere.'

The first spatters of rain were cold on David's neck.

He ran into the house at once. And they started looking. They found José and Fermina in the damp sitting room, sullen and silent. Like peasants in a medieval Flemish painting. Like two ragged survivors of a terrible winter, huddled against the enduring cold.

'José. We can't find Eloise. Have you seen her?'

José mumbled a 'No'. His face was set in the same expression he had worn since they came here. Self-pitying and resentful, and barely concealing his sorrowful fears. Of what?

Amy gasped with exasperation.

'Let's try upstairs.'

But there was nothing: Eloise really was gone. They tracked through all the many bedrooms. Nothing. They explored the garden, the front garden, the back garden. They walked a few nervous paces into the darkening woods, that fed into the ravine, whose stern and brutal stone walls rose behind the house.

Nothing.

Slowly, a cold unpleasant idea overcame David. Had she been snatched? Had she wandered into Campan proper? Eloise had said several times that she desperately wanted to use email and she desperately wanted to go to church for confession. Either of those tasks would have taken her over the bridge. Had she taken a stupid risk? Had she gone into the village?

They stood in the dim light of the hallway and discussed their options. They had no choice. They had to go and get her and bring her back. Amy volunteered to explore the village; David insisted he would do it.

He ran out, and up the rutted road that led to the bridge. He was in the centre of the cagoterie, the ruinous ghetto. Calling Eloise's name, he sprinted past the shattered houses and barns. Was she inside one of the ruined Cagot hovels? But surely not: the black sockets of their empty windows were silent. The battered doors of the cagoterie hadn't been opened in fifty years. Rusted scythes lay in the grass unused. A larger house had a goose foot *painted* on the wall: crudely spray-painted. And next to it a cackling teenage graffito:

Fous les camps Cagot!

David crossed the bridge. The rain was drenching now but he didn't care. He was at the end of the lane. By the walled churchyard. He walked past a slumped and grinning rag doll, with its head burst open, showing the yellow straw stuffing inside; he pushed the gate, negotiated the path, and entered the church.

It wasn't a Sunday, so he was surprised to see a service.

The congregation was tiny, half a dozen old people and a geriatric priest. And four mansized rag dolls. The service was some kind of harvest festival. A dismal little collection of tomatoes, corncobs, and tinned Del Monte pineapple was arranged by the altar. It took David two seconds to work out Eloise was not amongst the worshippers. The priest was staring at David but he ignored the hostile glare.

Striding outside the church again, he pushed the squealing gate, then ran through the punishing rain to the one place where Eloise might have gone, to maybe use the internet, a small *tabac* with a terminal or two.

The shop was shut; there wasn't even a rag doll in the window. Eloise had gone, completely gone. David felt a mixture of anger, worry – and an ardent empathy. Eloise's sadness, the terrible sadness of the newly orphaned, reminded him all too easily of his own sadness, his own orphaning. *She was like him. She had suffered like him.* He thought of her proud, defiant, silent tears, as she drove them away from Miguel in Gurs.

Eloise was brave. She deserved so much better than this. He had to find her before Miguel did. But he didn't know where to turn. Where had she gone? And why? What was happening to them all?

There were so many questions, falling on them, drenching them all, like a Pyrenean cloudstorm. They were drowning in puzzles and mystery. And they had to reach for the only answer, their only lifesaver.

José.

David ran through the teeming rain, past the war memorial, down to the bridge and the river, and the gutted cagoterie. The wetness slid down his neck, it damped his shirt to his chest. He didn't care. He was angry now: the flickering idea that Eloise had been taken by Miguel was all too gruesome and too angering.

He found Amy in the hall of the Cagot house, waiting: her blonde hair bright in the gloom. They talked for one minute, the conclusion of their debate was immediate. Amy agreed: they had to confront José. And David was the man to do it, because the conversation could be brutal and Amy was too close to the Garovillos.

David prepared himself as he crossed the hall: he focussed his angry thoughts. He was going to extract the truth. Whatever it took.

22

By the time David found José, after searching the many rooms of the old house, the shower had turned into a pelting mountain rainstorm, hammering the ancient slates of the Cagot refuge.

José Garovillo was alone in the kitchen, hunched over the stove, and pouring olive oil into a large earthenware dish. His wife was apparently locked in her room. José seemed locked in himself, just as he had been since they first found him hiding in the refuge house.

'Angulas,' said José, pointing to a saucer piled with slimy white worms.

David gazed at the dish, perplexed. His shirt was cold and wet on his back. He shivered and asked, 'An . . . gulas?'

'Elvers. But frozen of course. Fermina went into Campan – to the shop.'

'She left the house?'

'Do not worry. She was careful.' José turned from his cooking, and stared, momentarily, at David. His eyes were grey, and hollowed with sadness. Then the old man switched his attention to the earthenware casserole, adding some transparent slices of garlic, followed by a small half of red

190

chilli pepper. He turned up the gas. The garlicked spiciness filled the air.

'I just wanted to try them, Davido, *angulas bilbaina*. One more time. Just one more time.' José was trembling, visibly. 'The best little eels come from the Deva river, they are fished when there is no moon, and the water is tainted with tobacco . . .' His old hand reached out, with a weary flourish of expertise, and picked up the elvers, and poured them into the dish. For a minute the eels sizzled; José spooned them over.

'This is the crucial process. Too soon and they are no good, too late and they are ruined. Here we are . . .'

He picked up the casserole dish, and poured the fried angulas into a waiting sieve. A strange smell filled the kitchen – half fish, half mushroom. José concluded by draping the elvers onto a couple of plates.

'You will try.' He reached out and took some green herbs from a bowl, and sprinkled them on top. 'Fermina is not hungry. Join me?'

'I guess . . . OK.'

'You must use a wooden spoon, the metal of cutlery corrupts the flavour.'

There was nothing for it: the old man wanted to eat. The two men carried their plates into the gloomy sitting room, where an acrid fire in the humble hearth was giving off a pungent smoke.

José winced as he spooned the slithery little eels into his mouth.

'Aiii . . . Frozen. Not so good. But better than the fake ones. You know they now make fake angulas? *Sí*. It is true – they fake them because these real ones are so expensive, fifty euros for half a kilo.'

The impatient anger was rising inside David. The time had come.

'José . . . we need to talk. Now.'

'They make them from reconstituted . . . cod innards. Mackerel. Meat. Who knows.' José sighed, quite lyrically. 'All the real angulas are dying out, like the poets, like the Basque songs, like everything that is good . . .'

'José –'

'They even paint little eyes on the fake eels! Did you know that, Davido! Fake little eyes on the *txitxardin*!'

'Enough!'

José stopped.

Setting down his plate on the dusty floorboards, David began: 'Listen to me. Eloise's grandmother told me . . . something. It is painful, José. But I need to know.'

José shook his head, and examined his food, apparently ignoring David's questions.

'José! She said you were known at Gurs.'

The old Basque man gazed at his silvery angulas.

David persisted. 'They said you were known, by some people, as the traitor. Is it a lie? Or is it true? Is this why you have been silent these last days? Why all the mystery? What are you ashamed of?'

José sat motionless, the plate on his lap. Then he raised his watery eyes. The intensely anguished gaze made David flinch: something terrible had happened to José. Or maybe José had done something terrible.

'José?'

'It is . . . it is because . . .' His lips were almost white, his face the grey of morning mist on a river. 'Because it is true. Something happened at Gurs.'

'Were you imprisoned with my grandfather?'

José rocked back and forth, on his damp wooden chair.

David tried again: 'Were you imprisoned with my grandfather?'

'Yes.'

'But, José. Why didn't you tell us this in the first place?'

'Because of . . . things. That happened. I cannot trust anyone. When you know the secrets I know, the secrets I learned in Gurs, then you understand to be very careful. Forever.' He gazed mournfully at David. 'And yet . . . When I saw your face that day, when you came to the cottage . . . then I remembered my old friend· Martinez and I wanted you to know the truth, as much as I could risk.' The old man was sighing. 'I felt you deserved to know who your grandfather was. A Basque. But you needed to be protected, as well.'

'From Miguel?'

'From Miguel. From many others like him. But especially Miguel.'

'Did he kill my parents?'

The air was filled with the sounds of the downpour outside. 'Yes . . .'

This reply seemed to wrench something out of José, who closed his eyes and shuddered. Then he looked away from David: he was staring at the broken window beyond his questioner's shoulder. David spun, in sharp alarm – was that a shape in the woods beyond the garden?

The misty rain was deceptive: maybe it was just a *pottok*, one of the wild horses, drifting in that ghostly way, through the forest – but David couldn't help imagining it was . . . Miguel. Scoping them out, whispering to an accomplice, the rain dripping off his cap as he cocked his gun.

No: that was impossible. No one knew they were hiding out here. No one even knew they were in Campan, let alone concealed in the cagoterie over the river. And the house was incredibly sequestered: you only knew it existed, behind its screen of firs, by the time you knocked your head on the ancient stone lintel, with its goose foot carved cruelly and brutally into the granite.

But that raised another question. How did José know about this house? It was the ancient home and refuge of the Cagots, not Basques. How did José Garovillo end up here?

And then a cold new possibility gripped David – a claw around his thoughts. If José knew about the house, why shouldn't Miguel?

David sat forward. His interrogation needed some urgency. Maybe threats.

'José, does Miguel know about this house?'

'No. I never tell him, not the house. If he knew I would not be here! One day I knew I would have to run away from him, that I would need somewhere to escape, when he came looking, or when the police came hunting.'

'But how did you know about a Cagot safe house?'

José quickly spooned a tiny morsel of elvers into his white-lipped mouth.

David gripped José's other arm. Hard.

'Tell me. What happened at Gurs? Why did Miguel kill my parents?'

A frown of pain. David gripped harder. José grimaced, and exuded an answer:

'Because of what they were about to find out.'

'You mean what happened at Gurs. Your treachery?'

'Yes.'

David now realized, with an upwelling of contempt mixed with pity – that José was crying. Two or three tears tracked down the old man's face, as he explained: 'Yes I did something at Gurs. Things happened there. Miguel did not want people to know . . .'

'José, what did you do?'

The old man mumbled a reply; David leaned forward, unhearing. José said again, 'They torture us. You have to remember, they torture us.'

'Who?'

'Eugen Fischer.'

David shook his head.

'I've heard him mentioned, by Eloise's grandmother. Who is he?'

'A Nazi doctor.'

'And what did he do?' David felt the tingle of a bitter-sweet excitement: he sensed he was getting closer to the tragic core of this mystery. He was far from sure he wanted to know the answers; yet he wanted the answers more than ever.

'What did they do? José? How did they torture you?'

'They tested us. Many tests of the blood. And the hair and the . . . the blood. Testing the blood.'

'What else?'

'There were other doctors. And then the Catholics, many priests.' José was shivering. He was shivering like the oak leaves in the garden, pelted with cold mountain rain.

'What did the priests do?'

'They burned us. Some of us. Killed us.'

'Why did they do this?'

José took one more mouthful of the cooling, greasy baby eels. And then he said, 'They thought we were not human, they thought we deserved to be exterminated, like snakes. To die like pagans, or witches. Once they finished their blood testing . . . Eugen Fischer would hand some of us over to the priests and the criminals . . .' José waved a hand, despairingly. 'And they took us, and burned us. Many many people. In the swamps at the edge of the camp.'

'But why did they torture you?' David said. 'Was it like the witch burnings? Zugarramurdi? The burning of the Basques?'

José gazed with a profound sadness at David. And said, 'No.'

David's shoulders slumped. The mystery still eluded him.

He was angry now. Angry at himself for not working it out, and angry at his grandfather. And most of all David was angry at José. This old man could tell David everything, blow away the mist, trap the wild horse of the truth. José would have to confess. David had to know now.

Gripping José's arm, once more, David pressed on.

'José, people are dying. They're dying right now. What happened at Gurs? Why were you called the traitor?'

The brown eyes were closed, but José was nodding, muttering.

'*Sí* . . . you are right. It is time. *Sí* . . .'

David wasn't letting go of José's arm, not this time. He didn't care if he was hurting the old man. José spoke, his words dry and croaked: 'They did tests on us all, David. Many tests of blood types and skull sizes. The Cagots and the gypsies, the communists and the Basques, the French and Spanish too . . .'

José looked down at David's hand, wrapped around his upper arm. The old man spoke again: 'Fischer had tests from Namibia, his tests on the . . . Baster people. And of course the Bushmen. He told us all this . . . he told me this. Specially.'

'Don't get it. What's this got to do with Basques? Why you?'

'Because I became . . .' A tremble shook through Garovillo. 'I became his ally. Fischer's friend and helper.'

'That's why you are ashamed? Cause you helped Fischer!'

'Yes.'

'Why?'

'I thought I was Basque.' José was crying again. 'I was brought up Basque, speaking Basque. Proud to be Basque . . .'

A bright light shone on the puzzle. David saw.

'José, did they test you too? Test you . . . *racially*?'

'Yes.'

'Did they tell you that you weren't a Basque?'

The whispered reply was almost inaudible.

'Yes.'

'Did they tell you that you were a Cagot?'

The rain pattered on the windowsill. Then José Garovillo looked at the plate of half-eaten angulas on his lap – and he lifted the plate, and hurled it at the fire. The squidge of fried eels nearly doused the remaining flames.

José was babbling now.

'*Sí. Sí sí sí sí sí*! They told me I was not Basque, that in fact my descent was from the Cagots. The cursed people. The people of the goose, the goitre. The madness. The Saracens. The web-footed untouchables. *Yes!*'

David suppressed his shock and pursued the question.

'That's why you are here? In the Cagot house? That's why you knew where it was?'

'Yes, David. When Fischer had the results of my tests, they moved me from the Basque barracks to the Cagot division. The Nazis were obsessed with getting these . . . categories right. This race over here, this race in there. The Jews over there. They were like fussy old women. The racial hierarchy. Vile! But I was so ashamed of what they did to me, so ashamed.' José wiped another tear with the back of his liver-spotted hand, and stared at David. 'I was raised to . . . to despise, no, to abjure the Cagots. We Basques knew what it was like to be pariahs, to be a minority. We sympathized with the Cagots, yes. But still in our hearts, like the French and the Spanish, we thought the Cagots were lower, like the rats and the snakes. The shit people! Something wrong with them!'

'So Fischer told you that your blood was Cagot, not Basque. Then the Nazis put you in the Cagot section at the camp. But what happened then, José, how –'

'In the barracks I spoke with many Cagots. They told me of this house. They told me of many things about their people. My people. I tried to make them my people, I tried to believe they were my brothers, but –'

'You were too ashamed?'

'Yes.'

David felt the logic of the terrible story unfolding.

'So what did you do, José? Did you deny them?'

'That is the good word. *Deny*. Yes I denied my blood. Because I wanted to live. In the camp the priests and the Nazis were especially cruel to the Cagots; the priests called them the sons of Cain and they tortured and killed them more than anyone else, so yes I wanted to be Basque again, just to save my life. And I was raised as a Basque, I still felt I was a Basque in my soul.'

'So you went to Eugen Fischer?'

'I went to Fischer and the other doctors. I told them that if they pretended – forgot – pretended I was not Cagot, if they gave me back my Basque identity, I would help them.'

'How?'

The old man looked at the pitiful fire.

'I was a very young man, in my mid-teens, but I was a well known Basque radical. I had influence with the other young Basques in the camp. The real Basques.' He lifted his bitter gaze to David's. 'The Basques are a very brave nation, rebellious, indomitable. They were always brawling in the camp, fighting the Nazis, making things difficult for Fischer, trying to escape.' José shook his head. 'So I became a traitor to them. Yes a traitor. I told Fischer I would use my influence, make his work easier. I would persuade the Basques to cooperate. But only if he took me out of the Cagot division and gave me back my blood.'

'And that's what he did?'

José's voice dwindled to a whisper, once more.

'That is what happened. They pretended they had put me in the Cagot barracks by mistake. So I was restored, I was made a Basque once more! And then I used my influence. To . . . help Eugen Fischer do his terrible experiments . . . I persuaded other people to let Fischer test them. And so Fischer became a kind of friend to me. He told me too much. He told me of the Jews . . .'

'What? What of the Jews?'

José regarded David.

'The Holocaust. Eugen Fischer told me – why the Germans did what they did. The truth of the Holocaust. That is all I can say.'

'What?'

José's eyes were fluttering. Almost as if he was falling asleep. David reckoned the old man must be exhausted: confessing these murderous and long-buried secrets. He let go of José's arm. But continued the questioning:

'José, I need to know about Miguel. All this is the reason Miguel killed my parents. Right? He is ashamed of his Cagot blood. Yes?'

'Yes. This is the worst mistake I ever made. I told my son the truth, when he was maybe nineteen. He never forgave me. He was so proud to be Basque up to then. The great ETA activist . . .'

'So he was angry. And he thought my mother and father . . . were about to uncover his shame.'

'Sí.'

'And then he finds out I am on the same chase. And he needs to kill me, too.'

The wind rattled the dusty glass in the windows.

'Sí sí. It is so.' José grimaced. 'But there is still more . . . Davido.'

'My grandfather, you mean?' David felt the question hanging in the air, like the dampness of the house. A revenant of the past. A ghost he had to exorcise. 'Tell me, José. Was my grandfather . . . was he also a collaborator?'

'No!' The reply was fierce. 'Do not think that! Your grandfather was a good man. No . . . I mean Miguel.'

199

'What? What is it?'

'There is something strange and terrible about my son. You must be very careful. Sometimes I have thought about killing him myself. Before he kills me. Before he kills everyone. He will kill me one day.'

'Why?'

'It is the way he is made. By God. My son is . . . bad to the bone. Is that the phrase? And yet I love him. He is my son. Remember I am so old, I thought I would never have a child, but then young Fermina . . . we had a baby. A son. We were so happy. *Ena semea . . .*'

The old man's eyes were bright, for the first time in days; then they dimmed over again, dimmed unto darkness.

'But as he grew up . . . we realized he has the true shame of the Cagots. The true shame. But he is big and strong and clever. And he has friends, helpers. Powerful people you do not understand. The Society.'

'What is the Society?'

'No. I cannot say. Enough. Please.' The tears were rolling now. 'Leave me this last shame to conceal.' José wiped the smears of the elver grease from his mouth. 'I have told you far far too much. Too much, too late. If I tell you more no one will let you live. Because the secret Miguel is protecting is not just about me, about me and him and the Cagots. It is far far deeper than that, Davido, it is so terrible and dangerous, for us all, for all *la humanidad*. The secret will get you killed, if not by Miguel then by someone else. His friends. The Society. Anyone.' The old man looked, hard, at David. 'You understand? I am saving your life by not telling you any more!'

This was more than perplexing. It was bizarre. David sat in the half-lit dampness, trying to work it out. The rain was still nailing slates on the roof. Through the window he could see the fog, the votive mist summoned from the forests by

200

the downpour; the streams were brawling down the slopes, to join the torrential Adour.

David tried again, one more question. But José was resolutely unforthcoming. The old man, it seemed, had had enough.

Silence.

It was all an intense frustration, he had so many more questions. The death of his parents. Where the money came from. What was this about the Holocaust? What secret was so terrible it meant inevitable death?

Yet he wasn't going to get more answers, at least not now.

The door was thrown open: it was Fermina. The anger in her was blazing, she was shrieking at José, her bangles jangling, she was almost beating him with her words.

Her ferocious monologue was in Basque and Spanish, and yet the meaning was clear, she was asking José: what have you told him? You fool. What secrets have you revealed?

And then, in front of David, the younger wife came over – and she slapped the old husband – contemptuously.

José cowered under the blow, unresisting.

David was paralyzed by this ghastly scene. He watched, mute and inert, as Fermina slapped José twice, then grabbed her husband's frail hand, and hauled him to his feet – and dragged him from the room like a naughty infant. The door slammed. The stairs creaked.

Alone by the hearth of the old Cagot house, David heard another door slam, upstairs. The whole building shuddered in response; the dew-heavy cobwebs trembled along the cornices, dust motes flittered, unhappily, from room to room.

23

The light was sickly. Simon got up and walked to the window, pulled the curtains. He was greeted by the relatively quiet traffic of mid-morning. Twisting the watch on his wrist, he checked the time. *It was nearly 11 a.m.*; after a night of fraught insomnia, he had finally and evidently slept.

The silence from downstairs told him that he had missed Suzie and his son. He must have slept through it all – as she made breakfast, got Conor dressed, then took him to nursery school, before heading off for her own shift at the hospital.

He felt the acid reflux of fear and guilt. Again. The same feelings he had all night, the same feelings he'd had all week. Maybe he would never sleep well again? Not without a drink. Not without many drinks. He was scared, and guilty. And very very bored. He no longer had a role. Following Fazackerly's murder the *Telegraph* editor had taken Simon off the story, because it was all getting too hairy. *What if they come for you next, Simon? What if your articles are tipping off the killers?*

Lonely at the window, the journalist stared as the vehicles blurred past. One car raced to the lights then halted with a squeal. Simon got the usual surge of parental anger: slow down, you bastard, I have a little son. And then again he felt the pang of guilt: who was *really* threatening his son? *Really?* Who was endangering his young life? Who had brought death and mayhem so close to the family home?

Him. The father. The ambitious careerist. Him.

Simon knew he was in peril. Right now he wanted a drink more than he had in years. He was risking his hard-won sobriety. But what was he meant to do? He didn't have the motivation to get to a NA meeting. Yet he was bored and guilty, and scared.

Stepping into the bathroom, he showered in very hot water, brushed his teeth, chucked on some clothes and returned to the bedroom, feeling very slightly better.

Maybe it wasn't his fault.

Of course it was his fault.

Maybe it wasn't *all* his fault.

Opening his laptop, going online, he looked yet again at the emails from Tomasky and Sanderson, discussing Fazackerly's death, the strange parade of events and aftermath.

A few moments after he had found the professor, parboiled in his own laboratory oven, the police had rushed in, alerted by Simon's own call. They had swiftly escorted the stammering journalist away, then they had debriefed him, calmed him, interviewed him, they had even donated him a session or two with trauma specialists in the following days.

But Simon was still troubled by the appalling scene in the GenoMap lab, and he had sought succour and solace by emailing and telephoning questions to the detectives. He found Tomasky the best sounding board: the cheerful Pole had a sincere Catholic faith which helped; he had a dark Slavic yet Londony humour which also assisted: salty asides about death, which 'was about as bad as a weekend in Katowice'.

Tomasky and Sanderson had tried to explain the 'logic'

of Fazackerly's death to Simon, that killing him in the microwave was clever, and brutally efficient: silent and swift, leaving no gunshot wounds, no DNA evidence. The killers' only bad luck was that Fazackerly's powerful cellphone could get a signal inside a metal box.

And yet. It still seemed like a grotesque medieval torture to Simon – being boiled alive in a microwave. Your blood plasma literally boiling in your veins.

He shut down the emails with a heartfelt sigh. The thought of blood reminded him of his brother; the memory of his brother was perturbing and yet energizing. Right this minute, his brother was locked away. Simon was therefore the only Quinn with offspring and a future. He had a responsibility. To earn and work and pass on his name.

And now Simon felt a surge of returning pride, self-esteem – even anger.

To hell with this. He needed to shape up: Fazackerly's death *wasn't* his fault. So his articles may have pointed the killers in the direction of the professor; equally, they may not. Whatever the case: he, the journalist, was just doing his job, being a hack. Following the lead. His soul agonized for the danger to his family – but how else was he meant to feed them?

There was no other means: this was his career. But that still left the practical problem. How was he going to feed his family *now*? He was a freelancer, who lived off stories – but he'd been kicked off his best ever story. And now he had nothing else to do, nothing to write. No other commissions. What was he supposed to do today, tomorrow, next week? Go back to writing accounts of petty crime?

Idly, he Googled 'witch murders', just to see if there were any developments. Just in case.

The news this morning was subdued, compared to the furore that had greeted Fazackerly's murder last week: just one or two follow-up pieces. An American website was rehashing the entire chain of bizarre events for the delectation of its more prurient readers. Simon noted this American journalist had actually stolen some of Simon's lines, and shamelessly used Simon's quotes from Fazackerly.

Bastards.

He sipped water. And then he had an idea. Quite a fetching idea. There was *nothing* to stop him following the clues, chasing up leads, even if he actually wrote zero. He could still write, and research – if only for his own satisfaction. And even if he was barred from daily journalism on the story, at the end he could . . . do a book? Yes! If he had all the notes he could still write a book. And then he could make some real money, when it was all over. He could do a job and feed his wife and son and pay his debt to his conscience, and the bank, without annoying his editor, or the cops.

Simon flexed his fingers. Then he attacked the search engines.

The trick he deployed was one of his favourites when he was on a complex investigative story and he needed new leads: he would throw randomly associated phrases into the internet and online newsfeeds, juggling quote marks, seeing what came out.

For two hours he toyed with words. He tried various combinations of Scottish and Killing and Nairn, GenoMap and Fazackerly and Basque.

Nothing.

He tried some more.

Syndactyly, Witch, Cagot, Inheritance, Murder, Canaan . . .

Nothing.

He tried one more time, a whole host of words: Scoring, French, Nazi, Burning, Deformity, Torture, Genetic, Homicide, Gascony, Bequest . . .

And . . . There! Yes. He'd lucked out: two possibly related news items. *Two*.

The first was a murder in Quebec. A Canadian news website gave a brief resume. A very old woman had been killed three weeks ago in her house just outside Montreal. The woman had been shot, for no apparent reason. It was the very last line of the report that really made him pay attention: the woman was apparently Basque, and as a young girl she had been interned in a Nazi concentration camp. In Gurs. The French Basque Country. The murder was a total mystery, as nothing had been stolen, *despite the victim's wealth*.

This had to be linked. *Had to*. Even if it wasn't, it needed more investigating. He wrote down the details on his pad, then turned to the next news item. The article had been carried by a couple of newsfeeds a few weeks ago.

The headline was: 'Bizarre Bequest Leads to Million Dollar Basque Mystery'

A thirty-something man called David Martinez was staring out of a photo: he was holding a map. Martinez had an awkward grin in the photo, as he brandished the map, a kind of uncomfortable smile. The article said the map showed places in *the Basque Country*. Moreover it said the young man's grandfather had died and left him two million dollars – and according to the newspaper *this had come as a complete surprise*.

Simon scanned the article, feeling quite alive with excitement. He didn't want a drink any more. He wanted to know what *this* was about: a link to the Basques, a mysterious amount of money, a very old man – thousands of miles away – now dead.

The article gave him almost everything: it even explained that David Martinez had been a lawyer in London prior to his inheriting this mysterious sum.

It took two minutes on the net to find out the 'well known

law company' where David Martinez had worked: there were lists of lawyers of every company.

Walking to the window, Simon called Martinez's firm on his mobile. A clipped voice requested his name and credentials, he handed them over: Simon Quinn from the *Daily Telegraph*.

He was batted around the system for a few moments, put on hold, put through to HR, put back on hold . . . but then he reached a superlatively snooty man, apparently David Martinez's boss, Roland De Villiers, who was more than keen to hand out Martinez's mobile number. The boss actually added, for good measure, 'I do hope he's in trouble.'

The call clicked off, abruptly.

Simon looked at his notepad, resting on the windowsill. It was a British number that the lawyer had airily handed over. He keyed the numbers, but the ensuing ringtone was long bleeps – indicating that this guy Martinez was abroad – in Spain maybe?

Then a hesitant voice came down the satellite.

'Yes . . . Who is this?'

24

The smell of congealed eels hung in the air. Mist was sidling into the room stealthy and needy. David sat in the silence and the chill, wondering at José's words. Then he welcomed the return of his wits. *He needed to speak to Amy.* To tell her all of this.

'Amy!'

His voice echoed. He tried again.

'Amy?'

Where was she? He hadn't seen her for an hour. It was hard to believe she was outside in the rain.

He called again. His voice bounced off the mouldering woodwork, and down the empty corridor. Nothing.

A swift search told him there was no one on the ground floor: all he could hear was the incessant skitter of rat tails, as the vermin fled his approach through each unsavoury chamber.

How about the room they shared? He and Amy? Where they had talked through the night?

He had to take the stairs; he had to go up the stairs. The pounding of his feet matched the pounding of his pulse as he called Amy's name again – nothing, the hallway was empty.

He pushed the door and as he did his mind filled: the imagined scene of his parents, dying in their car, came suddenly and vividly into mental view. His mother's head crushed, blood drooling politely from her slackened mouth . . .

Maybe the same had happened to Amy. Everyone close to him was taken away: *everyone*.

David scanned the room he and Amy had shared. Empty. It was bereft even of rats, or ravens cackling at the window. The bunks were still shifted together; the old picture of a Jesuit saint was still askew on the peeling wall. Slumlike dampness seeped from the ceiling.

There was one bedroom left, Fermina and José's room. No doubt the door was locked and barred against the world.

Maybe she was in there?

David gathered his valour and stepped down the hallway and called through the door, Amy – *Amy* – but the returning silence was claustrophobic.

This was intolerable. He yearned to escape, to find the truth and find Amy – and then run away, get out of this awful house, this monument to oppression; the pains and terrors of the Cagots – branded, excluded, humiliated – seemed to have soaked into the bricks and mortar. David wanted to find her, and then fly.

He poised a fist to knock on the door. He would kick the door in, if necessary.

But his knock was stayed by *a voice* – right behind him.

'David?'

He swivelled. It was *Amy*.

'Where have you been?!'

'Downstairs –' Amy shook her head '– the cellar . . . to check –'

'What?'

'For passages. The *chemins des Cagots*. You remember? Eloise said there were passages, built by the Cagots – I thought if

we were in trouble, we could use them . . . but I only found
vaults –'

He put two hands on her shoulders.

'José told me, told me all of it – everything. He's locked
in there – with Fermina –'

He tilted a frown, leftwards, indicating the door.

'But why?'

He began to explain.

And he stopped almost at once. Their conversation was
slashed in half by a horrible and unmistakable sound.

A gunshot. And then another gunshot.

Inside the Garovillos' room.

They ran to the door and shoved against the rusted locks.
The wood and metal resisted for a minute, then two minutes.
But the planks were wormed, and the hinges were ancient,
the doorway began to splinter, and then it swung open. They
were inside.

David gazed across, and he felt his heart shrivel in bitter
disgust. Amy had a hand to her face, shrouding her tears.

Two corpses were sitting in two chairs.

José and his wife.

Fermina Garovillo had been shot at close range through
the temple, the side of her head was simply *missing*; the
obscene wound was echoed and amplified by a splattered
patch of blood on the wall nearby. José had shot his wife
first, it seemed – and then turned the gun on himself. And
his wound was worse: the entire top of his cranium, taken
clean away. Burn marks on his thin white lips showed how
he had done it, put the gun between his teeth, pulled the
trigger – blasting away his own brains.

More blood on the ceiling and the wall behind confirmed
the suicide. David took one quick look at the grey jellylike
stuff balanced on top of the chair – and he felt the rising
bile of nausea.

But why?

Why had they done it?

An answer, the answer, came immediately. The menacing slurch of tyres, outside.

David went straight to the window and scanned the scene, his muscles tense with alarm. And there. There it was. The reason for José and Fermina's suicide, maybe. A red car, driving slowly between the dripping trees. Miguel was surely inside the car. David recalled old José's words. *One day he will kill me.*

Amy joined David at the window. She cursed and shivered, simultaneously.

But there was faint hope. The red car slowed to a stop, then it started up once more, *going the wrong way.* David realized, with a tiny jolt of optimism, that Miguel must still be *looking* for them. The Wolf didn't *quite* know where it was, he was driving up and down. For how long he'd been doing this, who knew. However he had discovered their exile in Campan – torturing Eloise maybe? – he hadn't pinned down the precise location of the refuge.

But it wouldn't take him long. Eventually he would see the concealed turning. Miguel would drive past the bushes, and look in the right direction. And then discover the house. And then come and kill them. *Epa. Epa. Epa.*

'The gun!' said Amy.

'What?'

'There must be a gun.'

She was right. David scanned swiftly around the room for José's gun. The old man must have had a gun to shoot himself and his wife. And there – a glimpse of black metal in the greyish light. David reached between José's lifeless legs and picked up the pistol. It was still warm. He figured there must be bullets left inside. There had only been two gunshots.

He lifted the gun and held it, pointing the muzzle at the ceiling.

For a second the madness of it all gyred in David's mind: a year ago he was a lethargic media lawyer. Bored, safe, and incoherently sad. Commuting on the District Line tube, going home to a microwave chicken curry, maybe a pint with a friend. Maybe meaningless sex with someone he didn't love, if he was lucky. Now he was terrified, and angry, and hunted – and yet the paradox was there again: he felt *more* alive than ever.

He wanted to live now: he wanted to live so much. To find out the deeper reasons for his parents' murder, and to take revenge for their deaths. But the *first* thing was to escape.

'The back garden,' said Amy, her tears visibly repressed. She was being strong, she looked angry. 'Through the garden, the ravine? We can go that way?'

They hurried out of the door and along the hall; the damp old planks thudded and creaked as they took themselves downstairs, to the rear of the house – from there the garden and the gate led to the forests; but Amy pulled him back.

'Listen!'

He listened; she was right. Voices. Out there in the garden, maybe over the wall – in the woods.

'We can't risk it,' she hissed. 'The road?'

'Miguel's car.'

They sighed with frustration – and fear. David felt the rage inside. 'We're stuck. Dammit we're just stuck. He's got us trapped!'

'No. The cellar!' She grabbed his arm. 'I am sure there are passages down there. C'mon, we have to find them.'

She turned, and they ran down the musty hallway – and turned right. There was an old cellar door under the stairs. David reached for the handle.

The subtle growling of a car engine was distinct. Somewhere out there in the rain and the ruins the car was coming *very* close, prowling past the old cottages of the Cagots, taking the turning that led to the hideout. The voices outside, in the woods at the rear, were still audible. Closing in.

The door to the cellar opened on a dingy set of descending stairs, plunging into the dark dark underworld of the Cagot refuge.

They had no choice. David followed Amy down the steps, into the blackness. He turned and shut the door firmly behind them, immersing them in even deeper darkness. It felt like drowning at night.

'Amy –'

'Yes!'

'You're OK?

'Here's the floor . . . I think.'

David took out his phone and switched it on and used the light of the screen to see; the feeble glimmer illuminated the echoing black cellar. He surveyed the gloom.

'Wait.'

Amy had a finger to her lips. They stood still, and mute. Frightened. Male voices were discernible. *Inside the house.*

'The vaults!'

David squinted. Now that his eyes were adjusting, he could see the true size of the cellar. It was enormous – high ceilinged and enormous, stretching into the dark, a real medieval dungeon. Somewhere for storing a lot of food, maybe, when the Cagots had to hide out.

Giving off the main vaulted cellarspace was a series of massive wood-and-metal doors, leading, it seemed, to more dark, clammy chambers. Three of the doors were open, two closed.

'We need to search – the spaces –'

They peered into the first vault. It was so cold and sticky in this secondary cellar, their breath hung in the air, the spectres of words. David flashed the phone-light around. The goose's foot was carved on the lintel. The mark of Cain. David turned his light quickly this way and that, but the space was empty. A narrow stone bench ran along the side, empty. The smell was faintly rancid.

More noises scuffled upstairs. Then the thump of boots on stairs. The men were searching the upper floors of the house. They would find José and Fermina. That might delay them. David tried not to speculate on Miguel's reaction. He would come upon the grisly sight of his self-murdered parents: he would be more angered than ever before.

And then the terrorist would realize, he would descend. And find the cellar door.

Trying to quell his panic, David paced to the next vault. The second one was like the first, empty, long and obscurely pungent. His anxiety was like a drumbeat. Accelerating.

He stepped further inside, ensuring there was no concealed exit. There wasn't. The third vault was the same: it had no other doors. Now Miguel's dark voice could be heard – in the hallway above. Shouting. Soon he would see the cellar entrance.

They had come to the fourth and penultimate vault. It was sealed. The metal door was tall and mossed over with decay.

'Try it!' Amy whispered. 'We have to –'

'Hold the light –'

Amy took the phone and poised it – as he tugged, fiercely, at the cold metal handle. He tugged harder, and then again, even harder. The door began to slide, very slowly. It wheezed and complained, slowly yielding to his desperate struggles. The metal grated resentfully against the stone – and then it seemed to explode: it fell open and a swamping deluge of brown and rancid fluid came after, a wave of thick and malodorous soup that was so fierce it knocked them both to the cellar floor.

They were slipping now, slipping and gasping in the slimy water; and David could see, knocking and bobbing in the subsiding floods: yoghurty flaps of flesh, and grimacing human heads, and fibrous, amputated arms; the heads were half decayed, the hair on one face was like rusty brown wire; a protruding arm bone was sticking out of leathery strings of muscle –

'Amy?'

She was struggling to stand up, slipping in the juices of the corpses. He stared at her, suffused with horror. They were covered with brown-green, waxy slime. And then David succumbed to his gag reflex: he briefly puked into the pooling fluids, and puked again. Amy was coughing, violently, as she stood up; then she seemed to steel herself, and she closed her eyes, and she opened her eyes, and she pointed to the ceiling.

The voices above were sharper, nearer, angrier, the men were nearly done searching the house. She hissed:

'The last door – what choice –'

Skidding through the puddles, they approached the final door.

The insanity of the scene did not prevent the danger approaching. Together, they pulled at the door handle, the metal slipping in their greasy hands. The obvious fear was written on Amy's face – what if this was another flood, of fluids and bones? – but it wasn't. The door opened quite easily. It opened onto a dry and lofty space, and at the end of the vault gaped . . . a passageway. Clung with spiderwebs, long and dismal, and stretching into further blackness.

'The *chemin*!'

Amy was already inside, beckoning David to follow. He paused to shut the chamber door behind them. Quietly yet emphatically. It wouldn't stop anyone. It wouldn't stop the Wolf. It might delay their pursuers a few vital minutes.

'OK.'

The passageway was too low to walk properly: they had to crouch, and scuttle, desperately, like hapless large insects.

But they were escaping at last. The footfalls and voices grew faint. But when the men found the cellar door?

215

'Which way now?'

David switched the phone-light left and then right, the pitiful torchbeam revealed more passages branching off. The roof of the nearest passage was pierced by a worm, wriggling and pink. He could feel the clammy fluids on his jeans, he was covered with decaying human bodies, smeared with a scum of ancient human fat. The gag reflex tugged at his throat, once again.

'This one,' Amy said, her voice half-choked. 'Pointing left. It must – surely – it must – *go to the woods* –'

'Now!'

They made their way, in frightened silence, until a soft thunder halted their progress, joined by a tinkling: water was dripping through the soil above, dripping down the muddy walls.

'The Adour?' she said. 'We're going in a *different* direction.'

'It's too late now.' He grabbed Amy's wet hand. '*Quick* –'

A few metres further, the dirty passageway began to broaden, and gain height until it was almost possible to walk. Until it was almost possible to run.

They ran. The passage curved to the left and the right and then it stopped at some stairs of impacted soil. At the top of the stairs was a trap door.

'It could open anywhere,' said Amy. 'Someone's house. The *boulangerie*.'

'We're gonna surprise them –'

David climbed the earthen steps and shoved a shoulder violently upwards; the doorflap began to yield, a slant of light striped his face, and the trap door slapped open, with a bang. He looked across – as four faces stared back at him, grinning.

What?

But it wasn't four faces. It was four rag dolls: Campan *mounaques*. The family of rag dolls installed in the front pew of the church.

The dolls smiled forever. Smiling at David's soiled face as

he hoisted himself out of the trap door, then leaned down and hauled Amy to the surface. She gazed about.

'The church – *of course.*'

David nodded. 'We better get out of these – clothes – now, get out of them now – let's use these –'

He pointed at the rag dolls. Within a minute they had stripped themselves, extracted money and possessions, and jumped into the ordinary clothes of the rag dolls, the baggy jeans and jumpers; David kicked away his clothes, trying not to imagine what kind of . . . things . . . what kind of fetid silt . . . had touched his skin.

'OK?' he said.

Amy was using her discarded jumper to wipe her head. She shivered.

'Jesus. David. What . . . was . . . that stuff? In the cellar?'

'Body liquor.'

'What?'

'If you store bodies in an airtight space, for centuries, they decay . . . in a certain way. But –'

'They turn to *liquid*?'

'Eventually.' He glanced around the church, trying to work out what to do next. Amy pressed him: 'Explain!'

'The corpses slowly become adipocere – corpse wax. A sort of cheesy wax. Grave wax. Then over centuries they turn again, into . . . a . . .' He was trying not to think about it. 'A sort of soup. With flesh. I'm sorry. But that's what we found –'

'How do you know *that*?'

'Human biochemistry.'

She was trembling.

'Oh God. Oh God. Oh God.'

Her eyes were shut, absorbing the ghastliness. He decided not to tell her his darkest fears. One of the reasons you might store human bodies so diligently and carefully was if you feared they carried severe disease. Infectious disease.

'OK,' she said, opening her eyes. 'I'm OK. But José . . .' She inhaled deeply, to calm herself. 'Poor José.' Then she said: 'What now?'

'We get the fuck out of Campan.'

He crept to the main door, and creaked it open. They stealthily walked the path through the overgrown churchyard to the main iron gate. And gazed. There was not a person or a car to be seen; the only sign of humanity was one solitary old woman hurrying under an umbrella, way down the grey and lonely main street.

'Run for it –'

They sprinted out of the churchyard, hurling themselves down the humble main street of Campan, beyond the last dilapidated villa, running into the countryside. And still running.

After twenty minutes Amy called a halt, she had her hands on her knees. Gasping and gulping. Almost puking. David stopped, exhausted, and looked around, they had reached a junction, where traffic slashed past, burning down the main road.

But now Amy was running on.

'We can hitch! We need to hitch a lift –'

'Where?'

'Biarritz. Somewhere busy, with lots of people, where we can get lost. This road goes to Biarritz.'

He followed her, as she ran to the road, with her thumb out, hoping for a lift. David was desperate: who the hell would stop for them? Dressed like scarecrows, faces frightened, half smeared with some unspeakable effluent.

Five minutes later a French apple truck stopped; the driver leaned over, pushed the door open. They climbed in, profusely thanking the man. He glanced at their clothes, he sniffed the air, and then he shrugged. And drove.

They were escaping. Down the thundering autoroute to

Biarritz. David sat back, his arms aching, his mind spiralling, waiting for the sense of relief. But then he heard a beep. A message. He patted his scarecrow jeans: his phone! He'd forgotten that he'd turned his phone on, to use the light: he'd been keeping the phone off all this time, just in case Miguel was tracing his own number, too.

As he took the phone from his pocket, he felt the wild incongruity, a clash of modernity, and madness. He had been drenched with the vile distillation of many dead bodies, and yet his phone was bleeping.

The flashing number was British. He clicked.

And then he had one of the strangest phone calls of his life. From a journalist in England. A journalist called Simon Quinn. The phone call lasted an hour; by the time it was done they were in the depths of the Gascon hills, near Cambo-les-Bains.

David shut the call down. And then he rang a random number: and as soon as it answered he opened the window, and he threw the damp and mudded phone into the long grass of the verge, with a fierce relief. If anyone was tracing his calls, they would trace them to Cambo-les-Bains.

Amy was asleep in the seat next to him. The truck driver was furiously puffing a cigarette, oblivious.

He sat back, pensive. The phone call from the journalist. What did it all mean? Murders in Britain? Scientists? Genetics?

Deformity?

25

At the end of the bizarre phone call, his hand weary from scribbling notes, Simon thanked David Martinez and clicked off, falling back on the bed, his eyes bright with thoughts and ideas.

Extraordinary. It was truly extraordinary. And the tension in the young man's voice. What was he going through? What was happening down there, in the Pyrenees?

Whatever the answer, the phone call was a revelation. A breakthrough – and it needed celebrating. He almost ran downstairs. He needed to speak to Sanderson, and he needed a cup of triumphant coffee.

Spooning dark brown Colombian coffee grounds into the cafetiere, he called New Scotland Yard. It occurred to him, as he did so, that Sanderson might be angered by Simon's persistent pursuit of the story; it occurred to him that Sanderson would be *mightily* interested in this latest information.

But he couldn't reach Sanderson. Instead he was put through to Tomasky. The young DS seemed to listen with appreciative and gratifying interest; as he told the story, Simon felt almost exultant at his success. The best bit was the toes. They now had an explanation: the syndactyly. Yes.

Even as Simon explained his discoveries, he cursed himself for his own failure in not making this connection before – as soon as Emma Winyard had mentioned the Cagots, he should have looked them up! Then he could have strung the pearls himself: webbed toes. Cagots. The Pyrenees.

Still, he had at least got there in the end.

The coffee had brewed and the mug was full. It was Tomasky's turn to talk, as the journalist sipped.

'So, Simon,' the DS said, 'you're saying these people, the . . . Cackots . . .'

'Cagots. Ca-gots.'

'Right. You're saying these Cag . . . ots are all *deformed*? They all have webbed fingers or toes?'

'Not all. But some, certainly – and it is one of the characteristics of the Cagots. Since medieval times. That's why they were given the, ah, goose's foot to wear. To symbolize and epitomize their malformation.'

'Why? Why do they have webbed fingers and toes?'

'Genetics. They are a mountain people, inbred! Deformities like this are common in isolated communities with smaller gene pools. They don't get bred out. Fascinating right?'

'Sure.' Tomasky went quiet. Then he added. 'And you're saying our victims . . . are Cagots then. Someone is killing the Cag . . . ots?'

'Seems that way, Andrew. We don't know why, but we know that some of them are Cagots, and the ones who are Cagot and deformed get tortured. And the killings are happening all over. France, Britain, Canada.' He paused. 'And some of them are old, and they were in Occupied France during the war, maybe in this camp called Gurs. Maybe that's what links them as well. And some of them have lots of money . . .' Simon wanted to laugh at the bewildering evidence, but at least it was evidence. 'I need to speak to Bob Sanderson. He needs to *know* this.'

'Sure. I'm on it. I'll tell the DCI as soon as I see him.'

'Excellent. Thanks, Andrew.'

Simon rang off. He set down the mobile and stared out of the window. For half an hour he exulted in his discovery. Then his hymn of happiness was joined by the chime of the doorbell. The journalist breezed down the hall and opened the door. Behind it was Andrew Tomasky. Surprising.

'Hello, DS. I thought –'

The policeman pushed through the door and kicked it shut behind. Simon stood back.

Tomasky had a knife.

26

Tomasky growled with anger as his first stab of the knife missed Simon's neck – by an inch.

The journalist gasped as he sensed another slashing cut, and he swerved, again, batting away the blade – but Tomasky came at him for a third time, jumping forward, and this time he got a hand on his victim's throat and the knife was aimed directly at an eye.

Choking and spitting, Simon caught the stabbing arm at the last moment. The knife was poised just millimetres from the pupil, shaking with the violence of their struggle.

Tomasky was thrusting down, his victim was holding the wrist and grinding the hand upwards. They were on the floor. The knife was too close to see, it was just a menacing silver blur in his vision: a looming greyness. The knifepoint came closer, the journalist shuddered – he was going to be blinded, then killed. Drilled into the brain through the optical bone.

His eye was blinking reflexively, shedding tears. Loud noises rumbled behind. The bladepoint trembled with the strength of two men opposed. Simon screamed and made a final effort to force the blade away, but he was losing the battle. He shut his eyes and waited for the steel to sink into the softness, popping open the eyeball, then crunching into his brain.

Then his face was covered with splattering wetness, like he'd been slapped with heavy blancmange: and suddenly Tomasky was just a body, dead weight, sagging down, and he forced the dead policeman off his chest and he stared upwards.

Sanderson.

DCI Sanderson was standing in the door; next to him was a policeman with chest armour. The door had been kicked open. The chest-armoured cop had a gun.

'Shot, Richman.'

'Sir.'

Sanderson reached a hand down and pulled the journalist to his feet. But when he stood up he felt his knees go, trembling and buckling with the fear and the shock; he crumpled to the floor again. He was staring at Tomasky's body. The head had been blown apart, by a sidelong shot, at close range. The skull was in pieces. Actual pieces scattered across the hallway.

Then he sensed the wetness on his face. Smeary wetness. He had Tomasky's blood and maybe his brains on his face. His throat tightened with nausea as he stood; without a word to the policemen he hurled himself upstairs to the bathroom, where he averted himself from the mirror: he didn't want to see himself covered with brains and blood. Splashing water and more water on his face, he used a box of tissues, and half a bottle of handsoap, and finally he rinsed and nearly gagged, and rinsed again.

Now he checked the mirror. His face was clean. But there was something stuck in his cheek, lodged in its own little wound. Like a small piece of glass, burrowed in his flesh. Leaning close to the mirror he plucked the thing from his cheek.

It was one of Tomasky's teeth.

'League of Polish Families.'

The voice was familiar. DCI Sanderson was standing right behind, at the hallway door.

'What?'

'Tomasky. We've been watching the bastard for a while. Sorry it got that close. We've been monitoring his calls – but he slipped out of the building –'

'You –'

'Sorry, mate. Had to use lethal force. Waited too long –'

Simon's hands were still trembling with fear. He extended one into the air, experimentally. Watched it shaking. He grabbed a towel and dried his face. Trying to be calm and manly. Largely failing.

'Why *did* you suspect him?'

Sanderson offered a sad, sympathetic smile.

'Odd little things. The knotting. Remember that?'

'Yes.'

'You found out it was a witch torture, in an hour. Tomasky didn't. I put him on the job before you, and he turned up nothing like that. Yet he was a smart copper. That didn't quite . . . fit.' The DCI pointed at Simon's face. 'You're still bleeding.'

He switched his attention to the mirror once more. The wound where the tooth had impacted was indeed bleeding. But not badly. Rifling the bathroom cabinet, he found some cotton wool. He swabbed himself with water, then rinsed the woollen bud. White wool, red wool, clear water, stained water. Blood in the water. Sanderson carried on talking.

'When I noted that – the knotting, I mean – that's when I took an interest. I remembered he was keen to be assigned to this case in the first place. Very very keen. And then we found he was taking certain calls that were meant for me, and not telling me, like the call from Edith Tait. And he

225

wasn't following up other leads, either. So we looked into his background . . .'

The journalist gestured at Sanderson. He wanted to get out of the bathroom. He wanted to get out of the house. He could hear voices downstairs. More policemen, presumably. An ambulance outside, come to take the body away.

They stepped out onto the landing and leaned over the banister, looking down at the hall. The body was still lying there: with paramedics bustling around. Big splashes of blood, like bright red paint, were flung across the polished wooden floor. That wooden floor was Suzie's pride and joy. Simon wondered, incongruously, how angry she would be: about her floor.

'You said about his background?'

'Yeah.' Sanderson nodded. 'Likesay, Polish. Came here with his family about ten years ago. A cleanskin. No record of anything suspicious, even trained as a priest. Or monk. But his dad was big in the League of Polish Families. And his brother worked for Radio Maryja.'

'They are?'

'Hard right nationalist groups, ultra Catholic political parties. Linked to the Front National in France and various Catholic sects, like Pope Pius the Tenth. Lots of them perfectly legitimate but with . . . radical right agendas. At the edges anyway.'

'So he was a Nazi?'

'Nah. These outfits, from what we can tell, are not really Nazi. More hearth and home. The blessed Virgin Mary and a nice big army. They don't really go in for kicking shit out of black people. Or killing Anglo-Irish journalists. Not normally anyway.'

'I don't understand it.'

'Nor do I, mate, nor do I.' He squinted Simon's way, assessingly. 'But there may be some link . . . you know, your witch

226

theory. It alerted us. We're still checking Tomasky out. He was a passionate churchgoer. Witches and churches, churches and witches? Who knows.'

'So you listened in on the phone call I made to him?'

'We did,' Sanderson answered. 'He must have thought you were onto something, when you rang him, something he wanted hidden. So his only choice was to take you out.'

'The Cagots?'

'Yup. The gist of your call with Tomasky. And these poor bastards in France? Very interesting. What the fuck is all this about?'

'Sorry?'

The DCI looked momentarily sober, verging on reflective. Even maudlin. 'Remember what I said way back? How right I was.'

'What?'

This isn't any old fish and chip job, Quinn, this isn't a fish and chip job. This is something else. Who the heck knows . . .' His vigour returned. 'OK. Let's get sorted. Nuff rabbiting. Come on, we need to debrief you, Quinn. Then, I am afraid –'

'What –?'

'We're gonna assign you protection. Just for the while. And your close family.'

They descended the rest of the stairs. Past the body of Tomasky. Tip toeing through the bloodsplashes, apologizing to the paramedics and SOC photographers. The grey drizzly air of late September was enlivening. The sun was battling to be seen through the clouds.

Sanderson opened a car door for Simon, who climbed in. Sanderson sat alongside, in the back. The car began the long journey to New Scotland Yard. Finchley, Hampstead, Belsize Park.

'And,' Sanderson said, 'we will protect your family as

well. Your mum and dad, Conor and Suzie will be with you . . .'

'You're putting armed guards on my mother and father?'

Sanderson confirmed this with a curt 'Yep', then he leaned and tapped the driver on the shoulder. 'Cummings, this traffic is a bitch. Try St John's Wood?'

'Right you are, sir.'

He turned back to Simon. 'So that's it, wife and kid, mum and dad, there's no one else they can use. Right?'

The journalist nodded, then turned and stared out of the police car window, at the ordinariness of London. Red car yellow car white lorry. Pushchairs. Supermarkets. Bus stops. A knife three millimetres from his eye, a man bellowing with rage, forcing the knife down.

He rubbed his face with his hands, trying to rub away the horror.

'You will feel weird for a time,' Sanderson said, quite gently. 'I'm afraid you better get used to it.'

'Post-traumatic stress?'

'Well, yeah. But you can handle it, eh? The Fighting Irish?'

Simon attempted a weak smile. Then said:

'Tell me about the case, Bob. I need . . . distraction. What have you found, lately?'

Loosening his tie, Sanderson asked the driver to open the window. Cooler air refreshed the car. He said:

'We got some interesting leads on GenoMap. There's a Namibian connection. One of GenoMap's biggest sponsors was a Namibian diamond company, Kellerman Namcorp.'

'I remember Fazackerly mentioned them. *So?*'

'Seemed a bit odd to me. When I thought about it. A bleeding diamond company? What's that got to do with genetics? So I got a bod at the Yard to track down one of the scientists from GenoMap. A Chinese Canadian, Alex Zhenrong. We found him back in Vancouver. And he told us . . . quite a lot.'

They were passing the Regent's Park mosque. Its golden dome glittered half heartedly in the uncertain sunshine.

'Like what?'

'Like . . . a lot. He told us GenoMap found it hard getting people to fund the lab, at first, after what happened at Stanford.'

'But Kellerman were . . . keen?'

'They came on board after a year, and they were very keen *indeed*. Superfuckingduper keen. The only ones. Apparently they poured money into the lab. For several years. Genomics is not cheap but GenoMap got every machine they wanted. From Kellerman Namcorp.'

'And they are exactly? This corporation?'

'Diamonds, like I said. Big aggressive multinational, mining and export. They're up there with De Beers. They run their own part of Namibia, the Sperrgebiet. The Forbidden Zone. The owners are a very old Jewish family, South African. Jewish Dynasty.'

'Why were they so determined to finance the lab?'

'Because of Fazackerly and Nairn. According to Zhenrong anyway.'

'Say again?'

'Fazackerly was the best geneticist in Britain two decades ago. Big reputation. Nairn was maybe the best young geneticist in the world. Kellerman wanted their brains. And Kellerman wanted their results.'

'So that was good for GenoMap.'

Sanderson nodded. He glanced out of his window as they overtook a double decker bus. Crowded with shoppers.

'Yeah, but – so Zhenrong told us – Kellerman also wanted bangs for their bucks. They wanted some payoff for all that investment. So they pushed the research in . . . *a certain way* . . . If you see what I mean.'

'No. I don't . . .'

A brief silence. The journalist looked around the interior

of the police car. So calm and sensible and ordinary. So unlike the interior of his mind.

Sanderson explained.

'By the end, it seems Nairn and Fazackerly weren't just investigating genetic diversity in the way . . . you are supposed to.'

'Explain?'

'I'm no molecular biologist, Quinn, as you might have twigged. But my understanding is this. The initial idea behind GenoMap was . . . meant to be medical. Finding cures for diseases, through differering racial genetics.' Sanderson shook his head. 'That's why Alex Zhenrong joined, anyhow. But by the end, with Nathan Kellerman's strong encouragement, Fazackerly and Nairn, according to this Zhenrong lad, were just looking for genetic differences, *full stop*. They wanted to find and prove that there are large and serious genetic differences between human races. You understand.'

'Next stop Joséf Goebbels.'

'Yup. Maybe.'

'In which case . . . You reckon they are, or were, *racist*? Nairn and Fazackerly. A couple of Nazis? Fits with Tomasky.'

He shivered at the memory of the Polish policeman, teeth bared in rage; he looked across the car.

'Nope.' Sanderson shook his head. 'We don't think Angus was racist. According to all his mates, and Zhenrong, he just wanted to be *famous*, to be published. He was ambitious, *that's all*. Apparently he was pretty eccentric, as well as very smart. But he, at least, was not a Nazi.' Sanderson leaned a little closer to Simon, across the front seat of the car. 'And we think he and Fazackerly may have been onto something quite astounding by the end. Though they wouldn't tell anyone what it was. But it must've been something that the Kellermans *really* wanted.'

'So how do *you* know about it?'

'Fazackerly started boasting about it! In his cups.' Sanderson mimed a drinking hand. 'Zhenrong says Fazackerly was a terrible boozer. There was a genomics conference in Perpignan about six months ago when Fazackerly got rat-arsed. And he told everyone that him and Nairn, they were gonna publish something that would *amaze* everyone, that would make Eugen Fischer look like a nonce. That's not how Zhenrong phrased it, by the way, that's me.'

'Eugen Fischer? I heard that name. Recently.' Simon frowned. Exhausted by the mystery. 'The young guy in France, Martinez, he mentioned him.'

'That right? Well, Fischer was a race scientist. Worked in Namibia, and then for Hitler, one of the founders of eugenics. A real bastard. Thought Germans were supermen.'

'Namibia.'

'Namibia.'

'I remember . . .' Simon said, 'I remember there was, ah, a picture in Fazackerly's office of Francis Galton. He was a eugenicist . . . and he worked in Namibia.'

'You see?' Sanderson was broadly smiling. 'It all connects. The Namibian Connection! I'm only telling you all this because you had a detective sargeant's premolar embedded in your face this morning. Please keep shtoom for now. I guess you will wanna write a book when we're done, won't you?'

Simon found himself blushing.

'Hah.' Sanderson chuckled. 'Fucking writers can't resist. Make sure you give me a good haircut. Six foot two. Strong jaw. You know. And here's another thing. Nathan Kellerman, the Jewish heir to all those diamond billions, he and Nairn became very close. Kellerman and Nairn would have these . . . chinwags, apparently, when he used to come and visit London, see how money was being spent.'

231

'Conversations?'

'Yes. About the Bible.' Sanderson shrugged. 'The Curse of Canaan. Genesis 3 or whatever. Zhenrong listened in. Sometimes. To their . . . *chats.*'

'The doctrine of the Serpent Seed? The Curse of *Cain*?'

'Yeah. All the stuff you got from Winyard. Odd, eh?'

'When you say he and Kellerman were close . . . how close?'

'Well they weren't boyfriends. But a couple of years back Nairn started visiting *Namibia.*'

The car was now stalled on Baker Street. The sun was properly out; the streets were lively with people. Three Arab wives in turquoise hijabs were walking several paces behind the husband – attired in jeans and baseball cap.

'Right. And?'

'It's a pretty expensive place to go, the other side of the world. Nairn wasn't rich.'

Simon saw the clear light of logic.

'Kellerman paid for his trips!'

'Yup. We're pretty sure he paid, because Nairn went several times, in three years. Never told anyone why or what he did there.'

'Holidays?'

Sanderson's expression narrowed. 'Long way to go surfing.'

'You believe he's in Namibia now, don't you?'

The DCI smiled with a trace of smugness. 'I do. I even tried writing to him, on his email address. See if I could coax him out, tell him about the case. If he's down there he's probably still receiving emails. Reckon.'

Simon sat back. Sanderson confessed: 'I didn't get very far. Not good coppering. Tut fucking tut. But hey, at least I saved your Danish – just in time.'

The policeman's weary smile was warm: genuine and warm. Simon felt a little better. Then he remembered the expression on Tomasky's face. The growling anger. Ferocious. He felt worse.

Simon was quiet for the rest of the journey to New Scotland Yard. He was subdued during the debriefing; he was almost silent when he got home and hugged Suzie and embraced Conor with a fierce paternal love that almost broke his own heart, and his son's ribs.

The subdued feeling hung around like an unwanted, over-staying visitor, like the bloodstain that couldn't be removed from the hallway floor, no matter how many times it was sanded and polished. The journalist was melancholic and disquieted. He watched the fat housewife put out her fat housewifely washing. The fat black crow hopping along the garden. A policeman came to live with them, sleeping in the spare room. His radio buzzed loudly at odd times. He had a gun. He read football magazines.

Meanwhile, Simon researched Catholic sects and Polish skinheads. He drank too much coffee and researched genetics. He emailed David in France, and got a couple of emails in return. The emails were fascinating, and full of information, but they also added to his sense of danger and guilt. Simon felt guilty that he'd told the police about David: because Martinez and his friend – Amy – were, it seemed, suspicious of police involvement. Everywhere and everyone was suspect, unreliable, a menace.

And now Simon wondered if he could really trust *Sanderson*. Tomasky had, after all, seemed trustworthy and funny and decent; he had rather *liked* Tomasky – and Tomasky had tried to kill him. Who was to say that Tomasky's superiors were in the clear? How deep, how high, how far did this go?

This isn't any old fish and chip job, Quinn, this isn't a fish and chip job.

Five days later, sitting at his desk, bleakly daydreaming – yet again – he got a call from a distraught Polish woman.

Tomasky's sister.

Her English was appalling but her meaning was obvious: she was harrowed with guilt for what her brother had done, she wanted to apologize to Simon. She had tracked him down through 'The Scottish Yard policing man'.

He listened to her sincerely weepy, flamboyantly Slavic grief for several minutes, feeling his own awkwardness. Even if Tomasky had attacked Simon, the poor woman's brother had died. What could you say? *Never mind, it wasn't that bad?*

The woman was burbling again.

'Andrew was a good Polish man, Mister Quinn. Good man, regular guy! Regular.' Her words retreated into a taut, choking silence. 'He like *smalec* and *piwo*. He good. Normal. Like any men. But then the place change him, it change him.'

'Sorry?'

'Yes! Strasne. The monastery . . . the monastery Tourette in France.' Another suppressed sob. 'When he go there something happen. Something very bad like it change him. *Pyrzykro mi*. I am very sorry. *Pyrzykro mi.*'

The sobs came, and the phone call ended.

234

27

'*Bonjour!*'

Leaning out of his hotel window, on his tiny balcony, David returned a nervous hello to the affable, middle-aged French gentleman, sitting with his copy of *Le Figaro* on his lap, on the next balcony along. David weakly smiled – then turned resolutely away. He didn't want to talk, he didn't want to be recognized and acknowledged. He wanted pure and inconspicuous anonymity.

So he stared in the other direction, along the Biarritz seafront. The scene was boisterous: the beaches were wide and golden, hemmed by the glittering lace of the crashing waves; the architecture was a remarkable mix of Victorian townhouses, concrete casinos, and pink stucco palaces. The strange and clashing mixture matched his mood.

They'd been hiding out in this hotel for a several days, using only payphones, and occasionally sneaking out to cybercafes to send and receive emails. He'd got two emails from Simon Quinn, updating him. Which was useful.

But it was still a dislocating sensation. Being here. And the disorientation was compounded by one dazzling new fact: he and Amy had begun sleeping together.

It had happened their second night in Biarritz. They'd decided they'd had enough of skulking in their tiny adjoining hotel rooms, so they had quietly wandered to the Rock of the Virgin, the local beauty spot high on a promontory, and when they got there they had shyly stared at the lamps and the stars and the moon over the bay and the tourists downing oysters by the Porte des Pecheurs – and she'd started crying.

Her tears were unquenchable. She had cried for half an hour. Unsure what to do, David had escorted her to his room – and there she had shuddered and slipped into his bathroom to shower. He sat there, listening to the noise of the water hissing fiercely against the shower-curtain. He began to worry: was she OK?

Then she emerged, wrapped in white hotel towels, her face pink and her hair damp, her body shivering. Her blue eyes were filled with a depthless grief: she looked down at herself. Then she stared his way, her gaze honest, and brutally sad.

She said she felt dirty, and unclean. Tainted.

He asked why.

She started, then stopped; then she confessed, her words halting yet clear. She said she felt soured and bitter because she had *once loved Miguel*. And therefore it was all her fault. Everything. Because she loved him once, she had poisoned everything. She was the unclean one.

Amy was naked but for the towels. They were inches apart. He could smell the French soap on her roseate skin. Amy shivered again and then she turned to him and whispered *I shouldn't have loved Miguel* and the way she said *I shouldn't have loved Miguel* was so dark, so lushed, so violet and yielding, he'd felt commanded, he felt he had no choice: he leaned forward, and his lips had sunk onto her wet mouth, and the word *Miguel* became a kiss, a ferocious kiss, and then his hand slipped into her damp yellow hair, and between their kisses she whispered *make me clean* and then she said *make me clean* once again and then she said *fuck me*.

It had been one of the best moments of his life, and one of the most complex.

David was unnerved, and remained unnerved, because their lovemaking was so charged, so fierce, so freshly different. He had experienced nothing like it. The sex left them both breathless, shining with perspiration, with the balcony doors flung open to the cool night breezes off the sea, cooling their nakedness. And so it had continued ever since: agitated and wild. Fucking. Her scratches on his back were so deep they stung him when he showered in the morning.

Sometimes David wondered why their sex was so exquisitely savage – so tenderly brutal. Their twinned loneliness? The unhappy past they shared? The fact that death had seemed so close? Sometimes she talked of her Jewishness, her family, her dead father – even her relatives killed in the Holocaust – and he detected a kind of deep-rooted guilt. Survivor guilt. And maybe that's what he had too. Survivor guilt.

And maybe that was it – what drove them together with such passion. They were alone and they were survivors. They were like starving people falling on the first food in many weeks: they craved each other's bodies, feasted on each other, grabbed at each other, sometimes she bit his shoulder until he almost bled, sometimes he pulled her hair very hard, and often she swore when he turned her over, fighting him, then yielding, then fighting, her sweet brown legs kicking at the sheets. Screaming into the pillow, clawing the bedboard.

Harder, she said, do it harder.

And all of it, everything, was haunted by Miguel. The memory of Miguel ravishing her in the witch's cave. David wanted to deny it but he couldn't. Miguel was always there.

237

He was there even when they had sex. Maybe especially when they had sex.

Eusak Presoak! Eusak Herrira! Otsoko.

And now they had been here five days and he knew he was falling in love with her and he was wondering what to do next.

David turned from the balcony, and went back into the hotel room. He heard a key in the lock; it was Amy. He glanced her way – quizzically – she'd been to the internet cafe: she had been going there several times a day – they reckoned her fluent French and Spanish made her less conspicuous than David. So she went there more than him.

He could tell from Amy's face that she had news.

'An email?'

'Yes.' She sat down on the bed and slipped off her sandals. She was wearing slender jeans and a grey cashmere jumper; the autumn weather in Biarritz was sunny but cool. Gazing at her bare ankles, David repressed his desires, they had already had sex twice this morning: it was too much. It was all too much. It was wonderful. He was hungry. He wanted an enormous breakfast with brioche and baguette with sweet Bayonne *confit de cerise*. He wanted to see her naked, touch her there, the wounded pelt; the she-wolf shot by hunters, bleeding in the snow. Too much.

'*Eloise* emailed.'

She lay back on the bed. Staring up. Blue eyes staring at the ceiling like the blue sea laid out beneath the sun.

'You were right. She's in Namibia. She says she is OK. We mustn't worry about her . . . She says if we want to come, she can tell us where. She gave me . . . instructions.'

'What?'

'Namibia. She won't say exactly where but she promises we can be safe there. We have to meet someone in a hotel when we get there. He will tell us more.'

'She's with that guy. Angus Nairn.'

'Just like you guessed. Nairn gave her the money. Apparently –' Amy reached out as David came over and held his hand '– Nairn has been trying to persuade her to come to Namibia for a while.'

'Yeah?'

Amy held David's hand, tighter. And said: 'He wanted to do blood tests on her, and her family.'

'Because they are Cagots.'

'Of course. He'd been pestering her for months – but her mum and dad always said no, even though he offered money.'

Her hair smelt of citrus shampoo. David kissed her neck. She pushed him away, gently.

'And then after the murders, she got scared. And then, apparently, Angus Nairn offered her safety again – when she was with us in Campan, she sneaked off, read an email from him. And he offered to fly her straight out, to somewhere a long way away. Where no one can reach her.' Amy shrugged. 'Can't really blame her. The last known Cagot in the world . . . Of breeding age.'

'Apart from Miguel.'

She shivered. He touched her face.

'Maybe we should go there too,' he said. 'The beaches of Namibia. It might be safer . . . Gotta be safer.' He caressed her hair, cupped her cheek; he devoutly wished he wasn't falling in love with her. He knew it was dangerous. If he dived in the pool he could break his neck, because he still didn't know the depths. He kissed her again even though he didn't want to, he kissed her because he *had to*.

She pushed him away again.

'And she said something else. It reminded me . . .'

'What?'

'Of what José said to you.'

'You mean?'

239

Amy's expression was stern. 'She said this. She said the mystery, the Nairn stuff, the whole thing, it's bigger than we could imagine, bigger than anything. It's something to do with the Holocaust, the Nazis, the Jews . . . I don't know.'

'That's what she said?'

Amy exhaled. 'Sort of.'

Then she suddenly, and unexpectedly smiled.

'So we go there. So we don't. Come here!'

She was reaching for his shirt buttons.

But their lovemaking was halted by a brusque knock on the bedroom door.

'Monsieur! Mademoiselle!'

David immediately tensed. Rigid and wordless, he gazed at Amy, asking, with his eyes: *what shall we do*; she shrugged in return – a helpless, despairing shrug.

He got up, and swallowed his fears, and padded across.

'Who is it?'

'*S'il vous plaît. La porte.*'

They were cornered. They had no escape. They could hardly jump from the balcony. The next knock was louder and aggressive.

'Open the door!'

28

Behind the door was a policeman. He flashed a badge and told David in accented but otherwise perfect English that his name was Officer Sarria. The cop was in a smart kepi and dark uniform, and he had a colleague right behind him. The second man was in a black single-breasted suit, a very white shirt. Unsmiling. Wearing sunglasses.

Sarria pushed inside the room, past David; the policeman looked at Amy, sitting at the edge of the bed.

'Miss Myerson.'

'You know my name . . .?'

'I have been following you both across France. We need to speak. Now. This is my colleague –' He gestured behind. 'He is another policeman. I am going to talk with you. Now.'

David bridled at the idea of being interrogated, here. He felt cornered. Skewered. Something terrible would happen, hidden away up here. In the privacy of their room, on the top floor. He envisioned blood – flayed across the bathroom wall.

He glanced Amy's way; she half-shrugged as if to say *what else can we do?* Then he turned back.

'OK. But . . . downstairs. On the terrace. At the back. Please . . .?'

Sarria sighed, impatiently. 'OK, yes, downstairs.'

The four of them took the clanging hotel lift to the ground floor. In the lobby, David noticed another policeman, standing at the hotel door, in the sun: radio buzzing. The hotel was being *defended*.

They walked the other way, onto the al fresco terrace, towards an isolated table – almost nearer the sea than the bar. It was discreet, sheltered by potted fir trees. No one could see them.

Amy held David's hand, she was perspiring. The two policemen sat either side of the couple. David could feel himself sweating, as well. He wondered briefly if he was ill. What if they had caught an infection? From the bodies, in the vault, turned to liquor? Why had the corpses been stored so carefully?

The words *smallpox* and *plague* ripped apart what equanimity he had left. He tried to focus on the matter at hand. The policeman was talking.

'I was born . . . just up there in Bayonne,' said Sarria, apropos of nothing at all. He looked back at Amy, then David. 'Yes, I am Basque. Which is one reason why I *know* you need help.'

'So . . . what is it?' said Amy, bluntly. 'Why are you here, Detective?'

'We have been tracing Miss Bentayou. She is possibly a material witness to the criminal slaughter of her family.' His nod was sombre. '*Oui*. And we know she flew out of Biarritz, to Frankfurt.'

'So she's in Germany –' David replied, hastily.

'And from there, she flew straight to Namibia, according to the airline records.' His face showed irritation. 'Do not try to deceive me, Monsieur Martinez. We have been following this whole mystery for some time. The trail of chaos and blood . . . from the murders in Gurs . . . to that house in Campan, where someone heard *two* gunshots.' His words were terse. 'And the old priest in Navvarenx church told us your name. After that, it was easy to find out more. The news story about you, and so on.' The officer glanced at a tiny cup brought by a waiter: a delicate *cafe noir*. He didn't touch it. 'You may like to know the priest is quite well. He saved your life, I think. Shut the door just in time.'

Amy persisted.

'But how did you find *us*? Down here?'

'I am a senior officer of the *gendarmerie*. Part of my job is to maintain awareness of Basque terrorists.'

David flashed a brief glance at Amy; her face was composed, her blonde hair gently lifting in the breeze. But David could glimpse the turmoil of feelings under her concertedly impassive expression. He wondered if she was thinking of Miguel; he wondered *what* she was thinking of Miguel.

Sarria glanced sidelong at his colleague, then continued: 'We have contacts all across *Le Pays Basque*. Watchful contacts. We guessed you might be in Biarritz, because this is where Eloise flew out. I asked all the cybercafe owners to keep an eye, as you say – for an English girl. Of your description, Miss Myerson. Not so *difficile*.'

The silent policeman was scanning the terrace, and the beach beyond; like a presidential bodyguard, looking left and right.

Sarria elaborated: 'I also know, of course, that you are being hunted by Miguel Garovillo. One of the worst of ETA killers. Infamous and sadistic. I would like to arrest him myself. But he is clever. As well as cruel.' Sarria tilted his gaze towards David. 'And he has a lot of very . . . significant assistance. Important people behind him.'

'What do you mean?'

'Before I tell you, you need to know more. Of the history. You must prepare yourself.'

David looked Amy's way; the autumn light was bright on her hair. He turned to the suntanned face of the French cop.

'Tell me.'

'Very well.' He took a tiny, pouting sip of his *cafe noir*, then said: 'Do you have the map? The map mentioned in the news story?'

David felt a tremor of anxiety. 'Yes. It is here . . . I always keep it on me –' He felt in his jacket pocket, then pulled out the very worn road map.

Officer Sarria took it, and unfolded it; the paper was white in the sun, the blue stars almost pretty; he nodded, and glanced at his colleague, then he refolded the paper, and placed it on the table.

'I have seen this map before.'

'What?'

'It is your father's map, Monsieur Martinez. I returned it to your grandfather. After the murder.'

'I know it's Dad's map, but I don't understand –'

But even as he said this, the truth began to reveal itself in his mind. David stammered:

'You were – you mean –'

'I mean this.' He gazed at David. 'Monsieur Martinez, I may be a senior *flic* with grey hair, but once I was a young officer. In Navvarenx. In Gurs. *Fifteen years ago.*'

The reality kicked in; David's grief was painful in his chest.

'When my parents were killed?'

'I suspected it was ETA from the start. It had the hallmarks, if that is the word, of an ETA operation. The sabotaged car, a nasty explosion, it was similar to other ETA killings we investigated at the time. And I also suspected the young Miguel Garovillo was involved, we had eye witnesses.'

'So why the fuck didn't you arrest him?'

Sarria frowned.

'When I was at the Navvarenx police station we had a visit from the senior officer of the region.'

'Who?'

'It does not matter. What matters is this – he told me to conclude the case. He ordered me to finish the investigation, and mark it – unsolved. Yet we had evidence. I was very angry.'

'Why? Why would they do this?'

Sarria looked Amy's way. 'At first my immediate reaction was GAL.'

David also looked at Amy.

'Sorry? Who is gal?'

She replied:

'It's not a person, David. It's GAL.' Her face was white with anxiety. 'Capital G capital A capital L. *GAL*. They were a group set up by the Spanish state to kidnap and execute Basque radicals. In the 1980s and 90s. They had covert support from . . . elements inside the French government.'

'Exactly, Miss Myerson.' Sarria's nod was curt. 'This was the obvious answer. And my senior officer dropped hints, in that direction. A GAL killing – so you leave it alone. The authorities implied, to us, that your parents were Basque terrorists, Monsieur Martinez. Their death was therefore not a tragedy for the French State.'

David waited. Sarria sighed.

'But this made no sense to me. No sense at all. From what I could tell your parents had no link to terrorism. An American man and a British woman touring the area? And why would a known Basque radical, perhaps the fiercest ETA terrorist of all, *Otsoko*, the Wolf – son of the great José Garovillo – why would he suddenly be working for GAL? Suddenly a traitor to his entire cause?'

The question hung in the air, like the tang of salt from the sea, a hundred metres west.

'So . . .' Amy said, quietly. 'Why?'

'That is the question. Why the three murders.'

David interrupted:

'*Three* murders?'

'Yes. Of course . . .' Sarria's frown darkened. 'You . . . did not know?'

'I was fifteen. No one told me anything. *Know what?*'

'The autopsy. Your mother was five months pregnant with a daughter . . . when she died.'

The table was silent. David's soul churned with emotion. All his life he'd been an only child. Yearning for a sibling. And when he'd been orphaned, that loneliness, that hunger for a brother or a sister, had only intensified. And now this. *He'd almost had a sister.*

His anguished memories wove themselves, out of desperation, into a speculative reverie. Was this why Mum and Dad had gone on their strange holiday to France? Some desire to explore their roots? Following the revelation of her long-awaited second pregnancy?

Sarria spoke.

'I am very sorry, Monsieur Martinez. You can see I am here to help you. I knew your face as soon as I saw you a moment ago. Just like your father. In the car when we found him.' He looked briefly towards the sea, then returned his gaze to David. 'I would very much like to put Miguel Garovillo in a French prison cell, for the rest of his life. But before I tell you any more. I need to know your story.'

He shifted his little coffee cup to the side, and leaned his uniformed elbows on the table. '*Désolé*. You may not wish to trust me. I am sure you do not trust me. But I remember what it was like, discovering your mother and father. Believe me, that kind of memory, it does not fade. So my advice is tell me everything, now, and tell me quickly.' He paused, heavily. 'Because, let us face the truth: *what other choice do you have?*'

246

David gave Amy a long and significant look, her fingers interlinked with his across the table. She said:

'We have to. We have to be honest.'

She was, of course, correct. Their choices were narrowing down to nothing. So David nodded and drew a breath, and he told the policeman – *everything* – the whole story. The link to the British, French and Canadian murders. The journalist in England. The Cagot doors. The whole surreal roadtrip, crimsoned with blood every inch of the way.

By the end of this monologue, Sarria had taken off his kepi and laid it on the white paper tablecloth. His eyes had remained fixed on David the whole time.

'So . . . As I thought. *Les églises . . . La Societé.*' He was almost talking to himself – staring above their heads, searching for an answer in the sky over Biarritz.

Then he snapped from his thoughts and explained.

'It is the churches. It is not just the mobile phones, how he traced you. Monsieur Martinez. It is the churches. As the priest at Navvarenx implied.'

Amy spoke. 'What does that mean?'

'After I was taken off the Martinez murders, after the case was closed . . . I did some of my own . . . investigating. I looked into the background of those who had been stopping me. See if I could find this connection with GAL. Of course there was no such connect. *Mais –*' He paused, then continued: 'But there was a link with the church. Specifically, the Society of Pius the Tenth.'

Amy's face showed surprise.

'I've heard of them. Yes. And – and – and José was linked to them. He had that crucifix blessed by Pope Pius. Yes –' She clutched at David's arm. 'The priest, at Navvarenx.'

David recalled. 'He mentioned a Society. Said he had been asked to warn them . . . or someone . . . about us. And there

247

were portraits of that pope in some of the churches.' David struggled with the idea, he was at a loss. 'But who are they?'

Sarria elaborated.

'A large splinter group from the Catholic church, with strong support in the South of France. And in the Basque Country. Very *traditionale*. They were founded by Archbishop Lefebvre. They have links to the Front Nationale, to hard right-wing politics. Some of their bishops have denied the Holocaust. They have sympathizers across the state. They are . . .' He frowned. 'They are also active abroad. In Bavaria and Quebec, South America. In Poland they have political friends, the League of Polish Families. And the hard right in Austria. It is guessed there are eight hundred thousand members. Their own priests, their own seminaries, their own churches.'

Amy said: 'You are sure they are linked?'

'Quite sure. Everywhere I looked I found, mademoiselle, connections to the Society. *Un réseau, une conspiration!* My superior officer was a confirmed sympathizer. Very right wing.'

David gazed at the policeman, still deeply confused.

'But why would they be involved in this?'

The officer nodded, uncertainly.

'It seems to me the Catholic church wants to . . . suppress some knowledge. Which dates back to the war. Maybe to Gurs. Your parents were accidentally revealing the same . . . mystery. Perhaps by mistake. *Accidentellement.*'

'You say the Society is involved, but now you say the *whole* Catholic church?'

A shrug. 'This is my . . . hunch, is that the right word? My hunch. I have researched the Society ever since the first killings in Gurs. Some years ago the Society of Pius the Tenth was . . . *excommunié* . . . by Pope John Paul for rejecting the Second Vatican Council. And for their extreme views. But recently there have been signs that the Pope will take the Society back . . . into the warmth of Catholic communion. Peace overtures have been noted.' Sarria was faintly smiling. 'But I am thinking the church has asked the Society to do something, in return for healing the schism.'

'Close down this mystery. The mystery of Gurs. Once and for all?'

He sighed.

'Yes. Who better than the Society? They already know the whole story because their roots go back to Vichy, and *l'occupation*. When this began. Right-wing French priests were chaplains at Gurs. They tortured Cagots, and Jews, despite themselves.'

The picture, at least half of it, was now revealed to David. He gazed through the dark potted firs, at the blue Bay of Biscay. He talked to himself, quietly:

'Everywhere we went . . . we went into churches. Navvarenx, Savin, Luz. Eloise's house was opposite a church. She went into the church at Campan . . .'

'*Exactement*. The Society has maybe asked for help in their search for you . . . from the wider church. Priests and nuns and ecclesiastical officials, are maybe identifying you as you move from place to place. Let us say the average priest does not even know why he has been asked to do this. But he will do it because he is obedient. Loyalty means much, in this part of the world.'

Amy spoke up: 'And then the information would be passed to the Society? And then to Miguel?'

'*Et voilà*. But what else do we know? I do not have to explain one thing, do I? Miguel's motivation.' The policeman sipped his coffee, and flicked a glance towards the sea, then returned his attention to the table.

'Garovillo *fils* must have been brought up a Basque radical. Violently proud of his Basque heritage. And then – then one

249

day, he discovers from his father that he is not Basque, but a Cagot, a despised *Cagot.* Miguel Garovillo would have been shattered, destroyed. And then he must have resolved.' Sarria frowned. 'Resolved that he would do anything to keep this secret hidden, kill anyone who threatened to reveal the humiliating truth about his father – and about Miguel himself. Along the way his wishes happily coincided with the wishes of the Society. Maybe they recruited him at that point, maybe the two Garovillo men were already members. So it all folded into place.'

David spoke up. 'And on top of that his ETA status helped him. Right? He would have the guns and the bombs and the expertise. To kill.'

'*Vraiment.* And one day, Miguel found out that *your* parents were in France, researching the Cagots, and staying near Gurs. Asking questions at the Brasserie d'Hagetmau. That would have scared Miguel, alerted him to danger. The Wolf took action. *Alors.*'

The frail laughter of a child carried on the coastal breeze. A brief glimpse of personal emotion, of sincere sadness, crossed Sarria's face. He added:

'But this, of course, is all too late for your family, Monsieur Martinez. I am sorry I could not do more. I tried. Please forgive me?'

David quietly nodded. But he didn't really mean it: he didn't want to forgive, he didn't want contrition: he wanted answers. As many answers as possible. His determination was returning, he wanted vengeance for his mother and his father. *For his unborn sister.* But to do that he needed to see the whole picture. Before Miguel could destroy the evidence.

He spoke up: 'But, Officer Sarria, the link with Gurs? What happened *there*?'

Sarria shrugged his ignorance. 'That I cannot tell you –

because I simply do not know. No one seems to know. What I can say is this . . .'

He leaned to the centre of the table, his voice low and concerned: 'I can only protect you so far. You are in danger. Very serious danger. The Society, and its powerful political sympathizers, they still want you dead. They *need* you dead.'

'So what the hell do we do?' Amy said. Her arms were crossed. 'Where can we go? Britain's too dangerous. Spain likewise. Where else?'

'*Anywhere*. You do not know what danger you are in . . .' Sarria glanced significantly at David and Amy. 'Maybe this can assist. If you need motivating.'

He reached in a briefcase, and pulled out a large brown envelope. He opened the envelope and extracted a sheaf of photographs.

'These are the photos from the Gurs murder. Eloise's grandmother, Madame Bentayou. I was not sure whether to show them to you. But . . . but maybe you need to see them.'

David picked up a few of the glossy photos. Hesitantly. He was about to see what Eloise had seen through the window at the bungalow. What she could not, would not describe: the unspeakable murder of her grandmother.

He steeled himself, then looked at the biggest photo.

'Oh Jesus.'

The photo showed the entire murder scene.

Madame Bentayou's body was lying on the kitchen floor, a floor that was smeared with her own blood. Her body was identifiable from the clothes – and the tartan slippers; but there was no face to confirm this identification. Because her head had been cut off.

Not only had it been cut off, it seemed to have been *pulled* off. The jagged nature of the grotesque wound, the shredding and ribboning of the skin, the stretched elastic of the

251

tormented ligaments, they all implied that her head had been wrenched away; as if someone had sawn halfway through her neck, then given up in anger, impatience – or blood lust. David tried not to imagine the scene: the terrorist pulling at the living head, until the neckbone split and the ligaments snapped.

And that was not all. Someone – Miguel – surely Miguel – had also cut off the hands: the old woman's wrists were bleeding stumps, trailing veins and muscles. Puddles of blood extended from the stumps like flattened red gloves.

And then the hands had been *nailed to the door*. Several more photos showed the hands, impaled.

Two decomposing hands. Nailed. On the kitchen door.

Amy was hiding her face behind her fingers.

'Horrible. Horrible horrible horrible . . .'

Sarria murmured, 'I know. I am sorry. And there is more.'

David swore. 'How can there be more? How much worse can it be?'

The officer opened the envelope again, and pulled out a final photo. It was a close-up of one of the severed hands. He pointed to the left of the photo, with his pen.

David squinted, and scrutinized. There seemed to be . . . an arc of marks on the flesh. Faint, but definitely there. A curved row of small indentations in the pale flesh.

'Is that . . .' He fought his own revulsion. 'Is that . . . what I think it is?'

'*Oui*. A human bite. A bite mark. It looks a little experimental . . . as if someone has just, impulsively, tried to bite the human flesh. To see what it tastes like.'

Silence ensued. The waves were lullaby rhythms on the beach. And then the other policeman leaned in. And spoke for the very first time.

'*Allez*. Go. Anywhere. Before he finds you.'

29

The house was suitably quiet. The bored, yawning police constable – their guard and protector – was lying on the bed in the spare room, reading *Goal*. Suzie was working at the hospital: she'd refused to give up her work but allowed herself to be escorted on her commute. The au pair had fled back to Slovenia, two days ago, unnerved by the blood on the floor; Suzie's mother had come to stay, to help look after Conor.

And Simon was reading about Eugen Fischer.

The online biography of the German scientist was stark:

'Eugen Fischer (July 5, 1874 – July 9, 1967) was a German professor of medicine, anthropology and eugenics. He was a key proponent of Nazi scientific theories of racial hygiene that legitimized the extermination of Jews, sent an estimated half a million gypsies to their deaths, and led to the compulsory sterilization of hundreds of thousands of other victims.'

Simon sat ten inches from his screen, a metal savour of distaste in his mouth. Three intriguing aspects stood out in Fischer's extended life story. The first was Fischer's strong links with Africa.

'In 1908 Eugen Fischer conducted field research in

German Southwest Africa, now Namibia. He studied the offspring of "Aryan" men who had fathered children by native women. He concluded that the offspring of such unions – so-called "mischlinge" – should be eradicated after their usefulness had ended.'

Eradicated? Usefulness? Concluded?? The words were all the more powerful for being so dry and antiseptic.

Simon breathed in, and breathed out. And momentarily closed his eyes. Immediately, an image of Tomasky's surging anger filled his mental gaze, and he snapped open his eyes once again. He could hear Conor playing in the room next door, vroom vrooming his favourite toy car into its toy garage.

Listening now to his son's chatter, the boy talking to himself, Simon felt the fierce undertow of parental love: the painful protectiveness. Protect Conor. Protect him from all the evil in the world.

But the best way of doing that was by *staying focussed*. He returned to work.

'Hitler was an avowed admirer of Eugen Fischer, especially the professor's magnum opus *Menschliche Erblichkeitslehre und Rassenhygiene* (Human Heredity and Racial Hygiene). On his accession to power in 1933, Hitler appointed Fischer rector of Berlin University.

'The Nazi conquest of Europe (1939–1942) gave Fischer, with the ardent encouragement of Adolf Hitler, the opportunity to extend his racial research, which he had begun decades before in Namibia. In the concentration camp of Gurs, in Nazi-occupied southwest France, Fischer commenced a series of detailed studies of various European races: Basques, gypsies, Jews, etc.'

Simon was scribbling urgently now. Eyes on the screen, eyes on the pad in front of him. And more:

'The Nazi regime poured money into the "medical division" at Gurs. Rumours at the time spoke of significant discoveries achieved by the so-called Fischer experiments. However, the data recovered by Fischer at Gurs was lost in the chaos of the Allied invasion of Europe and the destruction of the Nazi regime (1944–1945). It has never been conclusively proved whether the Fischer experiments yielded scientifically valuable results. The consesnsus, today, is that the rumours of "racial discoveries" were Nazi propaganda in themselves, and that Fischer revealed nothing of importance.'

The final section on Fischer's life was tantalizing, yet even more mystifying.

'Many people were scandalized when, following the Allied defeat of the Third Reich, Eugen Fischer escaped serious punishment for his connections to, and research for, the Nazis. Indeed, he later became Professor Emeritus at Freiburg University, and in 1952 he was appointed as honorary president of the newly-founded German Anthropological Society.

'This extraordinary indulgence of a scientist seen as a founder and mentor of Nazi racial politics was by no means unique. Many of Fischer's colleagues at Gurs and elsewhere also escaped punishment, or endured at most a few weeks of "deNazification" in prison. For example, Professor Doctor Fritz Lenz, the head of eugenics at Berlin Dahlem, and a co-author of key works on Nazi racial theory, returned to work immediately after the war, and was offered the chair in human heredity at the University of Gottingen.'

These last assertions were so bizarre Simon read the whole passage twice. Then he read it again. Then he checked it on another website, which repeated the statement word for word.

Word for word? Simon began to wonder if the remarkable claim was simply a lie, perpetuated by the lazy scholastic standards of the internet.

He got up, opened the door, and walked into the living

room. Conor was playing on the carpet with his toys, transfixed by the adventures of Derek the Diesel Engine.

There – the bookshelves. High up on the highest shelf, gathering dust these ten years, was his father's old *Encyclopedia Britannica*. Simon pulled down the volume, paged quickly to Lenz, Fritz.

It was true. This beast, this horrible man, this expounder of eugenics, this friend of Mengele, this thinker behind Nazism, had calmly returned to work in 1946. *He hadn't even gone to jail*. The Allies didn't even put him in jail.

Why were all these doctors just . . . let off?

He tousled his son's blond hair, then returned to his study and shut the door. Again. He was excited. The mystery was coming alive, but it was coiled upon itself, like a snake, a cobra, hissing. Concealing what lay within.

His afternoon was nearly done. He went over the facts by writing down the words in an email to himself – one of his favourite ways of resolving a puzzle. Like an artist turning his own drawing upside down, to see it afresh, to spot the flaws, assess the quality.

Simon sat back from the computer, and sighed. His thoughts were incoherent, they were drivel, they were utter nonsense. Money, Nazis, Cagots, possible collaboration, so what? He had no overarching explanation for the murders: which now seemed almost random.

He felt his momentary excitement subside. He was almost back to where he started. He needed to speak to David and Amy. He needed to speak to David. Where were they? What was happening down there in southern France?

He remembered Tomasky's sister. What she had said. A monastery in France.

In France? A monastery called Tourette.

Hunched forward, Simon typed.

The screen returned his answer at once.

256

The monastery of La Tourette.

Built between 1953–1960, at the instigation of Reverend Father Couturier of the Dominican Order of Lyon. Architect Charles Edouard Jeanneret-Gris (known as Le Corbusier).

Simon paused.

The Dominican Order?

He remembered what Professor Winyard had told him. The Dominicans. The Dogs of God. The burners of witches. The hammer of witches. The *Malleus Malleficarum*.

Now his pulse quickened, dramatically. This monastery was apparently near Lyon. *Near Lyon?*

David Martinez had told Simon about the map that had been owned by David's father and handed on by David's grandfather. On that map, as Simon recalled, was one curious outlier, one hand-drawn blue star that was way beyond the Basque region, way outside the purlieus of the Cagots. Wasn't that near Lyon? Or was it Marseilles? It was Lyon, wasn't it?

The mystery coiled and hissed.

He read on.

Le Corbusier, the websites told him, was the greatest architect of the last century. He was also renowned for his purity, his cleanliness of vision: utilizing the precept *form follows function*. Everything he did was deliberate. He was also known as an atheist, 'therefore the commission to design this post-war monastery of La Tourette came as a surprise'.

But many things about this monastery were, it seemed, a surprise. Where the money came from – in impoverished post-war France. Why the Dominicans suddenly decided to construct a large priory when so many old and war-damaged buildings were in need of repair. Most of all, why the building had such a strange design.

As one book phrased it: Le Corb's idea was that living in this building, 'La Tourette', should be, in itself, a penance. The daunting nature of the structure, the difficulty of living

257

within it, should be part of the austerities of the monastic life.

These austerities, it seemed, were more than theoretical. The building was 'largely finished' in 1953. By 1955 'half the initial community of monks had mental disorders'. These included nervous breakdowns and major depressions, and they occurred precisely 'because the building was so oppressive'. The jarring spaces and the brutalism of the design apparently tipped the denizens over the edge.

Another factor, one critic claimed, in the 'outright unpleasantness' of the building, was the acoustics. At night 'every single sound in the building was amplified'. Every breath, every whisper, every snore. This was apparently 'a function of the concrete fabric and the inherently echoic spaces': in other words, the hostile nature of the building was a deliberate feature, *designed to disorientate*.

There was one more website. It was an architecture blog. A simple, humble blog, written by an architecture student from Brisbane. Who had apparently stayed at La Tourette a few summers back, after years of research on Le Corbusier.

The essay began with a short autobiographical note. And then launched into a blistering attack on the architect.

The basic allegation of the student was that Le Corbusier was a Nazi. During the war years, it seemed, Le Corbusier was very close to Pétain, the leader of the puppet French fascist regime of Vichy. Le Corbusier was also, the author alleged, a big fan of Hitler. The essay quoted one 'notorious' remark, when the architect said the Führer was 'marvellous'.

The blog attempted a counterbalancing argument. Admitting that Le Corbusier was not alone, that many architects had fascist or Marxist sympathies: because architects are utopians. *Architects want to change society. It doesn't necessarily make them Nazis or communists or killers . . .*

The blogpost drew to a close with another barb. It made the

claim that Le Corbusier's famous building in Marseilles, the *Unite d'Habitation*, was the most popular place to commit suicide in the South of France. And yet, the essay said, the monastery of La Tourette was even more oppressive – the only reason it didn't see so many suicides was because visitors tended to flee after a few days. The monks had to stay, and suffered terribly, and yet their religious vocations prevented self murder.

And then the essayist asked the obvious question: Why? Why did the Dominicans mysteriously commission a man like Le Corbusier to build a mysterious structure like this?

Simon shut down the computer to listen to the silence in his study, and the major chord of logic in his mind.

The essay blog might have finished on a query. But the answer was obvious, to Simon. *Form follows function*: that was Le Corbusier's lifelong belief. The function of this building was maybe to shelter facts, maybe appalling facts. The building was a subtly authentic statement of that sinister function. Herein lies evil. Do not come near. Like the vivid and offputting colouration of a poisonous insect.

He recalled Professor Winyard's exact words about those vital documents: the materials relating to the blood tests of the Cagots and the burning of the Basque witches. The documents suppressed and hidden by the Papacy.

'They were kept at the Angelicum, the Dominican University in Rome. For centuries they were safe. But then after the war, after the Nazis, they were felt to be less safe, too provocative. There are rumours that they were spirited away, to somewhere more secure. But no one knows where.'

No one knows where? Really? How about a strange Dominican monastery, built after the war, and associated with Vichy and the Nazis?

The mystery was now a nightflower, slowly opening beneath the moon. Scenting the midnight garden.

But he needed one more confirmation. He had to reach

David Martinez and confirm the star on the map. Had to reach him *now*.

Simon tried to calm himself. He stood up, walked to the kitchen, and made himself a cup of camomile tea, as he had once heard that camomile tea was calming.

Fuck camomile tea. He hurled the tea in the sink, ran back to his study and pointlessly called Martinez's phone number. The tone was dead. He tried again three seconds later, as if that would change something. The tone was dead. As he well knew, David had junked his phone: very sensibly.

So what now? Surely David Martinez would ring again at *some* point, from Biarritz, unless he was unable?

Simon paced his study, from one wall to the other. Fretting about David and Amy, trying not to remember the attack of Tomasky.

Walking from wall to wall took him three and a half seconds. Their house was so damnably tiny. It was way too small. Maybe if Simon cracked this remarkable story he could write that great book and buy a bigger house and . . .

Enough. Simon sat down at the computer and sent David Martinez an email. Then he exited his study, and joined his son on the sofa in the living room, and they watched, for the seventeenth time, *Monsters, Inc.*

Then they watched it again.

It was seven p.m. and Conor was in bed when his mobile rang – with a French number on the screen. Trying to convince himself that his heart wasn't beating like a Burundi drum, Simon took the call.

'Yes . . . hello?'

'Simon?'

'*David?* Thank God you called. Are you OK? Are you and Amy OK?'

'Yes – we're OK – we're still in Biarritz, but we're flying out. But what about y—'

'Nothing. I'm fine, I mean, ah, there's something I need to know.' Simon felt guilty for cutting so brutally to the chase, but his anxiety allowed him no option. 'David, *tell me* – do you have the map on you?'

'Yeah, of course. Everyone wants to look at this map . . .'

'*Please*. This is important. Get it out. You said there was a star, marked near Lyon . . .'

'That's right. Near Lyon . . . We never managed to work out what it meant.'

'Please take another look.'

Simon could hear the obedient unfolding of paper, and traffic in the background. David was obviously using a landline. An anonymous payphone in a little Basque city.

David came back on.

'Here's the star. What do you want to know?'

The moment of tension dilated.

'Tell me,' Simon said. 'Where exactly it is. What, ah, village, what town . . .'

The journalist could almost hear David peering closely at the map.

David came back on.

'It's quite distinct. It's next to a tiny village called Eveux.'

'Eveux?'

A pause.

'Yes, Eveux . . . that's near L'Arbresle . . . northwest of Lyon.' David's voice was now sharpened. '*Why do you want to know this?*'

Simon didn't answer, because he was stooping to look at his computer screen, at the entry on La Tourette. The website gave the monastery its full and sonorous French title.

Le Priore de Sainte Marie de La Tourette.

De Eveux-sur-L'Arbresle.

30

The hire car was slotted in row 3B of the airport car park at Lyon Saint Exupéry. Bags stowed, Simon pulled out into the midday traffic, and made for the autoroute that took him away from Lyon.

North along the Rhone valley.

He considered his moody impulsiveness. Was this all a mistake? He had asked Suzie what she thought of this journey, this sombre adventure; and she'd told him, with a certain languish in her eyes, that she'd agree to him going because she loved him. And because they were safe with the policeman anyway. And because he was going mad in the house doing nothing, he might end up drinking again, and she was worried about that.

Simon stared at the cars ahead. The autoroute was busy.

He knew almost everything Suzie had said had been a lie. She *didn't* want him to go. She thought it was *irresponsible* of him to go. The only reason she agreed to his going was indeed because she loved him. He was lucky to have her.

And he was an idiot.

But he was here now. And, whatever his motives, the

excitement of the chase *was* stimulating, energizing. What would this place be like? The monastery that sent people mad? Would he find the infamous archives? Simon glanced at the autoroute signs as he slowed the car: Ecully, Dardilly, Charbonnieres-les-Bains.

There. He slowed to check a road sign: this was it. The N7 to L'Arbresle.

Simon spun the wheel and headed left. He was motoring through the verdant depths of the Beaujolais. His thoughts wandered as he reached for the big road atlas of France, to check his route. A few hundred miles southwest from here, in Biarritz, David and Amy were hiding, hoping, waiting, flying out to Namibia.

What could he do to help them? Maybe nothing, maybe something, maybe what he was doing right now. His mind was a turmoil of confusion – and curiosity.

The last of the route took him past more vineyards, and yellowing copses of oak. Then the lane gave out, onto a wide sweeping meadow. And in the middle was the monastery of La Tourette.

Alone in the car, he said:

'Wow.'

He'd done a few hours' research on this modernist building, quizzed his architect father about the designer, Le Corbusier, but the reality was still pretty startling.

In the middle of the greenery was this . . . *thing*. It looked like the offspring of a multi-storey car park mated with a sour medieval castle. The building was almost uniformly grey. The only colour came from the various big windows, adorned with bright red and orange curtains.

Slowly he rolled the car towards the priory complex. More unusual aspects came into view. A surreal concrete pyramid jutted primly from the centre. Several grey corridors seemed to be angled, haphazardly. The whole edifice was supported on one side by a bank of grass, and on the other by spindly, irregular concrete legs.

Simon parked, and sought the entrance: it was a kind of concrete gantry that led to the core of the building.

The exterior may have been shocking, but his induction into Sainte Marie de La Tourette was simple, almost flippant. The monastery and the monks were obviously used to visitors and pilgrims, especially people interested in architecture. Simon was greeted by a monk in blue jeans and grey T-shirt, in a concrete side room.

As Simon confirmed his bogus, telephone-booked identity – Edgar Harrison, a visiting British architect – he twitched with apprehension, and searched the monk's face for a hint of curiosity, or scepticism, or suspicion.

But the monk just nodded.

'Monsieur Harrison. *Un moment.*'

The monk jotted down the name and details, *on a computer.* Simon scanned this side room as he waited to be processed. The space was humdrum, an average office, with files and paperwork, cordless phones and a fax machine, and a big glass case with keys for various rooms, hanging from hooks with neat little labels. *Le Refectoire, Le Libraire, La Cuisine.*

Le Libraire? At least there *was* a library. But if its contents were so secret why was it just casually mentioned here? *Le Libraire?*

The monk had done his work; he stood and took a key from another case, then escorted Simon to the concrete upper floors to show him his allotted room, the monastic cell where he would spend his three days on 'retreat'. The stairs were steep. They didn't speak. They reached their upper-level corridor.

The doors were lined up and down the concrete corridors like tall soldiers on parade. It really was like a prison.

The monk handed over the key, then left the pilgrim to his own devices. Simon entered the room, chucked his bag on his narrow bed, and gazed around – in dismay. The cell was homicidally oppressive: little wider than a coffin, with a low, damp concrete ceiling. The room terminated in a glass door and window with rusted surrounds. And there were sullen noises everywhere. Rattles of water in the pipes. A cough.

Then a phone call: on his new mobile. When Simon pressed *Accept*, the worry in his chest was like an incipient heart attack. Only his wife had this new number. What had happened?

But it was David.

'Simon . . . Where are you? Suzie gave me the new number.'

The journalist looked around. At the grey concrete walls. Patched with ugly dampness. He stepped outside into the corridor, to get a better signal.

'I'm in that monastery.'

'With the archives?'

'Well I hope so, David. I hope so.'

A monk came striding down the corridor. A wooden cross hung around his neck, contrasting with the surfing T-shirt underneath. He smiled, vacantly, at Simon. Who smiled keenly in return.

David was whispering into the phone. 'We're going to Namibia. Now.'

'Eloise is already there? Correct?'

'Yes.'

'OK. Well . . .' The journalist sighed. 'Please be careful. It's, ah, clearly ludicrous. You're being pursued by a bloody madman. But . . . *Be careful!*'

A silence. Then David said: 'Same for you, Simon. I know I never met you, but . . . y'know . . . take care of yourself?'

265

'Thank you.'

The journalist closed the call. And began his exploration of the building. *Le Priore de Sainte Marie de La Tourette.*

Two hours of wandering told him that the rest of La Tourette was as bizarre, and intimidating, as the cells. Odd doors opened into misshapen rooms. Occasional skylights showed the grey clouds from startling angles. Concrete joists thrust into empty space: they seemed to have no purpose other than to knock an unwary pilgrim on the head.

It was intriguing enough, but also disappointing. There was no intimation of mystery, no *sense* of any concealed archives. And the library was just a library – on the third floor of the building. It was not hidden at all and the contents were thoroughly ordinary. There were no ancient texts chained to shelves. No papal parchments in mahogany chests. No musty manuscripts bound in goatskin. There was nothing but racks of regular books and large metal tables. Even a drinks machine.

It felt positively municipal.

Sighing, heavily, Simon sat down at one of the tables, to search in some of the books – but his lifeless research was interrupted by another phone call.

Why so many?

He stepped outside into another bleak concrete corridor.

It was Bill Fanthorpe, the psychiatrist from St Hilary.

'Hi, Bill, I –'

'Hello, Simon. I'm sorry to bother you. But . . .' The doctor's voice was tinged with anxiety.

'What is it, Bill?'

'I'm afraid Tim has disappeared.'

A faint rumble echoed through the building. The sound of the Lyon–Paris TGV rumbling in the forested distance.

'Disappeared?'

'Yes. But please do not concern yourself, not overly.'

'Jesus. *Bill* –'

'This happens all the time, of course.' Fanthorpe's tone of worry had quickly faded, replaced by studied calmness. 'Schizophrenics can be exceptionally perambulatory. And of course Tim wandered off before, two years ago.'

'But when? When did he run away? How?'

The doctor hesitated.

'We think last night. As I was saying –' A thoughtful pause. 'I understand you have personal concerns for the safety of your family. Your wife told me. Therefore . . . We have been in touch with the police but they assure us there is no question of . . .' Another, slightly awkward pause. 'No question of foul play, as it were. But it was a serious lapse in security. My apologies.'

'Jesus *Christ*.'

'Please. Calm down. We will find him. Quite likely by tonight. Just as we found him the last time.'

Simon stared at the damp grey patch on the opposite concrete wall. This was all his fault. He had run off. He had left his family unprotected *for no good reason*. Why was he even here?

He had quit the house in the early morning, not telling the cops what he was doing – taking a taxi, then the train, then the first plane from Heathrow to Lyon – just so he could chase the *wildest* of geese, the *ludicrous* dream that he was some Watergating superjournalist, going to crack the biggest story in a decade.

What a fool he had been. In reality he was just a second-division crime reporter, already in his forties, who'd wasted too many years on booze, and was all-too-desperate to catch up with his peers, by pursuing some deluded fantasy. He was going nowhere. And his brother was now . . . escaped, on the run, in the wilds. Doing what? How was he surviving?

Now he thought of Tomasky; he tried not to think about Tomasky. Tried very hard.

With a jolt, he realized he was still holding the phone in his hand – and Bill Fanthorpe was still on the line. He apologized to the doctor, rang off, and instantly called his wife.

She confirmed what Fanthorpe had said: it seemed innocent enough, Tim had indeed just wandered off, it was not the first time he'd gone walkabout, last time they found him within twelve hours . . .

But Simon was not reassured. He told Suzie he loved her, loudly, not caring who might overhear his conversation. Then he told her he was coming home as soon as he could.

'OK, Simon. Of course . . .' Her tone was solicitous. Loving. More than he deserved.

'I'll call you later, sweetheart.'

He made his second urgent call of the day. The airport. The information was not what he wanted. He had already missed the last flight of the day from Lyon to London.

The next flight was at dawn. That was the fastest way back to London. If he wanted to go back immediately – he would have to wait until dawn.

After the briefest hesitation, he booked the flight.

So that was it. He would stay today, then leave before sunrise, and fly home from Lyon. He had this afternoon, and the evening, to see if he could find anything. And then he must return to his family. Protect them.

Simon continued his doomed and hapless search. He felt like a jerk even as he explored. He made for the roof. The roof was flat as his mood. It was grassed over. Odd, boxlike structures formed modernist gargoyles.

Then he took the lift down. The depths of the building comprised the religious core of the monastery: a large, dark, enigmatic chapel, semi-submerged into the slope underneath, and illuminated by slender stained glass windows on one side only.

And that was it, that was the chapel, and that was the

monastery. Acceding to his nerves, he retreated to a concrete cloister and frantically texted Suzie the question: *any news?*

She texted back: *no news.*

Anguished, almost furious, he aimed himself at the library, yet again. Maybe there *was* something here. There were certainly lots of books. But they were boring books. French books. Irrelevant books. Books by Aquinas. A history of the Blackfriars. A life of St Dominic. A selection of architectural monographs for the architectural pilgrims. One slim French biography of Pope Pius the Tenth did pique his interest, but then he noticed maybe three hundred other books in the same series: lives of all the other popes in history.

There were two other people in the concrete room, besides himself. A young woman was immersed in a yellow jacketed volume by Le Corbusier: *Vers un Architecture Libre.* The other companion was a monk, wearing a cardigan and slacks, and glasses so thick they made him look like a nervous treefrog.

Simon drove the thought of Tim from his mind. The thought climbed back into his brain, through the window of his soul. Where was Tim? Wandering some road? Asleep in a stairwell? Buying a big fat knife?

There was nothing Simon could do, not from here, not right now. He needed to distract himself with work. Pessimistically, he leafed another text: a glossy modern volume about the monastery's unique design. It mentioned several interesting features: the book went into great detail about 'light cannons' and 'pilotis'.

Sitting back, he sighed, and looked around. The large tall windows of the library gave onto the endless farms and vineyards. The monastery was very isolated. Squat and strange and lonely under the grey-black Lyonnais sky.

An autumn storm was brewing: a grandiose affair. The first thunderclaps drumrolled across the Rhone Valley, making the building positively vibrate. Even the mute little monk looked up from his studies at the noise, his bug eyes rolling.

The noise of the booming thunder was like two parents arguing upstairs, overheard by a small and terrified child; it was like the muffled but ominous sounds of someone falling to the floor, in a bedroom.

Das Helium und das Hydrogen.

The journalist shuddered, and turned to the book at the end of the table. The visitor's book. It was a huge leather job: at least a thousand pages thick, with entries dating back decades. He flicked through the most recent entries, at least those written in English.

'The noises at night: unbearable.'

'An expression of pure genius.'

'The most beautiful building in the world. And also the ugliest.'

'I have found serenity here. *Merci.*'

Lightning flashed across the darkling valley, briefly dazzling the grey walls and the orange curtains. Vast curtains of rain were marching down the valley. Drenching the little hamlet of Eveux-sur-L'Arbresle.

Eveux and L'Arbresle?

Eveux . . . sur . . . L'Arbresle.

A stir. Something stirred in the middle of his whirring anxiety, centred on Tim; he realized he *was* forgetting something.

The star on David's map: the asterisk so carefully inscribed by David's father, Eduardo. The monastery might be a narrative cul de sac, but Eduardo *had* thought it was important.

Could he? *Had he?*

Quick and urgent, Simon paged back through the visitor's book, working out dates in his head. When was the accident that killed the Martinez couple? He recalled the information, and fixed the date in his mind, and then he turned to the correct page in the visitor's book. Fifteen years ago.

He was at the correct page. He looked down the list of names. People from France, America, Spain, Germany . . . Then a lot of people just from Germany and France. And then . . .

There?

His heartbeat matched the booming thunder in the valleys of the Beaujolais.

He'd found a piquant comment in English. The comment said: *To search is to find?*

Then came the details of the pilgrim. City: *Norwich.* Country: *England.* Date of visit: *August 17th.*

Then finally the name.

Eduardo Martinez.

31

It took three days for them to arrange flights to Namibia. At last they headed out of the hotel for their furtive evening flight to Frankfurt. From Germany they made the nightflight eight thousand miles south.

Across the equator, across all the darkness of Africa – to Namibia.

They remained quiet and subdued, even with each other. Even when they were safely on the plane to Africa they hardly spoke, as if the momentousness of what they were doing barely needed explaining. Flying into the unknown.

While the plane traversed the vast and lightless Sahara David wondered what they would find in Africa – would they locate Angus Nairn and Eloise? What if something had happened to them? What if they couldn't find them? What then? Just hide on a beach? Forever? That's if they survived any infection they had caught. From the corpses in the cellar.

He tried to stifle his fears. Whatever their fate, this mystery needed to be resolved – so seeking out the centre of the mystery was the right thing to do. If they were being chased they may as well try and outflank their pursuers, get to the solution first. Another reason to take the gamble, to fly to Namibia.

Amy was dozing next to him. David picked up the inflight magazine and flipped to the atlas pages: Namibia was a huge country. A big orange rectangle. He scrutinized the names of the few towns indicated.

Windhoek. Uis. Luderitz. Aus. Very German. Relics of the German Empire. But there were so *few* towns? A big empty nothingness.

For most of the twelve-hour flight, Amy slept. Sheer exhaustion. David watched her beloved face, and draped her with an airline blanket to keep her warm. Her breathing slowed into deeper unconsciousness.

Eventually David, too, shut his eyes, and waded into sleep.

The next time he woke, the sun was blazing hot through the opened portholes, and they were landing in an airport the likes of which he had never seen before.

It was desert. Even the airport was desert. A couple of pathetic palm trees fringed the grey dusty runway, but immediately beyond the tarmac huge sand dunes rose, like frozen orange tidal waves, with wisps of dust whipping off the top.

The groggy passengers descended the ladder – into the furious heat. The African sun burned as soon as it touched the skin. Amy lifted a magazine to shield her face, David turned up his shirt collar to protect his neck. The airport – the island of baking asphalt in a sea of hot sand – was so tiny they could walk to the terminal in two minutes.

Passport control was three impassive guys apparently speaking English; ten minutes later they were on Namibian territory. A smiling black taxi driver approached them as they exited the terminal building into the starkly sunlit car park. Where did they want to go?

Their furtive researches in the cybercafes of Biarritz had yielded some results: Swakopmund, the place Eloise was directing them, was on the coast, in the centre of the Namibian littoral. It was also, it seemed, where they might find people willing to take them into the deserts and the mountains. Trekkers and outfitters.

David said to the cab driver, 'Swakopmund. Please?'

'OK! Swakop!'

The bags were thrown casually in the boot. The taxi spun out of the car park and onto a road that cut through the desert. Through the dazzle of the clear African air, David could see a thin horizon of blue.

'Is that the sea?'

'Yes sir!' the taxi driver said. 'Walvis and Swakop by the sea. By the sea with many many flamingoes. But do not make schwimmen, very jellyfish and many many sharks.'

The car swerved, they were being buffeted by a fierce wind. The driver laughed.

'You come wrong season!'

'We have?'

'Winter is cold. Windy and maybe even rain.'

'Cold?'

'Yes sir. But Swakop always windy. But cold now. Benguela current.'

David stared out at the endless enormous undulating dunes; they were a harsh yellow-white in the remorseless sun. Sand was blowing across the road – orange snakes of dust, writhing and dissolving.

Now they were here, the desire to find Eloise seemed a rather forlorn decision, almost quixotic. They were in a land of nothingness, a country of mighty desolation, with a population of barely two million scattered across a sun-crushed vastness the size of France and Britain combined; they were looking for one man and one woman. In the wilderness. Would this hotel even exist?

The cab driver was pointing. 'Swakop!'

David stared at the cityscape as they rolled down the streets. The sense of dislocation was profound. Looming suddenly from the sand was a pastiche Bavarian town: gingerbread houses, spired German churches, little Teutonic shops with curlicued Gothic signs for German newspapers and Becks bier. Yet the pavements were busy with black people, and orangey-beige people, and a few couples that looked American or maybe Australian, as well as obviously German people wearing . . . lederhosen?

The cab driver took them to the hotel Eloise had named; he approved of their choice because of his brother who had once stayed there and 'had so many oysters he was sick'. The hotel was big, white, scruffy and the paint was blistered by the wind but it was right on the sea, overlooking the pier and the wild, blue-grey ocean.

Some white guys were fishing off the pier, in thick anoraks and jumpers. Bloodstained buckets of oily fish showed their success. They were talking in German and laughing. They were munching black cake.

When David saw the fish in the pail he thought of the elvers that José had cooked: his last meal. Then the gunshots, the suicide, the obscene blurt of blood on the wall. The body liquor squelched across the cellar floor.

They bought fleeces at the hotel shop. Then they showered and changed and began their quest. At once. They were tired, to the point of exhaustion – but the need to find Eloise was urging them on. Driving the weariness away with two strong coffees, each, they attempted to do what they had come for. Find safety, find Eloise, find an answer.

Their 'contact' was a deputy manager at the hotel: Raymond. After a few minutes' searching they located him, a small, rather sad looking Namibian, peering at an aged computer screen in the office behind Reception.

He took one quick look at them – a white man and a

white woman asking for information about Eloise – and he nodded, gravely. Then he said:

'I know what you have come for. But first you must tell me.' He almost bowed. 'What was Eloise doing the moment you first saw her?'

David came right back with the answer:

'She was in her house, with a shotgun, pointed at us.'

A knowing nod was their response. Raymond turned, and reached down to the drawer of his desk to retrieve, and hand over, a slip of paper. Written on it was a row of digits and letters. David recognized the style.

'GPS coordinates.'

'Yes.'

'But where?'

The deputy manager shrugged.

'Damaraland? The bush. That is all I know . . . Now please I work, I am sorry – we are very busy. Swiss tourists.'

He glanced at them – with a sharp, wary expression. He obviously wanted these worrying people with these strange arrangements out of his office. This was fair enough, but it didn't leave Amy and David much better off than before. A bunch of coordinates, pointing them into the wilderness? David knew from his reading that Damaraland was a truly vast expanse of desert and semi desert, north and east of Swakop. How could they find someone, one or two people, in the middle of that? Even with GPS?

They got straight to work, finding someone to take them in-country. But it was hard; it was impossible. They stepped into travel shops, car hire companies, outfitters for treks. When they explained their requirement, the shop managers and outdoorsmen openly laughed. One Australian guy, in shorts despite the cold, threw a manly arm around David's shoulder, and said: 'Listen, mate, *Damaraland*? There are no roads. You need an expedition. You need two or three

276

fourbys, and a fucking bunch of guns. This isn't Hyde Park. Try kitesurfing.'

And so it went, and so it continued, and then the fog came. They'd been there for two days of increasing anxiety and it was windy and cold throughout; and then the weather worsened. The Swakopmund fog descended: the infamous mists of the Skeleton Coast.

It was like Scotland in December: thick and dismal, shrouding the gay little cakeshops in dankness, sending the lederhosened German tour groups into their warm snug hotels, veiling completely the black factory boats that floated inert on the cold Namibian sea; only the yellow-orange men sitting on their haunches seemed impervious: narrowing their sunburned eyes, and sitting in their cardigans and holey jeans, staring at the grey damp nothing. They looked like the Basque men, in berets, staring at the mountain fog in the villages of the high Pyrenees.

On the foggiest night of all, as they were getting truly desperate, when they were shivering their way along Moltkestrasse, they found a bar they hadn't seen before: Beckenbauer Bar.

It was tiny and gabled and Bavarian-looking, and it was noisy, even from fifty metres away. Keen to escape the shrouding dampness they stepped inside the bar, which was giddy and packed; people were singing in German and ordering steins of lager and clashing the steins together. Chortling.

Amy and David found a table in the corner and sat down, warm at last. A black waiter came over and he asked them, above the noise of the singing German voices, if they wanted anything.

David said, hesitantly: *'Ein bier . . .?'*

The man smiled. 'It's OK. I speak English. Tafel or Windhoek?'

'Ah,' said David, slightly blushing. 'Tafel, I guess.'

Amy was staring, with an expression of perplexity, at the exuberant and warbling German men. She motioned to the barman as he turned to go.

'Excuse me?'

'Yes, miss.'

'Why . . .' She was talking quietly. 'Why are they so happy?'

The waiter half shrugged.

'I think it is Ascenscion Day. I believe.'

Amy frowned.

'Ascension Day, that's forty days after Easter, isn't it? Usually in May.' Her frown deepened. 'This is September.'

The waiter nodded.

'No, not Jesus. Hitler.'

32

Simon tried not to shout as he read the visitor's book: to shout in triumph. David's father *had been here*. His father had actually been here. Fifteen years ago. He'd worked out the same link. He was halfway through the same mystery.

The last thunderclap abated. And then Simon's excitement faded. So David's father, Eduardo Martinez, was here fifteen years back? So what? That didn't mean he found anything.

To search is to find?

Why the question mark? What did that mean? If Eduardo Martinez had actually found something surely he would have put *To search is to find*. Just that – with no question mark. But then, why did he leave a comment at all? He must have felt he was at least searching for something. It was no *co-incidence* he'd been here.

Simon was glad when a buzzer sounded the monastic signal for dinner. He was hungry, as well as confused. And he could still hear the ceaseless prayer of his conscience: go home, go home, go home. Find Tim, find Tim, find Tim.

At the rasping sound of the buzzer the whole monastery had come alive. From all the concrete corners, from the chapel and the roof and the cells and the gardens, monks and pilgrims and retreaters were all gathering in the big refectory, to drink from jugs of local wine and eat salad and lamb from the long steel buffet.

Feeling an almost first-day-at-school bashfulness, Simon sat at the longest table with the most people. His shyness fought with his anxious need to get information. Quickly. He had one evening. Then leave before dawn. He wanted to drink wine. He drank water. Between courses he texted his wife: *any news?* She texted back: *no news.*

At the other end of the long table, the monks sat and ate. Some conversed with the visitors, some stayed quiet and contemplative; one bald monk in his sixties with a sorrowful face talked, very passionately, with a young blond man, evidently a visitor. The monk was in his ordinary day clothes like the other monks; the sad old monk seemed to be drinking a lot of wine.

Simon spoke with people on his own table. A Slovakian artist, seeking inspiration. A Belgian dentist having a religious breakdown. Two Danish students who were apparently here for a lark: the scary monastery that sent people mad! A couple of earnest Canadian pilgrims. Believers.

The storm had passed; blue and purple darkness enveloped the depths of rural France. Simon had finished his dinner and was again despairing. He had a few hours to go. He was sitting forward, feeling lonely, sipping coffee. Yet again he texted Suzie.

Sorry no news.

But then, as he sat there, hunched forward, muscles tensed, he overheard it, the telling phrase: *Pius the Tenth.*

The journalist edged slightly nearer this overheard dialogue, even as he stared resolutely ahead.

Two people were chatting next to him. A fortyish monk, and a pilgrim: an older woman. American, or Canadian maybe. He listened in.

'Brother McMahon has been here eight years now.'

'Uh-huh?'

'As I said, Miss Tobin, the previous librarian was . . . well . . . rather a bad influence. Member of the Society before they were excommunicated.

'Gotcha. And this was when? When you were a seminarian?'

'Yes. Many young monks trained here in the 1990s. But the librarian was like a malignancy, in his teaching. The Society had a lot of influence here, in those days. He taught injudiciously. From inappropriate texts and materials. But now we have Brother McMahon. And we are no longer a teaching institution. Would you care for some more wine?'

The woman proffered her glass. Their dialogue dwindled.

Simon finished his coffee, not even tasting it; he tasted a very small triumph instead. So that was it – the explanation. Tomasky had been here, an eager young Catholic seminarian. And he'd learned something from the librarian.

But what was it? What *changed* people? There were supposedly secrets in this monastery which could induce a severe religious militancy, even murderous violence.

And yet there was no sign of the archives themselves.

He stood up and got ready to leave the refectory – maybe he should do another search through the books in the library. Perhaps the archives were hidden in the books: in a foreign language. Greek. Arabic. Or in *code*?

Of course this was desperate, but he was desperate. He had one evening and that was that: go home and hug Conor and find Tim. Simon turned for the exit – and he saw the young blond visitor, the man who had been chatting with a monk, was now sitting at the long table, on his own.

Pensive.

What had the two of them been discussing so passionately? The man and the monk?

The journalist took the opportunity and extended a hand. The young man smiled cheerily.

'*Guten tag*. Julius Denk!'

'Sssimon ah . . . Edgar Harrison.'

A stupid mistake. But Julius Denk didn't seem to notice or care. He was animated – and yet distracted. His thin-rimmed spectacles reflected the lamplight. He spoke good English; he said he was a trainee architect from Stuttgart, interested in Le Corbusier. The journalist knew just enough about architecture, from his father, to sound like he was also an architect, albeit a pretty stupid one. They swapped opinions.

Then Julius talked of the balding monk: their conversation at dinner.

'That monk. Very unhappy. American Irish. He drinks. Has been here seven years.'

'Yea?'

'Ja. I think he is the archivist. He says he is having a crisis of faith. He is losing his faith in God. Not so good for a monk I think!' The young German laughed. 'I feel sorry for him you know. But he talk too much. The wine is good, *nicht wahr*?'

Simon agreed. With a pang of wild surmise. The archivist is *losing his faith*. Why?

Julius was still talking.

'You have not told me, Herr Harrison, you are here to admire Le Corbusier? What you think?'

'Ah . . . er. Le Corbusier. Yes. I think he's OK.'

'Ja? What aspect of his work is it that you like?'

'The, er, villa in Paris.'

'Savoie?'

'Yes that one. That one's OK.'

Julius beamed.

'True. I admire the Villas. And perhaps Ronchamps. But this building, it is a disaster. No?'

Now Simon shrugged. He couldn't manage an intricate discussion about 'roughcast concrete', or 'the modulor' – not when he was so alarmed about things at home.

But he made a stab at sounding coherent.

'The building is rather . . . disconcerting. That is true. Those noises everywhere in the . . . ah . . . the top bit.'

'Every sound amplified. Yes yes! And I think it is worse at night. I think I hear the monks masturbating.' The German chuckled. 'So. I wonder why it is designed like that, *ja*? To punish the soul?'

'Yes . . . or to stop you doing anything bad in the first place . . . a security thing. So someone will hear you . . .'

Julius had stopped laughing. Simon tried to push the conversation along. *One last go.*

'So, Julius, I'm *guessing* you don't like Le Corbusier.'

'*Nein*. I do not. And this place confirms it.'

'Why?'

'Because Le Corbusier was a liar!'

'Sorry?'

The German frowned behind his glasses.

'Remember what Le Corbusier said, in English.' Julius Denk's expression was pensive, and almost contemptuous. 'Remember?'

'No.'

'He said form follow function. *Ja?* But did he mean it? I think not.'

'OK . . .'

'And I can show you something. Can prove it! *Hier.*'

Julius Denk reached in his bag, and took out some paper. Simon stared.

It appeared to be . . . a blueprint.

The German gestured. 'An example. I bring this with me. A schematic of the whole building, from the Corbusier museum in Switzerland.'

A schematic. A blueprint.

This *was* interesting. This was *very* interesting. An entire plan of the monastery. The journalist's eyes widened, he tried not to show extreme curiosity.

'And . . .?'

'Here.' The German pointed. 'You see. If everything is so functional, what is that?'

'That' was a mess of complex dotted lines and faintly traced angles, with numbers and Greek letters attached. He couldn't see what Julius meant. He'd been pretending he was an architect for six hours. He couldn't keep up the lame and feeble illusion.

'Looks alright to me.'

'You do not see?'

'Why don't you tell *me*?'

Julius's smile was triumphant.

'I have been studying the building. But this section here makes no sense.'

'The . . .?'

'The pyramid. The pyramid has *no apparent function at all*. It just sits there doing nothing, in the middle. I have checked, there are no heating ducts, no engineering purpose. No one can explain it. I have therefore concluded it is mere decoration. You see?'

Simon hesitated, his throat slightly choked.

'I see.'

'It means he was a liar! The great Le Corb was a fraud. He added this *pyramid* as pure ornament. A purely decorative addition to the architectonics. The man was a charlatan! Form follow function? – it is nonsense!'

Picking up the schematic, Simon looked close. The pyramid

284

sprang from the basement. If it was accessible, it must be accessed from the lowest floor of the monastery. The dark and mysterious underchapel.

This had to be it, if anywhere: this had to be it, the only place he hadn't looked.

The pyramid.

33

'Disgusting, isn't it?'

David turned. A large blond man in a rugby shirt had sat down at the next table; he was staring at the roistering Germans.

He had a kind-of South African accent. David shrugged, not knowing quite what to say.

'Sorry.' The man burped. 'But I overheard your conversation. The waiter is right. Those bastards are celebrating the Nazis. The ascension of Hitler to power.'

He ran fingers through the thick blond hair; he was tall, tanned, vigorous, about thirty-five.

'And I am German! At least by descent,' he said. He extended a manly hand. 'Name is Hans. Hans Petersen. Only come here for the Tafel, best beer in Swakop.' He smiled again. 'My people are from Otasha. Cattle farmers.'

David offered his own name, and he introduced Amy.

'So . . .' David tilted a glance at the partying Nazis. 'Why . . . do they do it? Is it a joke?'

'For some of them, yeah.' Hans swigged from his Tafel. 'They fly here from Germany and make a big joke of it. They say it is . . . ironic. Shocking the bourgeois. But for others it is no joke. Some of them are descended from Nazis, or Nazi families, who fled here after the war. Some are from old colonial families – they've been celebrating Hitler since 1933.' He wiped the beer from his lips with a thickly muscled wrist. 'So what about you?'

The Germanic singing had subsided; many of the 'ironic' Nazis were departing the bar, cold blasts of air slapping the room every time the door swung open.

'We're . . . trying to get a lift to Damaraland. To meet someone. Seems kind of . . . impossible.'

The German's stare was almost unblinking.

'You say Damaraland?'

'Yes.'

He surveyed them.

'Well, could be your lucky day.'

'How?'

'I can take ya. Maybe. I'm heading up there with some conservationists tomorrow, do some work with the ellies.'

'The what?'

'Desert elephants. S'what I do. I left the farm to my brother. Too boring.' He chuckled. 'I help ecologists, the government. Safaris for tourists, run a fleet of 4 by 4s. Namibia is not the easiest place to get around.'

Amy smiled, anxiously. 'We noticed.'

Hans nodded and laughed and bought a beer. He asked a couple more searching questions, then a couple more questions – and then he stood and laid some Namibian dollars on the table, and waved at the waiter. 'OK. Let's call it a deal! Happy to give you a hand. Sounds like you need it.' He walked and paused, at the doorway. 'You'll have to get up early though, guys. Seven a.m. start. It's a long old drive.'

'But . . . Where?'

'Meet by the Herero Monument. You won't miss us – we'll be the guys with the DEP Land Rovers.'

David stared at Amy as Hans disappeared into the night. They had lucked out. They sighed their relief, paid the tab, caught a cab, and headed back to their hotel.

But their optimism was swiftly checked.

As they were passing the reception, the bashful, defeated face of Raymond appeared: barring the way to the elevators.

'Hello.'

'Raymond.'

The man was evidently concerned: he waved a hand across his mouth, indicating they should be very quiet. A second gesture beckoned them to a darker corner of the lobby.

He hissed. 'Please please. Please come. Please listen.'

'Raymond.'

He frowned in the shadows. 'People are looking for you!'

'Who?'

Amy's eyes were wide with alarm. Raymond shrugged, still frowning. The entire hotel was darkened, and hushed.

'A short man. Quite fat. Almost a beard. Accent Spanish.'

Amy whispered, David's way: 'Could it be . . . Enoka?'

David snapped the question: 'What did he say? This man?'

'Not much. He say he was just looking for a white couple. Your descriptions. I tell him nothing . . . but he is looking for you. Tattoo on his hand. Like a German . . . swastika.'

'Enoka,' Amy confirmed.

Enoka.

David felt like he was being force-fed a diet of terror. The burning images had never left him. Miguel's servile accomplice in the witch's cave, scuttling away. And then Miguel. Raping Amy. Not raping Amy.

Amy was already making for the lifts.

'Let's get inside.'

They fled to their room and double locked the door – and lay fully clothed on the bed – and barely slept.

When David woke, he had only the memory of a bad dream in his mind, like the bitter aftertaste of some sleeping pill. A dream with sexual elements. A dream of Amy and Miguel. He was glad he could not remember the details.

The fog had quite gone. They shoved their kit in their cases, gazed at the sea – now shining in the sun – and snuck out of the hotel and cabbed the few hundred metres to the Herero Monument. They sat low in the car seats as they drove. Frightened and cowering.

As promised, Hans and his cars were unmissable: two big ochre Land Rovers with 'Desert Elephant Project' stencilled on the side. The Land Rovers were piled high with equipment. Hans greeted them with another manly handshake, and gestured at the second Land Rover.

'Second car is full. You better come with us.' He took their bags and shunted them in the boot of the first car. Then scrutinized them with a wry smile. 'You guys OK? You look . . . kinda rattled.'

'We're fine. Just . . . wanna get going.'

'Least the fog's gone AWOL, eh? Like I said, you'd better come with me and Sam. Unless you want to talk about zoology for twelve hours. Hey. My Herero lieutenant! Sammy!'

A young black guy turned and grinned. Hans jerked a thumb at Amy and David. 'These guys are with us. Dropping them off past the Ugab. Gonna sit them with us.' He turned to David. 'OK, let's saddle up.'

David and Amy immediately climbed in the Land Rover. They held hands. The seconds dragged past. The cars remained stationary.

'C'mon,' Amy was whispering, to herself, very quietly. 'What's the problem? Can't we just go?'

They waited. And sweated. Trying to look as invisible as possible in the darkness of the car. Six minutes passed, then six and a half minutes, then six and three quarter minutes, and then Hans vaulted on board and slammed his door and whistled loudly and the cars rumbled into life. They were doing it, getting out of town, trundling out of the Swakop suburbs; passing some red and blue painted bungalows, a hint of shanty town, the last dusty supermarket, a disused railway track: and then – then the desert.

The silence and vastness seemed to swallow them. David felt a headrush of relief. The cars had seemed big and important and all too conspicuous in the amiable Swakop streets; now they were two tiny specks in an austere immensity.

Good.

David and Amy were in the back, Sammy and Hans were chatting in the front. Speaking in Herero, or so David guessed: some tribal language anyway. Hans had the GPS coordinates given him by Amy. Every so often the German cross-checked them with his satnav, and nodded, apparently content.

The gravel road was nearly empty in the diagonal morning light. Occasionally a rusty truck or big new 4WD would pass them coming the other way, kicking up its own dust trail, making orange smoke signals in the empty blue air. Some pick-up trucks had black workers in grey overalls lying in the back, smoking, or sleeping. The glossy SUVs generally contained a solitary white man who lifted one lazy finger in acknowledgement as they passed.

David wondered: had Raymond really seen Enoka? Maybe it was just paranoia, a mistake, an innocent mistake? But the tattoo was unmistakable. He had seen Enoka.

The car was hot; he was sweating. David rubbed at his brow. Trying to work it all out. It was probable that Miguel and the Society had calculated where Eloise had gone. The Society was, self-evidently, well aware of the GenoMap connection. The Society had killed Fazackerly in London, precisely because he was connected to GenoMap. They knew all about GenoMap, they were closing down GenoMap with extreme violence; just as they were killing anyone with a connection to Gurs, and the Cagots. At the church's bidding?

So they were surely aware of the Namibian connection – the links with Fischer and Kellerman Namcorp.

Putting the simple sums together produced a fairly obvious answer: Nairn and Eloise were in Namibia. David and Amy too. *And Miguel had come after them.*

David stared around, teetering on the edge of despair. Would they ever be safe? Violet-black mountains shimmered on the horizon. Mirages came and went: lakes of illusion, glimmering in the imperious sun. The heat was already impressive. Everyone in the car was drinking plenty of water.

The mountains reminded him of the Pyrenees. The Pyrenees reminded him of the map, still in his pocket, still folded and faded. David reached in his dusted jacket and pulled out the map. Amy was half asleep next to him.

He unfolded some of the soft paper leaves. Every star on the map had been explained, even the one near Lyon. But there was still that tiny line of writing on the back. He flipped the map over and looked. It was so faded, so barely legible, so small. Not his father's handwriting. David squinted as close as he could: was that maybe a German word? *Strasse*? As in street? *Maybe?*

Possibly. Or possibly it was just the Teutonic ambience of Namibia, leading him down that cognitive pathway.

Carefully, reverently, pensively, David folded the map. With its one last clue. And then he kissed Amy's sweet, bare, sleeping shoulder, hoping she wasn't dreaming of Miguel.

At length Hans turned, one hand on the wheel. He nodded at David.

'Empty, right?'

'Sorry?'

'I said, Namibia is empty. You know why?'

'No.'

'My people did this. Emptied the damn country.' He frowned. 'The Germans. You ever heard of the Herero Holocaust?'

He apologized: no, he hadn't.

Amy stirred on his left. Rubbing sleep from her eyes. And listening to Hans.

'Incredible story.' Hans glanced at Sammy. Who was silent. The big German driver turned and fixed his eyes on the pot-holed road, and gulped some more water from a little bottle, as he elaborated:

'In 1904 the Herero people rebelled, and massacred dozens of German settlers. My great great great uncle nearly died.' Hans suddenly pointed out of the window.

'Ostrich!'

Amy and David craned to see: three or four large ungainly birds were running down the road in front of them. With their flustered big black and white behinds, they looked like alarmed Victorian spinsters fleeing a minor sex offender. The sight was comical. But Hans was not laughing.

'Where was I? Yeah. The Germans saw this revolt as a serious threat to the potential of their diamond-rich colony, so they despatched a Prussian imperialist, Lothar von Trotha, to deal with the uprising.' Hans drank some more water. 'The Kaiser told von Trotha to "emulate the Huns" in his savagery. Von Trotha promised he would use "cruelty and terrorism". Nice bunch of guys, the German imperial classes.'

Hans steered a left and a right. 'And that's exactly what happened. Cruelty and terrorism. And genocide. After several battles, where the Herero were slain in large numbers, lovely von Trotha decided to finish the job once and for all and destroy the entire Herero people. In 1907 he issued his notorious extermination order, or *vernichtungsbefehl*. He decided to kill them *in toto*. Every last one. An entire nation.'

'Jesus,' said Amy.

'Yah,' said Hans. 'So the Herero were driven west, into the Kalahari desert, to *die*. Guards were stationed at waterholes so the people couldn't drink; wells were deliberately poisoned. You have to remember this was desert, searing desert, the Omahake. They had no food and water, an entire nation of people with no food and water. They didn't last long. Some women and children tried to return, but they were instantly shot.'

He jerked the wheel to avoid a small gaggle of little birds.

'And there are eye witness accounts of this holocaust. Unbearably harrowing. Hundreds of people just lying in the desert, dying of thirst. Children going mad amongst the corpses of their parents; apparently the buzzing of the flies was deafening, paralyzed people were eaten alive by leopards and jackals.'

Amy asked, quietly: 'How many died?'

Hans shrugged. 'No one's entirely sure. Reliable historians estimate that maybe sixty thousand Herero were killed. That's seventy to eighty percent of the entire Herero people.' He laughed, very sourly. 'Oh yes, the numbers, we do love our numbers, don't we? Makes it all easier to bear for white men. A nice sensible percentage. Seventy-five point six two percent!' He waved an angry hand, gesturing at the desert. 'The slaughter affects Namibia's demography to this day. Helps explain the emptiness.'

David was silenced – by everything – this horrible story, the stirring desolation of the landscape, the extraordinary heat – and the mighty sun. Namibia just seemed to dwarf . . . everything.

'Uis. We're nearly in Uis.'

The town of Uis, which had appeared to be significant on the map, turned out to be barely a village. A couple of caged liquor stores stood next to three petrol stations. A grey concrete building, apparently a restaurant, advertised Snoek, Meat Pies and Greek Salad. Several iron shacks, a few big houses with big fences, and some huts and bungalows comprised the sunburned residential district.

There were lots of men sitting on their haunches around the petrol stations, staring into the burning emptiness, staring at the Land Rovers. Unpaved roads straggled off into half-hearted woodland. The shadows cast by men and buildings were stark, etched into the dust. Black black black then blazing white.

Hans stopped the car at one of the gas stations; the other Land Rover did the same. David and Amy got out to walk about for a moment, to stretch aching legs, but the heat of the scorching sun was punishing – driving them back towards shelter. Hans looked at the pair of them sceptically as he paid the petrol attendant.

'You guys got hats?'

They both said no.

'Guys! In Namibia there are three rules. Always wear a hat. Take every opportunity to refuel. And never drink whisky with a Baster.' He laughed. 'OK. We're getting near – if your coordinates are right. Maybe another coupla hours.'

The car headed deeper into the thickening bush. David had never experienced this kind of terrain: it made the Pyrenees look like St James's Park. He was glad they were losing themselves in the wilderness: it made them that much harder to follow. If they were being followed. Were they being followed?

'These are the Damara wetlands,' said Hans. 'Underground rivers, coming to the surface. This water is what everyone relies on. We've gotta go straight through.'

It felt contradictory. From scorching desert they were shifting, abruptly, into an emerald paradise of sudden rivers. Waterbirds squawked, toads and frogs croaked. And the car was rocking right down the middle of it all, wheel-arch deep in muddy water. It was like they were tunnelling into Eden.

Reeds cracked against the undercarriage, ducks fled the splashing wheels; more than once it seemed they were going to get stuck in the sucking black mud and would have to be towed free. But, just when the car was about to give up, Hans did some manly manoeuvre with the wheel and the gearstick and they lurched from the sucking swamps – charging back up onto dry land.

David wound the window open. They were on much firmer territory now; lush yet dry. Big orange cliffs stood on either side, they were rumbling down a dusty canyon.

A gazelle, or an antelope, stared quizzically at them from a rock.

'Klipspringer,' said Hans. 'Beautiful things. Always remind me of Russian girl gymnasts . . .' He checked the GPS co-ordinates given him by Amy. 'We're nearly there. I hope your woman has given you the right numbers. But I can't see anything. I'd hate it if you guys have come all this way for nothing –'

'There,' said Amy.

34

David followed her gaze, and her pointing arm. Down a shallow side canyon he saw a group of tents – a largish camp of parked vans, pink tents and people. One of the men stood out, he had bright red hair. He was injecting a black girl in the crook of her arm; she was covered in grease and her breasts were quite bare.

'That must be Nairn.'

The Land Rovers pulled up, David and Amy climbed out and approached the red-haired man – only then did he turn to look at them. He was still drawing blood from the black girl.

'OK. I've nearly finished this bunch.' Angus Nairn's voice was loud, exuberant. He smiled at the visitors, then turned to a colleague and carried on issuing commands. 'Alphonse! Alfie. Stop faffing about or I'll be forced to get von Trotha on yer arse. Ask Donna to get the tables laid. And I want some kudu steak too. Excellent. Splendid. OK. You must be David and Amy? Eloise told me all about you. Give me a sec, we're just finishing up. Alright, laydeez –'

David and Amy stood there feeling spare, and stunned, as the business of the camp continued. David contemplated Nairn as he chattered. Where was Eloise?

Hans came over, rubbing driver's stiffness from his shoulders. As he shook Angus's hand, the Scotsman smiled, quite warily, his green eyes gleaming.

'And you are?'

'Hans Petersen. Offered these guys a lift.'

'Apparently so. Think I know your work with the ellies. Save the desert ellies, right?'

'Yeah.'

'Know the accent . . . Dorslander? Northern Dutch? Not an original thirstlander?'

Hans smiled at Angus.

'Sorry, no . . . German Dutch. Otasha.' He made his goodbyes to Amy and David. 'OK. We gotta make the Huab by nightfall. Glad I could be of help.'

Nairn nodded, Hans retreated. The Desert Elephant Land Rovers departed, trailing clouds of orange dust, like cannon smoke drifting over a battlefield. Angus picked up a big steel syringe and beckoned over another tribeswoman. David felt absurd standing here, doing nothing. Where was Eloise? Was Enoka with Miguel?

Miguel and Enoka.

'Mister Nairn. We think we may have been followed. To Namibia.'

The geneticist nodded, pensively. He continued drawing blood as he talked.

'Call me Angus. Followed how?'

'We're not sure. We just think maybe someone was looking for us in Swakop. A friend of Miguel's. Might be wrong.'

Angus sighed.

'Eloise told me about Miguel. Garovillo? Yup. I knew they'd come for us. But we're nearly done anyway. And we're pretty safe out here in the bush.'

'Where *is* Eloise?'

Angus lifted a hand.

'Wait. Let me finish. Just a few Nama and Damara to go. And the ever delightful Himba.'

David watched as Angus took samples from the last tribespeople. The process of collecting blood was simple, it seemed. The locals queued patiently in the sun, then exposed their black and brown arms for Angus to plunge a shining needle in the soft veiny crook of the elbow. In return for the extracted blood samples, he then offered a brief medical examination, and dispensed medications – antibiotics, analgesics, antimalarials – to his sardonically mystified but apparently grateful customers.

Now he was almost done. One girl remained, her hair and her bare body smeared with a reddish ochre substance – a form of grease, Angus told them, made from dust and butter.

'The topless ones are the Himba – don't know why bras are taboo. OK, that's it, just unfold your arm. Less jouncing would be good.'

The syringe glittered. The glass tube filled with blood, deep crimson blood, rubescent in the fading yet still burning sun. The shadows of the Damara canyon walls were long against the rocks; squawks and chirrs of birds and hyrax trilled through the air. The desert was returning to life after the infernal heat of the day.

'There,' said Angus. 'One more *fluid* ounce and we're finished.'

He turned and squirted the blood into a sealed glass vial, which he handed to Alphonse, who escorted it away with ceremonial care. Like a newborn being taken to the scales. Angus swabbed the girl's arm with a cotton wool bud. 'Alright love. Thank you very much. Here's some medicine for the kiddo. Do you understand? *De Calpol juju?*'

The girl smiled, in shy puzzlement, and took the bottle of medicine, then turned and followed her family homeward through the acacias, assimilating with the long dark shadows of the trees.

'Finally!' Angus almost cheered. 'Finito Benito! Now let's have some Tafels and tucker. Guess you're a bit confused, come all this way to see me and you can't see Eloise? All can be explained, but first we drink. And eat!'

He was right. In the centre of the camp some trestle tables had been laid for a meal. There were big steel bowls of kudu steaks with cold pepper sauce, golden Windhoek and Urbock lager already poured into glasses. Fruit sat next to chocolate bars.

'Courtesy of Nathan Kellerman, such a generous bene- factor, albeit a Zionist hoodlum. Come on, sit down for fuck's sake, you two came a long way in one drive. Damaraland from Swakop? Mad men! Amy, your name is Amy Myerson right? Eloise told me everything.'

Amy nodded, and said firmly: '*Where is Eloise?*'

A mosquito whined and Angus shot out his hands and clapped. A squished mosquito was black on his fingers. 'Howzat!' He squinted closely at the insect's corpse. '*Anopheles Moucheti Moucheti*. The day ones are arguably more dangerous, they carry dengue –'

'Please. *Where is Eloise?*' Amy repeated. 'She told us to come here –'

'She *was* here, you're quite right. But I got a bit angsty. Decided to send her south.'

'Where?'

'The Sperrgebiet. The Forbidden Zone. Safest place in the world – for the world's last breeding Cagot.'

'Apart from Miguel.'

Nairn's eyes brightened.

'So he is a Cagot as well? The terrorist! How is that? Tell me how. Tell me everything. The Urbock is cold and the desert evening is long. Tell me!'

Over half a dozen beers, and plates of cold kudu steak and okra, Amy and David relayed the story to Angus Nairn.

They were getting used to telling this story. There seemed increasingly little point in concealing the story from a potential ally. Miguel was the enemy.

At length Angus sat back, the desert breeze riffling his red hair.

'This explains a lot. It explains the murders, the ones you mention!'

David said, 'But . . . why? It doesn't explain why Miguel . . .'

'Don't you see? He's involved in the killings where torture is involved. The first two victims, the poor old girls who turned out to be rich.'

The logic unfolded in David's mind. Dimly.

'I guess . . . He was just back from abroad. When he came in the bar – Amy –?'

She nodded. 'And after Miguel was back in Spain, the killings changed. Right? The man in Windsor – he was just killed. Not tortured. And Fazackerly, the scientist, he was also . . . just killed. Cruelly but . . . efficiently. I suppose. But then when Miguel got *another* chance, in Gurs – Eloise's mother. She *was* elaborately tortured . . . Miguel again. But why?' Her blue eyes gazed Angus's way, full of questions. 'Why would he kill *and torture* – where others just kill?'

Angus stuffed another morsel of bread and chewed, exuberantly. 'Think harder. One reason is obvious.'

'Is it?'

'Yes!' A broad smile. 'Why is he so murderously cruel to the Cagots? In particular?'

The truth unpetalled in David's mind.

'Because . . . he knows about himself?'

'*Zakly.* He's a fucking self-hater! Like that Basque witch burner.'

'De Lancre?'

'Yep. That's it! He can't face his own reality, his own race,

300

his terrible identity. Can't deal with it. Sublimated self-hatred becomes externalized violence. That must be the answer. Like Freud said! And Miguel Garovillo is a Cagot! So he takes his violent feelings, and inflicts them on the hated Cagots who embody his self loathing, his misery. He uses the tortures once inflicted on the deformed people. The witches and outcasts. The pariahs of the forest who he cannot accept as kin.'

'But –'

'And he probably heard about the Basque witch burnings when he was a kid, all the stories. And that's *gotta* affect you. Tales of fire and torments! They fuck you up, your mum and dad, especially if they are terrorists. He probably has a psychosexual neurosis about the witch tortures.'

There was a momentary silence. David turned Amy's way, and he flinched. Because he'd noticed. Amy had just that second – briefly, subconsciously, surreptitiously – put her hand to her head.

As if she was hiding the scar. The marks of the witch. David considered that scar, the interlocking curves. Was the scar simply more evidence of Miguel's obsession, his sexual hang-ups, of the killer's psychic need to revisit these witch tortures? But why did Amy let him *do* it? Cut her living skin? Why?

He remembered her words in Arizkun.

We do not exist, yes we do exist, we are fourteen thousand strong.

Angus was talking again, his face shadowed yet animated in the long Damara twilight.

'And Miguel probably has his own strange urges, anyway. One or more of the nasty syndromes of the Cagots. The violent urges. Poor Cagot bastard. No doubt the church told its agents to despatch with swift efficiency. Yet when Miguel had a chance he snuck in a bit of medieval mutilation, couldn't help himself . . .'

A large moth flickered in the lamplight: lanterns had been

strung from trees around the camp. David gawped: 'You knew it was . . . the church?'

'Well, I presumed. Am I right? I'm right, aren't I? Uh-huh?'

'Actually,' Any interjected, 'it was the Society of Pius X.'

'Aha. The Lovely Zealots.' He slapped a hand down on the table, gleefully. 'Chalk one up! I should have guessed. Bigtime zealots. With lots of money and powerful sympathizers. If not them then another church sect. Yep, the Catholic church was, as you know, one of the prime movers in the closing of Stanford; they hated us, too. Totally hated GenoMap. And of course, thinking about it, the Society would be the obvious people to do the dirty work for Il Papa. And I mean dirty work. Left footers versus web footers. Hah.' He gulped beer, and continued. 'Always fascinated me, the infinite human capacity for violence. Where does it come from? Frankly I blame the girls. The chicks. If it wasn't for them men would just sit around having a nice pint and a chat about the fitba.'

'Sorry? *Girls?*' said Amy, a defensive tinge in her voice.

David stared at the Scotsman, who was chewing almost as fast as he was talking. Nairn was consuming an enormous meal; yet he was so skinny. Angular cheekbones, wild red hair, green eyes a-glitter in the gloaming of the semi desert.

'Yep,' he said, tearing off another fistful of flatbread. 'Women. The female of the species. They're the ones who guide human evolution. Via sexual selection, no? And how do they steer our evolution? Towards nastiness – by choosing nasty guys. True or not? OK, yes, they all *pretend* they like metrosexual chardonnay sippers but they really go for the ruffians, don't they? The bastards, the bad boys, the Miguel Garovillos – and so these bastards reproduce and so the evolution of man tends towards ever greater cruelty, perhaps explaining the pageant of blood that is twentieth-century history.' He burped. 'Thank God I take the Tube not the bus.'

An animal barked in the gloomy depths beyond the camp.

A jackal or a hyena. Angus was momentarily quiet, eating, drinking, smiling broadly and knowingly at Alphonse, his gracefully handsome helpmate. The rest of the camp dwellers seemed to have fled with the dying of the day. Disappeared unto their villages.

Amy was asking questions: 'So Eloise is safe but you're still camped out here. Why?'

'Coz I'm testing the last racial variants.' Angus shrugged, contented. 'Dotting some genetic i's and crossing some chromosomal t's. And we're nearly done. The Spanish fucking Inquisition are too late. I've got the Namibian blood tests in the car, ready to go.' He slugged some Tafel and burped robustly. 'We just have to pack up tomorrow, head down to the Sperrgebiet. Get to safety.' A pause. 'We've got all we need down there. Kellerman Namcorp have been preparing for this, for years, just in case they closed down GenoMap. We've been setting up parallel facilities, in the Sperrgebiet, so we could finish off, if it came to it.' He chortled. 'And so it goes. We need a few more days, do the last tests on Eloise, and . . . Canasta! The Fischer experiments are reiterated.'

He turned and looked solicitously at Alphonse.

'Alphonse, have a bloody beer. You work too hard.'

'Sure, Angus.'

'Alfie, I mean it. C'm'ere.' The Scotsman pulled the young ochre-skinned man towards him; Alphonse had glittering feline eyes, slender limbs. Angus kissed him on the lips.

Alphonse laughed, and pushed him away – 'Mad Scotsman!' he said, and gestured at the diminishing food. 'Did you eat all the kudu . . . *Again?* You'll get fat!'

'Me? Get fat? As if.' The Scotsman lifted his T-shirt and slapped his white stomach. 'The six-pack of Apollo!' Then he glared at Alphonse as he sat down again. 'Don't make fun, my little *bambusen*, or I shall be forced to wield the sjambok.'

'No. No, sir. White massa he very kind. He give me de good job picken de cotton.'

The two men guffawed, then kissed again. Angus turned and offered Amy some of the kudu steak from the big steel bowl. David stared at Alphonse.

Angus was turning:

'Jesus, jesusfuck. What's that?'

The Scotsman stared down the valley. Now the noise was discernible. David realized he'd been hearing it for a while – but in the back of his mind he'd thought it a distant growling animal, or some effect of the wind in the thorn trees.

There were cars. Big dark cars were sweeping suddenly, up the dry river bed: heading for them. A roar of engines and lights. David stared. The fear was like a physical pain.

'The tents – the guns are *in the tents* –'

Angus was up and moving – but then a rifle shot split the still and sultry air. It whipped the sand between the tables and the tents. A warning shot.

Angus sat down, very slowly.

David looked the opposite way. More dust clouds. More. Two more. Coming at them. From every direction, looming out of the murky shadows. The largest car, a black car with black windows, swept up to the camp and parked in a savage curve. Spraying sand over the food with a kind of bullying contempt.

A tall lean figure climbed out, his gait and his twitch and his pale scarred face quite distinctive, even in the darkness.

Miguel stared at them.

'Found you.'

35

The last Vespers had been sung in the chapel. The last pilgrims had retreated to their cells.

Simon crossed the refectory, and climbed the sloping corridors. He shut the narrow door of his cell; and waited. Mind racing, mind racing. The pyramid. He'd got lucky. He'd got very lucky. He had maybe found in a day what Eduardo Martinez had failed to find in a week. The pyramid. The archives. Concealed in the prim and creepy pyramid, peeping from the centre of the building. Obvious yet discreet.

For a moment he admired the dark artistry of the design. It had a sinister genius.

Then he lay back on the bed.

The first snores and echoes of the nightwatch rattled through the priory. Simon sighed, and fretted about Tim, as he stared at the absurdly low ceiling. It felt like the ceiling was actually *descending* upon him – if he looked away, then looked back, he got the distinct impression the concrete ceiling was edging down, millimetre by millimetre.

Eventually it would crush him. Like a witch killed by the laying of stones. Squassation. He could feel the pressure of the stones on his chest. More and heavier stones. Till the ribcage collapsed. Like Tomasky lying on top of him, pressing down the knifepoint.

Enough!

He had to do his task. Just do it. Have one attempt. Then go home and protect his son and wife and save his brother.

He rose and stepped outside. The corridor was midnight dark. The monastery was creaking and whispering, like an Elizabethan galleon riding the oceans. Creaks and groans and weird distant noises. From this vantage, he could hear a hundred people breathing in their sleep. Like the entire building was respiring. Like it was a huge concrete lung. With a malignancy at its heart. A black mass on the scan.

The walk to the reception room took him two minutes. And yes, the key was hanging there, from its hook, it was actually marked *Pyramide*.

But the glass keycase was locked. Of course.

Simon looked left and right and, absurdly, up and down, and he unclasped a Swiss Army knife. He prised at the latch of the door. He heard a noise. He turned. Sweating. The rooms and corridors were empty. Clammy with tension, he returned to his task: he jemmied the knife-blade viciously.

The glass door swung open. Half panicked, he grabbed at the key on its hook, then scuttled out into the dark empty corridor.

He was ready. Running very stealthily he made his way down the darkened steps, down some more empty steps, down towards the longest sloping corridor.

A sharp voice stopped him. It froze through him, made him shrink against a wall. He stared, panicked, into the gloom. But then Simon realized: *this stupid building*. The voice was probably three floors up. Maybe just the drunken archivist, yelling in his faithless sleep. Cursing the god of nightmares.

The concrete ramp led to the huge bronze door of the basement chapel. It was unlocked; it didn't even seem to possess a lock. Indeed it swung open to the touch, with surprising grace and ease: beautifully balanced. As it turned on an axis, in the middle of the door space, it became a vertical bronze line.

Behind the door was a horizontal window, filtering silver moonlight. The two lines formed a cross.

An electrifying sensation.

Simon gazed about him; he couldn't help it – this was the first time he'd had a *serious* look at the chapel, when it was quiet, and solemn, and unused – and now he realized: it was purely beautiful. The lofty concrete space was set with serene wooden pews, and an archaic altar; on the far side, the slots of stained glass windows tinted the external starlight – speckling the imperious chamber with exquisite parallels of colour.

He felt a strange desire to pause. Here. Forever.

But his conscience stabbed at his heart.

The Pyramid.

The chapel ran the length of the building, and there had to be an entrance somewhere in the rear, which would direct him to the mysterious inner sanctum of the building.

He searched for two minutes, and found it quite easily: a small metal door, in the dry shadows of a corner. Simon reached in his pocket, and slotted the key. He could hear another noise. From somewhere. An edgy scraping noise. Echoing down the concrete corridors.

Come on, come on, come on.

The lock yielded. He stepped down the narrow, almost totally blackened passageway. Advancing into this space was like squeezing into a tube. Simon wondered if this was what it was like: being in his brother's mind. The walls closing in, the darkness pressing on all sides, every day and forever.

The walls tapered so severely he had to turn edgeways to

shuffle through, then at last the passage concluded at another rusty steel door, barely visible in the gloom; Simon pushed it.

He fell into a bright pyramidal whiteness.

Simon protected his dazzled eyes with a hand.

Sitting on a chair in the middle of the room was the archivist monk. Brother McMahon. His teeth were red from wine.

'There are two keys to the pyramid, Mister Quinn.'

36

In the gloom of the Damara twilight, Miguel looked older, more savage, even feral. The *jentilak*. He had a gun levelled at David's head. Boots clattered on the sand as four, six, and now eight men got out of the black-windowed cars. One of them spoke, with an American accent. Enoka lurked at the back.

'So that's Angus Nairn,' the American said. 'And David Martinez and Amy Myerson?'

Miguel nodded. 'Yes. But the Cagot girl, Eloise? Where is she?'

The accomplice shrugged.

'Can't see her – anywhere.'

Miguel spat the words:

'Check! Check the cars and the camp. Alan! Jean Paul! Enoka!'

The men did as they were ordered; they moved swiftly between the Land Rover and the pink nylon tents, pitched along the dry river bed. The search took them barely half a minute, to confirm that it was just Alphonse and David, and Amy and Angus.

The tallest accomplice, Alan, spoke up. 'Sorry, Mig. No sign. Must've moved her.'

'We will find her. *Mierda. Pincha puta!* We will *find her.*'
Miguel scowled at the sky – and then seemed to master
himself. *'Cuff them.'*

Someone came at David from the side. He was pulled to
his feet, and his hands were yanked down and roughly handcuffed behind his back. The same was happening to Alphonse,
Angus and Amy. Then he was rotated, facing away from the
table, so he couldn't see what was happening. Now he was
staring out into the nocturnal silence of the desert; the blackness was darkened by the contrast of the car headlights.

'Amy?'

'I'm here,' she said, her voice directly behind. 'What are
they doing? David?'

Her question was overcut by a louder voice. Miguel was
interrogating Angus. Slapping him. David could just about
see this for himself: it was happening to his left.

'Tell me. Where is Eloise?'

Angus shook his head. Enoka came over. Once again the
squat little man appeared painfully subordinate to Miguel –
a cub seeking the approval of the alpha, the dominant male,
the leader of the wolf pack. Miguel nodded.

Enoka grabbed Angus's hand and bent back the fingers.

Angus grimaced with the pain.

Miguel stood close. 'Tell me. Where is she? Have you done
the testing yet? Have you?'

Angus spat a dusty answer: 'Get to fuck.'

'Just tell us. Or we will hurt you. More and more. *And more.*'

'If you kill us you will never know. Do what you like.'

Miguel's face twitched; he walked a few metres away,
then turned.

'Why are you in Damaraland? You haven't finished the
tests . . . have you?'

David craned to his left to see.

There were men surrounding the Kellerman Namcorp

310

Land Rover, searching inside. A different voice, this time French accented, called across.

'*Nous avons!* We have the blood samples, Miguel.'

Garovillo smiled. '*Milesker*. Make sure you get all the test tubes.'

The men continued their search.

Again David called, quietly: 'Amy?'

He still couldn't see her, she was right behind him. The dazzling headlights shone in the darkness, trained on the central drama. It was like a spotlit stage-set, in the very darkest of theatres.

And Miguel was the actor, the tragic hero, smiling wistfully into the moonlight. He gazed at David. He looked at Alphonse. His smile widened. He looked at Alphonse again, as if confirming a suspicion. He spoke, to no one in particular.

'*Ezina, ekinez egina* . . . All we need to do is find Eloise. They *haven't* finished the experiments. They still have the blood tests from their Namibian researches, still here – still to be analyzed. This much is clear.' He moved towards Amy. 'This is good. And yes . . . Amy Myerson, very nice of you to let my father kill himself. And my mother. *Jakina* . . . the little *Zulo*.' Amy was visibly trembling, perceptibly terrified.

Miguel spat his anger.

'*Aizu!* We need to *persuade* Angus Nairn to tell us where Eloise is. And for that we need help. I see you have a bonfire ready. The desert night is cold, no?' The terrorist frowned and smiled, at the same time. 'Let us go and warm up . . .'

David observed, quite helpless. Amy was being brusquely shoved along; then he felt a kick at his own calves, forcing him to move. They were being shunted into the wider clearing, away from the table, into the space between all the cars. A large unlit campfire had been set, already, by Alphonse and the other assistants. David stared at the pyre of dry wood, and wondered where those other camp-helpers might be. Probably sitting happily in their village huts, asleep or eating. Oblivious to this fatal encounter several miles away, way up the shallow canyon.

They were alone with Miguel and his men. They had no chance of rescue.

The four of them were forced to kneel in the dust. Like captives of some Islamic cult, kneeling in the dust, waiting to be decapitated. Nearby was the unlit bonfire, the pyramid of desiccated firewood.

They waited. The desert wind was cold now. Their captors were sitting and smoking in the doorways of their vehicles; still other men were minutely searching the Namcorp Land Rover.

'Are they going to kill us?'

Amy's voice was strained with tension. David felt a yearning to hug her, protect her, save her. The same old hunger. But he was handcuffed and kneeling. All he could do was lie. He lied to Amy.

'No. They need us to find Eloise . . . What's the point in killing us?'

'What the fuck are you talking about? *Of course* they will fucking kill us.' Angus was laughing. 'We're dead. We're geology. We're French fucking toast. You were witness to his father's suicide! He probably thinks you caused it. He knows you know his terrible secret. The darkness of the Garovillos!' His laughter was replete with anger. 'They will torture us first, try and find out where Eloise is. Then they will murder us. Out here in the desert. But, hey, there are worse places to die. Cumbernauld. You ever been to Cumbernauld?'

Amy was crying.

Angus laughed: 'In fact I'd rather fucking *die* here than *live* in Cumbernauld.'

Garovillo had returned.

'Good. *Jenika. Noski.* And now . . .' He looked at Angus

Nairn, and then at Amy and Alphonse, and David. Then back at Angus. 'Doctor Nairn. We really need to know where Eloise is, so I am going to rip it out of you. Rip it out of your fucking heart.'

'Fuck you.'

The terrorist's smile flickered with barely repressed anger, then he pointed at Alphonse.

'Take him. The boyfriend. The *sexuberekoi. Him.*'

Miguel's assistants dragged Alphonse to his feet. The young Namibian's knees were trembling. Miguel glanced at each of the captives in turn. And spoke.

'I always wonder . . . the witch burning stories, just a legend, no?'

A shrivel of fear tightened inside David.

'But now I wonder –' Miguel's smile was deep and sad '– what was it like? Watching someone burn to death? Haven't you ever wondered? You must have done your research? *Ez?* The witch burnings?'

Miguel put his face two inches from Angus's face.

'If you don't tell us where Eloise is, we shall tie your little beige bumboy to a stake. And burn him alive. You like the pretty Baster boys, don't you? The little *ecru* bastards? The *marikoi* coon?' He swivelled. 'So we cook him! A real faggot, fresh on the fire.'

David flashed a glance of horror at Angus. The Scotsman's face was impassive, and yet riven with fury.

Then Angus spoke: 'Cagot *cunt.*'

Garovillo's eyes burned.

'*Que?*'

'We know you are a Cagot. A shit person. Like your dad. Cagot.'

Miguel's face was twitching.

'Absurd. But what do I care?' He gestured, wildly. 'Burn the boy. *Agur.*'

313

Behind him his men were hammering a stake into the dust, in the middle of the dry tinderwood. A big wooden stake.

Alphonse was writhing in the clutches of the silent men. His protestations were incoherent mumbles: he seemed overwhelmed by the horror, he was bleating, mewling. The stake was driven further. The moon was bright. Nightbirds scattered from dark trees somewhere out there in the wilderness. The Damara riverlands of dry canyons and camelthorns stretched all around, in the intensity of the dark.

Angus was shouting:

'What's the point, Miguel? You can't hide it, we know it. Everyone fucking knows you are a cack person. Look at your twitching eye. What Cagot syndrome is that? What disorder do you have? Alperts? Hallervorden? What? Fasciculation. Twitching eye. That's Cagot. The madness of the mountain –'

Garovillo struck Angus hard across the face, so hard a flash of blood spat from the Scotsman's mouth, a gobbet of blood and spittle that glistened in the dust, illuminated by the car headlights. Then the terrorist barked.

'Torch the black. Now.'

Alphonse was dragged to the stake. David watched, horrified, mesmerized. They were really going to do it.

Amy cried out: 'Miguel. *Stop*. Please. What's the point?'

'The *Zulo* speaks? Yes? *Bai? Ez? Tell me where Eloise Bentayou is* and I will stop. Until then, I shall burn the fucking half caste – like they burned my people – tortured them – burned the Basques like witches –'

'You're not a Basque, you fucking moron.' Angus spat the words. 'You're a Cagot. A shit person. Look at you –'

'Angus, help me! Help me please!'

It was Alphonse, calling and wailing. He was now lashed to the stake; the sky was dark behind him. Amy's face was wrenched with anger:

'Stop this – Miguel –'

'Only if you tell me. Where Eloise is? Eh?'

Angus spat: 'Why? Cagot asshole. Why should we give her to you? You'll just kill her, too. Won't you?'

Miguel motioned a hand.

'*El fuego. Mesedez . . .*'

David stared, appalled. One of the accomplices was stooping to the dry timber gathered around Alphonse's feet. David noticed that Angus's boyfriend was wearing Nike trainers. He found himself wondering if they would melt. David clenched himself for what he was about to witness. Enoka was flicking a Zippo. The tiny flame began to catch.

'Angusss!'

Alphonse was screaming, his voice carrying like a church-bell, echoing up the canyon.

The first flames licked, hesitantly, as though they were investigating Alphonse – testing the flesh. Young predator cubs.

'This will keep us warm,' said Garovillo. 'The roasting of the bastard. The toasting of the *sinotsu*.'

The flames rose, gaining confidence; they rose higher. The desert wood was very dry. The flames crackled in the cold clear air. A smell of woodsmoke filled the night. The desert moon shone down. Alphonse was crying out, shrieking, stretching against his bonds.

Garovillo sighed, expressively.

'So there we are. Angus Nairn, the scientist Angus Nairn. Now you must tell me where she is. Alphonse is about to be die, to be cooked, pot roasted. You won't want him then, will you? When he's just a side of beef? So much . . . crackling?'

Angus looked directly at Miguel.

'You're going to kill us anyway. You can do what you like. What does it matter?'

Alphonse cried out. He was writhing, and yelling: 'Angus – no, Angus – please tell him!'

Miguel smiled again.

'He wants to live, Doctor Nairn. He doesn't want to have his . . . boyish limbs toasted and grilled. And I feel sympathy. I am vegetarian. *Barazkijalea naiz!*' He sighed. 'So tell us.'

Angus said nothing. David saw a profound tremor in Angus's cheek: the grinding of his teeth. Alphonse was wailing.

'It hurts! Angus! I'm burning! Please!'

The flames were higher, a stray spark had caught in Alphonse's hair; his hair was smoking, singeing, the smell of burnt hair mixed with the woodsmoke. Alphonse was catching: catching on fire. He was beginning to burn.

The seconds of waiting dilated in the darkness.

'OK! *Stop it!*' Angus was shouting. 'I will tell you where she is! Eloise. *Stop the burning.*'

Miguel spun – and snapped:

'Tell me now!

'She's in the Sperrgebiet.'

'Where?'

'Twenty-six kilometres due south of Diaz Point! Stop him burning, stop it –'

'Where exactly?'

'The Tamara Minehead. The Rosh road. Disguised as mine offices. Garovillo –'

Miguel smiled. And pivoted.

And gestured at his men.

'Pour a little gasoline, onto the flames. It's going to be a very cold night and we need a nice big fire.'

The following hour was the most grotesquely prolonged and awful hour of David's life. It was worse than anything he had yet witnessed these last violent weeks.

Alphonse burned, slowly, and profoundly, and agonizingly.

First his trainers smoked, and charred, and melted into stringy plastic, and then his cotton trousers dropped, blackened, from his brown limbs: charring rags of smoking cloth. Finally the flesh began to roast. Obscenely. The brown skin flashed away, showing the fat and muscles. And then the fat of the boy's thighs began to melt, spitting in the fire. And all the time Alphonse screamed. The shrillest, cruellest scream David had ever heard. A shriek that carried across the silent desert, a man being slowly burned alive.

Then the screaming stopped, and resolved into a low, sussurating moan. The flames were big and monstrous but Alphonse was hymning his own death, almost singing. The hair was a mass of burned and charring black dreadlocks, the smell of roasting flesh was evil and sweet: a crematorium smell, a barbecue smell.

Bats winged about the smoke. David saw the eyes of desert animals attracted by the smell and the glow – jackals skulking in the gloom. Hoping for food. The smell of burning meat was attracting the shiny-eyed jackals.

Standing hard by the fire, Miguel gluttonously inhaled the smoke. The terrorist leaned to the roaring flames, and poked at the blackened body with a stick. Alphonse twitched. Still alive. Still alive. The fire roared.

'Puerca? Urdaiazpiko?'

Amy was puking. She was leaning to her side and vomiting. David felt the same gag reflex. On his left, Angus had his eyes shut. The Scotsman's face was blank and impassive. And yet it somehow expressed the deepest emotion. Utter desolation.

And then, at last, Alphonse died. The dark head lolled. The fire had wholly engulfed him. The deed was done. The fire began to subside. The body was a mass of red embers, glowing bones and meat. A black and scarlet effigy of a man, in the black desert night. The ribcage had collapsed and the heart was exposed: a vermilion knot of muscle.

Miguel was still greedily inhaling the smell of burning flesh. And Angus was watching him. Eyes narrowed. There was a cold yet incandescent fury in the Scotsman's gaze, a shrewd and calculating anger. Ferocious anger.

David noted that even Miguel's accomplices seemed repelled by the immolation.

They were looking away, glancing surreptitiously at each other, and shaking their heads. But they were obedient. There was no sense of disloyalty. More like fear. They were scared of the Wolf.

Garovillo gazed at David, assessingly.

'That was impressive, Martinez.' He ran fingers through his long black hair. 'You are a man of some . . . courage. Or uncaring cruelty. Only you watched the whole show. Only you. And you did not vomit like Amy. You have a strong stomach. Strong constitution. You are stocky, like a bull. A wild boar.'

Then Miguel glanced at the sky. The woodsmoke was drifting across the heavens, turning the moon into the pale face of a young widow – veiled with funeral grey. The smoke was dwindling, the fire was nearly done.

'We need to build another fire. Yes we are all warm and *tostada* now. But the flames are nearly gone. So we need a big new fire. To barbecue our next course. The big man . . . the American Basque-burger.'

Alan shook his head. 'Ain't got no wood, Mig.'

'But we need to burn him. Burn him next!' Miguel's voice was stilted: with a hint of frustration. 'If we kill and burn the *Amerikako* then Eloise will be offered up to us.'

David felt the rough hands of Miguel's accomplices drag him to his feet. His knees were weak, he was sagging with the horror.

He was going to be burned alive. Like Alphonse.

318

37

The journalist stood there, utterly stunned. And trapped. 'You know my name?'

'Heck.' The monk laughed. 'You think we don't read the newspapers? You wrote about those murders in England, didn't you? Seen the photo.'

He sagged: 'But . . .'

'I've been watching you since you got here. We've been warned that someone might come . . . Name's McMahon. Patrick. Paddy Thomas McMahon.'

Simon leaned against a stack of books. Now he stared around: he saw that many shelves were bare: it was like the library had been ransacked.

The bald monk nodded.

'And . . . hey . . . as you can see, you're too late anyway.'

'What?'

'The papal authorities came two months ago. Took nearly everything.' He lifted a bottle of wine from the side of his chair and poured into a steel cup. 'Want some?'

Simon shook his head, and gazed across. Right now Brother McMahon looked less like a monk than anyone he had ever seen: with his old brown corduroys and a scruffy jumper, dirty sneakers. And quite obviously drunk.

'They took *all* the documents?'

'All the important files, yep.' McMahon laughed, unhappily. 'All the stuff that would make you go *hmmm*. They said they were a security risk. They had permission from the Vatican. So important, the Pope agreed! And when they were here they said that some people might come looking for the documents, and if they did I was to tell the authorities. And here you are. Welcome to my pleasuredome. Not much left to see.' The monk took a confirming gulp of wine. His gaze narrowed, as he surveyed the high wall of empty shelves. 'You wanted to know what was in the documents. Right?'

'That's why I came. And I'm too late.'

'Sure . . .'

McMahon's expression was drunkenly sardonic.

Simon felt a twinge of hope, returning.

'You can tell me, can't you?'

Silence.

The journalist repeated. '*You can tell me? Can't you?* You know what was in the documents, correct?'

'Well . . .' He sighed. 'I can tell you *some*. What does it matter now . . .'

'Tell me about the Basques? The Cagots? The Inquisition stuff?'

The monk nodded. And tilted his head. For a second he seemed to think, to consider his options. Then he said:

'Don't recall the whole lot, but I can tell you the reason they stopped the Basque witch burnings. That was one document they were very keen to take away.'

'And?'

A mournful, tannin-stained smile.

'They did it . . . Because the church was worried that the Basques might become *the second Jews*. More sons of Ham.'

320

'Sorry?'

'It's church speak.'

'Explain.'

'The Inquisition and the cardinals were worried by . . . "Divisions in the indivisible choir of man." That was one phrase I read in the archives. Striking right? Of course the fear's based on those . . . hidden ideas in the Bible, and the Talmud. Patristic texts.'

'Curse of Cain? Serpent Seed?'

'Yup.' McMahon smiled, drunken giddiness mingled with melancholy. 'You got it in one, good man. For two thousand years scholars and priests and cardinals have wrestled with the terrible and . . .' He burped, politely. 'Terrible and confounding implications of Serpent Seed, of non-Adamite humans. A different line of man. But they have never resolved it. Indeed their explorations made things worse.'

'The physical tests, on the Cagots?'

'Yes of course.'

'What did they discover?'

'Again, challenging stuff.' The librarian gargled some wine, and went on. 'The king's physicians even tried to test the Cagots' blood. But that proved zilch. Didn't have the science – this was the seventeenth century. But the *physical* examination of the Cagots caused consternation with the clerics and bishops. The precise line I remember was: "It is feared the class known as Cagots may not be of the children of God." That was the Bishop of Bordeaux, to the King of Navarre. After he'd seen the results from the doctors.'

The phrase resonated in Simon's mind, he could sense it echoing along the bleak concrete cloisters. Doors opening one by one.

He had a final question – then he had to leave. He really had to leave. He couldn't help remembering Tomasky. The tooth embedded in his cheek. If he was found here by someone less affably drunk than Brother McMahon, then *anything* was possible; the very worst was very possible. He needed to get out fast – after he'd asked one more question.

'So. What is it that made you lose faith? You encountered something, in here, that made you lose faith.'

'Did I . . .?'

'What was it?'

The strange concrete pyramidal space seemed to shrink around them. The mad angles, the intensely leaning walls, seemed to narrow and darken. And at the centre of it: this burbling, drunken monk, who no longer believed in God.

McMahon rubbed a sad hand across his eyes.

'In 1942, the Pope did a deal with Hitler. Kind of peace treaty.'

'What?'

The monk's voice was soft.

'The archives about the arrangement were kept here. Alongside the Basque and the Cagot documents. Because . . . they were related.'

'What kind of treaty?'

The librarian kept rubbing his eyes. Obsessively. Like he wouldn't look at anyone.

'You ever wonder why Pope Pius the Twelfth stayed so quiet during the Holocaust? Throughout World War Two?'

Simon frowned.

'Yes. I mean, of course. Yes.'

'Exactly! It's been seen as one of the great shames and scandals of the Roman church ever since. Maybe the greatest ever. There was total inertia in Rome when Hitler slaughtered the Jews. The Catholic church didn't even *condemn* the Holocaust, just made vague noises of . . . *unhappiness.*'

Simon asked again.

'So, this treaty?'

'Hitler discovered something. Through his scientists, in the camps in southwest France.'

'You mean Eugen Fischer at Gurs?'

The monk nodded, and sat back in his chair and stared upwards at the tapering mad roof of the pyramid. As if staring at his own disappearing faith.

'Yes. The deal was just *that*. Hitler agreed not to reveal what his scientists had found. Because what they had found somehow confirmed, scientifically, what the Inquisition and the Cagot examinations had previously implied. This thing that had so embarrassed the church, centuries ago – stuff so embarrassing they needed to keep it locked away. First in the Angelicum. Then here. Stuff that kept sending the archivists mad, or crazy. Stuff that made the monks neurotic, at least – those poor bastards that weren't deranged by the building in the first place. Stuff too disturbing to understand, yet too important to destroy.'

Simon interrupted: 'So you don't know what it actually *was*? The revelations from Gurs?'

'Nope. After the last librarian at Tourette joined that bunch – the Society of Pius – the deepest secrets were locked away in a further box, in here. Personally, I never saw them. Not directly.'

'But you know some of the background.' Simon was unravelling the knot in his mind. 'You know that, in return for Hitler not revealing this secret – what they discovered at Gurs – the Pope agreed to stay silent. During the Holocaust? *Right?*'

The librarian lifted a steel tumbler full of wine and did the bitterest of toasts.

'That's it. You got it. The Pope did a deal with Hitler, he did a deal with the very *Devil*, and six million fucking people died.'

Then the monk added:

'By the way, you've got one hour. To leave. I can't just pretend you didn't fetch up. I still have a job here. I may think these weird zealots who took the documents are a shitload of mothers, I may think the whole damn thing is a hateful charade, and the treaty a grotesque betrayal – but I'm sixty-five and I don't want to go anyplace else. What would I do? Live in Miami?' He shook his head. 'So. I'm gonna tell them you broke in and overpowered me. That means you need to run away from here very quick. I will call them in an hour. In return, for my being so good as to not turn you in . . . I want you to tell me.'

'What?'

'If you ever find the truth – what Hitler found – what scared the church. Tell me? I spent a life believing in this shit and serving the Dominicans and suffering in this fucking madhouse of a building and hell's teeth I'd like to know why I've lost my faith. Because I was born a believer, I was meant to believe. And yet now I am alone. So very alone.' He stared at the metal cup of wine in his hand. 'Blood of Christ, body of Christ, body of lies. *Cheers.'*

38

Miguel's expression was distinct; weary yet sated yet triumphant. David realized it was the same expression the terrorist had worn just after copulating with Amy in the witch's cave of Zugarramurdi.

'Wait. Wait wait . . . I am *sleepy*,' said Miguel. His breath was visible in the cold night air. 'We can wait. *Bukatu dut!* The American will warm us in the morning.'

Angus gazed at the terrorist.

Miguel gave orders for his men: Angus, Amy and David were tightly chained to an acacia tree, with their backs to the trunk. Guards were allotted. Then the terrorist very suddenly bedded down: so fast it was as if he had fainted. He was now lying deadweight on a canvas sheet, by the dying fire, faintly warmed by the glowing body of Alphonse.

'Klein Levin,' said Angus, blankly, and quietly.

David whispered to Angus, who was right beside him, chained with his back to the same tree.

'What?'

'The syndrome, Garovillo's condition . . . Hypersomnia, facial tics. Violence. I think it is Klein Levin.'

'And?'

325

'It's just . . . interesting.'

Silence. Then Amy spoke. Her voice tremulous with emotion:

'Angus. Whatever. We need – need – need to do something – just something –'

Angus nodded. 'I know. But . . . what? *What can we do?*'

No one spoke.

It was a cold and grotesque night, twisted with agony. David couldn't sleep. His thoughts stared down a black tunnel at one singular horror: he was going to be burned in the morning. At dawn. He was going to suffer like Alphonse. He hoped that death would come quickly.

He was the only one who didn't sleep. Angus and Amy whispered words of comfort to him, but in the end the sheer exhaustion weighed too heavily: they nodded out. Heads sagging.

David stayed awake. Staring into the desert black. Bitten by mosquitoes. Moths flickered against his face like tiny frightened ghosts. Even they departed as the night grew ever colder.

But then, in the grey weary hour before dawn, something moved. Something human. David stared.

Miguel was surreptitiously approaching the almost-dead bonfire. The accomplices were all asleep. Miguel had replaced the guard, and taken over the duty. Now he was creeping towards the sad smoking heap of the bonfire.

The ETA terrorist looked left and right, to make sure he was not being observed. David was in the shadows, beneath the tree, away from the lanterns. Miguel evidently didn't realize that David was watching.

But watching what? What was Garovillo doing? There was something simultaneously awkward, and terrible, in the lonely drama.

José Garovillo's son crawled up to the bonfire and reached

out a hand, across the charred and smoking embers. And he pulled at the roasted body of Alphonse. Tugging at the sagging dead meat of the man.

He was pulling on a leg. The broiled thigh of the poor Namibian youth – it came away easily from the hip bone. Like a chicken leg from an overcooked bird. Miguel laid the roast leg on the sand. Then he reached in his pocket, and he unclasped a sharp big knife. He was drooling now, a line of silvery spittle caught in the moonlight; David watched as the terrorist sliced and dug with the knife, carving a chunk of the charred and broiled flesh, from Alphonse's leg.

Miguel glanced left and right one more time: the Wolf Nocturnal, guarding its prey. Then he stabbed the meat with the blade and lifted it greedily to his dribbling mouth, the salivating maw of the wolf.

Otsoko.

David retched.

Miguel looked up at the noise. The terrorist saw David. Saw that his attempt at cannibalism was observed.

A flash of guilt seemed to cross his face, inexpressible shame and guilt. The terrorist dropped the knife to the dust as if he had never meant to be holding it. Abruptly he stood, and disdainfully kicked the meat and bones into the dirty embers of the fire. Then he wiped his face with a sleeve, and sneered at David. Silently. But the sneer was unconvincing; the shame was still there. Terrible shame.

Miguel retreated into the shadows, dragging his blanket. And slept again.

David stared. Transfixed by the horror of what he had just witnessed.

Alone in the wilderness, he gazed at the desert sky. Dawn was summoning the worshipful earth to life. It tinged the horizon with green and cool blue, and the palest apricot. Faint dark shadows began to stretch across the canyon floor.

The slender trees bowed like courtiers in the freshening breeze. David was still the only person awake.

He squinted, watching a big cat a few hundred metres along the dry river valley; the cat was tawny and gracile, with tufted ears and a long pert tail, prowling between the camelthorns. A caracal.

Further down the shallow canyon, he could make out large moving black shapes. Desert elephants. Making their unique pilgrimage, across all the thirstlands of Namibia, searching for water.

He wanted to cry. Because he was about to die. And the world was so beautiful. Cruelly beautiful. Savage and deathly and beautiful. He had never felt so vividly aware of everything. Every beetle, ebony black on the golden sand, every chirp of every desert bird that trilled in the soft green acacias. And he was about to die.

Miguel's voice echoed across the camp.

'OK. Come on. It is *fucking* cold. We need to burn him. Come on! *Egun on denoi!* Wake up.'

Suddenly the clearing was alive with people. Shivering men waiting for their orders.

'We need wood, Miguel?'

'Get them to do it.' Miguel barked at his men. 'Use Amy and Nairn. Let them gather the firewood to roast their friend. We can brew coffee on his brains.'

'Alright.' Alan was nonchalantly pointing a pistol at them. 'As he says. Don't see why we should sweat. *You* go and gather some wood. We'll be right behind you.'

Amy and Angus were unchained. A jabbing motion of the pistol gave them the direction. David watched from his bonds. The two prisoners shuffled down the canyon; Amy bent and picked up a small dead acacia branch. The men were smoking and laughing, swapping obscene jokes about the upcoming execution.

He noticed that Angus was talking to Amy. Whispering. Alan barked across the dust at the toiling captives: 'Shut the fuck. Just collect the wood.'

Angus turned, and apologized, then stooped to the sand and wrenched at a small dead tree, with a few remaining green leaves. Amy copied him: wrenching at a similar tree, a few yards away.

The day and the task had begun. Angus and Amy did their slow and sombre duty, piling the wood high in the clearing; a chilly breeze was kicking across the wastes, the sun was already shining, but it was still cold.

Miguel's voice was loud in the dawnlight.

'Alan, get the fire lit. It's freezing. Put our friend in the middle.'

'Yes, Mig . . .'

David felt himself torn apart by the accumulating horror. Even though he had been preparing himself all night, the reality was too appalling to bear. This mustn't be. *This mustn't be*. But now they came for him. He fought and writhed, but he was one and they were many; he tried to bite one of his captors, but they slapped him into silence. Inevitably and inexorably, he was dragged across the dust to the waiting heap of wood.

'Got the ropes?'

With brutal force he was half lifted, half shoved – hoisted into the middle of the firewood. For a moment his hands were unlashed and he tried to use his fists to hit out, hit someone, anyone – but the men grabbed his flailing fists: he felt them knotting his wrists behind the stake, and then the same happened to his ankles: they were roping his ankles too. Roping him to the big wooden stake.

Wood was stacked all around him, he was knee deep in distinctive grey desert wood. Dry and waiting.

He stared at Amy; she stared at him. Tears were running

down her face, yet she was silent. David sought out her blue eyes: he was searching, in his final moments, for a confirmation, some proof that she loved him. And there *was* something in her expression, something distantly gentle, and wistfully pure. But what was it?

'*Basta!*' said Miguel. 'Let's go. Breakfast. *Torrijas*. *Kafea*.'

'Wait.' Amy spoke: 'Let me kiss him goodbye.'

Miguel looked at her, sceptical and wry – almost laughing. The sun was up and David could feel the first real warmth on his face. Soon he would be boiling, the blood would boil in his veins.

'*Aii*. Why not? Kiss him goodbye. Say *agur*. Taste him one more time. And I shall watch.'

Amy nodded, subserviently. She walked to the bonfire. And she stepped over the wood and she leaned to kiss David, softly, on the lips, and as she did she whispered, very quietly, and very clearly.

'Try not to breathe the smoke. Euphorbia wood. Just try.'

David was biting back his own terrified sadness. He nodded. Mute. He accepted a second kiss, then Amy retreated and Alan stepped forward.

'Gas mark five?'

Someone laughed.

'Who's got the lighter?'

The Frenchman, Jean Paul, was chucking petrol from a can on the dry firewood. David felt the cold splash of the gasoline on his ankles, the heady smell of raw petrol rose to his face and then Enoka took the lighter. The squat Basque man clicked and cupped the lighter flame with a hand, protecting it from the desert breeze, like a little bird, like a baby chick, and then he knelt and tended the lighter and he stepped back slowly, inquiringly, carefully – and then with a polite *woooof* of an explosion, the gasolined firewood burst into flame.

It was really happening. Here. Now. In the yellow Damara riverlands. With the Lanner falcons wheeling over the wistful Huab. He was going to burn alive.

The desert timber was so dry it burst into vivid flame at once: big roaring yellow flames. Angus and Amy were crouched around the fire, warming their hands. Miguel laughed.

'That's good. Warm your hands on your cooking friend! Me too.' Miguel flashed a glance at his colleagues, and snapped an order. 'Keep a gun on them.'

Miguel stepped near to watch his victim's ordeal. David's eyes were watering in the smoke; his feet were hot; he could feel the heat on his own legs, flames crawling up his body, like the arms of loathsome beggars. He tried not to breathe the smoke. Euphorbia. Was there some plan? He was almost passing out with fear. He was going to die. His mind swam with terror and tiny hope. What were they doing? Amy and Angus were upwind of the thick oily smoke issued by the dead, crackling branches. Glancing at Miguel, who was downwind.

Miguel was inhaling the smoke. Breathing in and smiling serenely.

'The smell. Smell of the meat, like lamb. A little like lamb, no? You can smell the wood and soon the meat? Yes? *Ez? Bai? Amy?* You can smell? That is . . . that is your friend . . . burning – and –' Miguel began to mumble, through the fire-heat and the smoke – 'Yess . . . *Marmatiko* . . . he will be . . .'

David gazed from his own lashed and burning execution: astonished.

Miguel was stumbling, sideways. He was slurring and toppling – and then Miguel fell to his knees, half conscious.

The ETA terrorist was down.

And now Angus was on him like a predator; before anyone saw a chance to respond, Angus had leapt round the fire,

grabbed Miguel by the neck; at the same time he snatched
Miguel's own pistol – and put it to Miguel's lolling head.

The killer slurred a mumbled curse, barely conscious.

His guards were frozen with shock. Angus snapped: 'Stop!
Or I kill him!'

The moment jarred. Hands on guns. Men half out of cars.

Now Amy grabbed the knife lying in the dust, the knife
Miguel had used to slice the human flesh. Diving into the rising
flames, she slashed the ropes that tied David to the stake; as
the cords fell into the fire, he leapt away, Amy pulling him
free. Angus was shouting:

'I will kill Miguel. *Don't move!*'

No one moved. Apart from Amy: who slapped at David's
clothes, his smoking jeans and boots. The fire roared, as if
in anger, denied its food. Amy put a hand to his face.

'You're OK?'

'I'm OK – I'm OK –' He could barely hear her, over the
blaze of the flames and the sound of his own choking coughs:
he was spitting the vile taste of his own burning clothes.

A few yards away, Angus was dragging the semi-conscious
Miguel through the dirt – as Miguel's men threw glances at
each other. But their faces, in the clear morning light, flashed
with extreme confusion. What to do, without Miguel?
Without their commander?

Angus yelled: 'Come any closer he won't have a head,
you fucks. Amy – grab all the car keys. And get the case
with the bloods. David – get a gun and get to the car – *get
in the Land Rover* –'

Again the men glanced at each other, confused, angry,
and helpless. A few seconds, and Amy was done, brandishing
a fistful of car keys in her hand.

'Angus. I got them! And the bloods.'

'Go to the car! David!'

Obedient, suppressing his fears, he raced to the car and

jumped up and sat at the wheel. His burned, painful hand was poised on the key. Ready to flee the first moment Angus was safe.

The Scotsman was pulling the deadweight of Miguel closer to the Land Rover. Muzzle of the gun still close to his temple. Amy was in the seat next to David, watching. Ready to go. To escape. *Ready.*

But Miguel was stirring from his torpor, whatever the effect of the euphorbia smoke, it was wearing off – he was fitfully struggling in Angus's grip; David could see in the headlights – Miguel was trying to wriggle free.

'Angus!'

The scientist had the muzzle on Miguel's head, at the temple. David knew what was going to happen. Angus Nairn's face was set with grim satisfaction.

David watched, appalled, as Angus pulled the trigger: a point-blank execution.

But his grip was unsure: at the last possible moment, Miguel writhed, violently. Again he was the *jentilak*, the giant of the forest, unkillable, legendary: Angus got off a shot, and blood spat from Miguel's head, but it was a wound, just a wound in the scalp. The Wolf was alive, and down, and free. *And signalling his men.*

The first shot of a rifle zinged the morning air. David slammed the gears – then another shot spat against metal, with a chiming crack. The car door swung open and Amy grabbed at Angus – who leapt into the back seat: David floored the pedal, churning the sand, and then at last the wheels got a grip and they lurched forward, picking up speed. Faster. And *faster.*

The rear window smashed into a hundred shards as a bullet zapped the glass; Angus fired back, through the jagged void, random shots; one and two and three. One man seemed to fall, a squat figure: Enoka. Dead.

Angus screamed: 'Go!'

Swinging the car, wildly, David shouted: 'But where –'

'There!'

They jerked over a hillock at speed, a tongue-chomping vault into the air – then crashed into the sand and raced onwards, rattling everyone and everything: sliding in the gravelly dust, fishtailing. David gripped the wheel as they veered left and right through the dry river plains – slaloming between the camelthorns –

'David!'

Amy was screaming.

A huge elephant loomed ahead – they were going to crash into the elephant – the slow grey beast was crunching a branch in its mouth; it turned and looked at them, maudlin and pitying –

David tugged the wheel just in time and the car tilted, at speed, and he knew they were going to flip, right over, and pancake. They were going to be crushed, but then the car slammed back onto all four wheels and they raced ahead.

'The river. Take the river!'

It was an order from Angus. David obeyed.

The car slashed down the mudslide and cracked along the river bed, the wheels churned and the ducks and geese and weaver birds squawked and flailed. David crunched at the gears and accelerated. The big white car was fast and new.

For ten, twenty, thirty, minutes they scythed down the river road. Oryx, drinking placidly from the water, looked up at the noise, and fled. Springboks pronked in fear as the car came splashing over boulders and careering around riverine bends, dangerously fast.

'This way!'

Angus pointed; David took a fork along a dryer river bed. He grabbed the chance to check behind, once more – and his hopes climaxed: they really were doing it.

They'd escaped.

David felt an urge to sob in horror and scream in triumph at the same time. He did neither. He drove. Silent. The car was silent. They pulled over for a few minutes and Amy found ointment in the car's first aid box, and she anointed his half-burned hand. As she did he looked at her. She was not crying, but her eyes were clouded, she was subduing her terror. The car started, they continued their escape.

The sun was up, already hot. David tried to get a grasp of his own fear, his own terror.

Why? Why was Miguel even *there*? Always he kept finding them. It was like they were being hunted by Death itself: sleek, brutal and merciless. *Otsoko*. The Wolf. *Relentless*.

He thought of the smell of his own clothes burning. He was silent. Amy clutched his arm. Also silent.

An hour of river driving ended – Angus ordered a change of direction; David nodded, and spun the wheel hard to the right – and they growled up onto proper dry land. Rocks and sand. They drove on, and on. No one spoke.

They were driving due south. There wasn't any road. The relative lushness of the Damara riverlands was devolving into pure and tormented aridity. Sand dunes rose on either side.

Angus was the first to properly speak. It felt like a day since anyone had really spoken.

'We're in the Namib Naukluft,' he said. 'We're back in real desert. This stuff goes on for hundreds of miles.'

David gazed out at the enormousness of the wasteland. Great dunes, almost ice-creamy in consistency, were skirling dust from their soft and orangey crests; between them were flat dusty saltpans burned into eerie whiteness; and then, stark and black, the spars of dead trees. They looked like trees in a very bad dream.

Enough. David shivered himself out of his reverie. The

335

bad images crowding his mind were too awful to bear. And yet, amidst the cacophony of horror, something was rhyming: there was a harmony here, a frightening but authentic harmony.

He pieced together the images in his mind: Miguel eating the flesh of Alphonse. Old man Garovillo's stuttering confession in the Cagot House: 'Miguel bears the true shame of the Cagots.' And then the horror of the body liquor in the cellars beneath the house.

What if the ancient, now liquified corpses had been sealed in an airtight vault, not to prevent infection, but . . . to store them?

As food?

Taking a sip of water, he asked the scientist. Straight.

'Angus, were the Cagots . . .'

'What?'

'Were they . . . *cannibals*?'

Amy stared across the car, white and horrified.

39

For a kilometre or more, Angus was silent. David tried again. More silence. For the third time, David asked the question. This time Angus cleared his throat and said, with an uncharacteristic tinge of nerves in his voice, like he was choked on desert dust:

'What makes you say that?'

David didn't want to say: *I saw Miguel cutting up your boyfriend.* But he felt he had no choice. Prefacing his answer with a warning, he told the Scotsman. About Miguel in the night. And then the events in the Cagot House. The body liquor of the stored and decomposed bodies.

Angus stared out of the car window, at the desolation of the great Namib. Then he said, without turning:

'Yes, of course. And that's why the smoke trick worked.'

Amy interrupted.

'Sorry? What?'

'It seems . . . somehow cruel. Discussing it. The Cagots are almost dead. Why heap this ordure on their grave?'

'But –'

'But now you've guessed. Now you've actually . . . witnessed . . . I might as well be fucking honest. Yes it's true.

Miguel is cannibalistic. *Because he's a Cagot*. Part of their cursed genetic inheritance.' He leaned forward. 'The Cagots were cannibals.'

Amy shook her head.

'Please . . . please explain.'

'They were accused in early medieval times of eating human flesh, and the reputation stuck. Of course it could have been nonsense, like the Jewish blood libel – yet it was true. They really were . . . the Serpent Seed, the Curse of Cain. A race apart, a breed of cursed people. *All of it true.'*

'How? I don't get it!' Amy was pale with anger; her white face framed by the yellow sands of the Naukluft, through the window. 'Eloise? She is no madwoman. And she never said any of this?'

'Well, she wouldn't, would she?' Angus spat out his sarcasm. 'It's the great wild shame of the Cagots, not something you mention to the neighbours – why don't you pop round for a dinner, bring a fat friend –'

'But what's the science?' David steered the car between two dead and spiky trees. 'Cannibalism? How the hell does that . . . evolve?'

Angus frowned. 'It's because of the inbred isolated nature of the Cagots. Take their syndactyly, webbed toes and feet. This is typical of mountain peoples, with small gene pools. Syndactyly is associated with many chromosomal disorders. Some of them lead to psychoses, violence, strange sexual urges – who knows – you see?'

Any flashed a glance at David, then at Angus.

'Miguel was highly . . . sexual.'

'Excess libido, yep.' Angus was actually smiling. 'Hypersexuality, satyriasis. And the hypersomnia.'

'He always fell asleep after sex.'

'Typical man. What can you do.' Angus gazed at nothing, then went on: 'So, I suspect, Miguel has some obscure

338

combination of Klein Levin and Hallervorden-Spatz syndromes, not unknown to the average Cagot. This syndrome will get worse over time. And one of the psychosexual symptoms can be anthrophagy. Cannibalism! I realized he had cannibalist urges when I saw him sniffing the smoke . . . last night.'

David checked the mirror: there was some obvious and shocking sadness in the Scotsman's aggressive humour, his determined smile.

Amy said: 'So that's why the euphorbia worked.'

'Exactly. After I watched him with poor Alfie, I knew he would want to sniff the smoke again, the smell of burning . . . human flesh. I realized he would do that when they started to toast you, David. Wouldn't be able to resist.'

'And euphorbia?'

'*Euphorbia virosa.* Also known as Bushman's poison. Eating the leaves will kill you quickly. The woodsmoke can kill over time and knock you out very quickly. My gamble was that Miguel would step forward and inhale, try and smell the delicious scent.'

David felt a profound queasiness, like vertigo:

'But Angus. If Miguel hadn't stepped forward and . . . inhaled . . . the euphorbia smoke would have killed *me*.'

'Yes, well. I figured you wouldn't mind dying quicker by poison rather than waiting to be chargrilled.'

The car was quiet. The old dirt track turned onto a proper road. Black and tarmacked and murderously straight: like a fine needle of jet pointing due south. The sun was azimuthal in the sky, the shapes of running ostriches spotted the far and desolate horizon. David thought of his frail grandfather, back at the hospice in the desert: *desolada, desolada, desolada.*

The sadness and shame of his grandfather; the terrible fate of his parents.

Amy spoke: 'Where are we going?'

'Rehoboth. City of the Bastards.'

'Sorry?'

David checked in the mirror, Angus was still wearing that odd, cocky smile.

'I'm going to see Alphonse's mother, just for a minute. To tell her what happened. Alphonse was a Baster. A Bastard. His mother lives in Rehoboth and we need to get there *soon* because Miguel is not dead and his men will find a way out of the desert and they will come to the Sperrgebiet, they *will* come for Eloise –'

Amy interjected: 'Why didn't he believe you? When you told him Eloise was in the Forbidden Zone? Why did he continue to . . . do what he did? He had his answer.'

Angus scoffed.

'You still don't see? This man is driven by his shameful urges, his Cagot cannibalism. Probably he has kept a hold on it for years, but as the syndrome worsens the most primal and evil of his desires are surfacing –'

'He bit the hand of the Cagot woman he killed in Gurs. *Eloise's grandmother.* The cop called it "experimental" –'

'There you are. In one. He's yielding to these base desires, at last, as he goes finally mad. The syndrome tightens and grips. You can overtake this car – we need to keep moving.'

It was the first vehicle they had seen in an hour. David sped by, the car driver was a big, German-looking man. Who flashed his headlights as they passed: two blinks of silver in the shimmering heat.

Angus continued: 'So you see, Miguel used our predicament as an excuse to . . . cook someone. He had his answer but his impulses were predominant. What he really wanted was human flesh. As much as possible. A chance to feed his worst urges. He couldn't help himself.'

'And now?'

'He will be after Eloise. He still has a job to do, after all. Destroy the experiments and stop our tests and then kill Eloise, the last of the Cagots.'

A terrible thought struck David.

'Angus . . . Is Eloise also mad?'

'No. Not every Cagot suffers these syndromes. She's fine. And plenty of Cagots are – or were – perfectly healthy. Especially at the beginning of their . . . isolation.'

'But then?'

'As the gene pool dried up, over centuries, the bad genetic stuff recrudesced, healthier Cagots became rarer, and so the poor mad Cagots were shunned with ever greater severity, as a pariah tribe, and so the vicious genetic circle *tightened*. They were forced to inbreed, due to lack of partners; perhaps they were reduced to incest. Thus creating more cannibals and cretins and web-toed rapists. We better get petrol.'

The fuel station was a sudden outpost of sophisticated business in the bleak empty desert. One minivan was decanting half a dozen nuns, black nuns with smiling black faces, laughing. A couple of motorbikers were sitting in the shade, pouring bottles of water over their sunburned foreheads.

Watered and refuelled, they bought nuts and wizened apples and sticks of biltong. Then they climbed back in. The endless black strip of the road unfurled through the wastes.

Angus was still talkative: it was as if he saw conversation as a way of avoiding any contemplation of what they had been through. David was happy to go along; he, likewise, didn't want to consider what they had so recently endured.

'So tell me. You two.' Angus sank some water. 'We need to know who betrayed us.'

'Yes . . .'

'I think it's pretty obvious. Don't you?'

David said: 'No.'

Angus tutted.

'You were obviously set up in *Swakop*. By that guy. *Hans Petersen*. He was waiting for you. Like you just bumped into him and he kindly drove you to see us? *Och right*. I had suspicions when you showed but I was a halfwit, got distracted, didn't do anything about it. *Didn't think*.'

David protested:

'I don't think he'd betray us – No –'

'Fuck that, it was him. The elephant man. He is known in Namibia, hates Nazis, any hint of racial science. They probably told him we were doing the Fischer experiments, he agreed to help – do a set up – I *should have guessed*.'

'We didn't tell him why we were going.'

'He knew *already*. They had someone in Swakop tell him, so he was ready to befriend you, so you would give away Eloise's whereabouts, lucky for us I moved her –' Another slug of water. 'Anyfuckinghow, here we go. The City of the Bastards.'

They were driving into a largish town, ringed with fuel stations and metal bungalows. Telephone masts stood whitely on shallow dusty hills, the streets were wide and languid in the heat and blessed with German names: Bahnhofstrasse; Kaisersstrasse. Big dogs ran behind tall wire fences. Dark orange girls laughed outside a pink bungalow called Viljoen's Pool Hall. David rolled down the window and stared at the shoppers stepping inside one supermarket, Spar.

The people were strikingly beautiful. Like Alphonse. Coffee-coloured skin, slanting eyes, extraordinarily elegant cheekbones.

'So who are the Basters?'

Angus explained. 'The crossbred descendants of strapping Dutch settlers and petite khoisan tribesmen: the famous Bushmen of the kalahari. The Dutch and the Bushmen inter-married in the eighteenth and nineteenth centuries. In the Cape Colony. Take a left here. This is where –' His voice cracked for a second. 'This is where Alphonse's family live. I met him at Windhoek University. I needed an assistant. He was so beautiful, a beautiful bastard of Rehoboth.'

Amy glanced at David. Then she said: 'Angus, if you want to . . . be alone for while . . . we can . . .'

'No no no. I'm fine. I'm *fine*. Let me talk. Let me explain. Amy, the Basters were hated and despised from both sides because they were such unusual half castes, such extreme hybrids. The racial prejudice they faced drove them north, across the thirstland, into Namibia. So they settled here on the high plateau south of Windhoek. And they farmed cattle.' Angus gestured through the car window at a passing butcher's shop, with fiercely caged windows. 'They actually founded their own nation with its own flag and anthem. The nation of the bastards. That's what *Baster* means. Bastard.' Angus chuckled. 'And they're still here today. A precious genetic remnant. The unique inheritance of the Basters makes them *rhapsodically* beautiful – cocoa coloured, high cheekboned, sometimes blond yet simultaneously dark. Literally the most beautiful people in the world. As you can see – look at that girl there, by the post office. Stunning. They also like a drink, and they gamble. And they brawl. All the time, whenever they get drunk. Clock the fences. OK, here's the house. Alfie's mum. Five minutes.'

It was a bright blue bungalow, with a basketball hoop over the garage, and another tall wire fence around a neat if austere grass space. It could have been a house in America, but for the burning African sun and the acacia trees on the street and the strange slender beautiful cheekboned people laughing on the stoop of the Lutheran Church with the lurid green Le Palace gambling hall next door.

David and Amy said nothing. They sat in the car in the heat and she touched his hand and he squeezed her hand and they said nothing.

343

The Scotsman emerged.

'That was . . . fun.' He waved away any inquiries, and ordered David to drive on. 'Drive south. Let's just get there. Just get to the Sperrgebiet as fast as we can. Go!'

As they drove he talked – and talked. He talked of the Basters and Eugen Fischer. He spoke, it seemed, as a therapeutic measure. David listened to the mesmerizing babble of Angus's talk. Half soothed, half alarmed. The deserts were encroaching again, as they sped south along the straight back road at a hundred miles an hour. The road was so empty and straight and good and flat it felt like they were doing thirty, across the wilderness. They saw virtually no other cars.

'So you want to know why Fischer was here. In Rehoboth. In Namibia. Right? Yeah?'

David shrugged.

'I guess.'

'Simple answer. Because it's such a paradise for someone interested in genetics, like Fischer. There is more human genetic variation in Africa than anywhere else on earth. And there is maybe more in Namibia than anywhere in Africa. From the Nama to the Cape Malay to the purebred Boer. And I've sampled them all. I got them all. I've even sampled the khoisan, the Bushmen! Alfie's ancestors . . . They are very important, to the Fischer experiments. Now we need to go right, off road. Use the track.'

The wastes swallowed them, at once. The car growled along a dead valley, another *vlei* of dust and flattened salt. The dunes were smaller than before.

Angus went on: 'So what was Fischer doing here? Fischer believed that, technically, the Bushmen were a special kind of human. Certainly they are a unique adaptation to the dry desert lands. They are very small, and nimble, but they have all the necessary features, as it were. They have been

344

cleverly miniaturized by evolution. Like Japanese electronics. I call them the Sony Bushman.'

'In what way? How are they different?'

'The Bushmen have distinct genetics and physiognomy. Take the . . . steatopygia –'

'Steato – what?'

'The enormous buttocks. They are an adaptation to climatic harshness and regular famine. Like a camel's hump. And the women also have something called a Hottentot apron. Francis Galtony the great eugenicist, called it hypertrophy of the nymphae. Which is very delicate. He actually examined the women's vaginas with a sextant.'

'Are you saying,' Amy asked, her voice tremulous, 'that the women of the Bushmen, the Hottentots or whatever, that they have different . . . *genitals*?'

'Yes. They do. Different labia. They are distended and slightly askew. If the Bushmen were, like, seagulls, a taxonomist would probably put them in their own category. A subspecies.' Angus smiled in the car mirror at David's appalled and astonished face. 'Incidentally isn't it weird that Eugen Fischer, the greatest eugenicist after Galton, was called *Eugen*? It's like Charles Darwin's parents calling him *Evolute* Darwin instead of Chas.' He paused. 'Not that Fischer was the most consistent racist. He wasn't. When he was here he befriended the Kellermans. He liked nice cultured intelligent millionaire Jews in Johannesburg and Cape Town – with beautiful Jewish wives. He was less keen on Zulus. OK where are we?'

Angus stared at the drifting sands ahead. The dunes were nearly all gone now, they were entering a flatter, slightly greener landscape; still desert, but with the odd little camelthorn tree, and yellow acres of pristine dust. David checked his watch. They had been driving for many hours. Hundreds and hundreds of miles, right across central Namibia. They hadn't seen one other human being.

345

Angus said: 'We should head for Aus. Then across the desert to Rosh.' Angus squinted at the sun. 'Though we're not gonna make Aus before dark . . . Yes take that track there, by the ranch gates.' He sat back. 'So I was saying about the Hottentots. The Hotties are the sedentary version of the Bushmen, the Khoisan. Anyway, they had these creepy habits that the early researchers found *altogether* disturbing. Like the priest urinating on the newly wed couple, that wasn't too popular. And the worshipping of grasshoppers. And of course the constant eating of intestines was a big winner. And when they get married the Bushmen have one single teste removed. How weird is that?' He grinned, with a certain wildness. 'I always used to . . . tease Alfie about that. Told him to come and live with me in Scotland with his one teste. So he could be Monorch of the Glen.'

Amy spoke up, her voice full of emotion: 'Angus, I don't think this is funny.'

'No?'

'Are *you* simply racist? Or just a *bit* racist?'

A huge plume of dust was riding behind them, like a bridal train of orange-grey floating on a breeze.

Angus snapped his reply: 'I *despise* racism. I hate it. Racism is stupid. It's like hating donkeys for not being sheep. Besides . . . we are all the children of God. All brothers and sisters.'

David was startled.

'You believe in *God*?'

The scientist was almost angry.

'How can you *not* believe in God? In a place like this? This is the last and greatest Namibian desert. The Succulent Karoo. Look at it, the driest place in the world, arguably, but watered by the fogs that come off the sea – thataway. Check the *farcical* trees. Entirely different ecosystem.'

He was pointing at a fat thorny awkward sapling, with massive spikes stark against the cloudless blue.

346

'*Koekerboom*. The fauna and flora here are remarkable: lunatic cacti, insane beetles, thousand-year-old trees that burrow *underground*. There are also hyenas: a uniquely vicious subspecies called the strandwolf. Saw one once near Luderitz, frightened the living shit out of me. They prowl the beaches eating seal pups. Look like stage villains.'

David thought of Miguel, out there, hunting them down. *The strandwolf.*

Angus was still talking, a determined monologue. 'But this is why I believe. Look at it. Look at it! It's not an accident so many religions come from the desert. And this is the most daunting of all deserts. Look at this landscape!' He waved, quite furiously, at the wilderness. 'I'd like to drop a planeload of atheists at Luderitz airport and send them out across the wastes with a packet of cashew nuts. Within ten days they'd either be dead or believers. Atheists. Fuck 'em. *Adolescent wankers.*'

David was perplexed. He simply couldn't work out Angus Nairn. He was like no one he had ever met. Angus was still talking.

'Of course that doesn't mean God is this nice guy. He ain't. The universe is fascist. It is a tyranny, a mad dictatorship. Stalin's Terror. Saddam's Iraq. It's all so random and scary. We all lie there at night thinking, when will death come for *me? Don't we?* And one by one, we disappear. The Death Gestapo comes, and they drag you away, and you are expertly tortured, with lung cancer, heart failure, Alzheimer's.' Angus was talking to himself, almost. 'And people whisper, they tell each other, "You hear about so-and-so? He's gone. He's gone as well. They took him last night . . .".' He shook his head. 'Alphonse, poor fucking Alphonse . . .'

The car motored south. Angus was, finally, quite silent.

David thought of his grandfather, and that eagle circling the Arizona sky. The Sonora desert was beautiful, but Angus was right: this desert, the Succulent Karoo, was even more stirring, in a haunted way. The green and yellow bushman's grass, the pale acacias, the pink acid wastes scarred by long disused railways. It was desolate but transfixing: and the violet and purple mountains, the sudden inselbergs, they floated above the hazy and aethereal sands like a kind of memory; a memory of mountains, in the ghost of a landscape.

He stared and drove, and thought of his grandfather. His grandfather's strange and guilty shame.

Desolada, desolada, desolada . . .

Three hours later the sun had gone, and the violet-purples had turned to grainy black, and they were racing, silently and very fast, through the darkness. The true and noble darkness of the desert.

It was cold.

They were quiet and exhausted. Every so often the eyes of a nocturnal animal would catch in the headlights – a bat-eared fox, a desert hare. Then darkness. And then the headlights illuminated a big sign: *Sperrgebiet. Diamond Zone 1. Extreme Danger.*

'OK,' said Angus. 'Down that dirt road.'

Two hundred metres further, sudden lights blazed. Two armed black men had emerged from a wooden hut, with rifles cocked. They had torches: their faces were grim and determined.

'Stop!'

Angus leaned out of the car.

'Solomon. Tilac. It's me!'

A silence.

'Angus?'

Now the men were smiling.

'Angus. You de bloody mad man. We could have shoot you!'

'Sorry – sorry –'

348

The guards stepped back. One of them was flamboyantly waving them through.

They sped past; the untarred road was rumbling and rocky. Though it was hard to tell in the silvering darkness, the landscape seemed to have changed. The night air was still cooler.

David realized he could smell the sea, salty and pungent.

And there indeed was the ocean, glittering malevolently in the moonlight. The road ran up and over seaside rocks, bare grey rocks. Ahead of them was the twinkle of more lights: the silhouette of structure, a large complex of buildings, bristling with antennae and satellite dishes.

'Tamara Minehead,' said Angus. 'Park here.'

The reaction to their arrival was immediate: several men came straight out, one of them a tall and languid white man, in an intoxicatingly impractical grey flannel suit.

'Nathan,' said Angus, very wearily. 'This is Amy . . . Myerson and David . . . Martinez. Friends . . . those friends of Eloise. Friends, this is Nathan Kellerman.'

Nathan Kellerman stepped closer. He was young and handsome.

'My God, Angus, what happened to you all? You look terrible.'

'We're fine. Just need sleep. Fine.'

'And Alphonse, where is Alphonse? Everyone else? What the hell happened?'

Angus shrugged; a painful silence enveloped them.

Nathan Kellerman lifted a manicured hand. His tone sharpened. His accent was faintly American.

'Do you have the blood samples? The last blood samples, Angus!'

'Yes.'

'Then –' David could see Kellerman's relieved smile, his perfect white teeth. 'Then all is well. Let's go inside. Robbie, Anton. Help the good people.'

Slowly they shuffled through the bright modern building: offices, corridors, bedrooms. The cleanliness and modernity made an intense contrast to the privations of the desert. Expensively thin TVs, gleaming white kitchens. Cold steel fridges with glittering test tubes. It was another stunning dislocation, like stumbling on a Venetian palazzo in the jungle.

David and Amy were led to a bedroom. He tried to look calm and normal as they undressed, but some uncrystallized thought was troubling him. Something. Something. What was it?

He looked at his hands. Were they twitching? Maybe there had been some infection. From the body liquor.

He thought of Miguel sniffing the meat. He thought of Amy's eyes as she looked at him; would she still look at Miguel the same way, sometime? David was bewildered by the absence of Eloise. Amy came close and kissed him.

'Hey –'

'Eloise,' he said. 'Where is Eloise . . .?'

'I know,' said Amy. 'I know. But . . . I am *so* tired. I can't even think . . . Let's just . . . Tomorrow . . .'

Amy was nuzzling close. Scared and close and exhausted. The bedroom looked out onto the sea; a sharp salty breeze was lifting the curtains through the open window. The moon was high. It looked like a white screaming face, the face of someone being tormented.

They lay together in the moonlit bedroom, quite still, for a few moments.

Then they quickly fell asleep.

And he dreamed.

He was eating some meat, chewing on some gristly biltong; the dried meat was really gristly and bony. He was in his grandfather's hospital room, the desert was blinding outside. Then Granddad reached from his bed and pointed. David turned, with a mouthful of biltong, and he saw a naked girl, standing outside in the desert. And then he saw: she had no hands. And the reason she had no hands was because David was eating her hands. He realized he was *eating her hands*.

David woke with a jolt of terror; it was the middle of the night, he was staring at the still-screaming silent desert moon, through the square windows, with Amy snoring courteously beside him.

At last he had the truth. David now realized the truth: why he had been thinking about his grandfather. His grandfather's shame and guilt. The inability to explain, the terrible furtiveness.

He was in the Forbidden Zone in his mind, he had crossed into the Forbidden Land.

Granddad was a Cagot. It was the only explanation that made any sense; that explained it all. *Granddad was a Cagot*. An untouchable. A pariah. A cannibal of Gascony. The Cagots were indeed cannibals. And David was descended from a Cagot: he was one of them.

Amy snored and turned over; her bare young shoulder was soft in the moonlight. Soft like a succulent peach.

40

Simon was standing at a payphone, by a bunch of exiled smokers just outside Gate A of Lyon Saint Exupéry airport. A watery October sun was rising over the terminals. The first planes were rumbling and ascending into the grey morning air.

The journalist weighed the shining euros in his hand. He'd tried calling Suzie through the night but got no reply. Were they safe? Where was Tim? His heart confessed his guilt – with a nasty stab of pain. He'd got some information out of the monk at Tourette, but was it worth it? What if something *had* happened? Where was Suzie? She could just be at work. But it was so early. And Conor. What about *Conor*? Where was his mother-in-law? And Tim?

The questions raked his soul.

There was no one left to call. But he'd also tried his parents, and they too were out –

So he had no choice. He had to try the police. Simon stared down at his euro coins. One, two, three . . .?

Fumbling with the change, he fed the phone. It rang. And it was answered.

'DCI Sanderson.'

Simon paused – took a breath of diesely air – and then he gabbled his questions. Tim. Conor. Suzie. Conor. Tim.

The policeman interrupted:

'OK, Quinn, OK. I'm with you. Calm down. Are you on a payphone?'

'Yes.'

'Where?'

The doubt crept into Simon's thoughts.

'Somewhere in France. I chucked my new mobile. Don't trust it. Don't know . . . who to trust . . . Tell me what is happening.'

Sanderson said, very gently: 'They're fine. Your wife and son . . . are fine. But . . . there's been . . . developments. Last night. I'm heading into my chief super's office now. We'll call you, I promise, in a few seconds. What's your number?'

'Developments? Is Conor OK? Have they found Tim?'

'Conor's totally fine. Suzie too. Safe as houses. *What's your number?*'

Simon swallowed his anxieties; his anxieties had the horrible savour of bile, as if he had recently thrown up. He pressed a finger against his other ear, to drown out the sound of the airplanes. And he spelled out the digits.

'Wait there,' said the DCI. 'I'm talking to the CS right now. Wait there and . . . trust me?'

Simon nodded and chunked the receiver. He looked at the dull steel payphone.

'*Bonjour . . .*'

He swivelled. An affable-looking French chap, in neat jeans, and a light turquoise cashmere jumper – thrown suavely over his shoulders – was standing behind; the man was gesturing at the phone and smiling.

'*Je voudrais utiliser?*'

Simon growled.

'Go away.'

The man stared at Simon. Perplexed.

Simon growled again.

'Go away! *Merci fucking beaucoup!*'

The Frenchman backed away, then actually ran into the terminal.

The phone trilled. Simon picked up.

'OK –' Sanderson's tone was clipped, yet sympathetic. 'I just wanted to get the latest from CS Boateng.'

'What are these . . . *developments*?'

'I've got extra men looking after your wife and son. And your mum and dad. That's why they are safe. No one can get to them – these religious geezers, no one. No one can touch *them*. We haven't rung you because we are being very careful, after what's happened . . .'

The journalist had a cruel sense, at last, where this conversation was going.

The policeman confirmed it.

'It's Tim. Simon. Yer brother Tim. Why didn't you tell us anything about *Tim*?'

'I . . . don't know . . . I just don't know why.'

Simon shuddered with remorse. Tim. Of course. Why *hadn't* he mentioned Tim? When Sanderson had asked about family members who could require protection, he *had not* cited Tim. Why? Was it because he was *ashamed* of Tim? Or because he just didn't want to *think* about Tim? Or because he really thought Tim was safe so it was irrelevant?

Maybe it was all three explanations. Tied into a knot of denial.

'What's *happened* to him? Jesus. Is he . . .'

'Not dead. But we know he's been taken. Kidnapped.'

'*How do you know?* Are you *sure* he hasn't just run away?'

Sanderson's voice was dry and cool. 'Sorry. No. We have proof. They took him.'

'Proof?'

'A video. In an email. The captors sent it to everyone late last night. It went to your wife, your parents, and you, I'm guessing. If you get a chance to look at your email. You'll find it. I suggest you delete first.'

'Sorry?'

'Don't watch it, Simon. Really. Don't watch it!'

'Why?'

'It's . . . bloody distressing.'

A plane was landing, with a malign roar. Simon pressed the phone closer: 'Are they torturing him?'

'No. But they are . . . using him. Manipulating emotions. And they do it well. They want to use your feelings, your guilt, to get at you. He's their purchase on you. They clearly know you are in touch with Martinez, and Myerson. They will want all this, they want everything you know. Tim is in a lot of danger.'

'So what do I do now? What can I do? Come *home*?'

'No.'

'Then what?

'Hide.'

Simon pressed the phone closer to his ear, to make sure he was hearing correctly. '*Hide?* You just want me to . . . hide out?'

'Just for now. Yes.' Sanderson's voice dropped a few tones. 'I'm sorry but there it is. You chose to do what you did. You're out there now. I don't blame you for that. But . . . haring across France. Not telling us. Less than brilliant. But you've made your decision. And now you're probably facing a bigger risk if you come back to London. You might be spotted *en route*, they will expect you to try and find your family. Your friends out there said we can't trust the police in France, right? So it's very bleeding tricky. Who knows where they will have people.' He sighed, fiercely. 'Main thing is – your wife and son are safe: I can vouch for that. My men are good. And there's nothing you can do to help us find Tim.'

'So I stay here?'

'Stay there, for now, until we work this out. Stay quiet in France or Germany, you can cross the border unseen thanks to Schengen. Lie low. Very very bloody low. You know to use payphones only.'

'Yes.'

'Don't even use the same payphone twice. Call me direct as before . . . Call Suzie on this special number.'

Simon patted his pockets and found a pen. He wrote the number.

The DCI sighed.

'Simon . . . I'm sorry about this. But you should . . . prepare yourself for the worst. And don't watch the video. You know how ruthless these bastards are. Speak soon.'

The phone clicked and brrrd. Simon thought of his brother.

I made a dog hope you like it.

41

The morning was bright and unutterably dazzling. David was woken by a knock on the door. Another employee, explaining:

'Mistah Kellerman want you to join him on the terrace.'

David glanced across. He must have fallen asleep again, and the exhausted sleep had been profound: they hadn't noticed the sun rising behind the flimsy curtains.

He tried not to think about the nightmare as they showered.

But Amy sensed something.

'Are you OK?'

'Yes. Yes of course . . . Thank God we made it.'

She looked at him.

'Let's go and find Eloise.'

They changed into clean clothes, sourced from a wardrobe, then they exited into the corridor. Immediately the assistant appeared, and guided them out onto a sunlit terrace, overlooking the sea.

The wind had dropped. The view was austere but pristine: an entirely empty beach, a couple of small rocky islands in the bay. The barking of distant seals. South and north stretched rocky wilderness, echoing coves and cliffs. Only the hulking metal shape of a diamond mine interrupted the abject desolation, far in the distance.

A table was set up on the terrace. Angus was there, drinking coffee. Kellerman was beside him, dressed in a cream linen suit, and a discreet silk tie.

And Eloise was sitting across the table.

Amy ran over, and hugged the young Cagot girl.

Nathan gestured in David's direction.

'Please sit.'

They sat. They talked animatedly with Eloise. She seemed relaxed, even happy. Or at least, not afraid.

Someone served a basket of pastries, and more fresh coffee, freshly squeezed juice, and cold meats and bread. The luxury was sumptuous and startling: like they had just checked into a surprisingly good hotel in Hell.

David and Amy both fell upon the food: instantly realizing how hungry they were. But then David stopped, and paused, and shuddered – and slid the glistening pink ham off his plate back onto the serving dish. He chose more fruit and bread. Not meat. He didn't want meat.

Kellerman watched them, sipping his coffee from a china cup. Silent and aloof. His slender cellphone resting on the table. David had never seen such an anorexic cellphone.

Angus spoke first: 'Guys. We're safe here for the moment. I've been talking with Nathan. They won't dare to come into the Sperrgebiet. Not past the guards.'

'Are you sure?'

Angus flashed a glance at Nathan. Who nodded, rather casually; he was checking something on his phone.

Angus turned back.

'So we can relax. For a day or two.'

David nearly laughed, with open and outright contempt, at the word *relax*.

Relax?

The image of Alphonse was cut into his thoughts, tattooed on his neocortex. A man burnt to cinders, screaming his death agony: Miguel inhaling the scent of the meat. The Cannibalistic Cagot . . .

He suppressed his shudder and finished breakfast. Bread and fruit and cheese. No meat. They talked about the penguins and the seals on the islands offshore. Eloise said she had found a sandrose on the beach the previous day, a beautiful sandrose.

'And there are agates too!'

Her enthusiasm was touching, and teenage, and winning, but David couldn't cope. It was all too much. He just couldn't make small talk. Just couldn't. He pushed back his chair, and stretched and apologized – he needed to be alone. Amy looked his way and he tried to smile and failed, but he didn't say anything. He didn't want to talk about anything.

David walked across the terrace, down some concrete steps onto the empty beach. A big factory ship was way offshore, beyond the islands. The sands were grey and shining in the hot sun. The coastline, as far as he could see, was lunar in its sterility. The coastline of the Forbidden Zone. Last refuge of the Cagots.

'Hey?'

He swivelled. It was Angus, joining him.

'David. You OK?'

A brief and piercing pause.

'I'm fine.'

The Scotsman's answering smile was sad, and sceptical. He said nothing. David could bear it no longer. He had to confess; he needed to confess.

'Angus . . . do you think it is possible . . .' He had to force the words out of himself. 'That I am a Cagot? Of Cagot decent, at least. I've been thinking about my grandfather.

His guilt and shame. The only thing that makes sense is . . . that he was a Cagot too. Maybe he found out at Gurs, like José Garovillo.'

The scientist tilted his head, his pale white face even paler in the harsh Sperrgebiet sun.

'I had wondered if you would reach that conclusion.'

'So? What do you think?'

'To my mind, you do not present any of the obvious Cagot syndromes, but you do have, maybe, the colouration.'

'S'what I thought. Jesus.'

'It doesn't mean you will go mad. Not definitely. You may be fine, like Eloise. And then again you may not be.'

'Christ.'

'The only way we can know for sure is genetic testing. If you want. If you want I can do that here, in the labs. Do you really want to know?'

The truth was close, yet utterly unbearable. Like an HIV test, but infinitely worse. David stared out to sea. A smaller boat was floating there, closer than the great factory boat. Maybe a skiff, belonging to local fishermen.

David exhaled.

'I don't know, Angus. It's . . . so fucking difficult. I'm frightened, if I'm honest. I don't want to know that . . . I am like Miguel. How could I tolerate knowing that?'

'Of course.'

The two men kicked stones, and walked further down the beach, talking quietly. Angus was in pensive, discursive mood: speaking of the Serpent Seed, the Biblical tales of separate races of men. Then the scientist stopped, and stared at the virulent blue sea, the little islands offshore; he was speaking of earlier forms of hominid, *Homo antecessor, Homo habilis*, and then *Homo floresiensis*, a dwarf-like relative of man.

'You know they may have lived into recorded history,'

Angus surveyed the rocky islets. 'How creepy is that? Lost on the islands of Indonesia: an elf, a hobbit, a goblin . . .'

David barely listened. Silent and brooding.

Angus pointed out to the waters.

'Sea nettles.'

A few metres out, the coastal seawater was patched and dotted with dozens of diaphanous scarlet jellyfish, some of them a metre across, their fronds and tentacles pulsing organically.

They were beautiful yet repulsive. Angus elaborated.

'*Chrysaora Hysoscella.* Namibian sea nettles. They always remind me of vaginas. The colour and movement. The peristalsis of female orgasm.' He gazed. 'But now they remind me of floating . . . wounds. Big floating red wounds.'

Angus looked at David. And then the scientist said, quite fiercely: 'I just let him die. Didn't I?'

'Sorry?'

'Alfie. My little Alfie. I let them kill him – that fucker Miguel.'

'No, Angus. You tried to save him.'

'But I failed. I *failed* . . .'

The Scotsman looked vulnerable; the chutzpah was gone, the persistent smile, the chattering self confidence. His face was twitching, close to tears.

'I was trying to think of a better way out! I really was. I was. And I did. The euphorbia. But it was too late.' The Scotsman knelt and picked up a beautiful seashell, a whorl of creamy porcelain veined with pink and yellow, and a thread of tenderest red. Tender and vulnerable.

The seashell lay nestled in his palm. Angus gazed down; he was choked, almost sobbing.

'This is why I believe in God, David. I mean. *Look at this shell.* Why is it so beautiful? Why? It's pointlessly beautiful, isn't it? Purposelessly beautiful, why make a seashell so beautiful? Who does that benefit? What's the point? It's excessive. Evolution is itself *excessive*. This is where creationists have it *wrong*, the universe isn't designed – it is *inspired*.'

He dropped the shell. He kicked it away. Again David didn't know what to say.

Angus was still talking.

'I lied back then, David.'

'What do you mean?'

'At breakfast, I lied.'

'How?'

'I'm not sure they will be stalled by the guards. The Society. Not for long.'

'So . . .' David felt the horror of the inevitable thought: Miguel still out there, coming for them. 'What do we do?'

'Nathan is too arrogant to listen. I tried to tell him earlier but he wouldn't listen. He thinks he is impregnable here, the Forbidden Zone. Safe in his dynastic fortress. The great Kellermans of the Sperrgebiet. But he *isn't* safe. Kellerman Namcorp is powerful, but not *that* fucking powerful. The whole church? If they want to get at us they will find a way.' The sunlight made Angus's red hair almost coppery. 'We need a plan. Because they will come. Tomorrow, a few days, next week. They are coming for us as we speak.'

David stared across the tarnished silver of the sea. The Scotsman was surely right: they needed a means of escape.

The barks of the seals on the island were carried by the hot and savoury breeze. Penguins were chittering in their colonies on the smaller islands. It was, David realized, a world of unwitnessed beauty, the beauty of nothingness, no one ever saw this: the dead quartz and glittering ashes, the agates and buried sandroses: a wasteland of loveliness.

Out there on the blue severe waves, someone was observing. David looked, hard. It was a man, standing on the deck of the skiff. A man with a pair of binoculars, or something.

The man was standing and gazing through the binoculars –
at the buildings on the shore.

This man was staring straight at them. And there was a
man next to him, pointing. But the man wasn't pointing.

David felt the uncomfortable prickle of anxiety.

Now he realized: the man had some kind of . . . device.
A long black shape. Directed their way.

Angus was heading for the sheltering rocks.

'Run! David! *Run!*'

But David stood on the beach, gaping with the horror.

The first missile streaked eagerly through the clear blue
sky.

42

The fireballs were huge and billowing: monstrous black clouds tinged with Satanic tangerine. Towers of pungent smoke filled the sky.

'Amy! Amy!'

David edged up over the parapet of sand: the complex of buildings was *gone*. Replaced by a hideous wall of flame and devastation; the air was shuddering with the heat of the blaze; secondary explosions added to the surging noise.

Angus was prone beside him. Lying on the sand. He put a hand on David's shoulder.

'It's the oil generator – the fuel's gone up.' The Scotsman turned on his back, and looked towards the sea. 'The boat . . . The bastard boat . . . *Fuck* –'

David was staring in horror at the destruction: anyone in or around the building would have stood no chance. No hope. No chance.

Angus muttered:

'They must have come from Walvis Bay? Maybe Oranjemund . . .'

'David?'

A softer voice. David swivelled.

It was Amy. She was unharmed. Standing in the sand. Trembling.

And behind her was Nathan Kellerman, bleeding profusely, and staggering.

Amy sank into David's embrace.

'I was coming down to see you . . . then I got knocked over . . .'

He hugged her close. Angus asked Nathan:

'Eloise?'

Kellerman's voice was slow, and wearied:

'She was engulfed.'

His suit was smeared with a tar-like substance; David realized it was *blood*. Kellerman was bleeding from a chest wound.

And now a new noise joined the tumult, cars were screaming to the shoreline, and men in blue overalls and desert boots were jumping out. David recognized Solomon and Tilac, the Kellerman Namcorp guards. Nathan lifted an arm:

'Shoot.'

The men obeyed: they unhoisted rifles and knelt in the sand, and took aim. The boat was already departing, churning south – job done. But the Namcorp men fired anyway, and the echoes of the crackling rifle fire joined the roar of the burning fuel dumps, and the soft explosion of buildings crumpling in the flames. The smell of burning petrol was vicious, greasy black smoke was fogging the oceanic sky. Amy was shivering now. Angus was remonstrating with Nathan.

David could barely hear their conversation. He caught the odd word: *Amsterdam, helicopter, dinghy*. He looked between the two of them. Nathan was handing something to Angus. It looked like a gun, a pistol – and something else: a small black velvet pouch. Despite his deep tan, Nathan Kellerman had a notably white pallor; and the blood was still oozing from some hideous wound, staining his soft linen jacket a blatant burgundy. Angus, by contrast, seemed energized; he turned to David and Amy.

'Nathan wants us to use the company boat, down there.' He pointed. 'He's right. We actually have a chance – let's take it.'

'What?'

Angus gestured at the wide black cloud now drifting down the beach. 'They'll have zero visibility for an hour or two. The guards can hold them off with gunfire.'

David protested:

'Eloise . . .'

'She is dead, David. Nathan wouldn't lie. *Come on.* They'll be watching the roads out of the Forbidden Zone, but if we take the boat to Luderitz –'

Amy said, very softly: 'I think he's right.'

Angus was already hoisting Nathan's sagging arm over his shoulder, assisting him down the beach. David and Amy swapped glances, then followed, stunned and frightened. A few more rifle shots smacked the hot air behind them.

Behind the next cove was a small pier, and a tethered rubber speedboat with a powerful looking engine.

Angus got in, and assisted his benefactor into the boat. But his boss's head was lolling, unsteady on its axis. Amy climbed in alongside; David swiftly followed. The oily smoke from the explosions blotted out the sun, turning the desert day into twilight. The Scotsman ripped the cord, the motor growled, and moments later they were speeding along the coast.

Flames and burning buildings receded behind. For a while they were silent, watching the dismal spectacle slowly dwindling, the dinghy buffeted through the blue choppy waves. They passed a disused diamond mine: a skeleton of eroding steel looming above the cliffs.

Nathan was almost whispering, as he lay back on the black

rubber of the boat. His face wet with sweat, a Navajo smear of red blood across his cheek.

'So Eloise is dead. The last Cagot . . .'

'Yes.' Angus wore a regretful smile. 'They won, Nathan. Miguel is no damn use.'

An anxious pause. Nathan Kellerman reached out a hand, and touched Angus's wrist. The gesture was delicate, gracious, refined.

'Angus. There is one more way.'

'What?'

'Find the Fischer results.'

'What?'

The glittering green eyes of the Scottish scientist were fixed on the pained and twitching face of his boss, Nathan Kellerman. David leaned close to try and overhear this pained and fraught conversation. Angus asked Kellerman, 'You know where they are?'

'No. But . . . Dresler maybe. Maybe he does. He was the last option. If we failed at Tamara that was my very last option – I think he knows where they kept the data – but he will – it will be difficult to get it out of him.' Kellerman coughed, into his own hand. He looked down at his palm, now cupping his own blood. The Jewish dynast fell back, and gazed at the sky, a kind of wild acceptance in his eyes. Accepting the sky and the sea. Then his barely focussed eyes turned to Angus, once more.

'So Dresler knows, I think. And I always felt I could force it out of him, if I was truly desperate, but you'd have to take him . . . very close to the edge. I never wanted to risk it before, he was too useful.' Another anguished cough. Then he continued, grimacing. 'But now? What does it matter? Try it. Nothing to lose.' Kellerman was sweating in the sun. 'And this is my stop, Angus. Here's where I get off.'

Angus grabbed at Kellerman. 'C'mon, Nathan.'

'I am fucked, Angus. Look.' Nathan opened the jacket, like a prostitute letting fall her nightgown; a huge glistening oval of blood, like a red scarlet sea nettle, pulsed in his chest. Amy and David stared at each other. Angus had turned, he was trying to slow the boat; but even as the motor puttered out, Nathan Kellerman lifted himself to the side of the boat.

David shouted, reflexively:

'No!'

It was too late. Kellerman was over the side and slipping into the water, into the cold Namibian waters. David stared, aghast. Kellerman's white face was a sad oval in the blueness; Angus was steering the boat to a halt.

But Nathan was already half under, slipping deeper into the waves. His chest smoking blood.

And now the sharks were on him. The water was crazy with dorsal fins, evil and swooping. David glimpsed a vicious serration of teeth, already stained red. The devouring fish were tearing in a frenzy at the bleeding and flailing body, pulling it under. David couldn't help watching: the sight was transfixing. The sharks were ripping at the arms and the legs, like a kind of obscene children's game. Tagging and taunting the scapegoat. And then moving in for the kill.

Nathan Kellerman didn't scream. He seemed to accept his hideous death as he was torn apart, and pulled under the waves for the final time. David stared down into the sapphire fathoms; the sharks were pirouetting around the dim black corpse. A belch of blood and gas burst to the surface, foaming the waters red.

And then silence.

Angus said nothing. He started the boat, once again, and they cruised through the anxious waves, under the dignified sun.

They motored past the desolate coves. Sea birds wheeled,

their cries like dying falls. David stared at the black rocks and yellow sands.

He thought of the blood in the water; a man being eaten alive.

Then the Scotsman spoke.

'All the data and the bloods were in that building. And Eloise. Everything's gone. And he thought we'd be safe . . .' Angus was shaking his head. 'Kellerman was so stupidly stupidly wrong. Poor bastard.' The Scotsman adjusted the rudder, to steer them closer to the shore. 'We'll be in Luderitz soon.'

David voiced the obvious question:

'And then?'

'We've got a few hours' grace. But the Namibian authorities will have to intervene. So it will become common knowledge that we got out.'

Amy said, 'And we'll be stuck in Luderitz. What good is that?'

'There is a means of escape.'

'How?'

Angus explained, quite calmly.

'The diamond shipment. Nathan reminded me. Every other day, Kellerman Namcorp transports rough diamonds to Amsterdam. Just like De Beers, flying gems into London.' Another tilt on the rudder. 'The shipments go via Windhoek.'

David protested:

'But –'

'I can get you on. They know me. And passport control is essentially run by the company itself. You'll be landed at Kellerman HQ in Amsterdam. Back in Europe. Home safe and sound.'

'And you?'

'Dunno. Might take brunch . . . *Whatever.*'

'You're just gonna give up?'

The red-haired scientist gazed down the sunlit coast. The smoke storms were a long way away now.

'What do you expect me to do? Go back and start over? I'm done. I'm finished. It was my stupid ego that got me this steeped in blood. I thought I could repeat Fischer, get his data, then get the Nobel, God knows. With Nathan's help. But were they ever really gonna give me prizes for revealing something so apocalyptic? For guaranteeing war? I was an idiot. Race is the curse, the curse of God on man. And Kellerman had his own motives. Leviticus 25. I was so bloody *stupid.*'

'What are you talking about?'

'Work it out. My ego got Alphonse killed, Eloise killed. Nathan is dead. You guys nearly killed. Fazackerly is dead. It's so fucking over. I'm moving on. Turning a new leaf. Drawing a line. Might take up golf.'

'*But I'm not done.*' It was Amy talking. The two men looked at her; blonde hair floating on the hot salty breeze.

'Remember what José said?' She looked first at Angus, then at David. 'When he said I know what happened to the Jews – that's the whole key to this isn't it, Angus? Whatever this . . . secret is . . . that you were working towards. It explains why the Jews died in the Holocaust, doesn't it? Eloise told us that. You told her something.'

Angus piloted the boat without a word.

But Amy's face was set in that determined expression. She insisted:

'That's the big mystery, isn't it? Why the Holocaust? That's what this is all headed towards, isn't it?'

Angus was still silent, but Amy was fired up: 'Tell me this is it, Angus. *Tell me.* Hitler could have used the Jews as slave labour – and he had plans to put them in some homeland, in Russia or Africa, right? But then suddenly he changed his mind.' She gazed at Angus. 'Suddenly he decided he had to kill them. All of them. Even if it crippled – overextended and destroyed – the German war effort. Why did he do that?'

Angus was quiet, then he sighed.

'Yes. Sort of. It does explain the Holocaust. Maybe. Who knows. I only mentioned it to Eloise . . .' His expression darkened. 'Because I felt sorry for her. The last Cagot in the world. She was in pain. She deserved a little explanation for what was happening.'

'So what is it? What did Fischer find?'

'*Can't fucking tell you.* Because I have no proof. I never make a statement without proof. I am a scientist.' He gazed their way, angrily. 'Why not cut me some. Eh? My boyfriend is dead *and* Eloise's blood is also on my damn hands. Enough. *Enough.*'

'You won't tell us.'

'No. *Because I don't know for sure.* I never did the fucking Fischer experiments. But . . . but if Kellerman was right, there is a man who can maybe help. *That's what Nathan was saying.*'

The switchback moods of the Scotsman were bewildering. He was now staring ahead. David followed his gaze along the austere coast. He could see buildings, the spire of a church, brightly painted houses. Another surreal German town perched on the desert coast, overlooking the brutal sea.

David returned to the conversation.

'What man?'

Angus slowed the boat as they began their approach to the port. And said:

'Nazi. Cancerous old Nazi named Dresler, who worked with Fischer at Gurs. Knew Grandpa Kellerman. And as you heard – just here on the boat – *Dresler knows.*'

Amy said:

'Please explain. Knows what?'

'Herr Doktor Dresler fled here from Europe, in the 1990s.

371

He was uncovered somehow. Don't know how. So he came here. Good place to hide, Luderitz, million miles from the next *kartoffelsalat*. And he already knew the Kellermans.'

'And?'

'Remember. Rewind. Go back.'

'Sorry?'

'In 1946 Eugen Fischer got in touch with his old friends, the Kellermans, and told them what he had found at Gurs. And *naturlich* the Kellermans were . . . very excited by the news of what the Germans had discovered.' The boat was slowing. 'But the Kellermans had no proof – they didn't have the actual data. So they have been waiting for genetic science to catch up with the Germans – for six decades.' Angus smiled, laconically. 'They take a long view, these dynastic Jews. They've been waiting since the Babylonian Captivity, you might say. Anyway the Kellermans had hopes of the Diversity Project at Stanford but *that* folded.' He blinked as water splashed the boat. 'Then GenoMap kicked off – and so they basically took us over, and used us. To repeat the Fischer experiments. Then Dresler was coaxed south, he came to live here in the 1990s and he was able to help, with lots of info. People to bloodtest and so forth. Routes to explore. And eventually . . . the Cagots.'

He looked at David.

Amy asked: 'But . . . how can Dresler help us *now*?'

'Because. If what Nathan said is right, then Dresler also knows what the doctors did after the war. He knows the lot.'

'*After* the war? What does that mean?'

A shrug.

'Angus!'

The Scotsman slowed the dinghy further. Sea birds wheeled behind. He gazed at Amy, then at David: 'The Nazis discovered DNA – during the war.'

David was so stunned he felt the boat wobble beneath him. He gasped: '*DNA?*'

'Yup. They'd been onto it a while. Fischer, and so forth: he got the first intimations in Namibia, studying the *Khoisan* and the Basters. Then he clinched the proof at Gurs. But that's not key to what I'm saying. It's what the Nazis did with this technology. Because of what they *then* found, *within and between human genetic variation* – that's the key. It was a discovery so . . .' Angus shrugged. 'I mean *allegedly* – I don't have proof, and probably never will now – but it was a discovery *allegedly* so devastating that it led to the Holocaust. And it was *so* powerful it gave the Nazi doctors leverage – after the war.'

'I still don't get the whole picture . . .'

Angus tutted, impatiently, but explained. 'At the end of the war, the Nazi doctors from Gurs had one bargaining chip, which they could swap for their lives and freedom. And that bargaining chip was the Fischer results. The rumour is they hid the data somewhere . . . inaccessible. In Europe is my guess. Probably in central Europe, as the Allies pressed in on the shrinking Nazi empire.' He eyed the shallowing waters, then went on: 'The Allies couldn't imprison them, or try them, let alone execute them. In case one of the other doctors revealed the results.'

Amy interrupted: 'So the doctors were freed. Exonerated. Fischer became . . . professor at Freiburg, in 1945, despite everything he'd done.'

'Yes.'

'So this doctor in Luderitz? How does he fit in?'

'Well, if what poor Nathan said is right, Dresler knows where the results are hidden.'

David felt the surge of excitement. Angus raised a hand.

'Sure, it is compelling . . . But remember the Nazis must have hidden the data somewhere wildly inaccessible. Plenty of people have tried to find it. Who knows though.' Angus paused. 'Maybe we will?'

David was curious.

'We? You're coming along?'

He ran his fingers through his red hair. Eyes bright. 'K, I confess, you got me, it's a fair cop. I'm piqued. I'm intrigued. You shoot, you score. Maybe Dresler *does* know. And if so . . . *I want to know too*. I spent five years on this, I want to know if my hunch was right, about the Jews, Hitler, the Holocaust, the Basters.'

He leaned and flung a rope as the dinghy bumped into the pier. 'But first we have to go see Dresler. And torture the truth out of him.'

43

Simon walked nervously down the cobbled high street. Autumn in the Bavarian Alps was quiet. The ski shops were shut; and tourists were few, mainly hikers huddled over big maps, flapping in the breeze. It was a cold and greyish day and the kitsch, gilded streets were largely deserted.

But he still felt nervous. He'd have preferred the anonymity of a hotel in a big city, but didn't dare use credit cards or show his passport: so he'd chosen here, Garmischpartenkirchen, as a compromise. Suzie and he had been here on holiday years ago.

Suzie.

Suzie and Conor.

Suzie and Conor and Tim.

He was lodged in a cold austere cottage, in an ugly new development, in the silence of the Alps, just above the little town. But every minute of every day he'd felt the need for information. An overwhelming need.

So he'd spent half his time in the little town, on payphones to Sanderson and Suzie, or sitting in the internet cafe, with its tinkling bell above the door, and the wall full of red pennants for Bayern Munich FC.

He greeted the girl at the till; she smiled, with a polite nod of recognition, and returned to her magazine. Selecting a terminal amongst all the other dusty, unused terminals, he opened his webmail account. He could feel his own nervousness, like a bad taste in his mouth. Was there any news from Tim? About Tim? David and Amy? *What about his wife and child?*

There was just one email of interest. There were two *unread* emails but there was just one email he *wanted* to read. He didn't want to read that other message. Because he knew it was the communication about Tim, from Tim's captors. The email Sanderson had warned him about.

Don't watch it, Simon. Really. Don't watch it.

So instead he clicked on the other unopened email. It was from David Martinez. He read it twice, absorbing the very serious information, writing some notes in his pad. Then he stood and went to the girl at the till. She charged him a few cents and he paid the money.

The doorway swung open to the street. He stared over the shops and houses at the grey Alps beyond. They were a row of snowy faces, white and sombre: like a jury of elders looking down at his guilt.

Tim. The email about Tim?

The email about Tim.

It was becoming too much. He had managed to avoid opening the Tim email for three days now, and each time he came here it got harder, and harder, to resist clicking on it and watching, to resist the terrible temptation: the desire to know, to behold the worst.

He couldn't resist any longer.

Twisting on a heel, he stepped back inside and, with an embarrassed nod at the cybercafe girl, he returned to the screen.

He sat down, and opened up his webmail account. He clicked on the email.

Subject: Your brother.

He steeled himself. Dry mouthed.

The email was empty except for an icon. An icon that linked to a little movie. It buffered for a second, then cleared: and there was Tim. Sitting in a chair. Half smiling at the camera with his chubby face. Nervous.

It was the video of Tim.

A masked man was standing beside Simon's brother.

The captor spoke.

'That's right, Tim, look at the camera. Say hello to your brother.'

'Hello!'

Tim was waving. Anxiously.

The masked man nodded. And said: 'You have something to say to him?'

Tim's smile was crinkled. He was probably hearing the voices again. Tim spoke through the voices.

'Sorry Simon but hello. How are you. I am sorry the men are detaining me, we have been detained. Rather wrong. What can I say. Hello.'

The masked man said:

'Good. What else, Tim? What else do you want to say to Simon?'

'The dog. Gusty. They want me to mention Augustus. Do you remember when we went to the stream with Augustus, we were happy then weren't we? Doubtless. Because I understand why, doing everything like this.'

Tim swallowed. The masked man waited. Simon's mad older brother gazed right at the camera.

'Simon can you tell Mother I'm sorry for what I did, stabbing her was wrong. So very wrong I understand. Mummy?'

Simon felt the prickle of tears; he fought them.

His brother's face was fat and vulnerable.

'Just wanted to say I remembered the football, too, and

I believe we had a nice time when we were boys and if I ruined it, thus, because it was my fault my fault. Then if if . . . sorry Mum. Tell Mum sorry Simon, OK? Thank you.'

The masked man leaned closer to Tim and said quite loudly:

'Tim, do you know why we are here? Talking to Simon?'

Tim shook his head.

'I went to Oxford and after that it was very different. Believe me I undoubtedly . . . something happened.'

Tim turned and looked at the masked man. 'I no longer want this. Why are we here?'

'We're here because your brother won't tell us. We want him to tell us everything. Give us David Martinez and Amy Myerson. Tell us where they are. Tell us what he knows. Hand himself over . . . or else he will suffer just as you are about to suffer.'

Tim attempted a dreadful courageous smile. He was trying to smile, bravely, for Simon.

The pathos was unbearable.

Another man moved behind Tim. He had a rope and a piece of wood. A looped rope and a piece of wood?

The first man spoke calmly through his facemask. He had the faintest trace of an accent.

'So, Tim, I am so very sorry we have to do this but it is because of your brother, he doesn't care about you. So say goodbye to Simon, your brother who doesn't care.'

The man slipped the garrotte over Tim's head.

Tim began to choke, almost at once. His legs thrashed out, kicking and scraping, heels squeaking against the floor. The garrotte was tightened further, and harder. Now Tim's face was going pink, then red, then almost blue.

The impassive man, standing right behind, just kept the garrotte tight, saying nothing. And then the killer released the garrotte, and Tim gasped, and gasped. He was still alive. Tim was *still alive*.

The first man leaned towards the camera.

'Next time we kill him.'

The screen went dead.

Simon stared at the blackness. He pushed back the chair, and turned away, ready to go – to go anywhere, just anywhere else; he hurled some euros at the puzzled girl and then he strode out onto the cobbled street. He needed the fresh air to stop himself screaming.

Tim . . .

A police car was slowly rumbling along the cobbles of the main street. Heading uphill past the Gasthof Fraundorfer. Heading in the direction of the chalet.

Simon watched the car. Then he remembered David's information. He turned the other way, and started running.

44

In front of them was the strange skyscape of Luderitz itself: stern Lutheran churches sat atop dirt roads, which ran past gaily gabled Black Forest villas and scruffy miners' taverns. Rolls of barbed wire guarded wooden piers that jutted into the cold blue harshness of the sea.

David followed along, as Angus walked quickly, turned left – and gestured. 'Dresler's house . . .'

They were confronted by one of the most vividly painted houses; its walls were a bright, Baltic red. Big white jeeps were parked down the deserted road. Scorching hot metal in the sun.

Angus knocked, and paused. He had a hand poised in an inside pocket. David knew why. Angus knocked again, louder and harder, and waited.

Then, a noise. The door was slowly unlatched, and a very old man peered around it. Angus instantly whipped out Nathan's gun, shoved through the door and pushed the man, roughly, angrily back into his own hallway.

The muzzle of the gun was pointing at the old man's orange cardigan. Amy and David exchanged glances. Alarmed and frightened.

Angus showed no such fear or doubt. He spat his words:

'Dresler, listen, everyone is fucking dead. And I want to know where you guys put the Fischer results. Now. Tell me.'

The old Nazi shrivelled away, but Angus loomed over the old German, pinning him to the wall. Dresler was staring at the gun, and at Angus, and then at David. Three times he blinked, staring at David, as if he found David *more* frightening than the gun.

'Dresler. Tell me. Just fucking tell me.'

Dresler was stammering; Angus was growling his questions.

'Tell me now!'

'Ich weiss es nicht nein nein –'

'I know you speak fucking English, you cocksucker –'

The old man was dribbling. He was so frightened and shocked he was dribbling.

David felt a desire to intervene. The scene was too hideous; just too hideous. He stared around, as Angus shouted and yelled. They were standing in a hallway straight from Alpine Bavaria. There was actually a cuckoo clock ticking on the wall. Some ancient walking sticks, with yellow horn handles.

And a portrait of Pope Pius the Tenth?

Maybe Angus was right to terrorize this Nazi into confession.

Dresler's old mouth was opening and closing. Angus leaned nearer. David surmised the gun must be hurting the old man, the muzzle pressing hard in his chest.

'Where are the Fischer results? Next time I shoot.'

The old man pushed feebly at Angus; and the Scotsman casually pulled back, aimed the gun at Dresler – and he shot in the air, millimetres from his target. Almost grazing the doctor's face. Terrifyingly close.

Amy gasped. David looked away. He looked anywhere else. He noticed something: a little address book on the hallway

381

table, next to a phone. A little address book with hand-writing on the cover. What was that? Another echo in his mind. Something. Something there?

Then he looked back.

Dresler had sunk to his knees in fear.

'Listen, Herr Doktor. You have two fucking minutes. Where are the results?'

Angus lifted the gun again, and he set the muzzle to the man's shoulder. 'Next I will shoot your arm, here, at the shoulderblade. Might take the whole arm off –'

The doctor was trembling.

'*Ja!* OK OK!' The old man lifted a liver-spotted hand. 'Shark Island.'

'Where?'

'I tell you. Shark Island. Go and see.' He was still terrified. There was a moist dark patch in his trousers. Fear had voided his bladder.

'Shark Island? What does that mean? Why? That doesn't make sense.' Angus pressed the gun harder into the shoulder. 'Tell me more.'

'Aber . . . Aber . . .' The old man shivered. He shut his eyes, like someone about to be executed. He was mumbling words. What were they? Prayers? They sounded like prayers.

And then Dresler opened his old sad eyes. And then he looked at David, then at Amy. He shook his head. 'I do not believe this . . . I do not believe you.'

'What?'

'You . . . you people will not kill me. You do not have the courage. *Nein.*'

Angus swore, and shot again, this time at the floor. A few centimetres to the left of the old man's legs. Splintered wood spun in the air.

But the Nazi had found some determination. He shook

his head, and his eyes gleamed with a sullen defiance. Or maybe it was just a different kind of *fear,* maybe he was more scared of talking, of confessing, because of what might happen to him *then*.

Amy was protesting.

'Angus – you just can't shoot him –'

Angus swore, and waved the gun.

'But Kellerman said, fuck this, Kellerman *said* –'

It was an impasse. They were stuck. Angus had the gun aimed at Dresler's head but David knew the German was right, Angus couldn't do this. Not in cold blood. Couldn't kill this sad old man with his spidery writing.

The spidery writing? With a well-oiled click the mental machinery of the puzzle began to turn. He gasped aloud. Of course. The address book.

'Stop!'

Faces turned. David explained:

'He knows me.'

Angus was incredulous: *'What?'*

'I've worked it out. This guy Dresler. *He knows me*. He must *recognize* me.'

Amy went to speak; David interrupted: 'Angus. Where was this guy living – before he came to Luderitz?'

'France. Provence.'

'There. That's it.' David gestured, fiercely, at the kneeling old Nazi. 'He recognized me when I walked through the door. I saw it in his eyes.' He leaned very close to Dresler's sweaty face. 'You know me, don't you? Because you met my father. He found you. Someone in the Basque Country, a Gurs survivor, gave my father your details, your name, and Dad traced you to Provence.' He was leaning even closer to the quailing old German. 'And my dad threatened to reveal your past to the world – so you confessed – or you helped him – I'm fucking right, aren't I?'

Dresler was shaking his head. Mute. Determined and mute. But his silence was unconvincing. Amy whispered: 'I think you're right. Look at him.'

David didn't need any encouragement.

'It's the only thing that makes sense. *Someone* must have told my father about the monastery, someone who knew secrets. Who had an interest in the story, like an old Nazi, from Gurs. Who became a member of the Society of Pius . . . He would *know* where the archives were kept. It was you. You told my father – and then you had to flee, to Namibia, and this – this here –'

David grabbed at the address book. He waved it under Dresler's face.

'I recognize this handwriting! This tiny precise scrawl. You wrote on the back of my father's map. Didn't you?'

Again Dresler shook his head. And again it was unconvincing.

Angus was visibly excited.

'OK. So let's say that's it. You must be right. Let's put the clues together –'

'How?'

'Shark Island. That's what this fucker said. Shark Island.'

'Where's that?'

'Just down the road. Luderitz! By the fish wharves.'

Angus swivelled on Dresler. For a second it seemed Angus would strike the bowed and silent head of the Nazi with the butt of the pistol. Then he seemed to think better of it. He spat with contempt, but lowered the gun.

'Come on – we haven't got much time and Miguel could be anywhere, that chopper leaves in *two hours* –'

They ran to the door, leaving Dresler burbling and shivering in his hallway. A Nazi kneeling in the contents of his own emptied bladder.

The brutal noon sun was like a punishment, a fierce

chastisement. Angus gestured south. They ran down the dusty road which doubled back to the wharves.

Two black men were sifting listlessly through piles of white dust on a corner. The smell of fish and decay was overpowering. Bleak white dust and hot blue sky – and an old Nazi wetting himself. David's mind was alive with fears and anxieties, and hope. Maybe they would find the secret. He realized, now, at least he was *beginning* to realize, that he needed to find the secret. The secret of himself. The terror of ignorance was too much.

The road terminated at a gate.

'*That* is Shark Island.' Angus indicated a kind of peninsula, jutting out into the sea. 'We take this path . . .'

They paced along a hot burning track that hugged the shoreline, hemmed in by broken concrete walls. Then they paused. A windswept and derelict warehouse loomed to their left, providing shade. The smell of the cold rich Benguela current was intense in the burning air.

Swift and concise, Angus explained.

'Shark Island is where the Germans did a lot of their killing, in the 1900s. Used to be an island, now it's attached by a causeway. This is where the Germans herded all the Witboii to die. In the Holocaust.'

'Not the Herero?'

'Nah. Different Holocaust. *Another* Holocaust. I know. I know.'

'Jesus.'

'I'll explain sometime. Show me the map, with the writing.'

The precious old map. David pulled it from his jacket. The blue sad stars, the sad old creases. And the writing on the back.

Angus squinted at the tiny scrawl, and exhaled, his eyes barely an inch from the paper.

'You're quite right. It's his handwriting. Dresler.'

Seagulls wheeled above them; a Namsea fish-truck rumbled in the distance, backing into a vast warehouse.

'I think it might be an address,' David said. He pointed. 'See. Isn't that "strasse"?'

'Yes. But . . .' Angus frowned. He twisted, looking around, the sea-wind tousling his rusted hair. 'This is an address, a German name I don't recognize – there is no Zugspitzstrasse here. In fact, not anywhere in Luderitz. How does it link to Shark Island?'

Amy spoke: 'Maybe he was just . . . decoying. A lie?'

'No,' Angus replied, very firmly. 'Dresler was *petrified* when he coughed that info. You saw him. Pissed himself like a baby. That bit is true. There is something here . . . on Shark Island. But I don't see if it connects with what's written on the map . . .'

Again, he gazed around at the yellow scene, at the haze of dust, the scruffy grey road, the derelict sheds and wharves. The hot wind ferried the elegiac coughs of seals from beyond the cliffs. 'We need something German. Here. Connected with the Germans.' His gaze fixed. 'There. The Holocaust museum. That hut . . . must be.'

'Holocaust museum?'

Angus shrugged. 'I know. Doesn't look much. But yes, that's a museum, it's tiny, this is Africa – but it's very important to the Namibians. It's usually closed. I mean – so remote, they get no visitors. You book by appointment and –'

David advanced.

'Come on!'

The museum was a low wooden building, battered by the brutal Benguela winds, at the very end of the promontory. The museum door was shut. The air was somehow cold and hot at the same time. David could feel his skin burning, the sunshine was truly painful now.

Angus turned a handle and pushed. Locked. David stepped

alongside, and briskly kicked at the door. It succumbed with ease, the lock shattered.

They were inside. The hot wooden space was full of shelves and cabinets and glass cases ranked along the walls; and three large skulls grinned at them from the top of a large plinth.

'Christ,' said Amy.

Angus explained: 'The Herero Skulls. Fischer had them scraped clean by Herero women, they had to flense the skulls of their own murdered husbands. He wanted to examine them, compare skull sizes. Bless his little callipers. But we need to find – I don't know – where would the Fischer data be – they are here – there must be something here –'

They searched. Frantic and determined, they searched and scoured, they ransacked the dusty display cases, they overturned shelves of old books with titles in Gothic script, flicking desperately through the pages. *Die Rehobother Bastards und das Bastardierungsproblem beim Menschen.*

But nothing. They sorted and sifted through scientific instruments, somehow gynaecological and ghastly in their pristine steeliness. Nothing. David shunted aside a box of desiccated human bones, feeling guilt and horror as he did so. He was mistreating the evidence of two forgotten genocides, the hideous relics of a lost racial empire.

There was nothing. They were confounded. It was done. The three of them knelt in the centre of the little hut and shared their despair: whispering and quick. Angus was looking at his watch.

'That chopper goes in forty minutes – if we don't get it –'

Amy stared around, her eyes bright and hostile. The Herero Skulls grinned at them, from the tragic plinth in the corner. She coughed the dust and said.

'Horrible place. Horrible. I don't *understand,* Angus. There is nothing here from Germany, nothing at all, it's all Namibian.

German Empire but Namibian. How could the Fischer data be here anyway?'

Angus nodded, his voice low and resigned. 'You're right. It's all Namibian . . .'

David listened. Saying nothing. The skulls smiled at him, laughing at the Cagot. Was he a Cagot? They were mocking him. He tried to drive the thought from his mind. Focussed himself on the map. The clue.

'Zugspitzstrasse. What does it mean?'

'Nothing obvious.' Angus sighed, and shook his head. 'It's a common German street name. I've heard it before . . .' His expression stilled, and changed, and flashed, and was transformed. 'I've heard it before! Jesus!' He stood up. 'I've heard the name before. David. The map! One more time, yes yes, this is it –'

They all stood. Life quickening in the veins.

The map was unfolded in the dusty light. Angus held the paper a fraction from his face, reading the tiny line of writing.

'It's the address of the Kaiser Wilhelm Institut. In Berlin! Zugspitzstrasse. 93. The store rooms.'

'How –'

'Famous in . . . eugenic circles. Not really known to anyone else. This was a note made by Dresler for your father, right?'

'Yes.'

'So he's given him an address. Where to find the Fischer data, maybe, or some clue as to where the data might be . . . This is the Institut.'

'But it's in Berlin. How does it relate to here –'

The scientist's smile was triumphant. Even in the pure and horrifying drama, he was helplessly exulting in his own cleverness.

'I worked it out! There *is* something in this room from Germany.'

He turned and pointed. At the Herero Skulls.

'Them?'

'They were *repatriated*, from Berlin, in 1999. After years of wrangling. They used to be kept in the Kaiser Wilhem Institut. Now they are here. *They* have been to Germany. They were in Fischer's possession throughout the war, and after at the Institut. The answer must be in them somehow.'

Angus moved quickly to the plinth and picked up the biggest skull. He turned the sad and smiling cranium in his hand.

'An obscene joke. The Nazis loved obscene jokes, they paved Jewish ghettos with Jewish gravestones, so the Jews would trample their own dead. And –' He was examining the skull, closely. 'And where better to hide something very, very . . . important . . . than a skull like this? A sacred relic of a terrible genocide. Fischer must have known no one would *ever* smash it open, retrieve the secret, unless they *definitely* knew what they wanted, where they were seeking.' He lifted up the skull, squinted inside, then he lifted it higher, talking quietly to the skull. 'Sorry, brother, I am so very fucking sorry – but I have to do this. Forgive me.'

He dropped the skull on the floor. The dry aged bone shattered at once, almost gratefully. Crumbling in the dust, adding dust to orange dust.

A tiny steel cylinder glinted on the floorboards, amidst the scattered shards of bone. Angus picked it up.

'Hidden in the olfactory cavity.'

Amy and David gathered around. Faces tensed, and perspiring.

Angus ripped the top off the slender metal tube, and pulled out a tiny, exquisitely rolled piece of paper, almost leathery in consistency, like parchment but somehow finer.

The Scotsman focussed and examined the yellowed slip of paper. Etched across the paper, in faded old ink, was a tiny map.

'Zbiroh!' A sigh of exultant relief. '*Zbiroh . . .*'

Any explanation was truncated. A shadow had just

flickered the dusty light of the hut. A Namibian security guard had passed the window, and was standing at the door, pushing his way inside.

Angus shoved the map in the tube, pocketed the tube, and ran to the entrance; he flung the door open, and confronted the guard – waving his gun at the terrified guard's chest.

The guard stepped back, retreating into the dazzling sun.

'No! No trouble! Want no trouble!'

'Good,' said Angus, as he advanced, and patted the guard's pockets. He drew out a pistol and phone, and handed them to David. And tilted a head at the sea.

Grabbing the items with gusto, David hurled the gun and the phone into the crashing waves, just metres away. Seagulls fluttered and shrieked in alarm.

Angus was gesturing at the guard. 'OK. Stay here. Don't move. We're going. Take a staycation. *All-fucking-right?*'

They sprinted down the path to the mainland; David glanced behind – the guard was indeed standing there, black and statuesque in the sun, staring at them, perplexed, immobile, a silhouette of doubt.

The path turned onto the road and they ran right into the traffic – Angus waved a wad of South African rand at the very first Toyota sedan. The driver grinned and squealed his brakes.

The three of them jumped in, sweating and cramped. Angus snapped.

'Airport! Fast as you can.'

The drive took ten minutes: swerving and racing through the sun-dusted streets. They tilted past the Bank of Windhoek, an old pool hall, and a Shell garage – and then they were out of town: on the surrounding flats. David was remembering Miguel. The big black cars, roaring up the canyon.

The thought was horrifying. Miguel could be around here,

right now. Any minute he could just show. The big black car door flashing open.

Found you.

The whirring yellow sands were writhing across the road, making serpents of dust. They were out in the desert again. They were motoring through the wilderness. Angus took out the map and scrutinized it. And then he sat back. And yelled.

'Look!'

Terrible panic filled David: he looked, and saw nothing. *Miguel?*

Angus was still pointing: 'Look at that. That's a rare and precious sight. *Look at the horse!*'

It wasn't Miguel. David felt absurd relief, as he and Amy stretched to see through the scratched car window. But what were they looking for?

At first there was nothing. And then he saw: a horse, thin and solitary and loping across the dirt road. Then David saw more – dozens, then hundreds. Curvetting and playing in the sandy heat-haze.

Angus was rhapsodizing.

'The wild horses of the Namib. I *love* these animals. They're the last remnants of the *Schutztruppe* – the German colonial army. The horses escaped and turned feral.' He gazed, almost serene, at the dreamlike spectacle. 'Now they are the only wild desert horses in the world – becoming a new species, specially adapted to dryness.' Angus sat back. 'I always think they look like the souls of horses, roaming free in the after-life . . . That's why this place is so hard to leave. Things like *that*. But here's the airport. Just past the dunes.'

The car prowled around the last of the soft Barchan dunes. They were slowing onto a wide flat space. The driver stopped at the perimeter of a surreally bleak airstrip.

A small plane and two helicopters sat on some asphalt amidst acres of sun-scorched dust. One of the choppers had

Kellerman Namcorp inscribed on the side. Its propellers were already turning.

David turned to Angus and said: 'But where are we going?'

'Amsterdam –'

'Yes, but then?'

'Zbiroh! An SS castle. Bohemia! I'll explain later – mate, we gotta hurry, *Miguel is still out there –*'

They ran across the flatness. A man with a low slung sub-machine gun was standing by the helicopter, he stared at them, astonished, as they ducked under the whumping blades.

'Angus?'

'Roger!'

The black man smiled.

'Angus my man!'

Angus was shouting above the loud churn of the spinning chopper blades. Something passed between them. Something from the black velvet pouch? David guessed it was diamonds. Maybe. Roger did a nodding salute.

'Get in!' said Angus.

Roger was shouting at all of them, gesturing them into the chopper. *Quickly!*

David and Amy climbed in, and sat on the first seats they could find. Angus joined them, his face strained and exhausted. They strapped up, and even as their safety belts clicked, the chopper lifted up.

They were flying.

David stared down. Roger was a small figure now. Looking up at them with a hand to shield his eyes from the sand. David blinked and looked a kilometre south. A wild horse was cantering across the wasteland.

Then the clouds of dust intervened, and all was blank.

45

2.58, 2.59. 3.00.

There was no sign of him. David glanced warily at the station clock.

3.02, 3.03, 3.04.

Angus was by his side, saying nothing – for once. The tension evident in his face. Amy looked pensive to the point of depression.

What did she know? She had been noticeably *different* since they landed in Amsterdam and made their way across Germany, to Nuremburg Station where they had agreed to meet Simon. Why? Maybe she now suspected he was Cagot, or maybe she was merely reacting to his changed mood, his sudden intense anxiety. His distant chilliness, his violent moodswings, as he ransacked himself for answers or solace or quiescence.

He'd stopped making love to her. He couldn't do it any more. Once they had been rough, playful, sharply passionate. And now? He could see himself biting her, that white female flesh, and drawing blood.

It was an abyss, and he had to look into it, he had to reach far inside his soul, to get a hold of his essential self.

Because he needed his last reserves of equanimity, for the crucial hours ahead. The crucial days, the crucial minutes.

3.07, 3.08, 3.09.

Maybe Simon wasn't coming. They had sent one email from Amsterdam, and had got one quickly in return: *Yes.*

There had also been one other email in David's inbox, a very surprising email – from Frank Antonescu. His granddad's old lawyer in Phoenix had been doing some research of his own, and, through a contact at the IRS – who apparently owed him a favour – had eventually, 'after a lot of grafting and grifting!' worked out where the money came from.

The Catholic church.

The money was, Antonescu wrote, 'Paid not just to your grandfather but to a number of people immediately after the war. It was known as "Gurs money". I have no idea why. The fellow at the IRS was similarly mystified.'

So that was another joist of an answer – in the rising structure of a solution. But the full edifice would only be revealed when they got to Zbiroh. And found the Fischer results.

3.16, 3.17, 3.18.

Was Simon ever coming? Maybe something terrible had happened to him. Maybe Miguel had got there first.

'There!' said Amy.

A slightly scruffy, breathless, freckled, fair-haired man of about forty came running along the concourse. He stared at Amy and David –

'David Martinez!'

'Simon Quinn?'

The older man, the Irish journalist, glanced at the three of them, and smiled, shyly.

'You must be Amy. And you . . .'

'Angus Nairn.'

Hands were shaken, formal introductions made. But then

David and Simon looked long and hard at each other and the absurdity of their formality became apparent to both of them – at the same time.

They hugged. David embraced this man he had never met – like a lost brother. Or like the sibling he'd never had.

And then the tension, the spiralling terror of the situation, recrudesced. Amy reminded them, as she had reminded them repeatedly for the last three days:

'Miguel is still after us . . .'

Amy's fear of Miguel seemed to have *grown* since they fled Namibia. And maybe, David surmised, that was adding to her depression. The relentlessness of their pursuer was destroying her will. Perhaps she was actually resigned to Miguel's triumph. He always found them in the end; maybe the Wolf would find them this time, and finish the job.

Unless they got to the data first.

They went quickly to the hire car.

Angus was in charge of the map. He directed them out of the suburbs of Nuremburg, into the undulating country-side, and onto the Czech border. As they went, Simon confessed: he told them of his brother being held by the Society. Kidnapped and brutalized.

Even from the driver's seat, David could see the grief in Simon's eyes. The grief – and the guilt. No one spoke for a good few minutes when Simon finished his confession. The fate of this man, Tim, was also in their hands.

It was too much.

The frontier approached. The old Iron Curtain. In nearby fields, useless and rusting, stood derelict watchtowers and old coils of barbed wire. But the contemporary border was just one bright glass office – entirely empty. They didn't even have to show passports.

Simon spoke:

'Why Nuremburg? Why meet there?'

Angus explained that they wanted to convene in a big anonymous city, across the border from the Czech Republic. To confuse anyone who might be following.

Simon nodded.

'And this castle?'

'The map shows it's in a town called Zbiroh. But the entrance is two miles away, a little village called Pskov. Some kind of tunnel. The tunnel itself leads from a synagogue in Pskov.'

Again Simon nodded. His demeanour was enormously subdued.

They drove on. The Czech side of the border was a notable change from the German prosperity next door. Everything was a little more hunched, grubby, and humble. And the road to Plzen was lined with thirty-something women in tiny skirts and blonde wigs.

Angus explained:

'Prostitutes.'

'Sorry?'

'Came here for a conference a few years back, in Prague. The women here are working girls . . . the punters come over from Germany. Truck drivers and businessmen. They also sell gnomes.'

Amy queried this: 'Gnomes?'

The Scotsman pointed at a shop by the road. An entire rank of garishly painted garden gnomes was set up in front of the store.

'Because of some tax law, the gnomes are cheaper here, so again the Germans come over. For hookers and gnomes!'

He laughed drily. No one else laughed. But David was glad that Angus was laughing. The Scot was the only one amongst them who seemed to possess any positive energy, any real optimism. His intellectual need to know the Fischer results, his sheer curiosity, his selfish desire to know if he'd been right, was – rather ironically – keeping them all going.

But soon the car was silent, once more, as they sped along the motorway to Plzen. Angus had the map on his lap. Thick forests encroached. The drizzle was turning into proper rain.

'OK,' said Angus. 'Enough fucking *brooding*. Let's do something. Let's help Simon! Tell him the story so far. Poor guy's a freelance hack, he needs a story, to help with the mortgage. Let's pool everything we know.'

The mood in the car was so tense, so depressive, so frightened, David welcomed this impulsive idea. Talk. Just *talk*. Talk about anything. So they did: as David drove, they put together every segment of the puzzle, each adding their portion to the pot. And as they discussed, Simon scribbled in his notebook.

Then the journalist sat back. His voice was cracked with emotion, but at least he was managing to speak.

'OK. This is, ah, how I see it. What we know so far.'

David felt the flutter of his own anguish; he had an absurd fear that Simon would turn and point to him, and say *You, of course, are a Cagot.*

Simon began.

'The beginnings of the mystery go back three thousand years, when the Bible was being written in Babylon. At various places in the Book of Genesis, there are passages which hint at human beings *other than Adam and Eve*.'

Amy was staring out of the window. Looking at the cars behind and ahead, with anxious intent. Looking for red cars, maybe.

Simon went on:

'The problems caused by these insidious Biblical hints have always been with us. But they truly came to a head, in Christendom, in the fifteenth and sixteenth centuries, during the persecutions of the Basques and the Cagots.'

He glanced at Angus. Then went on:

'The Basques are truly a breed apart, with a unique language, culture and society, unusual blood type, and so forth. Their race possibly dates back to pre-Indo-European times – 30,000 BC. They have long suffered persecution for being . . . different. These persecutions peaked with the witch burnings of 1610–1611, the so-called Basque Dream Epidemic.'

Their hire car was speeding past a tiny Skoda, an old car from the communist era. A farmer sat in the front with his fat wife at his side. The Skoda was doing thirty kph.

Simon continued:

'The case of the mysterious Cagots is similar – yet more severe. The Cagots are, or were, a crossbreed. They lived in the same region as the Basques. Indeed they probably descend from Basques who intermarried with dark Saracen soldiers in the eighth and ninth centuries. As such, they were, from the beginning, very isolated within Christendom – but with an additional and fatal taint of the infidel.

'So they were persecuted. And by the seventeenth century these repressions were reaching homicidal levels: Cagots were being nailed to church doors. One byproduct of this persecution and isolation was the intensification of genetic problems within the Cagot community –'

David interrupted: 'It wasn't their fault.'

Simon replied, with a puzzled frown, 'No, of course, it wasn't their *fault*. However, the reputation they had for psychotic tendencies, cretinism, even cannibalism, was, tragically, not entirely unjustified. Many Cagots were afflicted with various syndromes which led to bizarre and even repellent behaviour.'

Amy asked: 'That was why the King of Navarre instituted the tests – to see if the Cagots were truly "different"?'

'Yes. Moreover, primitive though science was at the time,

it seems the King's doctors did observe the syndactyly, the web-footed deformity, and other physical manifestations of the Cagots' inbred genotype. They concluded that the Cagots *were* indeed different to the rest of humanity, in a very significant way.'

He flipped a page of the notebook.

'The discovery alarmed the Pope and his cardinals in Rome. The idea that God would actually be creating Serpent Seed, new kinds of men, *different* kinds of men, *men who are not men*, was pure anathema. It threatened the very basis of accepted Catholic doctrine that mankind is made in God's image. How can God have two images? Two kinds of children? Revelation of this truth would not only justify the worst persecution, *of a Christian and European people* – it would bring into question all of Catholic theology.'

'All Christian theology,' said Angus, 'for that matter.'

'This is why the church sought to end the persecution of the Cagots. For the very same reason the Spanish Inquisition decided to cease and suppress the Basque witch burnings. The Catholic elite wanted the "choir of Christendom" to remain "indivisible". The Basques and Cagots would be returned to the fold of humanity.'

'Yet there were, still, elements in the church that adhered to the bigoted, Curse of Cain philosophies. Especially amongst the lower clergy, the local peasantry, and some of the more rigorous church orders, like the Dominicans.

'Ever eager to avoid schism, the Vatican agreed to a compromise. The relevant and most controversial documents – relating to the witch burnings, and the blood test on the Cagots, and the ensuing papal conciliations – were not destroyed: they were secretly housed in the ancient archives of the Dominican University in Rome, the Angelicum. Centuries later they were carefully rehoused in a brand new monastery in central France.'

'Purpose-built,' Angus interrupted, 'by a far right architect, as a safe place to hide these documents. Correct?'

'And a masterpiece of functionality,' Simon replied. 'So offputting it sends people mad.'

Amy was still gazing out of the window. Her cardigan had fallen from her shoulder, exposing her bare suntanned skin. Gold and soft, and yielding.

David fixed his eyes on the road. Simon lifted his notes.

'Back in 1907 a brilliant young German anthropologist, Eugen Fischer, arrived in the desolate, diamond-rich German colony of Sud West Afrika, now Namibia. He was following in the footsteps of his hero, the great British scientist – and founder of modern eugenics – Francis Galton.

'What Fischer found amazed him. By studying the khoisan – the "Bushmen" of the Kalahari, and their close cousins, the Basters, a crossbreed between Bushmen and Dutch settlers, Fischer discovered that in the very recent past mankind had . . . possibly *speciated*.'

Amy said nothing. David said nothing. Angus was wearing a distant smile. Simon continued:

'The process of *speciation* – the dividing of one species into new species – is of course crucial to evolution. Yet the process is itself ill defined. When does a new breed or strain of an organism become a subspecies, and when can it be termed a truly separate species? Geneticists, zoologists and taxonomists still argue this point; but no one denies that speciation occurs.'

Simon turned a page.

'But hitherto nobody had expected that speciation might have happened to *Homo sapiens* within the last few thousand years. As Angus says, some experts believe a small form of human might have evolved *fairly* recently in Asia – *Homo floresiensis*. Hominids like this might even explain those Biblical myths of non-Adamite humans, implied in the first verses of Genesis. A genuine folk memory of small, dwarvish, almost-men.

'But that is still ten thousand years back. And yet, as Fischer investigated the Khoisan and the Basters he became convinced that something akin to speciation was *right now* taking place in Africa: either the Bushmen were a new species, or they were close to becoming so.

'This discovery affirmed the racism already present in Fischer's thinking. Like many scientists of his time, Fischer believed without embarrassment in a hierarchy of human races, with whites at the top, and aborigines and black Africans at the bottom. He now put the Bushman even lower than that, beyond the family of man.'

David changed gear to overtake a big red lorry with *Intereuropa* written on the side. He asked: 'Yet this guy Eugen Fischer liked Jews? The Kellermans?'

'Yes,' Simon answered. 'Fischer was, ironically, no anti-Semite. He appreciated the friendship of other clever men, especially if they were wealthy and glamorous. He became friends with the Kellerman dynasty, German-Jewish diamond merchants making millions from the mineral-rich sands of the Namibian desert. This friendship was to prove crucial in the following decades.'

Another page was turned.

'Then, in 1933, Adolf Hitler came to power. He had avidly devoured Fischer's books during his imprisonment as a young man. Now, as *Der Führer*, Hitler had the means to employ Fischer properly. First, Hitler made Fischer a rector of Berlin University. Then, in 1940, he despatched Fischer to a new German concentration camp at Gurs, near the genetically fascinating Basque corner of France.

'Adolf Hitler had a job in mind for the great scientist. To validate Nazi race science. And so, in Gurs, Fischer was told to gather the most interesting human genetic specimens in

401

one place, for intense medical testing: gypsies and Jews, French and Basques, Spanish and Cagots.

'By comparing the data derived from these subjects, with the data already derived from Fischer's Namibia research, the Führer hoped that his prize scientist would provide a definitive, authoritative and genetically provable racial hierarchy: final evidence that Germans were at the top, and Jews were at the bottom.

'Fischer was gratifyingly successful in these endeavours. In the first year, ably assisted by some brilliant German doctors, he discovered DNA. The basis of all modern genetics.'

Simon closed his notebook.

Amy said: 'But what did Fischer discover *then*? In his second year at Gurs? The frightening and terrible discovery? What was *that*?'

Angus was no longer smiling, he was frowning.

'Well . . . that's the motherlode, the ultimate question. And that is what we are about to find out.' He scanned the rainy road ahead. 'If we don't die first.'

46

Twenty minutes down the Czech motorway, they found the turning for Zbiroh. It curved between the hills and the woods and the scrappy Czech farms. David buzzed down his car window, feeling the need for cold wet air on his anxious face. Anything to drive away the deeper worries. He actively wanted some kind of physical pain – to mask the mental pain.

'Take a left here.'

They exited the motorway, swept around a final wooded turning: and they saw: Zbiroh Castle.

It was enormous. A vast, ugly, yellow, neo-classical palace, haughty and angular, sitting atop a rocky rise. The village of Zbiroh was sprawled in the dripping valley below, like a peasant prostrate before a Tsar.

David slowed the car as they stared.

Amy said: 'So . . . why is it so special?'

Angus provided the answer: 'The castle is medieval, and built on great silicic rock formations veined with jasper. When the Nazis occupied Bohemia they discovered that this stone, the jasper, perfectly reflects radio waves. So the SS installed a concealed headquarters for monitoring radio traffic. And after the war the Czechoslovak Army did *exactly* the same thing – used it as a secret tracking station. Following NATO aircraft. The castle was only opened to the public in the late 1990s.'

Simon spoke up: 'But why did the Nazis use it to *hide* stuff?'

'Can tell ya that too. Over many centuries that impervious stone beneath the castle has been turned into a complex of underground passages. And, at the very end of the war, the SS did something very strange. They plugged it all up, filled the passages with thick layers of concrete – nobody has been able to pierce it, even with big modern drills. The communists tried to dig through, but they failed.'

The castle gazed pompously across the village roofs. Angus continued: 'Of course many people have speculated as to the reason for the SS constructions. Why all the damn concrete? Was it stolen treasure the SS might have concealed? Some think the Russian amber room is down there. Who the fuck knows.'

There was a silence.

'Pskov,' Amy said. 'Remember we have to go to Pskov. The synagogue.'

Pskov turned out to be a little village in the shallow hills, just two klicks away. It was a dismal place comprising an orange-painted church, a small beer-hall with a grubby neon sign for Budvar, a few ancient and mouldering houses, and a Spar supermarket advertising London gin.

And that was that. It took them all of five minutes to walk the main streets, and walk back again.

They sat in the shelter of a bus stop. Amy asked the obvious question: 'Where is the synagogue?'

The rain was remorseless; it was a damp and ghastly October day. An elderly dog squatted across the road, defecating. David looked nervously at the church, which dominated the silent village. The church seemed deserted; but maybe someone was in there, right now, looking at them – and telephoning Miguel.

Miguel. The awful memory returned to David, with an extra tang of horror. He recalled how Amy had once said David looked like Miguel. 'Only Miguel is older and thinner.'

Could it be? Could he and the Wolf be . . . *related*?

Two Cagots together. Two cannibal cousins.

He shuddered. It just kept getting worse. Like he was drowning in vile truths, being sucked into the cess pit of reality. Deeper and deeper until he could no longer breathe.

Shit person.

He stared up and down the dismal grey road. And cursed his despair.

'Nothing. There's *nothing*. We're stuck. There is no synagogue – it's been *destroyed.*'

Simon agreed, the resignation raw in his words: 'You're right. That's it. We've lost.'

A decrepit Trabant sedan belched black exhaust fumes as it trundled down the road. Amy was wandering away from the bus stop, disconsolate in the wet, looking anxiously this way and then that.

Even Angus looked downcast.

'So we drink. Ach, if we're all gonna die, let's have a fucking drink.'

It was a ludicrous idea, it was a farcical idea, it was an idea. Their situation could not get any worse. Surely Miguel would find them, if not today, then soon. He would get them. So have a fucking drink.

They walked across the damp road and jangled the bell of the tavern door.

The interior of the pub was almost as dour as the neglected facade: a few wobbly tables furnished the bare space, with a single old farmer eating bacon in the corner. Four large

405

steel barrels of Budvar and Staropramen comprised the selection of beverages.

At least the beer would be good, David thought. Czech beer. Good Czech beer. A final beer. A fine drink to help them forget, to help them accept their fate. David realized he was dog-tired, bone-tired, spiritually tired: he was tired of running away. Let it happen, let it come, let it hurry up. He was tired, he was shattered, maybe even a touch suicidal. If he was a Cagot with maybe the worst of Cagot urges, he wasn't sure he wanted to live.

So drink.

The publican was unshaven, jowly, sixty-something and spoke a smattering of German. He served up four foaming lagers. Simon hesitated, and then he took a beer.

They sat at the table. Only Angus was talking. Only Angus had the energy. He was talking of Czech beer, in between gulps of Czech beer. 'The best pilsner should taste very slightly like horseradish. You know that? This one is a cracking example. You've gotta love Czech beer. The food is shite, they put whipped cream on everything, but, fuck, they know how to brew. They even have breakfast beers here, special beers for breakfast. Hah!'

Amy stood up and walked to the door.

'I need fresh air.'

David let her go. He could see why she wanted to be away from him, away from the cursed Cagot. Who would want to be his girlfriend? As the door shut behind her he realized that it was now sealed, the deed now done: he was utterly and finally *alone*. Everyone had left him, everyone had quit. He was lost in the desert of his own life. Like those solitary trees on the Skeleton Coast, living off the dew in the fog.

So let Miguel come and kill him, Cagot slaying Cagot, brother killing brother. It didn't matter any more.

Angus was talking about the Holocaust. He was on his second or third large glass of Staropramen and his conversation was seasoned with lunacy, a drunken nihilism.

'You know, what gets me is the fact that the Germans did three holocausts in the twentieth century. Not one, not two, but three: the Herero and the Witbooi and then the Jews.' Angus smiled angrily across the pub. 'So what's going on there then? I mean, OK, one holocaust, fair enough, we all make mistakes, could happen to anyone. Sorry my zyklon slipped. But then . . . two holocausts? Hm. That's a bit odd. That's a bit of a theme. Isn't it? Maybe we should try something a bit less holocausty next time?' He paused. 'And then . . . you do it *again*? For a third time? *Three holocausts in a row?* How does that work?'

He drank some more beer. Simon was staring down, staring at his shoes, staring at darkness.

Angus drank, and he ranted. 'And here's another thing. You know they built the best hotel in Luderitz right opposite Shark Island. That's nice, isn't it? So you get a view of the extermination camp from your balcony. So you can look at the graves – as you operate the trouser press. Do you think this was a deliberate feature, incorporated by the architects? I'd like to have been at the design meeting when –'

'Angus,' said Amy. She had returned to the bar. A determined expression on her face. 'Angus. Just shut the fuck up.'

The Scotsman laughed. And then he apologized. And then he laughed – sourly – and fell silent.

The talk of Shark Island reminded David of Namibia. That last scene, crouched in the hut. The Herero Skulls.

The obscene Nazi joke.

'You know . . .' he said, very slowly. 'Maybe . . . we're being . . . a bit *stupid*. There is no way a synagogue would still be standing here. In Pskov. The Nazis killed all the Jews.'

Amy said: 'But it's on the map. If it was demolished then why indicate it? I don't get it.'

David leaned nearer.

'So . . . maybe it wasn't demolished. It was turned into something else, probably before the war. The synagogue will be disguised as something else.'

'Like what?'

'Something insulting? Another joke, like in Luderitz.'

Angus nodded, firmly.

'Yes. *This is true*. The Nazis turned some synagogues into pigsties, some into nightclubs. To insult Jewish faith. Of course . . .'

Amy shook her head.

'There's no nightclub in Pskov. It's tiny – there's nothing bloody here, no dancehalls, no pig farms, no nothing.'

The farmer on the next table belched robustly as he finished his pig knuckle. And Simon was pointing.

'So what about that? *Look.*'

They all turned. At the top of the front wall was a small and grubby old window. It wasn't letting in much light because it was paned with dark stained glass, the colour of fortified wine.

But the dusty light, thrown by the Budvar sign outside, was sufficient to illuminate the window's leaded design.

It was a Star of David.

47

The publican was entirely uninterested in their bizarre request, and stranger questions – until David offered him three hundred euros.

Then he quickly brightened and took them to the back of the pub: where steel barrels concealed a wall.

It was painted with Hebrew script.

'Move the barrels,' said Amy. 'The Tabernacle must have been here.'

The steel barrels boomed and clanked as they were shifted. Under the barrels was . . . nothing. David felt a miserable disappointment, tinged with faint relief. Part of him actively didn't want to know what was under the castle. *The proof of his blood.* And part of him needed to know immediately.

The publican was staring at them. His arms were crossed. Beer stains dotted his white jacket. Then he said: *'Die Juden Tur?'*

'Yes!'

'Hier.'

He led them down into a dark corner of the back room. A small wooden door was set low in the wall. The publican gabbled an explanation in gruff German. Amy interpreted, her voice rising with excitement:

'He says . . . this is the door from the war. There is a cellar behind, a passageway beyond that. He used the cellar to store . . . something he doesn't want to talk about. Contraband maybe? He doesn't know where the passage ends. He has never explored further. Too bloody scared of the communists in the castle.'

Another hundred euros elicited an agreement to open the door – then to close it behind them. And to tell no one.

Another fifty euros bought a torch.

The door was creaked open. David felt a surge of queasiness as he peered through. Another small door, a little door, like a Cagot door. The door he was always meant to pass through.

Inside, a few steps led down into a room full of damp darkness and cobwebs – and stacks of beige and grey Marlboro cigarette cartons, and a dozen garden gnomes. The gnomes leered in the sudden light; one of them was frozen in a fishing position. With grinning scarlet lips.

'OK?' said David, trying to quell his nerves. Now he could almost sense Miguel – nearing. Hunting them down. Blood finding blood.

'OK,' the others replied, as one.

They stepped inside the low chamber; the bar owner looked at them for a final second, shrugged as if they were obviously mad, then shut the tiny door.

Darkness enshrouded them. Apart from their one feeble torchbeam. David flashed it down the chamber, which went on, and on. A long passage into the chilly blackness.

'Let's go.'

They knew they had two kilometres to walk: the distance to Zbiroh. They began in silence. The sound of their foot-steps slipping in the mud was the only noise they made. No one spoke.

Their hurried pace at last brought them to another door. An iron door. It was shut.

David slumped to the side. He could feel clammy mud on his back. He didn't care.

'Christ.'

Angus swore. Simon shook his head. David had his head weighed in his hands.

Another door. Just another door. That would stop them? He remembered all the doors he had been through these last weeks: the Cagot doors, the door in Navvarenx church, the door to the Holocaust museum, José's door in the Cagot house, all the many doors. And now another door, defeating them. Just one last door, one door too far.

Amy stepped forward, she turned the handle to the door. It opened.

48

As one they passed through the doorway into a dark, brick-walled room, with a concrete floor.

David spun the torch, left to right. It was a large space; wooden chests were piled in severely neat stacks on each side.

Angus walked across and directed David's torchbeam downwards, at one of the wooden chests. It had a motif burned into the surface: a large black Nazi swastika, clutched in the talons of an imperial eagle. And beneath it was an inscription, in Gothic lettering.

Die Fischer Experimente.

The lid of the first wooden case was easily prised off with Simon's pocket knife. Amy found a paraffin lamp, with a wick, sitting at the back of the chamber. They flicked a lighter and turned the knob: the wick sent a good light across the shadowy chamber.

And then, for an intense and concentrated hour, they sat in a circle – and deciphered the documents, by torchlight and lanternlight. With Amy interpreting the German, and Angus's knowledge of biochemistry and genetics, and Simon's appreciation of the politics and history, they were a tensely effective team.

As they speedily pieced together the last elements of the story, Simon wrote it down, once again, sometimes squinting close to see the documents proffered to his gaze. Every so often, Angus would exclaim, or swear – 'Fuck, so that's why, so that's what he found.'

Then Angus dropped the last document, and looked Simon's way.

'You're the writer. Finish the story.'

Simon looked nonplussed for a moment, struck by the horror of it all, their discoveries, and their predicament. Then he said, quietly, 'OK. So this is it. The last chapter.'

'Go on.'

'The first amazing discovery Fischer made was this: human speciation was happening. In Europe. Even as he watched. And it was the Cagots who were evolving.

'As a result of their linguistic, cultural and social isolation, the Cagots had become *a new kind of human*. A new species. They were still able to breed, with difficulty, with their close relatives, *Homo sapiens* – but they were genetically drifting away. Fischer guessed that in a few generations the last Cagots would die out, thanks to these breeding problems. Their speciation from normal humans would be a failure.

'Fischer relayed this information to Hitler, who was delighted. Here at last was proof that Nazism was just Applied Biology, as they had always boasted. Man truly differed from man. Indeed the racial differences within mankind were greater than even Hitler had speculated. Speciation was happening in Europe. It had happened to the Cagots . . .'

David glanced around, trying to contain his emotions. He wanted not to think of his own dark secrets, concealed in the vaults of his soul. Dooming him. Burying him under the concrete of his shame.

Then Simon turned a page.

413

'Through 1941, correspondence between the Führer and his favourite scientist became ever more enthusiastic. Money poured into the camp to accelerate Fischer's experiments. Hitler wanted proof that Germans were superior within the emerging hierarchy of races.

'But then Fischer made a discovery at Gurs which was even more profound – and complicated. He predicted that the Cagot process would be repeated; he told Hitler that another species would soon splinter off from *Homo sapiens*, as the Cagots had done.'

Amy interrupted:

'The Jews.'

'As we see in the documents.' Simon gestured at one of the open boxes. 'Because of their religiously imposed self-segregation, their strictures against outbreeding – which enforced genetic isolation from the wider family of man – the Ashkenazi Jew was gradually becoming a new subspecies, maybe a new species, with a unique genotype. And all this Fischer told Hitler in a letter. This letter.' He brandished the document, then returned to his notes.

'Indeed Fischer told Hitler that, paradoxically, Nazi isolation of the Jews was only going to *increase* the chance and speed of this speciation. When he handed over the information, Fischer knew that Hitler would be excited by proof of Jewish Otherness. The problem was, as Fischer reluctantly told Hitler, the Jews were becoming, in some respects, a *superior* species. Certainly in terms of intelligence. Superior even to the Germans.'

He flipped a page. 'How, ah, had this happened? Over centuries, Talmudic tenets and customs had emphasized the fame and renown of the scholar. For a Jewish girl in medieval Europe it was much more desirable to marry a brilliant rabbi than a successful merchant or a wealthy goldsmith.'

'So the brainy, rather than the brawny, had more kids.'

Simon nodded at Amy.

'The genetic evolution of the Jews was biased towards ever higher intelligence. Pogroms against Jews merely increased this effect. In times of great adversity and persecution only the most highly educated and adaptable Jews survived: the less bright Jews died off.'

He coughed, with a flicker of emotion. Then went on:

'The . . . *result* of these centuries of upward pressure on Jewish intelligence, and the simultaneous genetic isolation in ghettos and shtetls, meant that Jews were speedily evolving into a more intelligent kind of human. There were downsides: Jews were and are uniquely prone to certain genetic ailments, like . . . how do you pronounce this . . . Tay-Sachs disease?'

Angus nodded. Simon returned to his text:

'But the Jews were brighter. The syndromes might even have been the genetic price they had to pay for their cognitive gifts.

'This remarkable discovery, when relayed by Eugen Fischer to the Führer in Berlin, chimed with the darkest fears in Hitler's mind. Prior to this revelation, the Nazi leader had entertained other ambitious plans for Europe's Jewry – sending them all to Madagascar, or using them as gifted slave labour in some far-off Russian province. But with the Fischer data in his hand, Hitler realized he had little choice. He had to strike now, while he controlled Europe, before those clever and very different Jews became truly dominant and different – and enslaved Germany in turn.

'So in 1942 Hitler gave the go ahead for the Final Solution: the extermination of all European Jews, despite the huge cost and the possible crippling of the German war effort. Hitler had to end this menace to Aryan racial supremacy once and for all.

'But Hitler also decided to put his knowledge of speciation

to one further use: he employed it as a threat against the Catholic church.'

David spoke: 'The Milan Treaty.'

'Yes. In a secret accord signed in Milan in 1942 Hitler agreed to stay silent about human speciation, so threatening to Catholic doctrines, if the Pope agreed to stay silent about the Holocaust. It was a total bluff. Hitler had no intention of revealing the Fischer discovery that the Jews might be "superior" to the Germans. He simply intended to exterminate. But the bluff worked. The Pope stayed silent about the Shoah, thus assisting the Germans in their genocide; the shame of papal complicity has plagued the church to this day.'

Simon sighed, but continued.

'So . . . Between 1944 and 1945, the Allies slowly liberated Occupied France. The Nazi doctors who had worked at Gurs feared for their lives. But they had one grand bargaining chip: the mindblowing results of the Fischer experiments.

'Eugen Fischer realized that the western democracies would be just as keen as the Catholic church to suppress this knowledge – as it would destabilize the world, in so many ways, and of course lend disastrous credibility to Nazi racial theories. So Fischer and his colleagues had potential leverage over the Allies – but only if they could *preserve* the data. They therefore hatched a plan to conceal their results: in the labyrinthine vaults of an inaccessible SS castle, in Bohemia. The vault was hurriedly built – here – even as the Red Army marched across Slovakia.

'The plan worked. The doctors, many of whom had committed the most appalling crimes, threatened to reveal their experimental data if they were harmed; so they were hastily exonerated and returned to work at German universities by the fearful Allies. The Fischer data remained entombed and unknown. The conspiracy of silence had worked. Up to a point.

'At the end of the war, there was one *other* class of people who might reveal the terrible secrets of the Fischer experiments. *The survivors of Gurs.* Cagots and Basques, in the main. The Germans had been free and easy with the Fischer results in the camp. The few survivors therefore also had to be silenced: this was done with large sums of money. The Gurs survivors were bought off by the Catholic church – which was consumed by guilt at the behaviour of its chaplains in the camp. The church was also shamed by its cooperation with the Nazis. Blood money was paid.

'Some of the survivors then dispersed around the world, to Britain, to Canada and to America. But for many of these people the Gurs money was tainted: associated with the terrors of Gurs. Many of them never spent the cash, and endured a life of concealed shame.'

'So what happened afterwards?' Amy asked.

Angus answered. 'Nothing. At first. The plan worked: the Nazi doctors slowly died off, as did the Gurs survivors.'

'But everyone forgot about . . . the Kellermans?' she said.

Simon nodded:

'Yes. The Kellerman dynasty in far-off Namibia. They had been close to Fischer; Fischer stayed in touch with them after the war. Indeed some of Fischer's Nazi colleagues fled to Namibia, after the war, and were protected by Kellerman Namcorp.'

David gazed around the assembled faces. 'But what was in it for the Kellermans?'

Angus spoke:

'I can provide *that* answer. Truth is, the Kellermans were interested in the Fischer results *for the Jewish people.* Old Samuel Kellerman was a strict believer in Leviticus 25, that Jews were allowed by God to take slaves from the inferior Gentiles.'

Amy protested, 'But – *Nathan*?'

417

'Sure, yup, the younger Kellermans were different . . . they may have dispensed with these superstitions, but they were still ardent Zionists. Determined to create and then preserve Israel as a homeland for Jews.'

'So?'

Angus gazed Amy's way. 'Think about Israel, Amy. You're Jewish, you know this stuff. Through the 1970s, 80s, and 90s, demographics have been pointing to one outcome in Israel: at some point Jews are gonna be outnumbered by non-Jews even in their Jewish homeland. And then Israel will no longer be safe: and maybe another Holocaust will ensue.'

Simon interrupted: 'The Fischer results promised a philosophical escape route. If it could be proved that Jews were a different subspecies to ordinary gentiles – or at least headed that way – that would give a justification for treating non-Jews, within Israel, in a discriminatory fashion. Why should a different *kind* of man get the vote – in a homeland reserved for Jews?'

Amy shook her head. '*Homo judaicus*? *Shameful!*'

'But it makes sense,' Angus answered her, calmly. 'Universal human rights do not apply if humans are *not universally the same.* If the Jews are provably different, superior, then they deserve provably different and superior rights. If you really want to fucking push the point.'

'Therefore,' Simon added, 'the Kellermans wanted the Fischer results for their Zionist purposes – or, failing that, to repeat the, ah, experiments and get the same data. Right?'

'Uh-huh.' Angus was gesturing, in the lamplight. 'But the first option was closed. No one would tell them where the data were hidden. That left the second option. Science. Redoing the experiments. But it has taken seventy years for science to catch up with the Nazi discoveries at Gurs, and begin to prove them, all over again. And even now, when

418

science has caught up, there are still forces ranged against the whole concept of racial differences and eugenics. The Human Genome Diversity Project at Stanford was shut by pressure from western governments – and from the church.'

'So the Kellermans switched to GenoMap.'

'Exactly. The experiments we were doing at GenoMap were *directly* funded and abetted by Kellerman Namcorp. That old Nazi doctor, Dresler, fled to Namibia in the 90s, after he was uncovered by David's father. And he forwarded advice to GenoMap on how to reproduce the Fischer results. He even suggested blood testing the same people: Gurs survivors – Cagots especially.'

Angus continued: 'And you know what? This plan would have succeeded, if Fazackerly hadn't blabbed. At a conference in France, he boasted he was going to successfully repeat the experiments of Eugen Fischer at Gurs. I was there. It was mortifying. And I guess that's when the Catholic church was alerted, and began taking more serious steps. They recruited the Society of Pius X: because, as we all know, they are some zealous fuckers. And because they already knew the secrets of Gurs, so it involved no widening of the circle of knowledge. Their roots go back to Vichy France.'

Simon briefly glanced David's way, then looked at his notes.

'And sympathizers with the Society had already killed off previous attempts to unearth the Gurs secrets. *David's parents* – when they came to France, innocently seeking the truth of the Martinez's, ah, Basque ancestry . . .'

Amy interrupted, her voice fierce in the flickering shadows. 'And the Society was already using the most ruthless operatives to do this work: ETA terrorists like Miguel. Perfect! A highly trained killer, a devout Catholic. And he had a hatred – concealed self-hatred – for Cagots.'

Angus had returned to one of the cases. He lifted out a

document, embossed with several black swastikas, like rigid and futurist *lauburus*.

'It also makes sense . . .' David said, hesitantly. He was trying not to think of his parents; trying not to think of Granddad; trying not to think. He stammered his words. 'Using him. I mean Miguel. The Wolf. Cause he knows the crucial area: the Basque Country, where many Cagots and Gurs survivors lived . . .'

Simon concluded the story.

'The murders began anew. A number of Gurs survivors were deliberately killed. The few remaining provable Cagots were killed, some of them simply because they were Cagots.' He gazed around the dimly lamplit space, and closed his notebook. 'And that is the tragedy of the Cagots, isn't it? *They had to go.* They were living proof of human speciation, the speciation that might one day happen to the Jews. But take away the Cagots, at least anyone of provable Cagot ancestry, and the evidence for speciation is gone. Remove the Cagots, and the Fischer experiments can never be repeated. Catholic doctrine is safe. Multiracial democracy is safe. And so the last remaining Cagots had to die.'

They all sat back.

'That's about it,' said Simon. 'Jesus Christ.'

David spoke:

'OK. We need to go. We got the answer. We have some leverage. *We're gonna run out of light . . .*'

Angus was clutching that last document.

'David. You should see this.'

The dread crept through David's soul. The moment had come.

'Yes. *No.* Why?'

'I found it. A name caught my eye.' He paused. 'Martinez . . .'

He offered the paper under the torchlight.

David grabbed the single sheet and read it, avidly, his hand shaking, a tightening sensation in his chest. He read it twice. He looked at Amy, and then at Angus, and then back at the list of names. He had enough German to glean the meaning; his mind swayed with the shock. His own hand was shaking now. He handed it back to Angus. And said: 'Read it out . . .'

Nairn carefully took the document. And he read it out: it was the story José hadn't told David . . . *couldn't* tell him.

'Your grandfather . . . *thought he was a Cagot*. But of course he wasn't. It was a lie. It says it all here. After a year in the camp, he was seen as a troublemaker, a teenage Basque rebel. So the Germans humiliated him, and silenced him . . . by putting him in the Cagot section. The barracks of the hated pariahs. They convinced him he was of Cagot blood. *Yet he was Basque*. And so, David, are you. You are a Basque.'

David looked at Amy. He felt the most intense relief, a kind of shameful joy. But her face was strained, and tense: he saw no joy there, no gladness, he saw distraction and fear.

And then his own joy vanished, replaced by an equally intense terror. Provoked by just one word.

'*Epa!*'

49

Simon watched, aghast. Miguel flashed a brief smile, and a gun, at Angus and David. The terrorist was surrounded by men, carrying weapons, cans of gasoline and flat silver packages. Explosives maybe. The men set to work: in the shadows at the edge of the vault.

They had been so engrossed in their unravelling of the story, they hadn't even heard the stealthy approach of the Wolf and his men. And now here he was.

Smiling at Amy.

'Amy. *Esti. Muchas gracias, señorita.*'

She was gazing back at him; her voice was an eerie monotone. 'Yes . . . I did . . . what I promised.'

'You did.'

Miguel laughed a richly sad laugh. David felt the anger surging inside, like an oncoming storm:

'You. Amy? You? You betrayed us?'

She didn't turn his way. She couldn't even bear to look at him.

Miguel strode close to David. His breath was sweet, and fragranced with red wine. It mingled with the reek of the petrol, that Miguel's silent men were splashing over the wooden cases.

David was instantly reminded: the stench of the bonfire in Namibia. When Amy saved him. And now she had betrayed him.

Miguel nodded, almost sympathetically. 'Yes, of course, she betrayed you. She loves *me*. She always did. What is your life to her . . .'

David ignored the terrorist; instead he spoke, angrily, ferociously, at Amy. She was hunched and averting her eyes, maybe crying.

'So it was you? All along? Who told them where we were going? Namibia? You fucking bitch –'

Miguel intervened: 'Enough!'

David swore once again at Amy, who was now deep in the shadows.

Miguel's smile faded.

'Do not *blame* her. She is a woman. *Arrotz herri, otso herri.* And besides, Davido, she did the correct thing, the moral choice, she is correct. Because I am the good guy. The hero. We are the good guys. Do you not understand? *We are on the side of the good.'* Miguel's eye was faintly twitching. 'If the information in this cellar was ever to become known by others, then nations, races, tribes . . . would be forced into war. Humans who are not human? One race provably superior to another? *Imagine.* Human species fighting human species. Racial hierarchies confirmed. Nazi science vindicated. The democratic multiracial world – in ruins.'

Angus spoke up:

'But you can't stop science. One day a lab will repeat these results on genomic diversity, it is inevitable –'

'Is it, Nairn?' Miguel swivelled, turning on the scientist. 'Is it true? We closed down the Stanford Project. We closed down GenoMap. The Cagots are all dead, so the Fischer experiments can never be repeated. We have won. We have to win, or do you want us to be like animals, like rats, fighting each

423

other, fighting always? Do you want that? . . . *Umeak! You are children!*'

He glanced along the vault; his men had set the charges, the flat, sinister grey packages were tucked snug against the walls. The crates, doused in petrol, were ready to burn.

'Good. We are nearly done. *Bai.*'

Was there any way of escape? David urgently counted the number of men: there were seven or eight of them. Armed, dressed in dark clothes, and quietly efficient. Finishing their task.

There was no escape. *And what did it matter anyway?* They were finally cornered; they had lost; and he, David Martinez, was going to die, betrayed by the woman he loved. Even as he discovered the truth. A generous and bitter irony.

'Are we ready?'

One man turned.

'*Bai*, Miguel.'

'Excellent.' The Wolf turned back to the captives. 'I must also thank you for helping us locate the Fischer results. People, agencies – *governments* – have been searching for these for many decades.'

Miguel gazed first at Simon, then Angus, then David, as if he wanted to gain their entire attention for his following words, which he enunciated very carefully.

'Of course, you thought it was the church, didn't you? You realized it must be the Society of Pius the Tenth, and therefore you decided the entire church was involved, behind the scenes. The Holy Church.' He shook his head, with a contemptuous smile. 'Well, maybe we have a little help, some cooperation at a certain level . . . but do you really think Rome would have the money and the means and the will and the savagery to do all this, to take all these lives, mmm? Cardinals with guns and missiles? Really? *Bai?* Does that really make sense? Do you want to know where our money actually came from?'

The lamplight was dim, the air was stale. Miguel continued:

'The money came from much higher than that. Let us just say . . . Washington, and London, and Paris, and Jerusalem, and Beijing, and, of course, Berlin. Such a lot of money and assistance from Berlin. *There* is one government which sees it as its duty and, yes, its destiny, to make sure Nazism is never reborn in any form. They would do almost anything to rid Germany of her shame, and save the world from scientific racism. They would recruit any zealots or terrorists, for instance . . . They would make sure these zealots worked at a distance, in the darkness. So as to give everyone . . . in that succulent English phrase "plausible deniability".'

He stepped back. '*Bai* . . . David – and you . . . Angus Nairn . . . and you, the journalist. Quinn. Obviously we cannot let anyone survive. Consequently, you will be buried in here, along with the Fischer results, forever. *Nola bizi, hala hil.* The passage will be concreted. The barroom demolished and the passage filled in.' He held up a box, the trigger for the explosives. 'You will be in the most impressive of tombs. Which is nice for you.' He smiled in the torchbeams. 'But dead, nonetheless.'

Even as his last words faded, Amy stepped out of the shadows. Her face was alive, now, alive and angry:

'Miguel, you said you'd let them *go.*'

'*Mazeltov.* Of *course* I lied.'

'But Miguel – you said you'd spare them, for me – you promised –'

She stared at the terrorist. He scowled.

'You think I love you that much? My little piglet? The whore that fucked with the Amerikako? Eh?'

Amy's face was uplit by the paraffin lamp. There was a

425

glow there, a pleading in her expression. She stumbled over her words.

'But I never slept . . . with David.'

The statement was bizarre. Why was she saying this? Miguel dismissed her with a contemptuous wave. She repeated:

'*I never slept with him*, Miguel. And this is important . . . Because . . . because . . .'

Amy faltered, her hand to her face. She was trying to say something, and failing. But David could see, in the shadows: her other hand was gently placed on her stomach. Protectively.

With a rush of anguish, David realized. 'No.'

His word was so solitary, yet so firm, they all turned to him. He spoke again.

'You're pregnant?'

Miguel stepped forward. David repeated, staring at Amy:

'You're pregnant. And you know it's his. You know it's *his*?'

This final torment was too much. Amy's face was streaming tears. She nodded and took hold of the terrorist's arm, then she pulled Miguel's large dark hand to her stomach, and she placed his palm flat against her belly.

'It's yours, Miguel. It is yours.'

David's resignation was now tinged with the most horrible tragedy. She had betrayed him, betrayed them all, and now this? He looked left and right, at Simon and Angus. They were both waiting, staring at Miguel, at Amy, at the trigger for the explosives.

'So I have a son . . .' Miguel's voice was a rich whisper, hoarse and jubilant. 'So I have a son! A child. A daughter.' His eyes shone. 'The Garovillos live . . . the name lives on . . . ?'

He left her side, and reached to a crate, and took up his gun.

'Amy, just for you, I will merely shoot them. A better death than being buried alive. *Hauxe de lorra!* I will kill your friends now. To save them pain. They do not want to be buried alive.'

Miguel gestured with the gun at David. The other men were now virtually done in their tasks and standing to attention behind Miguel, hands behind their backs. The charges were set. Ready and waiting.

'Kneel!'

David shook his head. The gun insisted.

'Kneel!'

'Fuck you.'

Miguel went to David, and put a rough strong hand on his shoulder, and forced him to the floor. He had no choice. The gun was inches from his ear. His knees slowly buckled and he sank to the concrete, kneeling in the gloom.

Amy was staring at David. Her eyes glistening. He cursed her with a glowering stare. He felt pure hatred for her now. Was she enjoying this? Getting off on this? Had she never loved him ever? Had it always been Miguel?

Miguel crouched down directly in front of David. He put the pistol three inches from the condemned man's eyes. The terrorist's final smile was a pout of appreciation, like a gourmet's air kiss.

And then Amy shouted: 'I'll kill the baby. Stop. Stop it now.'

David glanced wildly across the chamber.

Amy had Simon's knife, and the blade was poised over her belly. The steel tip of the blade was aimed at her womb, the unborn. Ready to plunge.

David looked at Angus, who was gaping in amazement.

Amy said again, louder this time:

'Let them go, Miguel. Because I *will* kill the child. Your son. The last Cagot in the world, in my womb. I will kill him. Let them go and then blow the place, but *let them go.*'

Angry, roaring, wolflike, Miguel stood – and ran at Amy, trying to lean and grab the knife, even as she jabbed it towards her womb, to kill, to stab; and as she did this, Amy screamed at Simon:

'The lamp!'

It was already done. The paraffin lamp had been knocked across the wooden crates, smashing against the wall beyond. Instantly the flame of the lamp ignited the paper and wood, just soaked in gasoline. The chamber virtually exploded: a rush of flames flashed across, churning smoke, searing the air, choking the life from the cellar. One man screamed: his hair was on fire. Miguel was grabbing for Amy. She was shouting – at Angus. Where was he? Then David saw. Angus was swinging a torch at Miguel's skull. The impact was grue-somely audible: a tremendous crack.

It happened so fast in the fire and the smoke, David could not see what happened next. Was Miguel down? But where was Simon. The air was dusty and burning, the shouts loud, the flames were keen. Amy? And then he realized, someone was yelling: 'Run! The explosives!'

They were all running. Bodies running in the chaos. Everyone was turning, and running up the passage; but David lingered, and swivelled, and saw: Miguel was on the ground and bleeding. But he was reaching for something on the floor, between the stinking flames of the paraffin. The terrorist was seeking the switch – the explosive trigger. David was the nearest, he tried to lean and grab it. He was too late. The switch was pressed.

'No –'

'David!' Amy screamed.

Her scream was utterly drowned by a strange explosion, oddly broken, and partial. For a moment the room shook and concussed – but then came a blast wave.

It was like a sideswipe from God, hurling David into a corner, and slamming him to the concrete floor. All was smoke and blackness.

50

The pain was intimate and intense, somewhere deep inside
him. A pain that lived in the darkness, like an eyeless animal.
But then he opened his eyes, and discovered the truth: he
had survived. Yet he was half-buried under rubble and stones,
he could barely move, but he could breathe and see.

The chamber had collapsed. Rocks and earth had filled
most of the void, entombing the boxes, and stifling the fires.
A respectful silence reigned. David realized he had probably
been lucky. If all the charges had detonated, he'd have been
killed. Maybe the flames had destroyed the wiring, maybe
just one bomb had detonated.

So the fires were dying but he was still trapped under
rocks. And there was no sound of any other life, and certainly
no rescue.

A noise. He looked left and right; there was light filtering
from somewhere, up the tunnel. An aperture, letting in air,
inhaling sad grey smoke.

The earth moved again, a few metres away. A face emerged.

Miguel, brushing soil from his face.

Miguel had survived. The indestructible killer, the *jentilak*
from the forests of Irauty.

The terrorist was prone and he was bleeding copiously from a wound on the side of the head, with another vicious wound in his leg, a lavish gash, proudly glistening.

The smoke and dust of the explosion drifted, wistfully, as the light of the last gasoline flames died away.

Miguel saw David.

The terrorist frowned. He frowned and laughed and shook his bleeding head. And then he threw a plank of wood off his chest, and rolled free, and began dragging himself across the rubbled concrete floor, towards David.

David's blood was liquid cold. There was something unspeakable in the Cagot's slow, grisly crawl, dragging his ravaged leg. Dragging himself over to David.

Desperate to escape this human worm, this crawling, bleeding predator, David tried, again, to liberate himself, but the rocks and stones were too heavy. It was squassation. He was being crushed like a witch by the rocks. And now Miguel was on him.

And the terrorist was *salivating*. Miguel had ripped away David's shirt and exposed the flesh. A line of dribble spooled from the wide and scarred mouth; David's skin twitched, reflexively, at the sickly warmth of the spittle.

The Cagot flashed an exultant smile.

'*Jaio zara, hilko zara . . .*'

Miguel wiped his mouth and bared his teeth and then he stooped his mouth to the exposed flesh and he began to bite; David was being eaten alive; he could feel the teeth of the terrorist biting into his stomach muscles and then the gnawing, gnawing sound as Miguel tried to bite through, moaning with pleasure, biting into a man's living stomach, sucking at the pooling blood –

But a gunshot slapped Miguel away, and David gasped, and a second shot burst the terrorist's head open, like a great bloody flower, a vile carnation of red. He was shot dead.

And Amy was standing above him, and some other men. They had climbed through the hole with the light, and David looked, in terror and panic, at Amy and Angus and others, as they pulled the rocks away, and set him free –

'Come on,' said Amy, dragging him to his feet.

He looked down at his stomach. He was bleeding, there was a bite mark and some blood – but he was OK –

'Now!' Angus shouted. He jerked his head, indicating their escape. There seemed to be soldiers up there. Or policemen, way up the passage. Bright lights. Torches. Uniforms.

'But –' David protested. 'But –'

Amy squeezed his hand. Her gaze was ardent, and fierce.

'I did a deal with the police. They wanted Miguel, David. I gave them *Miguel*, and the archives – for us, you and me. Now try and run – the police have been fighting Miguel's men, in the bar –'

Angus yelled:

'We have to go!'

It was another rockfall. Blocks of stone and muddy boulders were slipping and groaning; the whole passage complex had been destabilized. They clambered through the hole and into the passage and then they ran: *for their lives*, a wall of mud was chasing them – everyone was running, sprinting, fleeing, as a tidal wave of slurry came after them like a wild animal, a devouring cave monster – a mouth of grey and black rocks – chasing them, trying to eat them alive, a wolf of rock.

And then they reached the little door and the booming sounds of the rockfall began to subside, and they wrenched open the *Juden Tur*, and emerged blinking and gasping and dirty into the bright light of the Bohemian *pivnice*.

Where several German policemen were standing and waiting. And Czech policemen too. And Sarria was there. And the other policeman from Biarritz. Some other guys in

431

plain clothes and sunglasses. Secret police? What? There were doctors tending men on stretchers. Signs of a gunfight.

One German officer came over to Simon, brandishing a mobile phone:

'Herr Quinn?'

'Yes – but –'

'A detective . . . in Scotland Yard. Here.' The German officer handed over the phone. The journalist took it and stumbled outside, into damp grey October air. David watched for a second: then he saw, through the doorway, Simon buckling into tears, and crumpling, and stumbling. A hand over his eyes, hiding his shameful sobs.

No doubt Tim was dead. They had been too late for Tim.

David and Amy and Angus walked out into the rain. Large shiny police cars were lined up and down the road; several ambulances were waiting, red lights flashing, others were racing up the hill. A platoon of soldiers in fatigues stood at the end.

It was mayhem: cops were running into the beer-hall. Carrying more explosives, or so it seemed.

He looked at Amy, her face streaked and smeared with dirt and blood. But alive. Intact. Was she pregnant?

She shook her head. And spoke.

'Listen. Let me talk. I knew he would catch us. By the time we reached Amsterdam I realized . . . Miguel would *never* give up. One day somewhere he would find us. We had to entice him. Entice him into a trap where *we* could kill *him*. Where the cops could get him. I couldn't trust you to know, because . . . I knew you loved me too much . . . And . . . because . . .' She blinked, and wiped her eyes with the back of a grimy hand. Then she said: 'You would never let me risk it, David – especially if you knew I was pregnant. And the pregnancy was my one trump card, if we needed to buy time in the cellar. And we did – I guessed right – we needed to buy time.' Her gaze was calm, yet rich with emotion. 'So, yes, I called Miguel. Betrayed us, told him where we were going. He believed me. He still loved me. He *wanted* to believe.'

'But –'

'But then I called the police as well, Sarria. He spoke to the German government and to the French government. He told them that they would get everything they wanted – Miguel, an end to all this, and the hiding place of the Fischer archives. So the data could be destroyed. And the Cagots all dead . . .'

'You did a deal with the police?'

'As well as Miguel. Yes, I had to, David. But it was so *difficult*. Miguel had to get here first, any sign of the police and he'd never have come. But the police have been following us for days. We're lucky. Very lucky. They've agreed to let us go, and we must commit to stay silent. Forever. That's the deal, that's the deal that kept us alive. *All of us.*'

She took his hand, and, just as she had done with Miguel, she placed his palm on her stomach.

'So that really was true? You really are . . .'

'Yes.'

He couldn't bear to ask the terrible and obvious question. Instead he turned away and stared down the dismal street where the police lights twinkled sadly in the rain like blue stars written on an old grey map.

51

Stepping from the shower Simon dried himself and threw on a shirt. He could still hear the mild laughter outside, the happy noises of a summer holiday.

Briskly he walked to the top of the stairs. Not for the first time this week, he stared out of the window at the blue and sunlit Pyrenees, across the valley, their summits confected with snow. Then he jogged down the sunny steps, into the villa's airy kitchen. He wanted to join his friends, in the sun, before the afternoon ended.

But his attention was snagged *en route*.

A package lay on the kitchen table. The address was Simon Quinn, *c/o* David Martinez.

The stamps were South African. And he recognized the scrawly handwriting.

Nerves jangled, he opened the package. Two items fell out. A clasp of hair. And a little toy dog. And there was a note.

Call me on this number.

Calming himself, Simon walked to the door that led to the riverside lawns. He dialled the number. The answering voice was quite unmistakable.

'Hello, Angus.'

'So you're holidaying with Mr and Mrs Martinez?'

'For a fortnight or so.'

'Excellent news. Soaking the rich!'

'And what about you?' Simon was desperate to ask the question; but he desperately didn't want to know the answer. He leaned against a sun-warmed wall. 'Why the sudden phone stuff? Thought you were still a bit paranoid?'

'Well I've calmed down now. I reckon they really *must* have agreed to Amy's deal. Our lives for Miguel. The Fischer data destroyed. If they were really planning anything it would have happened by now, three frigging years later. So, yes, I have opted to chillax. Move on. Get some putting practice. You know.'

'Well, good, glad to hear it. So . . .' Simon watched a heron gliding across the sky, down the long Gascon valley. 'So where are you?'

'Little town near the Cedarbergs. And I got enough diamonds to keep myself in biltong.'

'OK.'

Again Simon wanted to ask *the* questions yet he couldn't quite stomach it. So he asked something else:

'You know . . .'

'What?'

'You never told us. Did you ever find Alphonse?'

The thoughtful silence carried halfway across the world. Then Angus replied: 'Took me six months. I searched the desert. But, yes, I found . . . what was left of him. He's buried out there now, in the desert. Poor old Alfie.'

Simon wondered, 'Did it help?'

'You mean closure? Yeah maybe. Reckon I'll always feel guilty. But then I always did. It's probably *genetic*. Talking of which . . .' Angus's voice was quieter. 'I wanted to tell you this personally, rather than in some silly email. I'd like to have told David but . . . maybe it's easier through you.' He paused. 'I did both the tests, Simon. Successfully.'

'Well done.'

'*Dankie*. In fact, without shipping the entire horn section into the recording studio, I like to think I'm the only geneticist in the world who could have done some of that – got enough genetic material from the toy dog, for instance, but, yes, I managed it. I got your brother's DNA. And compared it to the DNA in your son's hair.'

'Where?'

'Borrowed a lab at Witwatersrand.'

The moment was coming. Simon felt the tension like a steel grip around his throat. Angus gave the answer.

'Timothy Quinn, your late brother, carried the classic genetic markers for schizotypal mental disorders, DNA sequence alterations in NRG1 and DISC1.' A sober pause. 'I can say with 99.995 percent certainty that your son Conor Quinn does *not* have the same sequential alterations.'

'That means . . .?'

'*He hasn't inherited it*. Of course yer little Conor might drop dead from a heart attack at fifty, I didn't check that. But no schizophrenia. He's fine.'

The sense of shocking relief was like diving into a cold pool in hot weather. Simon exhaled, and said: 'Thanks, Angus. And?'

'It's also good news. It was pretty damn unlikely that Miguel could have fathered a child, anyway, because of his congenital problems. But now we have proof. Little Miss Martinez is indeed the daughter of David Martinez. 99.99 percent sure. That's as good as it gets. And neither David or his daughter carry any of the markers of . . . the Cagots. He is Basque, so is his daughter.'

He stammered, 'OK, well . . . Well *thank you* – for doing all this.'

'Ach. Think nothing!' Angus said, rather wistfully. 'OK, I better go. Send my big love to David and Amy, when you give them the news . . . Tell 'em I like the name they chose. Maybe we'll meet again soon. See ya.'

The call ended.

Simon slipped the phone into his pocket, and walked outside. Amy and David were sitting in plastic chairs, by the riverbank; a scene of tranquil contentment.

The journalist felt a gladness, a lifting of his spirit. Yet the happiness was twinned with a pang of abiding and persistent remorse. As it always was, as it always would be. Conor was going to be OK; but Tim would always be dead. The harmony of life would never change: the sonorous bass tone of grief, and the purling treble of love.

He took a plastic seat by David. Who turned.

'Suzie's gone to the supermarket . . . with Conor. More wine I think.'

'OK.'

David continued: 'The package. I saw it. From Angus?'

'Yes.'

A pause.

'So?'

'She's *yours*. Just as you said. You said you were sure.'

David nodded.

'I just wanted to make *really* sure. Not that I would love her any the less. She is my daughter. But . . . medically, we needed to know. What about Conor? Is he . . .?'

'Cool. He's fine. Clean bill.'

'Good. That's really good.'

'Yeah . . .'

They fell silent. Amy was up and playing with her little girl; the blonde-haired two year old was giggling, jumping up and down, and pointing at the birds in the trees across the river.

'Funny thing is,' said Simon, quietly. 'Your daughter . . . she actually looks English. Of all things. She's got her *grand-mother's* genes . . .'

'And she's half Jewish *and* a quarter Basque. I guess she is the bright future of the world! And all she can say right now is – *Daddy go shopshop*.' David leaned over, and called to his little girl. '*Eloise Martinez*, be nice to your mother. She's teaching you about trees . . .'

Eloise smiled.

The breeze was soft in the riverine trees; the air was warm yet fresh with forest scents. David lifted his wineglass, and tilted it at the horizon, as if he was toasting the Pyrenees themselves.

'Of course this means . . . they really have died out. The Cagots. The poor *Caqueux*. They have disappeared forever.' He raised the glass higher. 'And now only the mountains remember.'

Simon nodded, and drank his juice, and gazed at the babbling water of the young River Adour. The scene was beautiful, and wistful, and serene. The river was racing jubilantly through the greenwoods, to the distant sea. It reminded him of a laughing little girl: running towards the waiting arms of her mother.